Hippocrene U.S.A. Guide to
UNCOMMON AND
UNHERALDED MUSEUMS

Hippocrene U.S.A. Guide to

UNCOMMON AND UNHERALDED MUSEUMS

Lincoln S. Bates
and
Beverly S. Narkiewicz

HIPPOCRENE BOOKS
New York

ISBN 0-87052-956-0

Contents

Introduction

In 1866, Jesse James robbed his first bank and began a notorious career that made him a legend in his own time. Still, when Bob Ford shot and killed him in St. Joseph, Missouri, in 1882, probably the last thing most folks imagined was that one day there would be a museum in memory of Jesse James.

One hundred fifty years ago, hunting whales was just a job, although difficult and dangerous, with little thought for the creatures themselves. Today, the future of whales is a worldwide concern. Nineteenth-century whalers could scarcely have conceived of such a turnabout or of museums devoted to their trade.

Tools that built the nation were simply tools. Buttons, no matter how elegant and diverse, were still buttons. Factories were just that. Horses, no matter how highly prized, were, nonetheless, merely animals. Museums for them? People plied their trades, played their games, immigrated and were assimilated. Museums were for grand collections of art and antiquities or belonged to the esoteric realms of science.

Somewhere along the line we began to preserve pieces of our past, and we're the better for it. Our lives have grown increasingly high tech and homogenized over the past three decades or so, and the rich and varied texture of the American experience has begun to fade. But it's still possible to glimpse and appreciate the threads and fibers and hues of our heritage in small museums across the country.

These museums are originals. They document our growth as a

I
NORTHEAST

Most of the furnishings, such as Eli Terry's accounting desk, in this restored 1801 house are related to clockmakers, but the main ingredient here is clocks—more than 1,500 of them. All are American made and are of all sizes and types, spanning clockmaking from colonial days to the present. Grandfather clocks—plain and fancy—abound, as do domed clocks, shelf clocks, hourglasses, Mickey Mouse pocket watches, and almost any other type of timepiece known to man. Grouped in rooms devoted to different eras, all are clearly labeled and accessible for close-up viewing.

Hartford

Historical Museum of Medicine and Dentistry, 230 Scarborough St., at intersection with Albany Ave. (203) 236-5613. Free. Open weekdays, 9 a.m. to 4:30 p.m.; weekends by appointment; closed holidays. Limited access for handicapped.

Three rooms of cases and wall displays hold 18th-, 19th-, and 20th-century artifacts of medicine and dentistry in this headquarters of the Hartford Medical and Dental Societies. Dental instruments with handles of mother-of-pearl or rare woods; a rural doctor's leather saddlebags containing pistol, wireclippers, and hammer along with medical instruments; terrifying trepanning tools—such outmoded implements are all on display as intriguing historical oddities. Of greatest interest, however, is that the exhibit's historical depth offers an excellent perspective on the rate of progress in dentistry and medicine over the last three centuries. A separate room is devoted to Horace Wells, the Hartford dentist who discovered the effectiveness of nitrous oxide as an anesthetic in dentistry.

Kent

Sloane-Stanley Museum, Rte. 7, 1 mile north of village. (203) 927-3849 or 566-3005. Adults: $1.25, seniors: $.75, children: $.50. Open May 15 through Oct. 31, Wed. through Sun., 10 a.m. to 4 p.m. No facilities for handicapped.

Close by the ruins of a 19th-century iron furnace is a replica log cabin built by Stanley Tool Works to hold the many Early American woodworking tools and implements collected by noted Connecticut artist and writer Eric Sloane. Sloane himself arranged them artistically to emphasize the ingenuity, design skill, and reverence for wood of our homesteading forefathers; most were handmade and all have been carefully preserved. And all—from augers to pikes to broadaxes to wood planes and tools no longer recognizable but for their labels—have an innate beauty that Sloane captured so well in his numerous books on Early Americana. The building's lobby contains exhibits on the furnace where pig iron was smelted.

New Haven

Yale University Collection of Musical Instruments, 15 Hillhouse Ave., on campus of Yale University. (203) 432-0822. Free. Open Sept. through May, Tues., Wed., and Thurs., 1 to 4 p.m.; June and July, Tues. and Thurs., 1 to 4 p.m.; closed for University recesses, holidays, and month of Aug. No facilities for handicapped.

There are few exhibits more beautiful than Yale's strong and balanced collection of fine musical instruments. Intended as a collection to document the history of music, most of the instruments can also stand as simple works of art: the peg box of a 1748 treble viol, for example, ends in a delicately carved head instead of a scroll; the harpsichords are carved, painted, and inlaid with fine woods; some pieces, such as a crystal flute, are unique as well as lovely. Works of famous instrument makers are part of the exhibit, and a second-floor room holds keyboard instruments.

Newington

American Radio Relay League Museum of Amateur Radio, 225 Main St., on Rte. 176. (203) 666-1541. Free. Open Mon. through Fri., 9 a.m. to 4 p.m.; closed holidays. Accessible to handicapped.

This is headquarters for ARRL, as well as a museum devoted to preserving historical and antique items connected with amateur (ham) radio. Among the fairly disorganized exhibits and groupings here, knowledgeable ham radio operators will recognize and appreciate such bits of radio memorabilia as an "Old Betsy" spark-gap transmitter (still in working order) and the Ralph P. Thetreau Memorial Antenna System. Of more general interest is the Elser

Mathes Cup, a trophy yet to be awarded to the first ham operator to communicate with Mars.

Old Lyme

The Nut Museum, 303 Ferry Rd., off Rte. 156 south. (203) 434-7636. Adults: $3 plus one nut, children 6 to 16: $2 plus one nut. Open May through Oct. 3, Wed., Sat., and Sun., 1 to 5 p.m. and by appointment. No facilities for handicapped.

One woman's special interest has led to a specialized collection; Elizabeth Tashjian is creator, curator, and whimsical tour guide of this personal tribute to nuts. Two rooms in Tashjian's Victorian house are given over to nuts in different guises—crafted into dollhouse furniture, jewelry, and toys—as well as used as motifs in furniture, art, masks, tapestries, and other decorative items. There is a fine collection of nutcrackers, a display of the 20 better-known edible nuts, plus some nut oddities, such as a 35-pound double coconut. Outdoors are sheet metal sculptures resembling nutcrackers.

Riverton

Hitchcock Museum, Rte. 20, northwest of Hartford. (203) 379-8531. Free. Open June through Oct., Wed. through Sat., 11 a.m. to 4 p.m., and Sun., 1 to 4 p.m.; during Apr. and May, Sat., 11 a.m. to 4 p.m. only. No facilities for handicapped.

The interior of an 1829 stone church is an effective setting for this collection of antique painted furniture. Featured are not only the painted, stenciled, rush-seated chairs of Lambert Hitchcock, whose work charmed so many housewives more than 100 years ago, but also work of other 18th- and 19th-century craftsmen of "fancy" furniture. Related exhibits display a treadle-powered lathe used for turning chair legs, other antique furniture-making tools, and a collection of antique crib quilts. A movie documents the history of chairmaking in Riverton.

Terryville

Lock Museum of America, 130 Main St., on Rte. 6 just east of Rte. 8. (203) 589-6359. Admission: $2, children under 12: free. Open

May 1 through Oct. 31, Tues. through Sun., 1:30 to 4:30 p.m. and by appointment; closed Mon. No facilities for handicapped.

This extensive collection of locks, keys, and lock hardware convincingly establishes Connecticut as the cradle of the American lock industry. Lighted glass cases in several rooms display cabinet locks of McKee & Co., Yale cylinder pin locks, bank and vault locks, locks from colonial days, mail locks, and even a large collection of handcuffs, leg irons, and prison locks. A mechanical display illustrates the workings of a pin tumble lock, and one room is devoted to cases of ornate hardware, knobs, and escutcheons.

Uncasville

Tantaquidgeon Indian Museum, 1819 Norwich-New London Tnpk., on Rte. 32 north of New London. (203) 848-9145. Donation. Open May through Oct., Tues. through Sun., 10 a.m. to 4 p.m. No facilities for handicapped.

Located in the heart of Mohegan Indian country and established by John Tantaquidgeon, descendant of Mohegan Chief Uncas, this museum is devoted to preserving Indian history and traditions, particularly those of the once-powerful Mohegan nation. In the museum's Northeastern Woodland section are bowls, baskets, ladles, and other items of stone, bone, and wood made by New England Indian craftsmen past and present; other areas display craftsmanship of Southeast, Southwest, and Northern Plains Indians.

Waterbury

Mattatuck Museum, 144 W. Main St., from Exit 21 of I-84. (203) 753-0381. Free. Open Tues. through Sat., 10 a.m. to 5 p.m.; Sun., noon to 5 p.m.; closed Mon. Accessible to handicapped.

During the Industrial Revolution, Waterbury was known as The Brass City and the Mattatuck Museum amply illustrates 19th-century America's love of that nonrusting alloy. Sleigh bells, saddle ornaments, kerosene lamps, pots, stove trimmings, belt buckles, hairpins, buttons, pistol cartridges, hinges, screws, wire, clock movements, and eyelets for shoes, corsets, and suspenders are the kinds of consumer goods made from brass that fill display cases in this former Mormon temple. Additional exhibits feature Connecticut artists and other aspects of local industrial history.

Winchester Center

Kerosene Lamp Museum, 100 Old Waterbury Turnpike, Rte. 263, on village green. (203) 379-2612. Free. Open daily 9 a.m. to 4 p.m. Accessible to handicapped.

This former general store and still-operating post office in a small New England village is the perfect setting for a collection of kerosene lamps and lighting devices. More than 500 pieces crowd one large room, hanging on walls and displayed in glass cases. All are shown as found, and most are utilitarian—no fripperies here. In addition to common and uncommon household kerosene lamps are such items as angle lamps, innkeepers' timed lamps, a boiler inspector's lamp, and a magic lantern kerosene slide projector dating from the 1850s. Most of the lamps are of glass, all are interesting, and they trace the period of kerosene lamp use from 1856 to 1880 when Edison invented the light bulb.

Maine

Brunswick

Peary-MacMillan Arctic Museum, first floor, Hubbard Hall, Bowdoin College. (207) 725-3416. Free. Open Tues. through Fri., 10 a.m. to 4 p.m., Sat., 10 a.m. to 5 p.m., Sun., 2 to 5 p.m.; extended summer hours; closed Mon. and holidays. No facilities for handicapped.

This small natural history museum focuses on Arctic animals, Eskimo culture, and the history of Arctic exploration, particularly Admiral Robert Peary's push to the North Pole and Admiral Donald MacMillan's Arctic explorations. All manner of exploration equipment is on view, including one of Peary's sledges, a fur suit worn by MacMillan, and the log of MacMillan's North Pole expedition. Artifacts tell the story of people who make their homes in the Arctic, and there are display cases of stuffed animals native to the region. Life-size photographs of the two explorers in full Eskimo regalia enhance this unique collection.

Caribou

Nylander Museum, 393 Main St., one block east of Rte. 1 (207) 493-4474. Free. Open June through Aug., Wed. through Sun., 1 to 5 p.m.; Mar. through May and Sept. through Dec., Sat. and Sun., noon to 4 p.m.; closed Jan. and Feb. Limited facilities for handicapped.

Olof O. Nylander was a natural scientist who contributed count-less specimens to museums in both his native Sweden and in this country. During his career he managed to amass the impressive personal collection housed in this museum. His large fossil collec-tion is recognized as one of the finest in the eastern United States. There are also a complete collection of Maine minerals, shells from all over the world, marine fauna specimens from five continents, and a display of local Indian artifacts. Adjacent exhibits include a medicinal herb garden and mounted birds, butterflies, and moths.

Island Falls

John E. & Walter D. Webb Museum of Vintage Fashion, Rte. 2, about 100 yards south of Island Falls Village. (207) 463-2402. Dona-tion appreciated. Open May 26 through June 8, July 21 through Aug. 3, Aug. 18 through 31, Sept. 15 through 30, Oct. 1 through 7, 10 a.m. to 4 p.m. and by appointment. No facilities for handi-capped.

Fourteen rooms in a turn-of-the century house display manikins wearing period costumes in a variety of settings—an 1890s bridal shop, a Roaring '20s room, Jim and Barry's Haberdashery Shoppe, Sheila and Diane's Millinery and Dressmaker Shoppe. Inter-spersed among the exhibits of ladies' clothing (circa 1830–1950) and men's haberdashery (circa 1858–1940) are accessories to complete and complement the ensembles. A children's room also features antique handmade dolls. Tea and crumpets are served by advance request.

New Harbor

Pemaquid Point Fishermen's Museum, Rte. 130 at Pemaquid Point Lighthouse Park, south of Damariscotta. (207) 677-2494. Donation suggested. Open Memorial Day through Columbus Day, weekdays 10 a.m. to 5 p.m. and Sun., 11 a.m. to 5 p.m. Ramp for handi-capped.

Fishing gear and techniques used by Maine fishermen past and present are the focus of the exhibits in this old lightkeeper's house situated next to a working lighthouse. Of particular interest is a room displaying different methods of harvesting the sea—scallop dredge, trawl, purse seine, eel trap, and a cunner net for catching bait. A lighthouse lens, made in France, is also on display, as are numerous pictures, models, half-hulls, and tools and equipment used for both lobstering and fishing.

Rockland

Shore Village Museum, 104 Limerock St., north of Main St., east of Rte. 1. (207) 594-4950. Free. Open daily June 1 through Oct. 15, 10 a.m. to 4 p.m., and by appointment. Limited access for handicapped.

Known as The Lighthouse Museum for its enormous collection of lighthouse artifacts, this old Grand Army Hall also houses a delightful mix of miscellanea. The lighthouse materials, complete with a lens big enough to walk through, are probably the largest such collection in the U.S. and feature hands-on groaning foghorns, clanging bells, and flashing lights. Other maritime articles complement the collection: scrimshaw, ship models, nautical instruments, marine art, and even a collection of more than 3,000 lighthouse postcards. Several other interesting, but unrelated, exhibits fill out the two floors of the hall.

Southwest Harbor

Wendell Gilley Museum, Main St. and Herrick Rd., on Rte. 102. (207) 244-7555. Adults: $3, children under 12: $1. Open May and during fall months, Fri. through Sun., 10 a.m. to 4 p.m.; June through Aug., Tues. through Sun., 10 a.m. to 5 p.m. Accessible to handicapped.

Wendell Gilley was a woodcarver of national renown who produced more than 6,000 bird carvings before his death in 1983. On display in this attractive modern building are 200 of Gilley's works—herons, owls, eagles, ducks, and other species of birds painstakingly hand carved from wood and accurately painted. Changing exhibits of wildlife art, Maine folk art, and the works of other woodcarvers complete the museum.

Wiscasset

The Musical Wonder House, 18 High St., just off Rte. 1. (207) 882-7163. Ground floor tour: $7.50; full house: $20. Open daily

Memorial Day through Oct. 15, 10 a.m. to 6 p.m. No facilities for handicapped.

Restored antique music boxes, phonographs, player pianos, and other mechanical musical delights share this elegant old house with fine period furnishings. Many of the music boxes are one of a kind, and all are in working order, which owner Danilo Konvalinka will happily demonstrate. They come in amazing variety—beautifully decorated boxes, a Louis XV-type drum table with musical works inside (made in New Jersey), an 1895 Swiss music box that features interchangeable dancing dolls, clocks, a German 16-bell box with accordian-pleated lid, even a 19th-century musical writing desk from Geneva. One room holds dozens of cylinder-type music boxes that range in size from a few inches to several feet and in mechanical complexity from simple to sophisticated.

Massachusetts

Boston

The Computer Museum, 300 Congress St., in downtown financial district. (617) 426-2800 or 426-6758 for recorded information. Adults: $6, students and seniors: $5, half price after 5 p.m. Fri. Open year round, Tues. through Sun., 10 a.m. to 5 p.m.; Fri. to 9 p.m.; closed Mon., except during summer. Accessible to handicapped.

It's fitting that Massachussetts, home of so many computer manufacturers and high-tech industries, should also claim the world's largest display of computers in a museum devoted solely to the history of information processing—from abacus to silicon chip. Both serious computer people and people with no knowledge of the subject can enjoy exploring 40 hands-on exhibits covering technological efforts, from the largest computer ever made (SAGE) to state-of-the-art computer graphics applications.

Cambridge

Hart Nautical Collections, Massachusetts Institute of Technology Museum, 55 Massachusetts Ave.; enter at 77 Massachusetts Ave., take right down hall; museum on left. (617) 253-5942. Free. Open daily, 9 a.m. to 10 p.m. Accessible to handicapped.

Although tracing the evolution of ship design is the purpose of this collection of scale ship models, the exquisite craftsmanship of the models themselves provides the real entertainment. In a variety of scales, fully rigged or spouting stacks, they offer the familiar—*The Half Moon, The Mayflower*—as well as such exotics as a Korean warship called *The Turtle* for its spiked cover, and an ancient Viking ship. Also on display are builders' half-models, whaling prints, working drawings, and engine models, all descriptively labeled.

Dalton

Crane Museum, South St., behind paper mill. (413) 684-2600, ext. 380. Free. Open June through mid-Oct., Mon. through Fri., 2 to 5 p.m. Limited access for handicapped.

Crane & Co. has been making fine rag papers since 1801, and its company museum presents the story of American paper making from Revolutionary days to the present. Among the many different kinds of paper displayed in glass cases are those used to make U.S. currency, American Express cheques, stock certificates, and men's old-fashioned paper collars. There is also a model of Crane's original paper mill. Exhibits are self-explanatory, but someone is always around to answer questions or offer interesting anecdotes.

Harvard

Fruitlands Museums, 102 Prospect Hill Rd.; take Rte. 2 to Rte. 110 toward Harvard, then Old Shirley Rd., and follow signs. (508) 456-3924. Adults: $5, seniors: $4, children 7 to 16: $1. Open Tues. through Sun., plus Mon. holidays, May 12 through Oct. 14, 10 a.m. to 5 p.m. Limited access for handicapped.

A hillside setting provides a spectacular view from the four buildings that comprise this museum. **Fruitlands Farmhouse** was the scene of Bronson Alcott's Transcendental Utopia and now serves as museum of that philosophical movement, containing mementos and memorabilia of its leaders—Alcott, Ralph Waldo Emerson, Henry David Thoreau, Margaret Fuller, and others. Shaker handicrafts and products—baskets, home utensils, and furnishings—are on display in **Shaker House,** office building of a local Shaker society in the early 1800s. Indian relics and specimens of historic Indian art and industry, along with interpretive dioramas, are featured in the **American Indian Museum.** The **Picture Gallery** has a selection of Hudson River landscape paintings and a fine collection of primitive portraits done by 19th-century itinerant artists.

New Bedford

New Bedford Glass Museum, 50 N. Second St.; take Exit 15 from Rte. 195. (508) 994-0115. Adults: $2, seniors: $1.50, children: $.50. Open Apr. through Sept., Mon. through Sat., 10 a.m. to 4 p.m.; Oct. through Mar., Tues. through Sat., 10 a.m. to 4 p.m.; closed Sun. and winter holidays. Ground-floor galleries accessible to handicapped.

The beauty of the glassware on display in seven rooms of this Federal-style mansion is hinted at in the pattern names: Peachblow, Lava, Mother-of-Pearl Satin Ware, Amberina. During the 1880s New Bedford Glass Works led the international art glass movement, and for nearly a century turned out quality glass items designed for almost every decorative purpose: vases, pitchers, tableware, powder jars, lampshades, even fountain pens and cribbage boards. Pieces were etched, cut, colored, silvered, or enameled as fashion dictated and as the firm diversified into porcelain, silverplate, and chandelier manufacture. Two thousand pieces of glassware are on exhibit.

North Andover

Museum of American Textile History, 800 Massachusetts Ave., across from Old North Andover Common. (508) 686-0191. Adults: $2, children and seniors: $1. Open Tues. through Fri., 10 a.m. to 5 p.m.; Sat. and Sun., 1 to 5 p.m.; closed Mon. and holidays. Accessible to handicapped.

During the 19th century, mills in New England's Merrimack River Valley produced textiles for the entire nation, and the industry revolutionized the lives of farm families throughout the area. The story of American cloth making and the people who made it are documented in this modern building on an old town green. Samples of different types and weaves of textiles, historic prints, and numerous examples of both industrial and preindustrial cloth-making machinery make up the bulk of the exhibits. Although tours are available, clear labeling makes for easy informal touring. This is a museum with a good sense of its subject and the people who were a part of America's Industrial Revolution; the roar of textile machinery in operation gives a sense of what life was like for 19th-century mill workers.

Orleans

French Cable Station Museum, Cove Rd. and Rte. 28. No telephone. Adults: $1, children over 12: $.50. Open July 4 through Labor Day, Tues. through Sat., 2 to 4 p.m. No facilities for handicapped.

Built in 1890 to receive a direct communications wire from Brest, France, the French Cable Station was the communications satellite of its day. Closed in 1959 because of automation in the telecommunications industry, the station was reopened in 1971 as a museum with much of the original equipment—telegraph keys, paper tape readers, and rather primitive amplifiers—in place. A rare Hently sound magnifier (only one of two such pieces of equipment still in existence) is part of the display.

Petersham

Fisher Museum of Forestry, Athol Rd., in Harvard Forest off Rte. 32, south of Rte. 2. (508) 724-3302. Free. Open year round, Mon. through Fri., 9 a.m. to 5 p.m., and also Sat., 10 a.m. to 4 p.m., May through Oct. No facilities for handicapped.

Dioramas in this unique museum depict typical New England forest and land use—from scenes of the heavily forested land that greeted New England's first settlers, through agricultural clearing, to the regrowth of forests today. A self-guided tour also includes exhibits of related items such as forestry tools, birchbark canoes, and photos of the 1938 hurricane that wreaked major havoc on New England forests.

Plymouth

Cranberry World Visitors Center, 225 Water St., ½ mile north of Plymouth Rock. (508) 747-2350 or 747-1000. Free. Open daily, Apr.

1 through Nov. 30, 9:30 a.m. to 5 p.m., and until 9 p.m. during July and Aug. Accessible to handicapped.

Southeastern Massachusetts is cranberry country, and the tiny tart cranberry—its culture, harvesting, and use from colonial days to modern times—is the focus of this attractive oceanfront museum that also overlooks a working cranberry bog. Antique harvesting tools, a working model of a cranberry bounce separator (a device for screening out bad berries), educational exhibits, and even a scale model of a typical Massachusetts cranberry farm, tell the tale of what has become a major agricultural product. Free cranberry refreshments complete the tour.

Sandwich

Thornton W. Burgess Museum, 4 Water St. (508) 888-4668. Donation suggested. Open Apr. 1 through Dec. 31 and the month of Feb., Mon. through Sat., 10 a.m. to 4 p.m.; Sun. 1 to 4 p.m.; closed Mon. in winter. Accessible to handicapped.

Thornton W. Burgess was a pioneer conservationist and early activist in wildlife protection, as well as author of such classic children's books as *Peter Rabbit and the Briar Patch, Old Mother Westwind,* and *Reddy Fox.* Housed in an historic home, this collection of the author's works, accompanied by natural history exhibits relating to his stories and his conservationist philosophy, makes an educational and entertaining visit for young families and a serendipity trip for oldsters who read and loved his books.

Sharon

Kendall Whaling Museum, 27 Everett St. (617) 784-5642. Adults: $2, students and senior citizens: $1.50, children over 5: $1. Open Tues. through Sat., 10 a.m. to 5 p.m., and most Mon. federal holidays; closed Sun., Mon., and most other holidays. Handicapped access available.

Housed in a converted turn-of-the-century hospital in a pleasant New England village, this is a whaling museum with international scope. Its broad collection, extending from Pre-Columbian times to today, boasts the largest assemblage of Dutch maritime paintings outside Europe, two galleries of fine scrimshaw, a diorama on modern whaling, galleries devoted to Japanese and Arctic whaling and sealing, plus British and American artworks. Children will take particular interest in a fully outfitted whaling boat on display.

South Lancaster

Toy Cupboard Theater and Museum, 57 E. George Hill Rd., off Main St., Rte. 70. (508) 365-9519. Admission: $.90. Open during puppet theater performances, Sept. through June, first and last Sat. of month at 11 a.m. and last Sun. of month at 2 p.m.; July and Aug., Wed. and Thurs. at 2 p.m.; or by appointment. Limited access for handicapped.

Along with dolls and toys, this private collection features an exceptional display of paper toys, pop-up books, and other paper items that don't usually survive childhood. Exceptional, too, are the many dollhouses, shops, stores, and other architectural miniatures in all scales and sizes, mostly furnished. The puppet theater, with a complete array of puppet characters and sets, is also open for touring.

Springfield

Indian Motorcycle Museum, 33 Hendee St.; take St. James Ave. Exit of Rte. I-291. (413) 737-2624. Adults: $3, children 6 to 12: $1. Open daily 10 a.m. to 5 p.m.; closed Thanksgiving, Christmas, and New Year's Day. Accessible to handicapped.

Motorcycle buffs regard the Indian Motorcycle Company, established in 1901, as one of the best motorcycle makers ever. One of the first Indians made is on display here, along with such interesting specimens as collapsible models used during World War II, motorcycles on skis, and a replica of the first motorcycle ever made. Interesting, too, are the displays featuring women motorcycle racers, the numerous miniature models, and a large collection of toy motorcycles.

Springfield Armory Museum, One Armory Square, on grounds of Springfield Technical Community College. (413) 734-6477. Free. Open daily 9 a.m. to 5 p.m.; closed Thanksgiving, Christmas, and New Year's Day. Elevator available for handicapped.

Originally an arsenal, then a site for developing and testing new small arms (starting with the 1795 flintlock and ending with the

M-14), the Armory now houses the world's largest collection of small arms. Exhibits favor Springfield products: muskets, the 1873 Trapdoor, the Model 1903 from World War I, the M-1 semi-automatic, and other Springfield contributions to the American military heritage. Weapons of other manufacture—from Winchesters to Gatling guns, from recoilless rifles to anti-aircraft guns—round out the collection begun in 1870. Particularly eye catching is the double-tiered display of rifle barrels immortalized as *The Organ of Guns* by poet Henry Wadsworth Longfellow.

Sturbridge

Saint Anne's Shrine Russian Icon Collection, 16 Church St., actually in village of Fiskdale, on Rte. 20, west of Rte. 93. (617) 347-7338. Free. Open daily May through Oct. Facilities for handicapped.

A simple white clapboard chapel in a lovely pastoral setting holds one of the largest collection of Russian icons in the U.S. Sixty tempera and gold-leaf portraits of saints and other holy figures are on permanent display here, many of them very old, all irreplaceable. The icons, collected over a period of years by Assumptionist priests serving as chaplains to the American Embassy in Moscow, were assembled as a collection in 1971. A brochure explains how icons were traditionally made, displayed, and venerated in Russia, Greece, and the Near East.

Watertown

Perkins School for the Blind Museum, 175 N. Beacon St., Rte. 20, in school library. (617) 924-3434. Free. Open Mon. through Fri., 8:30 a.m. to 5 p.m., but calling ahead is advised; generally closed during school holidays. Downstairs is blind- and wheelchair-oriented; upstairs inaccessible by wheelchair.

This is both a museum for blind people and about blindness. Downstairs, the Tactile Museum features "in-touch" exhibits of stuffed animals, shells, and other natural history specimens, as well as examples of modern technology, such as a model of the space shuttle. Upstairs, the Museum of Blindiana traces the education of the blind, starting with an ancient Egyptian bas-relief, and including early Braille and other reading and writing aids, as well as materials used by Helen Keller and Laura Bridgman, the first blind deaf-mute to be successfully educated.

Weston

Cardinal Spellman Philatelic Museum, 235 Wellesley St., on campus of Regis College. (617) 894-6735. Free. Open Tues., Wed. and Thurs., 9 a.m. to 4 p.m.; Sun., 1 to 5 p.m. Accessible to handicapped.

Because exhibits change every three or four months and range from deep philatelic studies to light topical groupings, there is always something on display here to interest all types of stamp enthusiasts. Glass frames containing several pages of stamps and accompanying explanatory texts may trace the postal route of a canceled cover, explain a set of block plates, or simply present a series of stamps on one subject—birds, flowers, Walt Disney, zeppelins, sailing ships. Dwight D. Eisenhower's personal stamp collection is mounted under the Presidential Seal. The museum owns other notable collections, such as those belonging to Enrico Caruso and to the Vatican.

New Hampshire

Bethlehem

Crossroads of America Museum, Rte. 302 and Trudeau Rd., 2 miles east of village. (603) 869-3919. Adults: $2.50, children 6 to 15: $1.75. Open June 1 through mid-Oct., Tues. through Sun., 9 a.m. to 6 p.m. No facilities for handicapped.

This museum's name refers to ³⁄₁₆-scale model railroad crossings, hundreds of them in this three-story former boarding house. Freight trains and passenger trains puff over a multi-storied trestle, wind their way through mazes of tracks, eject mail pouches from mail cars, and travel through a network of track, tunnels, mountains, buildings, and other structures built by owner Roger Hinds. Demonstrations and tours take place every half hour; there is also an exhibit of model cars, ships, planes, and trucks.

Franconia Notch

New England Ski Museum, Rte. I-93, adjacent to base station of Cannon Mountain Aerial Tramway. (603) 823-7177. Adults: $1.00, children under 12: free. Open mid-May to mid-Oct. and late Dec. through Mar. 30, Tues. through Thurs., noon to 5 p.m.; closed Wed. Accessible to handicapped.

Ski enthusiasts will be delighted with this museum devoted to their favorite sport. Its exhibits feature such rarities as skis dating from the last century, poles from the one-stick era, various types of boots and bindings, posters and trophies, as well as related items like stamps, pins, and badges. The themes of the exhibit—The Many Forms of Skiing, Ski Places & Ski People—change annually, but a multi-image film on the history of New England skiing is a permanent fixture.

Glen

The Grand Manor Antique and Classic Car Museum, Rtes. 16 and 302, 3 miles north of North Conway. (603) 356-9366. Adults: $4.50, seniors: $3.75, children 7 to 15: $2.75. Open 9:30 a.m. to 5 p.m., weekends mid-May to mid-June and mid-Oct. to Christmas; daily, mid-June to mid-Oct. Accessible to handicapped.

Classic cars of the 1950s and grand touring cars of the 1920s and '30s are the focus of Grand Manor's extensive collection of mint-condition and restored autos, including such classic makes as Duesenberg, Packard, and Pierce Arrow. Car buffs will particularly appreciate a 1930 Packard boattail speedster (one of five in existence), a 1936 supercharged Auburn Speedster, a 1927 Cadillac dual-cowl phaeton, and a "Happy Days" hot rod.

Laconia

Carpenter Museum of Antique Outboard Motors, Rte. 3, 5 miles south of Laconia. (603) 524-7611. Open by appointment only. Accessible to handicapped.

This is very likely the only museum of its kind, and for that reason may be of interest to boaters and nonboaters alike. Mounted on stands, more than 100 engines of 30 different makes trace 75 years of outboard motor history. There is a turn-of-the-century wooden hand-driven model, a 1945 Japanese motor, an Indian Silver Arrow made by the Indian Motorcycle Co., several models that work completely submerged, and other unique examples of marine engines. Related memorabilia—advertising signs, literature, books—are also on display.

Manchester

Lawrence L. Lee Scouting Museum, Bodwell Rd., at Camp Carpenter, 4 miles north of Rte. 93, Exit 5. (603) 669-8919. Free. Open daily, July and Aug., 10 a.m. to 4 p.m.; Sept. through July, Sat., 10 a.m. to 4 p.m.; and by appointment. Accessible to handicapped.

A rustic knotty pine structure at this lakeside Scouting camp contains an exceptional and handsomely mounted display of Boy Scout memorabilia. Scout founder Robert Baden-Powell's Boer War treasures are here, along with colorful pennants, uniforms, flags, neckerchiefs, jamboree souvenirs, badges, and insignia from Scout troops past and present from all over the world. Other unique items include a flag and patch carried into space by Alan Shepard, a belt buckle collection, and Scout stamp issues spanning the past 86 years. The museum also has a comprehensive Scouting library.

North Conway

Conway Scenic Railroad and Museum, Rtes. 16 and 302, in village center. (603) 356-5251. Free. Open early May through late Oct., 10 a.m. to 5:15 p.m. Accessible to handicapped.

This is an operating railroad museum of authentic restored antique steam and early diesel locomotives, plus cars of all types—boxcars, coaches, baggage cars, cabooses and snow flangers—set amid a century-old station, roundhouse, turntable and freight house. Plaques detail the history and origin of equipment, and artifacts—baggage carts, ticket cases, scales, telegraph equipment—fill the passenger station. One-hour train rides in restored antique coaches depart the depot several times a day.

Warren

Morse Museum, Rte. 25C; follow Baker River Valley Hwy. to Rte. 25C. (603) 764-9407. Free. Open daily June 21 through Labor Day, 10 a.m. to 5 p.m. No facilities for handicapped.

Ira H. Morse, farm boy turned shoe retailer turned big-game hunter, singlehandedly created this museum in 1928 to house his mounted safari trophies and curios collected during numerous trips to the African jungle, India, Ceylon, and China. One of the most interesting of the exhibits, however, is also the tamest—a collection of shoes. In his travels, and from associates who traveled even more extensively, Morse acquired samples of footgear representing cultures and fashions from all over the world and devoted a corner of his museum to their display.

New Jersey

Camden

Campbell Museum, Campbell Pl., off Rte. 30. (609) 342-6440. Free. Open Mon. through Fri., 9 a.m. to 4 p.m.; closed holidays. Handicapped parking available and "only five steps" into museum.

"Soup is good food," says the commercial, and soup tureens are elegant serving dishes. This collection, funded by the Campbell Soup Company, offers a unique look at the artistic and bizarre in soup service, mainly ladles, bowls, and tureens. The accent is on pieces from 18th-century European royal households, but the collection covers other regions, such as the Orient, and spans the centuries from 500 B.C. to the present. Here is a tin-enameled earthenware boar's head tureen from Denmark, circa 1770; there a huge hard-paste porcelain swan tureen from Saxony, circa 1745. Shapes range from ships to fish to flowers; materials from sterling silver to fine porcelain. Symbols of affluent dining, they give a whole different flavor to the contemporary "cuppa" soup.

Fort Monmouth

U.S. Army Communications-Electronics Museum, Kaplan Hall; take Exit 105 from Garden State Parkway. (201) 532-1682. Free. Open Mon. through Fri., noon to 4 p.m. Accessible to handicapped.

Always vital to campaigns, military communications have

evolved just as have weapons and tactics. This museum displays the research and development of military electronics at Ft. Monmouth and contains numerous historical exhibits, such as World War I air-to-ground equipment, the first walkie-talkie, the first helmet radio, the first Morse Code translator, and a model of the radar at Pearl Harbor.

Franklin

Franklin Mineral Museum, Evans St., off Rte. 23. (201) 827-3481. Adults: $2, children: $1. Open Apr. 15 through June 30 and Sept. 1 through Nov. 15, Fri. and Sat., 10 a.m. to 4 p.m.; Sun., 12:30 to 4:30 p.m.; Tues. through Thurs., groups by reservation; July and Aug., Wed. through Sat., 10 a.m. to 4 p.m., Sun., 12:30 to 4:30 p.m. Accessible to handicapped.

This region of New Jersey was the site of major zinc mines until the rich ore was depleted in the 1950s. At this uncommon museum, thousands of area mineral specimens gleam from display cases, colorfully fluorescent under different types of light. The museum also consists of a mine replica constructed and outfitted with timber, rails, ore carts, drilling gear, and ore scoops actually employed in Franklin's zinc mines. The equipment, tunnels, and lighting artfully convey the subterranean environment of the zinc miner.

Haledon

American Labor Museum, 83 Norwood St. (201) 595-7953. Adults: $1.50, children under 12: free. Open Wed. through Sun., 1 to 4 p.m. No facilities for handicapped.

The country's only such institution devoted to labor, this museum is located in Botto House, the only immigrant house designated a national landmark. The museum tells the story of American workers, their unions, organizing struggles, workplaces, and diverse ethnic heritages. The first floor contains four period rooms depicting life of an immigrant working family in the early 1900s. The upper floor holds a gallery for changing exhibits related to the labor movement. The house was a meeting place for striking workers during the 1913 silk mills strike in Paterson.

Jersey City

C.A.S.E. Museum of Russian Contemporary Art in Exile, 80 Grand St. (201) 332-7963. Donation requested. Call for schedule, which varies. No facilities for handicapped.

A unique institution (with a branch in Paris), the museum collects and exhibits unofficial Soviet art—paintings, sculpture, lithographs and other media—produced in the Soviet Union between the eras of Stalin and Gorbachev. This is art that does not glorify, celebrate or reinforce the state; rather it tends to celebrate freedom of expression or reflect reaction to oppression. Supported by the Committee for the Absorption of Soviet Emigres, the museum (both branches) claims some 800 pieces, most by emigres, but including some smuggled work of artists still living in the Soviet Union. Many of the works convey a sense of captivity, social stagnation, sorrow. They are nonetheless powerful, and they remind visitors why tyranny squashes those artists it can't co-opt.

Lyndhurst

Hackensack Meadowlands Development Commission Environment Center Museum, 2 DeKorte Park Plaza, west of New Jersey Tnpk. (201) 460-8300. Admission: $1, children under 12: free. Open Mon. through Fri., 9 a.m. to 5 p.m.; Sat., 10 a.m. to 3 p.m.; closed holidays. Accessible to handicapped.

The entire center is a multi-faceted facility focusing on the area's salt-marsh environment and other natural history topics, but the hot attraction is the nation's only museum devoted to trash. Photos, cartoons, games, and exhibits illustrate the mountains of garbage our throw-away society generates and the accompanying headaches in dealing with it. The dramatic entranceway consists of a wall of actual trash, a cross section of a dump, comprising plastic containers, glass bottles, old tires, rusted metal, detergent boxes, and other refuse. Beyond lie exhibits concerning migration of trash, recycling, biodegradability and composting. The aim is to raise awareness of the problems and encourage people to find solutions.

Madison

Museum of Early Trades & Crafts, Main St. at Green Village Rd., off Rte. 24. (201) 377-2982. Adults: $1, children: $.50, seniors: free.

Open Tues. through Sat., 10 a.m. to 5 p.m.; Sun., 2 to 5 p.m.; summer hours, Tues. through Sat., 10 a.m. to 4 p.m.; closed major holidays. Plans to install a wheelchair ramp.

"The Way We Worked" might be the overall theme of this museum, which displays early 18th- and 19th-century tools, utensils, and implements, the preindustrial technologies that built New Jersey's and the nation's foundations. Changing exhibits cover the trades of bookbinder, cooper, cobbler, eyeglass maker, nut and bolt maker, and weaver, among others. Additional exhibits focus on kitchen implements and early lighting devices. The museum is located in a former library, built around 1900 in the Romanesque style.

Millville

Museum of American Glass, Wheaton Village. (609) 825-6800. Adults: $4, seniors: $3.50, students: $2, family: $9. Open Apr. through Dec., daily, 10 a.m. to 5 p.m.; Jan. through Mar., closed Mon. and Tues.; closed Easter, Thanksgiving, Christmas, and New Year's Day. Accessible to handicapped.

This museum offers a comprehensive and crystal-clear view of American glassmaking history from the first factory in 1739 to modern methods and uses. On display are more than 7,000 objects ranging from paperweights to chandeliers, vases to prisms, Mason jars to fiber optics. Period rooms help place the items in evolutionary context, and pieces include elegant lamps as well as more mundane kitchen utensils, such as funnels and cheese graters. Contemporary decorative glass shimmers and gleams in a special wing. Also in the Wheaton Village complex is a 19th-century-style glass factory where skilled artisans blow glass and create bottles, pitchers, and other pieces.

Mt. Holly

Historic 1810 Burlington County Prison Museum, High St.; take Exit 5 from New Jersey Tnpk. (609) 265-5958. Donation requested. Open Apr. through Nov., Wed. tours 10 and 11 a.m., 1, 2, and 3 p.m.; Sat. tours 10 and 11 a.m., noon and 1 p.m. No facilities for handicapped.

A three-story stone structure designed by architect Robert Mills, this was the county jail from 1810 to 1965. There are grim reminders everywhere, from a scale model of a gallows to the top-floor maximum security cell with its floor-based iron ring for an ankle chain. On display are leg cuffs, skeleton keys, and equipment in the basement workshop—where debtors made brooms and shoes and, ironically, sharpened blades. Visitors can see the cell chambers and processing corridor. Some of the cell walls bear fading and peeling graffiti, including the Ten Commandments and profile illustrations of 1950s and '60s film and song idols. The museum hopes to eventually have cell exhibits that show how incarceration changed over time.

Port Monmouth

Spy House Museum, 119 Port Monmouth Rd., off Rte. 36 near the beach. (201) 787-1807. Donations welcome. Open weekdays, 2 to 4:30 p.m.; Sat., 1 to 3:30 p.m.; Sun., 2:30 to 5 p.m.

Geared primarily to children and some two decades abuilding, this museum comprises four 1-room pre-1700 structures (one Dutch and three English) and recounts the heritage of the fishing and seafaring families that settled on Sandyhook Bay in the 1600s. The collection ranges from handcrafted tools to photos and models of boat building, from ice saws to water pumps. Also on view are preserved and mounted animals of the wetlands; there are plans to install a salt-water aquarium and a fishing pier.

Teterboro

Aviation Hall of Fame of New Jersey, Teterboro Airport, near I-80 and I-46 and the Meadowlands Sports Complex. (201) 288-6344. Adults: $3, seniors and children under 12: $2. Open daily, 10 a.m. to 4 p.m. Educational center is accessible to handicapped, but old control tower is not.

Photographs, artifacts, and plaques relate the stories of aviation pioneers such as Charles Lindbergh and Amelia Earhart. Also on display are piston, jet, and rocket engines developed in New Jersey. Visitors can sit in a helicopter cockpit and board a 40-passenger Martin-202 airliner. The high point of this museum is the old control tower where visitors can tune into actual air traffic control, learn about the state's leading airports, and view the personal aviation collection of broadcast personality Arthur Godfrey.

Trenton

Old Barracks Museum, Barracks St., between Rtes. 29 and 206 and near the state capitol. (609) 396-1776. Adults: $2, seniors and students: $1, children under 13: $.50. Open Mon. through Sat., 10 a.m. to 5 p.m.; Sun., 1 to 5 p.m.; closed Easter, Thanksgiving, Christmas Eve and Day, and New Year's Day. Limited facilities for handicapped.

Dedicated to Revolutionary War life in New Jersey, the museum introduces visitors to period characters, issues, and furnishings. An authentic barracks built in 1758, it housed British troops during the French and Indian War and Hessian soldiers at the time of the Battle of Trenton. It later served as a hospital for Continental troops. Today, it contains a restored squad room replete with military gear and period rooms displaying 18th- and early 19th-century furniture, ceramics, and other items. Dioramas depict the Battles of Trenton and Princeton.

New York

Ballston Spa

National Bottle Museum, 20 Church Ave., just south of junction of Rtes. 50 and 67. (518) 885-7589. Adults: $1, children under 12: free. Open daily June through Oct., 10 a.m. to 4 p.m.; Nov. through May, open Mon. through Fri.; closed major holidays. No facilities for handicapped.

Collectors of old bottles, glass, and stoneware will feel right at home among this assemblage of antique bottles, glass-blowing tools, and glassware, and even non-collectors will be interested in such exhibits as an 1890s pharmacy, a doctor's office, and a display of bottles from all 50 states. The museum, which maintains a research library, is housed in Verbeck House, a fine example of Queen Anne architecture built in 1889. An annual Bottle Identification Day is held on the grounds.

Blue Mountain Lake

Adirondack Museum, 1 mile north of junction of Rtes. 28N and 30. (518) 352-7311. Adults: $7.50, seniors: $6.25, children 7 to 15: $4.75. Open daily, Memorial Day weekend through Oct. 15, 9:30 a.m. to 5:30 p.m. (no new admissions after 4:30 p.m.). Accessible to handicapped.

The very word "Adirondack" conjures up images of rustic outdoor furniture in woodsy resort lodges and such outdoor recreations as boating, fishing, and camping. This rather large—22 buildings on 30 acres overlooking Blue Mountain Lake—historical museum covers all those facets of the legendary Adirondack region, while also providing a look at the more workaday aspects of life in the area—mining, logging, and transportation—from colonial times to the present. Of special note is an opulently-furnished Pullman car, typical of the mode of travel that wealthy American families once employed to get to their favorite vacation spot. The scenery is rugged, and the exhibits are imaginatively mounted.

Brewster

Southeast Museum, 67–69 Main St., on Rte. 6W, west of Rte. 684. (914) 279-8124. Suggested donation: $1. Open Tues. through Thurs., noon to 4 p.m.; Sat. and Sun., 2 to 4 p.m.; closed Jan. and Feb.

A modest regional historic museum it may be, but among the permanent exhibits here are some genuinely unique collections. Notable are the Borden Condensed Milk Factory exhibit, a charming collection of 250 salt and pepper shakers, and circus artifacts dating back to when the town of Brewster served as winter headquarters for several of the small circuses that were eventually consolidated under the P. T. Barnum tent. Also on display, among regional Victoriana, is an interesting collection of local minerals, an exhibit on the Croton Water System, and memorabilia of the Harlem Line Railroad.

Buffalo

QRS Music Rolls, 1026 Niagara St., on Rte. 266. (716) 885-4600. Free. Tours offered Mon. through Fri. at 10 a.m. and 2 p.m.; closed weekends and the days surrounding most major holidays. No facilities for handicapped; children under 7 are discouraged from touring.

QRS bills itself as the world's largest piano roll manufacturer since the turn of the century, and while the company makes no claim to be a museum, a tour of the red brick factory building does include a look at a small collection of items manufactured by QRS over the years, displays of magazine articles and advertising from the 1920s and earlier, and a nice variety of player pianos. Most interesting of all is an exhibit on the actual manufacture of player piano rolls. Nearly everyone finds player pianos fascinating, and it is heartening to see that music rolls for player pianos—both antique and modern—are still being produced.

Cold Spring Harbor

The Cold Spring Harbor Whaling Museum, Rte. 25A, 3 miles west of Rte. 110. (516) 367-3418. Adults: $1.50, seniors and children 6 and over: $1. Open daily, 11 a.m. to 5 p.m.; closed Thanksgiving, Christmas, New Year's Day; closed Mon., Labor Day to Memorial Day. Accessible to handicapped.

The history of Long Island isn't just that of duck hunting and potato farming. Whaling also was an important industry there in the mid-1800s, and at one time the tiny village of Cold Spring Harbor boasted a fleet of nine whaling vessels. The central exhibit of Cold Spring's whaling museum is a fully equipped 30-foot whaleboat, but of equal interest are the more than 700 scrimshaw items. In addition, there are marine paintings, whaling implements, a hands-on marine mammal bones display, ship models and a tribute to the sailors hailing from all over the world who made up the crews of Long Island's whaling vessels.

Corning

The Rockwell Museum, Cedar St. at Denison Pkwy. (Rte. 17). (607) 937-5386. Adults: $3.50, seniors: $2.50, 17 and under: free. Open Mon. through Sat., 9 a.m. to 5 p.m.; Sun., noon to 5 p.m.; during July and Aug., open Mon. through Fri., 9 a.m. to 7 p.m., Sat. and Sun., 9 a.m. to 5 p.m.; closed Thanksgiving, Christmas Eve and Day, and New Year's Day. Accessible to handicapped.

In a city built on glass—the Corning Glass Company with its well-known museum is right across the river from this museum—one would expect to find exhibits of glassware here and there, and the Rockwell Museum doesn't disappoint. The 2,000-piece collection of fine Steuben glass housed on the second floor is stunning. Produced under the direction of glass designer Frederick Carder, the collection includes beautiful examples of Art Nouveau design, crystal art pieces, and studio works done by Carder himself. But glass isn't everything, for here is also one of the finest collections of art of the American West in the eastern U.S.—works by Frederic Remington, Charles M. Russell, Thomas Morgan, and others— along with Navajo weavings, antique firearms, and Indian artifacts. There is also an enchanting collection of antique toys to delight visitors of all ages. Assembled by the owner of Corning's Rockwell Department store, the collections have found a home for the last decade in the old city hall.

Croghan

American Maple Museum, Rte. 812, 10 miles north of Lowville. (315) 346-1109. Adults: $2, children 5 to 12: $1. Open Mon. through Sat., 11 a.m. to 4 p.m., mid-May to mid-Sept. No facilities for handicapped.

While the production of maple syrup in New York isn't as well publicized as it is in New England, the maple industry has a long history in the Adirondacks. The museum building is a former parochial school; inside are eight rooms devoted to the techniques of collecting and processing maple syrup and sugar, from Indian times to the present. One room is given over to the closely related logging industry, and there is even a maple hall of fame, with pictures of people recognized for their outstanding contributions to the maple industry. A gift shop offers maple products and souvenirs, and if you time things right, you can partake of a pancake dinner featuring pure New York maple syrup.

Deansboro

Musical Museum, on Rte. 12B, 14 miles southwest of Utica. (315) 841-8774. Adults: $3.50, children: $2.50. Open daily, 10 a.m. to 4 p.m., Apr. 1 through Dec. 31; closed Jan., Feb., and Mar. Accessible to handicapped.

"Please touch!" read signs throughout this museum's 14 rooms, and accepting the invitation means using hands, feet, and nose to pump, crank, grind, blow, and otherwise operate any of the hundreds of music-producing instruments on display here. Where to begin? With the violano-virtuoso that produces a combination piano-violin concert? The rare Welte Mignon automatic piano? Pump organs? Steam organs? Juke boxes, windup music boxes, mechanical dulcimers? Located in a specially built pavilion—because of its enormous size—is a huge 1,800-pound Wurlitzer band organ that creates the music of a 20-piece band. There are also toys, whistles, and photographs of musical instruments on display and a re-creation of a 1940s ice cream parlor with jukeboxes featuring Bing Crosby, Glen Miller, and the like. For those whose musical tastes run to an earlier era, there is dancing to nickelodeon tunes in the recreated Gay '90s bar room.

East Aurora

The Elbert Hubbard Museum, 363 Oakwood Ave., 18 miles south-west of Buffalo. (716) 652-4735. Admission: $1. Open June 1 through Oct. 15, Wed., Sat., and Sun., 2 to 4 p.m. No facilities for handicapped.

In the 1890s, impressed by the Arts and Crafts movement in England, Elbert Hubbard—writer, lecturer, entrepreneur, philosopher—established Roycroft, a community of artisans dedicated to producing fine handcrafted goods in the Arts and Crafts style. The community flourished until the Depression, producing books, furniture, copperware, leather goods, and other handmade products, many examples of which are on display in this bungalow-style house built by Roycrofters in 1910. Books, furniture, artwork, and artifacts abound here, all products of an era when it was still economically possible to produce fine wares by hand. The house itself, with its copper hand-hammered hardware, wood paneling, and many built-ins, is a nice example of Arts and Crafts design.

East Bloomfield

A.W.A. Electronic-Communication Museum, on Rtes. 5 and 20, 20 miles southeast of Rochester. (716) 657-7489. Free. Open June through Aug., Sat., 2 to 4 p.m., and Wed., 7 to 9 p.m.; May through Oct., Sun., 2 to 5 p.m.; closed holiday weekends. No facilities for handicapped.

Housed in the restored 150-year-old East Bloomfield Academy building is a collection of rare early wireless radio and telegraph equipment documenting the history of wireless from its nascent days. One room has been turned into a reproduction 1920s-'30s radio store, complete with parts department; another features equipment used by shipboard wireless radio operators; a third celebrates the Golden Age of Entertainment through the history of radio and television. Many of the displays are hands-on, and many are unique. For anyone who finds the idea of seeing an early Tesla spark coil in operation, watching television on a two-inch screen, or tuning up a vintage Atwater Kent radio, this is the place to be. Of special interest to ham radio buffs are a re-created antique amateur wireless station and its fully operational modern counterpart, code named W2AN.

East Durham

Butterfly Museum, Wright St. (Rte. 67), between Freehold and Oak Hill. (518) 634-7759. Donation suggested. Open June to Labor Day, Wed., Thur., Sat., and Sun., 2 to 5 p.m. Accessible to handicapped.

Set amid beautiful mountain views of the northern Catskills, the Butterfly Museum is the result of Max Richter's lifelong interest in raising and collecting butterflies and exchanging specimens with other collectors. An enormous number of butterflies are on display in specimen cases here, as well as a variety of beetles, other insects, and shells. There are also items made from butterflies, and upstairs is a gift shop specializing in souvenirs about and made from butterflies, insects, and shells.

Elmira

National Soaring Museum, Harris Hill Rd., in Harris Hill Park; take Exit 51 from Rte. 17. (607) 734-3128. Adults: $2, seniors and students: $1.50, children under 12: free with adult. Open daily, 10 a.m. to 5 p.m.; closed Thanksgiving, Christmas, and New Year's Day. Accessible to handicapped.

Occupying 28,000 square feet of display area is the world's largest exhibit of classic and contemporary sailplanes and gliders. Here is the only known full-scale reproduction of the Wright Brothers' 1911 glider, the Schempp-Hirth *Minimoa* sailplane, and numerous World War II gliders and artifacts, including U.S. Air Force and Marine training sailplanes. Alongside such actual motorless aircraft are exhibits on meterology, aerodynamics, and the history of flight. Visitors can also experience controlling a sailplane by sitting in the museum's cockpit simulator. Actual sailplane rides are available just outside the facility.

Gloversville

Fulton County Museum, 237 Kingsborough Ave., 9 miles north of New York State Thruway 90, east of Rte. 30A. (518) 725-2203. Donation. Open July and Aug., Tues. through Sat., 10 a.m. to 4 p.m.; Sun., noon to 4 p.m.; fall and spring, Tues. through Sat., noon to 4 p.m.; closed mid-Nov. through mid-Apr. No facilities for handicapped.

The world's largest leather glove—five feet long—is on display in this county museum, as well as numerous other, more normal-sized samples from the industry that gave this town its name. Gloves of all sizes and types—for men, women, and children—are featured items in this glimpse at what was once a flourishing local industry, the tanning of leather. Also on exhibit are tanning and cutting materials and equipment. In other parts of the museum are more general types of county memorabilia, such as local carvings and miniatures.

Ilion

Remington Firearms Museum, 14 Hoefler Ave., on Rte. 5S, just south of New York State Thruway 90. (315) 894-9961. Free. Open Mon. through Sat., 9 a.m. to 4 p.m. year round; Sun., 1 to 4:30 p.m. from May to Oct. Accessible to handicapped.

The rifle that helped settle America was a flintlock Remington percussion rifle, originals of which are on display here in the hometown of the famous Remington Firearms Company. The development of rifles and shotguns from 1816 to the present—from flintlock to repeater—is visible in wall displays and cases, in one exhibit. Even more interesting are exhibits of guns that belonged to the famous and infamous. There are target .22s like the one Annie Oakley used for her exhibition shooting, a 1865 double Derringer that tucked nicely into a gambler's vest pocket, plus various six-guns and other handguns associated with both good guys and bad guys. Added attractions are displays showing how firearms are assembled, and such off-shoots of the business as knives, farm equipment and typewriters—Remingtons, of course—including the model used by Mark Twain.

Liverpool

Salt Museum, Lake Dr., in Onondaga Lake Park, southwest of New York State Thruway Exit 37. (315) 457-5715. Donations accepted. Open May 1 through Oct. 31, Mon. through Fri., 10 a.m. to 5 p.m.; Sat. and Sun., 10 a.m. to 6 p.m. Accessible to handicapped.

Times was—from about 1770 to the early 1900s—when the city of Syracuse, of which Liverpool is a suburb, was nicknamed Salt City because of its importance in the salt industry. Taxes on salt financed the Erie Canal. Abundant in natural springs in the area, the salt was extracted by boiling and evaporating, and these procedures are documented in this reconstructed salt house—actually a new structure built on an old foundation and around an original boiler chimney. A 20-minute slide presentation entitled "Boilers, Barons, and Bureaucrats," narrated by a fictional 150-year-old salt manufacturer, sets the stage for a tour of artifacts and equipment used in the salt industry, including drilling rigs, a reconstructed boiling block, and coopering equipment used in making barrels in which the salt was shipped out of Syracuse by canal.

New York City/Manhattan

American Numismatic Society, Audubon Terrace, Broadway at 155th St. (212) 234-3130. Free. Open Tues. through Sat., 9 a.m. to 4:30 p.m.; Sun., 1 to 4 p.m. No facilities for handicapped.

The main function of coins may be as legal tender, but coins as hard evidence in the unraveling of the story of civilization is the theme of the American Numismatic Society's fine World of Coins exhibit. Display cases lining three walls of the main exhibition room document not the history of money, but 2,500 years of the history of mankind, starting in ancient China, India, and Asia and passing through Medieval times to today, with coins as the link among cultures. Coins are also portrayed as social, economic, political, artistic, and religious products of their societies. A special feature of the display is the chance to tap via computer terminal into the Society's extensive data bank for detailed information on any object on display. The Museum of the American Indian and the Hispanic Society of America Museum are also located in the Audubon Terrace complex.

Black Fashion Museum, 155 W. 126th St., west of Lenox Ave. (212) 666-1320. Suggested donation (adults: $1.50, seniors and children: $1). Open daily noon to 8 p.m. by appointment.

Associated with the nearby Harlem Institute of Fashion, this museum offers changing exhibits from its permanent collection. The focus of the collection is certainly unique: clothing that celebrates the contribution made by black people to the world of fashion, a contribution that runs the gamut from slave dresses to the winners of recent fashion design competitions. It is a strong collection culled from a rich and proud heritage, and among notable examples of clothing featured in changing exhibits are a copy of the inaugural gown made for Mary Todd Lincoln by former slave Elizabeth Keckley; dresses by Ann Lowe, designer of Jacqueline Bouvier's gown for her wedding to John F. Kennedy; costumes from such Broadway shows as "The Wiz" and "Eubie"; and clothing from the wardrobes of Diahann Carroll, Ruby Dee, Lionel Hampton, and other black celebrities known for their fashion flair.

The Con Edison Energy Museum, 145 E. 14th St., just west of Third Ave. (212) 460-6244. Free. Open Tues. through Sat., 10 a.m. to 4 p.m. Accessible to handicapped.

Among a goodly number of interesting exhibits proving that electric energy isn't such a dry subject after all, is one that fascinates both natives and tourists alike: a "walking" tour beneath the streets of modern-day New York City. This simulated tour opens up the fascinating world of The Big Apple's core, an underground tangle of utility lines, subways, and sewers, all colorfully illuminated—in this exhibit, at least. Among other informative displays are old-time kitchen appliances, examples of Thomas A. Edison's experiments, and a scale model of Edison's innovative Pearl Street powerhouse, circa 1882. There is also a question-and-answer panel with information on such electrical trivia as when the first New York major league night baseball game was played, hands-on energy-saving devices, and a depiction of Con Edison's efforts to stock the Hudson River with striped bass from its own hatchery.

The Forbes Magazine Galleries, 62 Fifth Ave., on corner of 12th St. (212) 206-5548. Free. Open Tues. through Sat., 10 a.m. to 4 p.m.; closed Sun., Mon., and all legal holidays. Two steps up at entrance, but otherwise accessible to handicapped.

Given the fabulous wealth of Malcolm Forbes, what would a person collect? Some nice art, certainly. And legions of toy soldiers. And toy boats of all types from all eras. And, just as a quirk, some oddball trophies? Or how about something truly fantastic, like *objets de luxe* crafted by Fabergé? Malcolm Forbes collected all such things, plus a number of presidential papers, and installed them in his magazine's building. Here, imaginatively and whimsically displayed, a flotilla of toy boats sails across an old-fashioned copper bathtub, toy soldiers mount sieges on turreted castles, and four miniature presidential rooms highlight a gallery full of Lincolniana, presidential signatures, and other documents. Added attractions are works of art that relate to the various collections, such as a panel from the luxury liner *Normandie* that enhances the toy-boat gallery. The collection of Fabergé eggs here is second in number only to that of Britain's Queen Elizabeth.

J. M. Mossman Collection of Locks, 20 W. 44th St., in offices of the General Society of Mechanics and Tradesmen, just west of Fifth Ave. (212) 838-2560. Free. Open Mon. through Fri., 10 a.m. to 4 p.m.; closed holidays, subject to change. Accessible to handicapped.

Even without the benefit of tour guides and the kinds of educational presentations offered by most museums, a visit to J. M. Mossman's collection is a satisfying side trip in midtown Manhattan. On view in 13 handsome-wood and glass-cases are such variations on the familiar padlock as grasshopper, snail, quadruplex pin tumbler, wheel, Renaissance, click, magic key, and even a so-called Very Complicated lock. A free booklet with detailed information outlines a self-guided tour.

Museum of Television and Radio, 1 E. 53rd St., just east of Fifth Ave. (212) 752-7684. Suggested donation adults: $4, seniors and students: $3, children under 13: $2. Open Wed. through Sat., noon to 5 p.m.; Tues., noon to 8 p.m.; closed Sun., Mon. and major holidays. Accessible to handicapped.

Watch and listen is the rule of the day at this museum, formerly the Museum of Broadcasting. With a repository of more than 40,000 radio and television programs spanning 60 years and covering all aspects of the field—entertainment, news, sports, documentary, variety—the world of broadcast is at the public's fingertips here. Choose a program from the card catalog, ask the librarian to retrieve it from the stacks, and Lucy or Jack Benny or the news of a particular day will come alive at one of the two-person consoles on the premises. This is the only museum of its kind. It is very popular, and space is limited, so there can be a wait to enter.

Museum of Holography, 11 Mercer St., just north of Canal St., 1 block west of Broadway. (212) 925-0581. Adults: $3.50, children: $2. Open Tues. through Sun., 11 a.m. to 6 p.m. No facilities for the handicapped, and exhibits are not aligned for people in wheelchairs.

To answer the most often-posed question by visitors to this museum, holography is a means of creating three-dimensional images with laser light. On permanent display in a landmark cast-iron building in New York's Soho district are films and exhibits describing the history and technology of holography. Changing exhibits offer a look at selections from the world's largest collection of holograms. What you see at first glance is not necessarily what appears with a closer look—from one angle a candle is unlit, but from another it flickers in flame; a shiny round apple materializes in a previously empty hand; Beverly Sills appears in full performance, lacking only the sound. It's all rather mysterious and somehow compelling.

Museum of the City of New York, 1220 Fifth Ave., at 103rd St. (212) 543-1672 or for recorded message -1034. Adults: $3, seniors and students: $1.50, children: $1, family maximum: $5. Open Tues. through Sat., 10 a.m. to 5 p.m.; Sun. and holidays, 1 to 5 p.m.; closed Thanksgiving, Christmas, and New Year's Day. Accessible to handicapped.

Founded in 1923, this was the first museum devoted to a major American city. Preserved here are objects revealing three centuries of the city's material culture, growth, and development. Collections range from costumes worn or designed by New Yorkers to decorative arts objects such as silver, ceramics, and furniture, as well as paintings and sculpture, prints and photographs, theatrical memorabilia, toys and dolls. Of special note are the Big Apple multi-media presentation, 10 exquisite dollhouses dating from 1769 to 1976, and period alcoves and rooms detailing interiors from several eras in the city's history.

Police Academy Museum, 235 20th Street, between Second and Third Aves. Free. Open Mon. through Fri., 9 a.m. to 3 p.m.; closed weekends and holidays. No facilities for handicapped.

A machine gun used by Al Capone's gang with lethal results, counterfeit money, a shotgun fitted into a violin case, exotic weapons with long-forgotten histories, souvenirs of celebrated criminal cases—exactly the kinds of things that the crime buff hopes to find in a museum detailing the rich and exciting history of New York City's Police Department fill display cases here. In addition, there are exhibits on the changes in uniforms, badges, nightsticks, handcuffs, fingerprinting, and other crime-fighting equipment of New York's Finest, plus engrossing evidence of the ongoing war against gangs and drugs.

New York City/Queens

American Museum of the Moving Image, 35 Ave. at 36 St., Astoria. (718) 784-4520. Adults: $5, seniors: $4, students and children: $2.50. Open Tues. through Fri., noon to 5 p.m.; Sat. and Sun., 11 a.m. to 6 p.m. Accessible to handicapped.

The art, history, and technology of motion pictures, television, and video are the focus of exhibitions, screenings, collections and interpretive programs here. Located in a renovated building on the site of the Astoria Studios complex, a former facility of Paramount Pictures, the museum features, in addition to a comprehensive view of the moving-image industries, a look at many of the behind-the-scenes professions, such as acting, directing, set designing, make-up, and sound engineering. Scale models, photographs, tools, and equipment tell of the many skills that go into making a film or a television production.

New York City/Staten Island

Jacques Marchais Center of Tibetan Art. 338 Lighthouse Ave.; from Rte. 278 south for 5 miles on Richmond Rd., right on Lighthouse Ave. (718) 987-3478. Adults: $2.50, seniors: $2, children: $1. Open Apr. through Nov., Wed. through Sun., 1 to 5 p.m.; Dec. and Mar. by appointment. No facilities for handicapped.

For people who think they've seen it all in The Big Apple, there is a little bit of tranquil Tibet on Staten Island. One of the two

Tibetan-style buildings here is used as a library. The other, a temple-like structure complete with granite altar, houses a collection of 19th-century dolls, figures, statuettes, wall hangings, artwork, bowls, wooden calligraphic blocks, robes, and other objects, most of which pertain to Buddhist religious practices. There are butter containers from which lamas replenish their lamps, aprons of carved human bones worn in rites aimed at calling up the spirits of the dead, and silver skull bowls studded with semi-precious stones. The collection was started by the sea-going grandfather of Mrs. Harry Klauber, who adopted the name Jacques Marchais and who later amassed most of the artifacts and designed the center's buildings and gardens.

Palmyra

Alling Coverlet Museum, 122 William St.; from New York State Thruway north on Rte. 21 to Palmyra, right at first light, then left. (315) 597-6981. Donations accepted. Open daily, June through mid-Sept., 1 to 4 p.m. Handicapped access to first floor.

The village of Palmyra is primarily known as the cradle of the Church of the Latter Day Saints, but thanks to one woman's admiration of local handiwork, it is also the repository of the largest collection of heirloom woven bed coverings in the United States. Over a period of 30 years, Mrs. Merle Alling assembled this collection of lovely hand-loomed spreads, most of them the work of local 19th-century farmwives who also spun and dyed the wool, cotton, and linen that make up the bedspreads. Colors are rich, and designs range from simple to sophisticated. In addition to the coverlets, the museum features numerous 19th-century handmade quilts, spinning equipment, and coverlets produced on multiple-harness looms by two 19th-century professional weavers.

Rochester

The Strong Museum, One Manhattan Square, in southeast corner of city inside Rte. 490 inner loop, off Monroe Ave. (716) 263-2700. Adults: $2, seniors: $1.50, children 4 to 16: $.75. Open Mon. through Sat., 10 a.m. to 5 p.m.; Sun., 1 to 5 p.m.; closed Thanksgiving, Christmas, New Year's Day. Accessible to handicapped.

It's too bad every American city can't have a museum like the Strong Museum. Many communities have exhibits devoted to the early farm-oriented way of life in this country, but this museum is unique in its exploration of a period—1820 to 1940—when American life was undergoing some very basic changes. Mechanization turned villages into cities, steam and electric power changed the very pace of the day, and new modes of transportation brought far-flung communities in touch. Seeded by the vast collections of Margaret Woodbury Strong, this museum offers close-up looks at popular taste and culture between the Early American period and World War II. Catalog files and comprehensive labeling permit real study of American art pottery, furniture, ceramics, glass, silver, export trade goods, lighting devices, timepieces, toys, mechanical banks, home crafts, and housekeeping equipment. Almost overwhelming is a collection of dolls—92 cases full. The familiar faces of Tweedledum and Tweedledee, the British princesses Elizabeth and Margaret, Shirley Temple, and Kewpie dolls peep out from among play-worn examples of wax, wood, rag, porcelain, plastic, and papier mâché dolls. There is also an exhibit-oriented activity center for three- to seven-year-olds.

Rye Brook

Museum of Cartoon Art, Comly Ave., between King St. and Pemberwick Ave., and between New England Thruway and Hutchinson River Pkwy. (914) 939-0234. Adults: $3, seniors and students: $2, children 5 to 12: $1. Open Tues. through Fri., 10 a.m. to 4 p.m.; Sun., 1 to 5 p.m.; closed Mon., Sat., Thanksgiving, Christmas, and New Year's Day. No facilities for handicapped.

As if this museum's focus—original works from the various genres of cartoon art—weren't unusual enough, it is also housed in Ward's Castle, the first house in the world constructed (in 1876) entirely of reinforced concrete, a cross between a Queen Anne cottage and King Arthur's castle. From the rug beneath the visitor's feet—featuring the likes of Mandrake the Magician, Henry, and Pete the Tramp—to the decor in the rest rooms, everything here is a delightful celebration of cartoons, comic strips, comic books, animation, caricature, and illustration. *Mad* magazine's Alfred E. Newman looks out from one display; television sets flicker with cartoons; and a papier mâché statue of Dagwood Bumstead soaks in a footed bathtub. Because so many of the characters are so very familiar—from the comics pages, the editorial pages, and both giant and small screen—there truly is something fun for everyone here. The museum is the brainchild of cartoonist Mort Walker, creator of Beetle Bailey.

Saratoga Springs

National Museum of Dance, S. Broadway, on Rte. 9 about 3½ miles north of I-87. (518) 584-2225. Adults: $2, seniors and students: $1, children under 12: $.50. Open May through Labor Day, Tues. through Sat., 10 a.m. to 5 p.m.; Sun., noon to 4 p.m.; Labor Day through Dec. 15, Thurs. through Sat., 10 a.m. to 5 p.m. and Sun., noon to 4 p.m. Accessible to handicapped.

In this, the only museum in the country devoted exclusively to dance, three large galleries of changing exhibits share space with the permanent hall of fame exhibit "Shaping the American Dance Dream" where photo murals, video presentations, and memorabilia augment biographies describing the work and influence of the great in dancing. George Balanchine, Martha Graham, Isadora Duncan, and Agnes deMille are all on show here, right alongside such other shapers of American dance as Fred Astaire and Busby Berkeley.

Stony Brook

The Museums at Stony Brook, 1208 Rte. 25A; north on Rte. 97 from Long Island Expressway to end, then left for 1½ miles. (516) 751-0066. Adults: $4, seniors: $3, students: $2.75, children 6 to 12: $2. Open Wed. through Sat. and most Mon. holidays, 10 a.m. to 5 p.m.; Sun., noon to 5 p.m.; closed Tues., Thanksgiving Day, Christmas Eve and Day, and New Year's Day. Almost entirely accessible to handicapped.

This complex of three museums offers a very satisfying mix, handsomely mounted all around. While the focus of all three is largely local (Long Island), that is not to say the works and items on display are in any way second rate. The celebrated 19th-century painter and draftsman William Sidney Mount was a local, and several of his beautifully-composed works are the centerpiece of the Art Museum's exhibitions on Long Island artists. Duck decoys, shown in the History Museum, are also of local origin, but this is one of the five best collections of decoys in the world, and Long Island decoy carvers were world renowned. Also in the History Museum are a nice selection of costumes and costume accessories dating from the mid-19th century to the present, as well as toys, textiles, and a fascinating group of 15 miniature rooms executed by Frederick Hicks and depicting interiors ranging from an Elizabethan room to a 1930s antique shop. A visit to the Carriage Museum is a remarkable experience—its 12 galleries are chock-full of plain and fancy carriages, pleasure vehicles, farm and delivery wagons, stages, sleighs, horse-drawn fire wagons, and such outstanding specimens as a gypsy wagon, the beautiful Grace Darling omnibus, and a gaily-painted stagecoach that plied the highways of France in the late 1700s.

West Point

United States Military Academy Museum, Olmsted Hall, on South Post of U.S. Military Academy, actually in town of Highland Falls. (914) 938-2203. Free. Open daily, 10:30 a.m. to 4:15 p.m.; closed Christmas and New Year's Day. Accessible to handicapped.

This is the granddaddy of American military museums, a gold mine for both military and non-military history buffs and the repository of many "once-owned-by" items—a pair of flintlock pistols once owned by George Washington, sabers of Gen. Winfield Scott and Gen. Philip Henry Sheridan, a uniform coat of Gen. Ulysses S. Grant, a sash worn by Gen. Robert E. Lee, swords and pistols once owned by Napoleon Bonaparte. More than 20,000 items are on view here, including guns, cannons, edged weapons, and uniforms. There are artworks by Thomas Sully, Frederic Remington, Winslow Homer, and the Weirs—Robert, John and J. Alden—among others. While the focus, of course, is primarily on the American military, there are exhibits on European and Asian military history as well.

Pennsylvania

Allison Park

Depreciation Lands Museum, 4743 S. Pioneer Dr., near Rte. 8 off the Pennsylvania Tnpk. (412) 486-0563. Adults: $1, children: $.50. Open Sun., 1 to 4 p.m. and by appointment. Accessible to handicapped.

Devoted to a little-known chapter of early national history, this museum focuses on the settlement of part of western Pennsylvania known as the Depreciation Lands, which represented a method of repaying Continental troops whose scrip or wages depreciated during and after the Revolution. An authentic log house and period artifacts—including tools, household implements, and a Conestoga wagon—provide a perspective of late 18th-century life on what was then the frontier. The museum holds a festival the first Saturday in October.

Ambridge

Old Economy Village, Rte. 65 west of I-79. (412) 266-4500. Adults: $3, seniors: $2. Open Tues. through Sat., 9 a.m. to 4 p.m.; Sun., noon to 4 p.m.; closed Mon. and holidays except Memorial Day, July 4th, and Labor Day. Limited access for handicapped.

A six-acre historic site, Old Economy Village displays the industry, culture, and life style of the Harmonists, a 19th-century Christian communal group known for their piety and prosperity. The homes, craft shops, storage buildings, and other edifices contain tools, furnishings and utensils used by society members. A green-house, gardens, and community kitchen also offer glimpses into the nature of the defunct sect. The site contains more than 16,000 artifacts and 17 restored structures. Special events include mid-summer Kunstfest and a 19th-century Christmas.

Boyertown

Boyertown Museum of Historic Vehicles, 28 Warwick St., off Rte. 73. (215) 367-2090. Adults: $2.50, seniors: $2, students: $1.50. Open Tues. through Fri., 8 a.m. to 4 p.m.; Sat. and Sun., 10 a.m. to 4 p.m. No facilities for handicapped.

As much as anything, transportation tells us about our past and how far we've traveled. This museum focuses on antique vehicles traditional to southeastern Pennsylvania. There are the expected steam, electric, and gasoline-powered cars and trucks, but also sleighs, surreys, huckster wagons, and Conestoga wagons. Two unusual pieces are the Hill car made in nearby Fleetwood and believed to be the oldest gas-powered auto in America and the first truck body built by the Boyertown Carriage Works.

Columbia

Watch and Clock Museum of the National Association of Watch and Clock Collectors, 514 Poplar St., off Rte. 30. (717) 684-8261. Adults: $3, children 6 to 17: $1. Open Tues. through Sat., 9 a.m. to 4 p.m.; closed holidays. Accessible to handicapped.

Time marches on here. Centuries of minding the minutes toll in the form of clocks, watches, tools, patents, records, and memoirs. There are European musical clocks, French timepieces, and jewelry, everything reflecting the precision and art that have gone into keeping time. The museum counts the country's largest collection of timepieces and houses some extraordinary works, such as Dr. Stephen Engle's monumental clock—11 feet wide by 9 feet high, it has 48 moving figures and two organ movements.

Coplay

Saylor Park Cement Industry Museum, N. Second St. (215) 435-4664 or 261-1200. Free. Open May through Sept., Sat. and

Sun., 1 to 4 p.m.; other times by appointment. Accessible to handicapped.

Dedicated to David O. Saylor, founder of the Portland cement
industry, the museum features nine vertical Schoefer kilns from the
late 1860s. The structures are connected at the base, through the
middle of which runs the museum proper. Here are photos, cap-
tions, and artifacts discussing Saylor's cement-making process. The
site was owned by the Coplay Cement Company until the 1970s
when Lehigh County acquired it to retain as a record of the area's
industrial development. It is reportedly the only museum devoted
to the cement industry.

Cornwall

Cornwall Iron Furnace, Rexmont Rd. at Boyd St., off Rte. 72 north
of Pennsylvania Tnpk. (717) 272-9711. Adults: $1.50, seniors: $1,
children 6 to 17: $.50. Open Tues. through Sat., 9 a.m. to 5 p.m.;
Sun., noon to 5 p.m.; closed Mon. except Memorial Day, July 4th,
and Labor Day; closed Thanksgiving, Christmas, and New Year's
Day. Limited access for handicapped.

Before the Revolution, the American colonies smelted one-sev-
enth of the world's iron, and Cornwall's furnace was a major producer. It ceased operations in 1883, but stands today as a unique
reminder of a young nation's iron industry. Preserved here are the
weighing and casting rooms, the steam engine and the air blast
mechanism with its huge wood-and-iron gear. Exhibits, graphic
displays, and artifacts tell the story of the region's early iron manufacture from mining ore to producing cannonballs. Within the
Cornwall complex are bins, ovens, smithies, shops, and other
features of a complete iron plantation.

Doylestown

The Mercer Museum, 84 Pine St., between Rtes. 611 and 202.
Adults: $4, seniors: $3.50, students: $1.50. Open Mon. through
Sat., 10 a.m. to 5 p.m.; Sun., noon to 5 p.m.; closed Christmas,
Thanksgiving, and New Year's Day. Limited access for handi-
capped.

Henry Chapman Mercer was a collector, and this museum represents his energetic attempt to retrieve and display the prein-

dustrial tools that built a nation. Some 40,000 implements, objects, and utensils encompass more than 60 trades and crafts, from farming to clockmaking to law. Crammed into a seven-story concrete structure that Mercer designed are not only hoes, tongs, mallets, chisels, strainers, pots, and urns, but also a whaleboat, wooden ballot boxes, a lap-held tape loom, a betty lamp, tavern signs, and a gallows—the last word in antiques. There is also a changing-exhibit gallery, and in May the museum hosts a weekend folk fest with demonstrations and sales of 18th- and 19th-century crafts accompanied by period entertainment.

Easton

Canal Museum, 200 S. Delaware Dr. (215) 250-6700. Adults: $1, children 5 to 12: $.50. (Canal boat ride $4 for adults, $2 for children; price includes Locktender's House Museum.) Open Mon. through Sat., 10 a.m. to 4 p.m.; Sun., 1 to 5 p.m. Canal boat has 2½-hour schedule and runs Memorial Day through Labor Day and weekends in Sept. Limited access for handicapped.

The museum gives glimpses of the construction, development, and operation of American canals—including Massachusetts' Middlesex, New Jersey's Morris, and New York's Erie—from the late 18th century to the 1930s. Audiovisuals and exhibits depict the technology and economics of canals, the water highways of early America. One room represents the interior bottom of a canal boat compete with living quarters. There are three hinged boat replicas plus actual pieces of old locks and gates. Visitors also can ride on a mule-drawn canal boat along a restored section of the Lehigh Canal and tour the 1890s Locktender's House.

Franklin

Antique Music Museum, 1675 Pittsburgh Rd., 12 miles north of I-80. (814) 437-6301. Adults: $4, young people 12 to 16: $2.50, children 7 to 12: $1. Open Apr. 15 to Oct. 22, Mon. through Sat., 10 a.m. to 4 p.m.; Sun., 1 to 5 p.m. Accessible to handicapped.

This museum is pitched to the ear as well as the eye. For fans of the Gay '90s and Roaring '20s, this tuneful collection zings the strings of the heart. Antique nickelodeons, calliopes, street barrel organs, carnival organs, monkey organs, and other sound pounders roll back the years. The museum has one of the two Artizan calliopes, which play by roll or keyboard, left in the country. And a rare Berry Wood A.O.W. Automatic combines 13 instruments in one machine. The owners give personal tours and play all the antique music machines.

Galeton

The Pennsylvania Lumber Museum, Rte. 6 between Galeton and Coudersport. (814) 435-2652. Adults: $1.50, seniors: $1, children: $.50. Open Mar. through Nov., Mon. through Sat., 9 a.m. to 4:30 p.m.; Sun., 10 a.m. to 4:30 p.m.; Dec. through Feb., Mon. through Fri., 9 a.m. to 4:30 p.m.; closed some holidays. Facilities for handicapped, including wheelchair on site.

A facility whose bite is as good as its bark, this museum displays all the tools and machines of Pennsylvania's 19th-century lumber industry. From saws and axes to log loaders and a Shay-geared locomotive, the museum cuts through the years to a bygone era. Perhaps the most dramatic exhibit is the site's period-designed operational sawmill that reduces logs to boards and trims them to standard lengths. The museum also hosts several wood-related craft workshops during the year and the annual Bark Peeler's Convention, a weekend of demonstrations, competitions, and entertainment.

Johnstown

Johnstown Flood Museum, 304 Washington St. (814) 539-1889. Adults: $3, seniors: $2.50, children 6 to 18: $2. Open May 1 through Oct. 31, Mon. through Wed., 10 a.m. to 5 p.m. and Thurs. through Sat., 10 a.m. to 8 p.m. and Sun., noon to 5 p.m.; Nov. 1 through Apr. 30, Mon. through Sat., 10 a.m. to 5 p.m. and Sun., noon to 5 p.m. Accessible to handicapped.

One hundred years ago a flood from a neglected dam all but destroyed the city of Johnstown. The surging wall of water killed more than 2,000 people and destroyed many buildings. The three-floor museum, housed in what was a Carnegie Library (circa 1891), contains retrieved artifacts such as ledgers and furniture. A 20-minute docudrama film, relief maps, and photos also help tell the story of the ruin and rebirth of Johnstown.

Kennett Square

Mushroom Museum at Phillips Place, 909 E. Baltimore Pike, on Rte. 1, 35 miles southwest of Philadelphia. (215) 388-6082. Adults: $1.25, seniors: $.75, children 7 to 12: $.50. Open daily, 10 a.m. to 6 p.m.; closed Easter, Thanksgiving, Christmas, and New Year's Day. Accessible to handicapped.

Pennsylvania is the leading mushroom-producing state and this region bills itself as the mushroom capital of the world. Dioramas, charts, slides, videos, and exhibits relate the history, lore, and mystique of mushrooms, dating all the way back to the Egyptians, Greeks, and Romans. A mushroom-growing room, recipes, and gift packs amplify the feast. Established in 1972, the museum was started in response to numerous questions about how mushrooms grow. It continues to evolve—one of the more recent additions is a diorama on the shiitake, an Asiatic mushroom gaining popularity in the U.S.

Lititz

Candy Americana Museum, 46 N. Broad St., off Rte. 501, just south of Pennsylvania Tnpk. (717) 626-1131. Free. Open Mon. through Sat., 10 a.m. to 5 p.m.; closed Thanksgiving and Christmas. No wheelchair ramp.

Operated by the Wilbur Chocolate Co, this museum tells the story of how sweet it was, and still is. The collection features hundreds of antique and unusual candy containers, such as porcelain chocolate pots, tins, and wooden holders. There are also molds, spoons, ladles, stirrers, and other implements of early candy manufacture. Antique production equipment sweetens an early 1900s candy kitchen and offers contrast to contemporary methods illustrated by a video. The museum's exhibits cover all phases of candy making, from manufacturing and processing to packaging and advertising. A candy outlet store provides relief to those afflicted with the proverbial sweet tooth.

Philadelphia

American Swedish Historical Museum, 1900 Pattison Ave. (215) 389-1776. Adults: $2, seniors and students: $1. Open Tues. through

Fri., 10 a.m. to 4 p.m.; Sat. and Sun., noon to 4 p.m. No facilities for handicapped.

Founded in 1926, the museum commemorates and preserves materials relating to Swedish-American and Scandinavian subjects. Twelve permanent galleries and one changing-exhibits gallery house arts and artifacts, including Carl Larsson paintings, Anders Zorn etchings, Orrefors glass, invention models, dolls, folk costumes, furniture, and more. Swedish traders arrived in the area in 1638, and colonists followed in the next decade—part of the museum's offering encompasses archaeological artifacts from this early settlement period. The museum also celebrates traditional Swedish holidays, such as Valborgsmassoafton to welcome spring and Midsommar to mark the summer solstice.

Mummers Museum, Two St. at Washington Ave., not far from the Liberty Bell and Independence Hall. (215) 336-3050. Adults: $2, students, seniors, and children: $1. Open Tues. through Sat., 9 a.m. to 5 p.m.; Sun., noon to 5 p.m.; closed Thanksgiving, Christmas Day, and New Year's Day. Accessible to handicapped.

The Mummers Museum, the only such institution dedicated to a single folk custom, reflects the rich history and pageantry of Philadelphia's famed Mummers parade on New Year's Day. It's nothing less than a colorful romp through layers of cultural blending in the City of Brotherly Love. Masquerade, music, dance, and art all find expression here. Learn to do the Mummers' strut, browse among the spangled, plumed, and vibrant costumes, and discover the origins of mummery via old-time movie viewers. The facility also houses a hall of fame and a research library.

Pittsburgh

James L. Kelso Bible Lands Museum, 616 N. Highland Ave., Pittsburgh Theological Seminary. (412) 362-5610. Free. Open Wed., 9 a.m. to 3 p.m. during the academic year and by appointment. Accessible to handicapped.

Named for a professor of Old Testament history and biblical archaeology at the seminary, this museum serves as a research and teaching facility as well as an informational resource. It features objects from Near East excavations dating back to the 1920s and illustrating the culture, commerce, and social structure of biblical times. Displays include ancient pottery, tools, figurines, and weapons, cuneiform tablets and Egyptian hieroglyphics, coins dating to the 4th century B.C., a 1st-century A.D. wooden comb from Qumran, and a fragment of linen wrapping from one of the Dead Sea scrolls.

Pottstown

Streitwieser Trumpet Museum, 880 Vaughan Rd., Exit 23 from Pennsylvania Tnpk. (215) 327-1351. Suggested donation of $3. Open 11 months by appointment, 8 a.m. to 5 p.m.; closed during Aug. No facilities for handicapped.

Established in 1978 and located in a restored 19th-century barn, the museum houses more than 700 instruments, sheet music, recordings, photos, books, and figurines relating to sounds according to brass. Founder Franz Streitwieser believes old brass instruments are as honorable in music as venerable violins. Trumpets, after all, have warded off evil, heralded royalty, and sounded "Charge!" The collection boasts Civil War bugles, 18th-century German steer horns, and copies of Viking instruments. Streitwieser has even found a gold-plated tenor horn from 1880 used in the Russian czar's orchestra. A spring and fall concert series allows the museum to blow its own horn, and antique instruments from the collection frequently find play.

Scranton

Pennsylvania Anthracite Heritage Museum, Bald Mountain Rd., off I-81 and the Scranton Expressway. (717) 963-4845. Adults: $2, seniors: $1.50, children: $1. Open Mon. through Sat., 9 a.m. to 5 p.m.; Sun., noon to 5 p.m. Accessible to handicapped.

The museum's purpose is to collect, preserve, and interpret the history of Pennsylvania's hard-coal region, looking at the interactions of economics, technology, and culture. Some 500 objects—including a full-size steam engine, vehicles, mining gear, and textile machinery—and 200 photos and illustrations fill a 22,000-square-foot exhibition hall. In addition, the museum abuts the Lackawanna Coal Mine Tour where visitors can don hard hats and board an underground rail car to follow a vein of anthracite coal some 250 feet below the surface.

Titusville

Drake Well Museum, off Rte. 8, north of I-80. (814) 827-2797. Adults: $2, seniors: $1.50, children 7 to 17: $1. Open daily, May through Oct., 9 a.m. to 5 p.m.; Nov. through Apr., Tues. through Sat., 9 a.m. to 5 p.m.; Sun., noon to 5 p.m. Limited facilities for handicapped.

In August 1858, energy entered a new era. The world's first oil well gushed at this site in western Pennsylvania and Edwin L. Drake became the father of the oil industry. The museum interprets the beginnings of this vital industry with some 70 exhibits depicting the production, refining, and use of oil, the geology involved, and the early oil companies. Also on the grounds are a replica of the first derrick and engine house, various wagons and oil rigs, and an early pipeline station. In August, the museum hosts its annual Oil Field Picnic celebrating the regions' oil field traditions in folk festival format.

Williamsport

Peter J. McGovern Little League Baseball Museum, on Rte. 15, 15 miles north of I-80. (717) 326-3607. Adults: $4, seniors: $2, children 5 to 13: $1, family: $10. Open Memorial Day through Labor Day, Mon. through Sat., 9 a.m. to 7 p.m.; Sun., noon to 7 p.m.; remainder of year same hours, except closes at 5 p.m.

Baseball brings out the kid in everyone, and this museum is home park for the Little League version of the game. Begun in 1939, Little League baseball now involves 2.5 million kids every year in some 7,000 leagues. This eight-room facility traces the evolution of uniforms and mitts through the years and shows team records and participants in the annual Little League World Series. One room is devoted to safety precautions in Little League play, and various videos address such topics as how baseballs are made. Batting and pitching cages test a player's skill and a question-and-answer board tests knowledge of the rules of the game.

York

Bob Hoffman Weightlifting Hall of Fame, 3300 Board Rd.; take Exit 11 from I-83. (717) 767-6481. Free. Open Mon. through Fri., 9 a.m. to 3:30 p.m., Sat., 10 a.m. to 3:30 p.m. Accessible to handicapped.

Pumping iron—or bending, twisting or otherwise wrestling with it—dates back to the 19th century, and strongman feats go back centuries. Weightlifting is now an important part of the Olympic games and a major element in sports conditioning. Via exhibits, gear, statues, photos, drawings, and memorabilia, this museum flexes the concept and practice of bodybuilding and honors the Mr. Americas, Olympic medal winners, female champs, and various legends of the sport such as Eugen Sandow and Bob Hoffman. The museum explains the finer points of competition and posing, and a display room features the latest equipment.

Rhode Island

East Greenwich

New England Wireless and Steam Museum, Frenchtown Rd. at corner of Tillinghast Rd. (401) 884-1710. Admission: $5. Open June 1 through Sept. 30, Sun., 1 to 5 p.m. and by appointment. Limited facilities for handicapped.

This is really two collections in one—exhibits on early radio, telegraph, and telephone equipment, plus a number of stationary steam, hot air, gas, and oil engines. Visitors with a mechanical bent will delight in the sheer variety, while others will enjoy wandering among the mechanical and telegraphic curiosities, or browsing through the reference library.

Newport

Naval War College Museum, Coasters Harbor Island; cross Newport Bridge to reach island. (401) 841-4052. Free. Open weekdays, 10 a.m. to 4 p.m., year round; also open weekends June 1 through Sept. 30, noon to 4 p.m.; closed holidays. Accessible to handicapped.

The history of the art and science of navel warfare is the theme of this spacious two-level museum. Both parts illustrate that history through exhibits of ship models, paintings, busts and statuary, uniforms, and weapons. Exhibits on the first floor concentrate on the history of the Navy in the Narragansett Bay region, starting with the first naval engagement of the Revolutionary War in 1775, and continuing to today. The focus of the second-floor exhibit space is the history of the Naval War College, which was established in 1884.

Vermont

Glover

Bread and Puppet Museum, Rte. 122, off Rte. 16, south of Glover. (802) 525-3031. Free. Open by appointment only. No facilities for the handicapped.

Two floors of a 125-year-old barn have been converted to a showplace for the vast collection of masks, puppets, paintings, and graphics created by the long-running Bread and Puppet Theater for use in its productions. Grouped according to size, color, theme, or pure whimsy, original theatrical characters in the form of figures and masks—from a tiny doll to a 20-foot effigy—hang from ceilings and walls and crowd the aisles, recreating scenes from past puppet shows.

Manchester Village

American Museum of Fly Fishing, Rte. 7A, on corner of Seminary Ave. (802) 362-3300. Suggested donation: $2. Open daily May through Oct., 10 a.m. to 4 p.m.; weekdays, Nov. through Apr., 10 a.m. to 4 p.m.; closed major holidays. Accessible to handicapped.

Exhibits of fishing rods and reels are interesting enough, but fishing flies—beautifully handcrafted bits of fluff, feather, and silk floss—can be absolutely charming. They are nicely mounted here in wood-framed glass pages accompanied by etchings depicting typical waterways where fish they are designed to lure might be found. Many were made by famous fly-tiers, the likes of Ray Bergman, Theodore Gordon, and others. There are rods and reels crafted by such masters as Orvis and Payne, and angling paraphernalia of many famous Americans—Bing Crosby, Andrew Carnegie, several presidents, and many more—making this the world's largest collection of fly-fishing gear.

Pittsford

New England Maple Museum, Rte. 7, 8 miles north of Rutland. (802) 483-9414. Adults: $1, seniors: $.75, children 6 to 12: $.50. Open daily May 26 through Oct. 31, 8:30 a.m. to 5:30 p.m.; Mar. 15 through May 25 and Nov. 1 through Dec. 23, 10 a.m. to 4 p.m.; closed Jan. and Feb. Accessible to handicapped.

The complete story of maple sugaring is presented in this typical sugar shack, starting with the making of the special wooden buckets used to collect sap from sugar maple trees, through the boiling down of sap into syrup, to candy making. Attendant displays include murals, paintings, artifacts, and a large collection of antique and modern equipment. A slide show and tasting counter amplify the presentation.

Proctor

Vermont Marble Exhibit, 61 Main St., on Rte. 3. (802) 459-3311. Adults: $2.50, children 2 to 12: $1. Open daily late May through Oct., 9 a.m. to 5:30 p.m. Access for handicapped.

A new all-marble lobby leads to an impressive Gallery of Presidents, with marble bas-reliefs of American heads of state, then on to other unusual displays concerning the geology, quarrying, and use of Vermont marble. Photographs and films do most of the explaining, but displays on the uses of marble are eye-catching and well labeled. A sculptor works in full view of visitors, and a nearby gallery features all manner of marble sculpture.

Rutland

Norman Rockwell Museum, Rte. 4 east, 2 miles from junction of Rtes. 4 and 7. (802) 773-6095. Adults: $2.50, seniors: $2, children 8

to 16: $.75. Open daily 9 a.m. to 6 p.m.; closed Easter, Thanksgiv-
ing, Christmas, and New Year's Day. Accessible to handicapped.

In a comprehensive and colorful exhibit of magazine covers,
advertisements, novel and short story illustrations, movie and war
posters, calendars, and other published works dating from 1912–
1978, illustrator Norman Rockwell's long career is commemorated
here. The museum emphasizes the years Rockwell spent in Vermont, but all 323 Rockwell covers for *The Saturday Evening Post* are
on display.

St. Johnsbury

Fairbanks Museum, 83 Main St., on corner of Prospect St. (802)
748-2372. Adults: $2.50, seniors and students: $2, children under 6:
$1.25, family: maximum $6; planetarium shows are an additional
$1. Open Mon. through Sat., 10 a.m. to 4 p.m., (summers, 10 a.m.
to 9 p.m.); Sun., 1 to 6 p.m. Limited access for handicapped.

More than 1,800 stuffed birds from all over the world are
perched in this handsome building, and include such exotics as
numerous species of gaudy parrots and what may be the largest
collection of hummingbirds anywhere. The museum also features
art exhibits, a display of Japanese netsuke figures, and science,
natural history, and anthropology exhibits. But the birds are most
captivating.

Windsor

American Precision Museum, 196 Main St., on Rte. 5. (802)
674-5781. Adults: $2, children 6 to 12: $.75; family: maximum $6.
Open May 20 through Oct. 31, weekdays 9 a.m. to 5 p.m.; weekends and holidays, 10 a.m. to 4 p.m. Accessible to handicapped.

Housed in an 1846 brick armory, this is a thoughtfully designed
collection of hand and machine tools, together with the products
they made—from typewriters to dynamos, from measuring tools
to computers. Exhibits are designed to be viewed from all sides,
and all are absorbing, whether they concern something as familiar
as an automobile or as unfamiliar as a 20-foot industrial planer.
Many tools are displayed in conjunction with the item they were
designed to produce. Thomas Edison's tools are here, as are many

other objects showing the progression of technological innovation and tracing the history of the American system of manufacturing.

Woodstock

Billings Farm and Museum, River Rd., off Rte. 12 north. (802) 457-2355. Adults: $5, children: $2. Open daily, early May through late Oct., 10 a.m. to 5 p.m. Accessible to handicapped.

The story of traditional farming in Vermont is told in this living museum through representations of typical rural Vermont life, circa 1890. Exhibits in restored barns document the rigorous labors that constituted farm life of nearly a century ago: providing feed for livestock, cutting firewood, building stone walls, cutting ice, maple sugaring, and such. Family and community pleasures and amusements—board games, quilting or corn husking bees where work and pleasure could be combined—have not been forgotten in the displays of daily and seasonal activities. The tour includes a visit to adjacent dairy buildings that are part of the farm established by the Billings family in 1871, which is still in operation today.

II
SOUTHEAST

Delaware

Dover

Delaware Agricultural Museum, 866 N. DuPont Hwy., on Rte. 13 just south of Delaware State College. (302) 734-1618. Adults: $3, seniors and children 10 and over: $2. Open Tues. through Sat., 10 a.m. to 4 p.m.; Sun., 1 to 4 p.m.; Closed Jan., Feb. and Mar. Accessible to handicapped.

When we think of American agriculture we generally think of the Plains states, parts of the South and Northwest, and California. But in the nation's youth, several eastern states were prime producers. Opened in 1980, this museum preserves the agricultural heritage of the Delmarva Peninsula. An exhibit building displays all manner of artifacts, from butter churns to threshers to the area's first broiler house. Eleven historic structures recreate a 19th-century farming community—a mill, wheelwright shop, schoolhouse, and country store, among others. Numerous temporary exhibits and special programs provide an even richer harvest. In 1990, these ranged from sheep-shearing and cider-making to photo exhibits and a Civil War encampment.

Lewes

Zwaanendael Museum, Savannah Rd. and Kings Hwy.; take Rte. 9 from Rte. 1. (302) 645-9418. Free. Open Tues. through Sat., 10 a.m.

to 4:30 p.m.; Sun., 1:30 to 4:30 p.m.; closed Mon. and state holidays. First floor accessible to handicapped.

The Dutch settled here in the 1630s, and this museum recalls that bold foray into the New World. The building itself, with an ornamented gable and decorative shutters, copies the town hall in Hoorn, The Netherlands. It contains artifacts, such as brick tiles of the type used during the early settlement period, and displays a model of this 17th-century community situated on Delaware Bay. Other exhibits and materials reflect the region's maritime heritage and local engagements during the War of 1812.

Wilmington

Hagley on the Brandywine, Rte. 141; take Exit 7 from I-95. (302) 658-2400. Adults: $8, seniors and students: $6.50, children 6 to 12: $3. Open daily, Apr. through Dec., 9:30 a.m. to 4:30 p.m.; Jan. through Mar., weekends only, 9:30 a.m. to 4:30 p.m.; closed Thanksgiving, Christmas, and New Year's Day. Limited access for handicapped.

Many company-type museums show products and processes but not all reveal how they developed; this one does. The Du Pont Company started here in 1802, manufacturing gunpowder. It erected a company town replete with mills, quarry, power plant, shops, schoolhouse, and family manor. Today, exhibits, dioramas, models, classic gardens, and restored buildings recount industrial growth and five generations of family splendor. Structures include barn, cooper's shop, office building, and the workshop where inventions and experiments began the firm's transition to the chemical industry. Machines and methods are demonstrated and tours explore ruins of original buildings. And the past is present— water still flows through the mill races, powering a waterwheel and a turbine.

Florida

Apalachicola

John Gorrie State Museum, 6th St., near the water tower, about 1 block from Rte. 98. (904) 653-9347. Admission: $.50. Open Thurs. through Mon., 8 a.m. to 5 p.m.; closed Christmas and New Year's Day. No facilities for handicapped.

In the 1830s, a young physician named John Gorrie settled in Apalachicola, a busy port on the Gulf. He was also mayor, city treasurer, and council member, but as a doctor his main concern was health, and that meant treating yellow fever. To keep his patients' rooms cool, he devised an ice-making machine that laid the foundation for the development of refrigeration and air conditioning. The museum not only contains a model of his ice machine, a sickroom, diorama, and a replica of Gorrie's office, plus portraits and memorabilia, but also depicts mid-19th-century life in the port community.

Fort Lauderdale

International Swimming Hall of Fame, 1 Hall of Fame Dr.; take Broward Blvd. from I-95. (305) 462-6536. Adults: $1.25, students, military, and seniors: $1. Open Mon. through Sat., 10 a.m. to 5 p.m.; also Sun., 11 a.m. to 4 p.m., Dec. through May. Easy access, but no facilities for handicapped.

This is a museum that truly makes a splash. Videos, artwork, medals, trophies, sculpture, and memorabilia, plus a research library and special exhibits, tell the stories of Olympic-caliber swimming, diving, and water polo. There are biographies of some 300 aquatic superstars, from Johnny Weissmuller to Mark Spitz. In the adjacent pool facility, you can literally follow the plunge of champion diver Greg Louganis who began his career here. The pool and diving well, with antecedents from the 1920s, are open to the public.

Key West

Mel Fisher Maritime Heritage Society Museum, 200 Greene St., downtown near Mallory Square. (305) 294-2633. Adults: $5, children: $1. Open daily 10 a.m. to 6 p.m. (last ticket sold at 5:15 p.m.) Accessible to handicapped.

It's a sort of word association—Mel Fisher and sunken treasure. The man has gained renown in recent years by successfully locating treasure troves from the heyday of the Spanish Main when groaning galleons carried gold, silver, and jewels from the New World to the Old. Many of those ships sank in the sea, victims of storms, faulty navigation, and buccaneers. One of the best of the modern treasure hunters, Fisher has recovered coins, ingots, and artifacts from the *Atocha* and the *Margarita*. Here, you not only learn the story of these finds, but you can indulge in some fantasies and heft a gold bar worth $40,000.

Wrecker's Museum, 322 Duval St., in center of town. (305) 294-9502. Adults: $2, children under 12: $.50. Open daily 10 a.m. to 4 p.m.; closed Christmas. No facilities for handicapped.

Wreckers were accomplished early salvage men, daring sailors and divers who disregarded dangerous conditions to save passengers and cargo from foundering ships. This museum, located in Key West's oldest house (circa 1829) and home of premier wrecker Capt. Francis B. Watlington, displays the wrecker's license, rules of the game, artifacts from the trade, paintings, antiques, and period furnishings. The house itself, a true sea captain's abode, bears a ship's hatch in the roof, displays models of vessels, and boasts an exterior kitchen.

Miami

American Police Hall of Fame & Museum, 3801 Biscayne Blvd., northeast corner of Rte. 1 and I-95. Adults: $3, ages 12 and under and 60 and over: $1.50, police officers: free. Open daily, 9 a.m. to 4 p.m. Accessible to handicapped.

The only national museum honoring U.S. law officers killed in the line of duty, this museum recently outgrew its Northport, Fla., home and now occupies the three-story former Miami FBI headquarters. Engraved on marble in the hall of fame are the names of more than 3,400 officers slain since 1960. The exhibit area contains some 10,000 law enforcement-related items, ranging from badges, weapons, hats, and uniforms to a 1960 Harley Davidson motorcycle and the futuristic car from the film *Blade Runner.* At a mock crime scene visitors are invited to examine clues and witness statements and solve the murder. There's crime and punishment—also exhibited are a jail cell, an electric chair, a gas chamber, and a guillotine.

Mulberry

Mulberry Phosphate Museum, behind City Hall, at junction of Rtes. 60 and 37. (813) 425-2823. Free. Open Tues. through Sat., 10 a.m. to 4:30 p.m.; closed legal holidays. Accessible to handicapped.

Fossils are the name of the game here, mainly animal fossils from Florida. Housed in a turn-of-the century railroad depot, the museum has more than 3,000 specimens—remains of sharks, mastodons, rhinos, proto horses, plus the world's only exhibit of a 10-million-year-old baleen whale. The bones and teeth were found in local phosphate deposits, among the most extensive in the country. To give this preserving mineral its due, the museum also exhibits photos of phosphate mining as well as samples of the raw mineral and its products.

Ocala

Don Garlits Museum of Drag Racing, next to I-75; take Exit 67. (904) 245-8661. Adults: $6, children 3 to 12: $3. Open daily, 9 a.m. to 5:30 p.m. Accessible to handicapped.

Opened in 1984, this sport museum is nothing less than a testimony to the American love of automotive speed—VA-ROOO-OOM! It contains over 100 cars holding a place in hot-rodding history plus mementos of Garlits himself, the "king of dragsters." There are photos, antique racers, even an engine room filled with the powerhouses that give muscle to the machines. A continuously-running video puts you closer to the action and includes early footage of drag racing.

Orlando

Tupperware Museum of Historic Food Containers, Tupperware International Headquarters, 5 miles south of Florida Tnpk. on South Orange Blossom Trail. (305) 847-3111, ext. 2695. Free. Tours available Mon. through Fri., 9 a.m. to 4 p.m. Accessible to handicapped.

If you have a refrigerator and leftovers, chances are you have a plastic food-storage container, both items perhaps taken for granted. But food storage has evolved along with other pedestrian aspects of life and living. This museum not only houses Tupperware's product line of over 200 pieces, it takes you back thousands of years to alabaster and earthenware containers of the ancient Egyptians, Greeks, and Romans. Ceramics, pottery, metal, and glass were the pre-plastic era's materials of choice, and the collection contains Venetian, pressed, and leaded glass pieces. There's also a 19th-century North African leather bottle, among less common containers. The whole illustrates that it is indeed a long way from open-hearth fires and corked jugs to microwaves and freezers.

Panama City Beach

Museum of Man in the Sea, 17314 Back Beach Rd., just west of intersection of Rtes. 98 and 79. (904) 235-4101. Adults: $3.50, children 6 to 16: $1.50. Open daily, 9 a.m. to 5 p.m. Accessible to handicapped.

Many of us became acquainted with undersea adventure via *Sea Hunt* or *20,000 Leagues under the Sea*, but people around the world have been diving in the ocean for food, fun, fighting, and finery in eras predating those tales. This museum examines that history, from the earliest days to scuba, hard-hat diving, and the establishment of underwater habitats (including the original Sea Lab I). In addition to permanent displays, there are temporary exhibits covering such topics as undersea treasure, aquanauts to astronauts, and deep diving with small submersibles.

Perry

Forest Capital State Museum, 204 Forest Park Dr., from Rte. 19 south. (904) 584-3227. Admission: $.50 per person. Open Thurs. through Mon., 8 a.m. to noon, and 1 to 5 p.m.; closed Tues., Wed., Thanksgiving, Christmas, and New Year's Day. Accessible to handicapped.

Florida means oranges, Disney, seashore and gators . . . but wood? Yes. The forest industry is the state's third largest, generating more than $3 billion annually. Wood figures in all the museum's structures—pecky cypress and red cedar walls, a dome of black ironwood and lignumvitae, display cases and a Florida map made of diverse species of native wood. Exhibits interpret the turpentine industry, modern forestry practices, and virgin forests. "Terry Tree" talks about the life cycles of trees, and two life-size habitats—a cypress swamp and a hardwood hammock—are located at the visitors center.

St. Augustine

Tragedy in U.S. History Museum, 7 Williams St., off Rte. 1 east and San Marco. No telephone. Adults: $3.50, children under 12: $1. No facilities for handicapped.

Spawned by the assassination of President John F. Kennedy, this museum grew to embrace a myriad representations of American agony. It covers both well known and little known, both crime and punishment. Regarding the Kennedy assassination, the museum claims Lee Harvey Oswald's bedroom furniture, the car he used on the fateful day, and the dramatic Zapruder film of the shooting. But it also includes the automobile actress Jayne Mansfield was decapitated in, Bonnie and Clyde's getaway car, a bill of sale from slavery days, a 1718 Spanish jail replete with skeletons, the whistle and engineer's watch from the wreck of Old 97, and Elvis Presley's last will and testament. Among other items are a whipping post, bear traps, whiskey still, antique guns, blacksmith gear, and old diesel engines—debatable tragedies, but here nonetheless.

Tampa

Ybor City State Museum, 1818 9th Ave.; take Exit 1 (21st St.) from I-4. (813) 247-6323. Admission: $.50. Open Tues. through Sat., 9 a.m. to noon, and 1 to 5 p.m.; closed Sun., Mon., Thanksgiving, and Christmas. Accessible to handicapped.

If you're talking cigars, but with an embargo on Cuba, Tampa may well come to mind. From the mid-1880s to the 1930s, the section of Tampa called Ybor City was the cigar capital of the United States. Housed in an old bakery building, with the huge beehive ovens still in place, the museum relates the city's cigar manufacturing history, with emphasis on hand-rolled cigars. The story involves several ethnic groups—Cubans, Italians, Romanians, and Germans—and exhibits embrace labels, boxes, molds, cutters, tables, and other artifacts. For an additional $.50 fee, you can tour a cigar-worker's house nearby, and guides will give you directions to a few remaining places where old-timers still roll cigars by hand.

Tarpon Springs

Spongers Museum, in the Sponge Factory, 510 Dodecanese Blvd., off Rte. 19. (813) 942-3771. Free. Open daily 10 a.m. to 6 p.m.; closed major holidays. Accessible to the handicapped.

Greek immigrants settled in the area in the early 1900s and fostered a sponge industry using traditions and methods from the old country. Tarpon Springs has been this country's sponge capital for decades, and in this small museum today you can view divers' outfits, knives, and related gear, plus learn about the biohistory of the sponge and something about the five sponges of commercial value among some 2,000 types of sponges that grow in the sea. For a modest fee, you can see a 15-minute film recounting the history of Tarpon Springs, and the shops nearby market all manner of Greek dresses, caps, and food plus coral, shells, and, of course, sponges. It is a dip into a different culture, and one where you need not get sponged.

Winter Park

Beal-Maltbie Shell Museum, on campus of Rollins College, intersection of Holt and Fairbanks; take Exit 45 from I-4. (305) 646-2364. Adults: $1, children under 12: $.50. Open daily, 10 a.m. to noon, and 1 to 4 p.m. Accessible to handicapped.

Nearly 100,000 species are represented here in a collection of some 2 million shells from around the world. The grand array dates back to 1888 when Dr. James Beal began gathering shells at Key West. A century later, the chambered nautilus, cabbage murex, Venus comb, measeled cowry, and scores of other graceful, colorful, intriguing shells beckon the eye and the spirit. Beyond aesthetics, there are shells for buttons, money, dye, cooking, religion, rank, domicile, and carving. No shell game, this is a gallery of nature's work at its finest.

Georgia

Atlanta

Federal Reserve Bank Monetary Museum, 104 Marietta St. NW, downtown, not far from Omni and Underground. (404) 521-8500. Free. Open Mon. through Fri., 8:30 a.m. to 4 p.m.; closed holidays. Groups and handicapped are advised to call first about facilities.

Ah, the color of money, to say nothing of the shape, texture and history of monetary exchange. The subject is concisely displayed here, in the most appropriate place, a bank. In the only such exhibit in the Southeast, some 30 display cases with descriptive labels trace the evolution of money from early means of payment to checks and credit cards. You can view a solid gold bar, $10,000-denomination bills, rare foreign and domestic coins (including one worth $250,000), stone money from Yap, and other riches. Exhibits also illustrate the minting and printing of coin and currency. A wealth of material, to coin a phrase.

Center for Puppetry Arts Museum, 1404 Spring St., in Midtown between Peachtree St. and I-75/85, not far from the IBM tower. (404) 873-3089. Admission: $2 per person, free with performance ticket. Open Mon. through Sat., 9 a.m. to 4 p.m.; closed Sun. and major holidays. Free guided tours throughout the week (call for times). Accessible to handicapped.

The world of puppets comes to life at the Center for Puppetry Arts, established in 1978. It holds performances such as *Hansel and*

Gretel and *The Snow Queen* as well as various puppetry workshops. Its museum houses one of North America's largest exhibits of puppets—more than 150 hand, string, rod, shadow, and body puppets. You can see ancient ceremonial clay puppets from Mexico, ritualistic African puppets, plus some of the original Muppets. There are also shadow puppets from Turkey made of painted animal skins and Italian rod marionettes in battle armor. A unique and age-old art form with a magical cast, puppetry deals with everything from religious beliefs to social commentary to plain old fun. And speaking of fun, the museum has a hands-on gallery where kids can operate rod, hand, and string puppets on stage. In addition, it features three special exhibits annually.

Cartersville

William Weinman Mineral Center & Museum, Culver Rd.; take Exit 126 from I-75 to Rte. 411. (404) 386-0576. Adults: $2, seniors: $1.50, children 6 to 11: $1. Open Tues. through Sat., 10 a.m. to 4:30 p.m.; Sun., 2 to 4:30 p.m. Accessible to handicapped.

Named in honor of a barite miner in the region, this museum tells the story of mining and minerals in Georgia, including amethyst, quartz, marble, staurolite, calcite, and granite. In addition to a Georgia room, there's an international wing. The museum features a simulated limestone cave, a fossil exhibit and Indian ornaments and weapons utilizing regional minerals. There's also an outside mineral garden with oversized geodes and old mining gear and related vehicles.

Columbia

Confederate Naval Museum, 202 4th St., near Rte. 80/280 and the banks of the Chattahoochee River. (404) 327-9798. Donation requested. Open Tues. through Fri., 10 a.m. to 5 p.m.; weekends, 1 to 5 p.m.; closed Mon. and major holidays. No facilities for handicapped.

This is the only museum devoted entirely to the history of the Confederate navy, which was an improvised force outgunned and outmanned by its foe, but nonetheless one which achieved successes. Major exhibits are the salvaged remains of the ironclad ram *Jackson* and the steamer gunboat *Chattahoochee*. Artifacts include anchors, hooks, shells, fuses, cutlasses, 32-pounders, utensils, and a torpedo. Also on display are other relics, weapons, and uniforms from the Confederate navy as well as ship models, dioramas, and prints and engravings of vessels and battles. The museum hopes to become the home for artifacts from the salvaged *Alabama.*

Dahlonega

Dahlonega Gold Museum, on the square, Rte. 19 north from Rte. 400. (404) 864-2257. Adults: $1.50, youth: $.75. Open Mon. through Sat., 9 a.m. to 5 p.m.; Sun., 10 a.m. to 6 p.m.; closed Thanksgiving and Christmas. First floor is accessible to handicapped.

The nation's first gold rush occurred in north Georgia more than 150 years ago, displacing the Cherokees and resulting in the establishment of a branch U.S. mint where more than $6 million in gold coins were minted between 1838 and 1861. Gold still shines here, but it's more in the form of tourist dollars than precious metal. This museum, occupying what was once a red-brick county courthouse (1836), chronicles the early days of gold fever, displaying a 2,500-pound safe, milling and refining gear, photos, old prints and documents, and gold coins and nuggets. On the second floor, it presents a 25-minute film of Georgia's gold-mining history. Special programs sometimes involve the staff in a gold-panning demonstration at a sluice box out front. It was from a speech delivered on this building's steps that Mark Twain borrowed some phraseology and concocted the famous line, "There's gold in them thar hills!"

Eatonton

Uncle Remus Museum, Rte. 441 south, 43 miles from Atlanta via I-20. (404) 485-6856. Adults: $.50, children under 12: $.25. Open Mon. through Sat., 10 a.m. to 5 p.m.; Sun., 2 to 5 p.m.; closed Tues. from Sept. to May. No facilities for handicapped.

Joel Chandler Harris, author of the famous Uncle Remus tales, came from Putnam County, Georgia, and this local museum honors the man and his work. Constructed from two authentic slave cabins, it has many mementos of the mid-19th-century locale—a fireplace, cook pots and kettles, walking stick, chairs (seating for the stories' Old Man and Little Boy). Shadow boxes contain wood carvings of the various critters mentioned in the tales. Also in the museum are several first editions of Harris's works and memorabilia related to his life and times.

Elberton

Elberton Granite Museum, ½ mile west of town on Rte. 72; take Rte. 77 Exit from I-85 or I-20. (404) 283-2551. Free. Open daily, 2 to 5 p.m., Jan. 15 to Nov. 15; closed weekends and holidays mid-Nov. to mid-Jan. No facilities for handicapped.

Granite is big business in northeast Georgia and Elberton bills itself as "the granite capital of the world." Some 35 quarries and 100 processing plants operate in the area. However, the first plant was built solely to complete a Confederate monument in the late 1890s; the statue fell, but the industry grew. Opened in 1981, the museum exhibits antique and contemporary stone-cutting tools and granite products, sculptors' implements, and photos illustrating methods of cutting, polishing, and sandblasting. You can also learn about the mysterious Georgia guidestones and about "Dutchy," the original Confederate statue recently exhumed and now proudly displayed.

Savannah

Ships of the Sea Museum, 503 E. River St., from I-16 to Bay St. (912) 232-1511. Adults: $2, children 7 to 12: $.75. Open daily, 10 a.m. to 5 p.m.; closed Christmas and New Year's Day. No facilities for handicapped.

Georgia's principal port, Savannah has a rich maritime tradition. This museum not only conveys that heritage, but sails beyond to broader oceanic ventures. Models and artifacts represent vessels of ancient Vikings and Koreans, Captain Cook's *Endeavor*, the tiny fleet of Columbus, and the nuclear-powered ship *Savannah*, among others. Its 60-piece ships-in-a-bottle collection, built by British naval commander Peter Barlow, is considered one of the finest in the world.

Maryland

Aberdeen Proving Ground

U.S. Army Ordnance Museum, off U.S. 40 at Aberdeen or off I-95 at the Aberdeen interchange, then east on Rte 22. (301) 278-3602. Free. Open Tues. through Fri., noon to 4:45 p.m.; weekends, 10 a.m. to 4:45 p.m.; closed all holidays except Armed Forces Day, Memorial Day, July 4 and Veterans Day. Accessible to handicapped.

Ordnance means weapons, ammunition and armor, and this museum means more bang for the buck. Its martial collection ranges from 16th-century body armor to 20-century artillery, from the 19th-century Gatling gun to the German railway cannon "Anzio Annie." More than 200 tanks and artillery pieces occupy an outdoor 25-acre park. Historically linked to the technical evolution of weapons, the museum also reflects the story of the Army's Ordnance Corps, the birth of which dates to the Revolutionary War and the new nation's armories, arsenals and powder magazines.

Annapolis

U.S. Naval Academy Museum, U.S. Naval Academy, east of Washington, D.C., on Rte. 50 or south of Baltimore on I-97. (301) 267-2108. Free. Open Mon. through Sat., 9 a.m. to 5 p.m.; Sun., 11 a.m. to 5 p.m.; closed Thanksgiving, Christmas, and New Year's Day. Accessible to handicapped.

Originating as the Naval School Lyceum in 1845, the museum has evolved into a caretaker of objects, documents, and art concerning the rich history and tradition of the U.S. Navy and its officer corps. Prints, paintings, books, swords and uniforms, ship instruments, and gear form the main body of the museum's collection. Among the more unusual materials are the Malcolm Storer Naval Medals Collection, composed of more than 1,200 medals from 30 countries and spanning the centuries from 254 B.C. to 1936, and the Navy's trophy flag assemblage of some 600 American and captured foreign flags.

Baltimore

Mount Vernon Museum of Incandescent Lighting, 717 Washington Pl., just north of a monument dedicated to George Washington. (301) 752-8586. Free. Open seven days a week by appointment only. Limited access for handicapped.

The theme here might be "A Thousand Points of Light." Started as a hobby by dentist Hugh Francis Hicks, this unique collection chronicles the development of electric lighting via displays of 8,000 different types of bulbs, only a fifth of the entire lot. Individual exhibits demonstrate Edison's first attempts at commercial illumination. Bristol board filaments evolved to pressed tungsten. There are international designs, miniature and decorative lamps, and medical/dental lighting devices. Also displayed are the world's largest, smallest, and longest light bulbs. After seeing these, you may never grumble again about changing a bulb.

Baltimore Streetcar Museum, 1900 Falls Rd., located under North Ave. bridge near Jones Falls Expressway and 2 blocks from Penn Station. (301) 547-0264. Donations welcome; modest rates for rides. Open year round Sun., noon to 5 p.m.; June through Oct., also Sat., noon to 5 p.m. Accessible to handicapped.

To some degree, a city is its transportation system, and this museum shows how Baltimore once moved. Established in 1966 to preserve a representative collection of streetcars, it is reputedly the only museum dedicated solely to a single city's once-common transportation mode. The facility exhibits 12 street railway vehicles spanning the period 1859 to 1963. An accompanying audiovisual presentation recounts the history of streetcars, and streetcar rides are available with drivers dressed in period garb.

Baltimore Museum of Industry, 1415 Key Hwy.; take Exit 55 from I-95. (301) 727-4808. Adults: $2, seniors and students: $1, group rates available. Open Memorial Day through Labor Day, Tues. through Fri. and Sun., noon to 5 p.m.; Sat., 10 a.m. to 5 p.m.; closed Mon.; rest of year open Thurs., Fri., and Sun., noon to 5 p.m.; Sat. 10 a.m. to 5 p.m.; other hours by appointment; closed Christmas and New Year's Day.

Although not strictly in the "uncommon" category, this museum boasts some singular attractions based on unusual collections and Baltimore firsts. Housed in an 1865 oyster cannery on the South Baltimore waterfront, the museum displays such developments as Ottmar Merganthaler's linotype and A. K. Shriver's industrial pressure cooker. Baltimore claims America's first power company, first tin can, and first packaged ice cream. Hammers on anvils and belt-driven machinery provide an audio backdrop to working antique equipment. The East Coast's only operating steam tugboat—the 1906 S.S. *Baltimore*—has been restored and awaits visitors at the museum's pier.

Babe Ruth Birthplace and Orioles Museum, 216 Emory St., off Martin Luther King Blvd. to Pratt St., near University of Maryland Hospital Complex. (301) 727-1539. Adults: $3, seniors and groups: $2 (children in groups: $1), under 12: $1.50. Open Apr. 1 to Oct. 31, daily 10 a.m. to 5 p.m.; Nov. 1 to March 31 daily, 10 a.m. to 4 p.m.; closed Easter, Thanksgiving, Christmas, and New Year's Day. Limited access for handicapped.

Established in 1983, this museum is about local baseball and a legend, perhaps *the* baseball legend. George Herman "Babe" Ruth was born on the second floor of this former row house which is now bedecked with period furnishings and family artifacts. There's even a family photo album with unfamiliar shots of the Babe—in a smoking jacket, swim trunks, tuxedo, as well as some from his youth. A 25-minute documentary tells of the New York Yankee slugger's career. But for baseball fans, there's much more—uniforms, bats, gear, awards, and photos of Baltimore Orioles players or baseball greats who hailed from Maryland, including Jimmie Foxx and Lefty Grove. You can see the oldest baseball in Maryland, the scorecard from Ruth's first professional game with the Orioles, and a history of professional ball in this city.

Ellicott City

Ellicott City B&O Railroad Museum, 2711 Maryland Ave., 4 miles west of Baltimore's Beltway Exit 13, via Catonsville. (301) 461-1944. Adults: $3, seniors and students: $2, children 5 through 12: $1. Open Memorial Day through Labor Day daily except Tues., 11 a.m. to 5 p.m.; other days and times available for groups. Limited access for handicapped.

Site of the first passenger terminus in the nation, this museum comprises two restored buildings (circa 1831 and 1886) containing railroad displays, photos, dioramas, model trains, and various mementos of the Baltimore & Ohio rail line. Rotating exhibits also play a part—such as women on the railroad, great tented railroad circuses, and the railroads during the World Wars. There's even a haunted railroad station for children.

Havre de Grace

Havre de Grace Decoy Museum, Market St., 5 minutes off I-95. (301) 939-3739. Adults: $2, seniors and children: $1, special tour rates. Open Tues. through Sun., 11 a.m. to 5 p.m.; closed Mon., Easter, Thanksgiving, Christmas, and New Year's Day. Accessible to handicapped.

This area calls itself the "decoy capital of the world," and if you like decoys you shouldn't duck this museum. Displayed in the three-story building are some 2,000 decoys made by regional and national carvers. You'll also see prints, paintings, and other artwork related to decoy making and duck hunting, plus related clothing, weapons, and bushwhack boats. Exhibits cover the period from 1870 to the present. Information panels discuss the use of decoys and how they are made. On weekends local carvers demonstrate the craft, and on the first weekend in May the town holds an annual decoy festival.

LaPlata

Afro-American Heritage Museum, Gynn Rd., Charles County Alternative School, from Rtes. 225 and 301 south. (301) 753-6102 or 843-0371. Free. Open year round, ok to visit during school hours; appointment advised generally, but necessary in summer months when school building is closed. Accessible to handicapped.

There is history and there is history, and sometimes the version you learn depends on the color of your skin, your national origin, your socio-economic class. William Digges has taken a view of the black experience in the United States with his family-oriented collection that is, well, uncomfortable. It stems from local rural heritage, but could easily represent the black experience throughout the South. Here you'll find bills of sale for slaves, flogging whips, and a ball-and-chain from slavery days. And if bondage weren't enough, there's lasting bigotry—Aunt Jemima dolls, "coon" sheet music, and postcards of "pickaninnies." You'll also see items of sustenance—farming tools, domestics' irons, log hut construction, cookpots and recipes, a black midwife's medical satchel. Also here are documents related to the Dred Scott decision and the 13th, 14th, and 15th Amendments to the Constitution. A resource for area schools, this museum is really a history book for us all.

Lutherville

Fire Museum of Maryland, 1301 York Rd.; take Exit 26 from the Baltimore Beltway. (301) 321-7500. Adults: $2, firefighters and seniors: $1, children under 12: $.50. Open May through Oct., Sun., 1 to 5 p.m.; weekday tours by appointment. Limited facilities for handicapped.

The evolution of urban life hasn't eliminated fires or the need for firefighters, and what was once a sort of civic trade is now a science. This facility displays more than 60 vehicles dating from 1822 when they were hand- and horse-drawn. Most of the equipment is operational, and pieces hail from New York, Pennsylvania, and Tennessee as well as Maryland. Also available for viewing are firefighting-related films and the country's largest working fire alarm display.

Rockville

Latvian Museum, 400 Hurley Ave., off Rte. 28 near I-70. (301) 340-1914. Donation requested. Open 8 a.m. to 5 p.m.; open by appointment only. Limited access for handicapped.

The Baltic lands of Latvia, Estonia, and Lithuania, seemingly forgotten by the rest of the world after their forced embrace by the Soviet Union half a century ago, made the headlines in 1990 with their determined efforts for independence. For Americans who know little of Latvia, this museum near Washington, D.C., recounts that small nation's history and heritage from the Ice Age to the 20th century and includes immigration to the United States. Photos, maps, artifacts, textiles, tools, hand-carved furniture, and dioramas bring this story, and Latvian culture, to life.

Salisbury

Ward Museum of Waterfowl Art, 655 S. Salisbury Rd., on campus of Salisbury State University, Rte. 13 from Rte. 50. (301) 742-4988. Adults: $2, seniors and students: $1. Open Tues. through Sat., 10 a.m. to 5 p.m.; Sun., 1 to 5 p.m.; closed Mon. Accessible to handicapped.

This museum is going to the birds, but not in the colloquial sense. Historically, decoys were used for hunting, and exhibits here range from Southwestern Indian reed decoys to the graceful decoys used by 19th-century market gunners. The carving grew into art and the working decoy became decorative sculpture. Wildfowl art soars here, and includes 20 years of world championship carving and numerous examples of regional styles. The museum also houses a replica of the Ward Brothers carving shop with its tools and artifacts.

Upper Marlboro

W. Henry Duval Tool Museum, Patuxent River Park, 16000 Croom Airport Rd., from Rtes. 301 and 382. (301) 627-6074. Free. Open Sun., noon to 4 p.m.; other times by reservation. Wheelchair accessible.

Located in the scenic and rustic Jug Bay Natural Area, the

museum presents a century of farm, home, and trade tools spanning the decades from 1850 to 1950. For some 50 years until his death in 1979, W. Henry Duval collected more than 1,000 tools from area farms. There are axes, adzes, saws, chisels, and other woodworking implements; dental instruments, such as a hand-pumped drill; cobbler's tools; and myriad others. A second building is designed for hay wagons, mowers, and other large farm equipment. In our automated, mechanized, electrified age, these basic, get-the-job-done tools recall the true meaning of the term "hand-made."

North Carolina

Asheville

The Health Adventure, 501 Biltmore Ave., just north of junction of I-40 and Rte. 25. (704) 254-6373. Adults: $2.50, children: $1.50. Open Mon. through Fri., 8:30 a.m. to 5 p.m.; closed weekends and major holidays. Necessary to schedule programs in advance. Accessible to handicapped.

A health education facility founded by the Buncombe County Medical Auxiliary in 1966, this museum offers something health-wise for all ages with a constantly changing variety of programs and exhibits. There's a glass lady that talks and giant teeth to brush. You can assemble a skeleton from real bones and plan a meal with giant foam food. A soft-sculpture heart provides hands-on learning, as do fetal models depicting human embryonic development. You can even see a digestive system and take an eyeball apart. The concept of preventive health is nowhere else so in touch and up front.

Aurora

Aurora Fossil Museum, Rtes. 33 and 306. (919) 322-4238. Free. Open Mon. through Fri., 9 a.m. to 4:30 p.m.; closed major holidays. No facilities for handicapped.

An ocean basin eons ago, this coastal region holds a hoard of fossilized bones and teeth of marine life in its rich phosphate deposits. The mining operations of Texas Gulf Phosphate Co. have provided this small museum with much of its exhibited material—shark and whale teeth 5 million to 15 million years old, walrus tusks, porpoise teeth, vertebrae, and more. Photos and exhibits complement the collection, and local folks have donated items such as a bowl of an Indian pipe. A 12-minute film conveys a picture of the area's geology, and across the street is a pile of mining debris where you can search for your own fossils.

Bailey

Country Doctor Museum, Vance St.; take Rte, 581 Exit from Rte. 264, 32 miles east of Raleigh. (919) 235-4165. Donations welcome. Open Sun. through Thurs., 1 to 5 p.m.; other times by appointment. No access ramp, but a low entrance step.

Remember family physicians, the docs who made house calls? Well, here's the only medical museum dedicated to that vanished breed, especially the rural variety. The quaint building is a restored composite of two area doctors' offices with an interior divided into an apothecary and library, a simulated doctor's office, and an exhibit of ailments and treatments. Artifacts include books, mortars, pestles, canisters, a Confederate operating table, amputation instruments used on Stonewall Jackson, portable microscopes, blood-letting devices, desks, and cabinets. Outside is an herb garden with 60 specimens of medicinal herbs. Authenticity was built in from the outset—the principal founder, Dr. Josephine Newell, practiced in Bailey for many years and comes from a long line of physicians.

Beaufort

North Carolina Maritime Museum, 315 Front St., on the Intracoastal Waterway just off Rte. 70. (919) 728-7317. Free. Open Mon. through Fri., 9 a.m. to 5 p.m.; Sat., 10 a.m. to 5 p.m.; Sun., 1 to 5 p.m. Accessible to handicapped.

North Carolina boasts an incredible coast, studded with bays, banks, port towns, lighthouses, and beaches that go on forever. Not surprisingly, it also has a maritime museum to illustrate all this, with special emphasis on natural history of the coast, indigenous small craft, and maritime activities ranging from oystering to lifesaving to shipbuilding. Diverse models include privateers, sailing skiffs, tugs, and other vessels. Old photos, navigational instruments, sailmaking tools, decoys, and salt water aquariums add other chapters to the story. Annual programs focus on regional specialties such as seafood and wooden boats.

Cherokee

Museum of the Cherokee Indian, on edge of Great Smoky Mountain National Park, near Rtes. 19 and 441. (704) 497-3481. Adults: $3.50, children 6 to 12: $1.75. Open mid-June through Aug., Mon. through Sat., 9 a.m. to 8 p.m. and Sun., 9 a.m. to 5 p.m.; Sept. to mid-June daily, 9 a.m. to 5 p.m.; closed Thanksgiving, Christmas, and New Year's Day. Accessible to handicapped.

No dusty relic from bygone days, this architecturally striking museum employs a combination of practical and ornamental objects and videotape presentations to tell the richly textured story of Cherokee culture. Here are beadwork and baskets, weapons and tools, garments and masks. "Hearphones" enable you to learn about Cherokee myths and legends and listen to the centuries-old spoken language while viewing the syllabary developed by Sequoyah. The Hall of Honored Cherokees pays tribute to outstanding figures in the Cherokee nation's past.

Kenly

Tobacco Museum of North Carolina, 709 Church St.; take Exit 107 from I-95 and go 1 mile north on Rte. 301. (919) 284-3431. Adults: $1, children and students: $.50. Open Mon. through Sat., 9:30 a.m. to 5 p.m.; Sun., 2 to 5 p.m.; farm tours offered in July and Aug. at 10 a.m. and 2 p.m. Mon., through Sat. Accessible to handicapped.

Whatever one's feelings about tobacco, there's no denying it occupies a prominent socioeconomic niche in North Carolina; indeed, one-half of the flue-cured tobacco in the United States reportedly is grown within 50 miles of Kenly. This 6,000-square-foot facility, as much community as industry effort, uses exhibits, videos, and tours to relate the region's tobacco-producing history. Planting and harvesting tools plus artifacts from turn-of-the-century rural homes, schools, and churches paint a full portrait of agricultural life and lifestyles. In season, you can visit fields, curing barns, and tobacco auctions.

Winston-Salem

Museum of Early Southern Decorative Arts (MESDA), 924 S. Main St.; take Rte. 40 to Old Salem Rd. (919) 721-7360. Adults: $5, children: $3. Open Mon. through Sat., 10:30 a.m. to 4:30 p.m.; Sun., 1:30 to 4:30 p.m.; closed Thanksgiving, Christmas Eve, and Christmas Day. Accessible to handicapped.

Situated in historic Old Salem, MESDA is the only museum devoted solely to researching and exhibiting regional decorative arts of the early South. Fifteen period rooms and four galleries display furniture, textiles, paintings, ceramics, metalware, and other materials made and used in the South from 1690 through 1820. You can view the work of America's first professional woman artist, see one of the earliest court cupboards made in the nation, and experience the environment of a Maryland plantation dwelling. Room settings range from rustic Tennessee frontier to elegant South Carolina seaport. Items include figurines, clocks, containers, candleholders, vases, draperies, and floorings as well as furniture and implements.

South Carolina

Charleston

Macaulay Museum of Dental History, 171 Ashley Ave., on campus of Medical University of South Carolina. (803) 792-2288. Free. Open Mon. through Fri., 8:30 a.m. to 5:30 p.m.; closed weekends and holidays. Visitors are advised to call ahead. No facilities for handicapped.

Named for a prominent Columbia dentist, Dr. Neill Macaulay, this museum covers nearly 200 years of American dentistry, including an instrument designed by Paul Revere, a century-old gold mill, and South Carolina's first dental x-ray unit (circa 1912). It displays a 19th-century dental office and features a series of dental chairs, including a folding type that traveled with itinerant practitioners along the region's country roads. Also exhibited are Civil War instruments, once-prevalent wall-based equipment, cabinets and molds, a mid-19th-century instrument chest, and an electrosurgical unit that decades ago was considered a cure-all for oral diseases.

Darlington

Stock Car Hall of Fame, Rtes. 34 and 151 west, 8 miles from I-95 and 1 mile west of downtown. (803) 393-2103. Adults: $2, children: free with adult. Open daily 8:30 a.m. to 5 p.m.; closed major holidays. Accessible to handicapped.

The American fascination for cars knows no bounds—antique autos, Indy racers, dragsters, and, yes, stock cars, too. This museum is devoted to cars that raced the stock circuit in the 1950s and '60s, starting with the hot machine that won the first Southern 500 in 1950. Here, too, are the cars of Fireball Roberts, Richard Petty, Buddy Baker, and many others. There are also trophy cases, memorabilia, and biographical tributes to 34 members of the hall of fame. In addition, your visit includes a simulated two-lap drive over the asphalt track.

Edgefield

Pottersville Museum, on Rte. 25 one mile north of town and about 25 miles north of Augusta, Ga. (803) 673-3333. Donation requested. Open by appointment daily, except Tues. and Thurs. No facilities for handicapped.

Regional history is thrown in clay at this unusual museum. A one-room structure (circa 1810) forms a museum dedicated to regional potters, such as Abner Landrum, Collin Rhodes, Lewis Miles, Dave the Slave, and T. M. Chandler, and houses one of the more prominent collections of Edgefield pottery. Many items displayed are signed pieces from the decades of the 1820s through the 1860s. Also featured are artifacts belonging to area families and politicians (Edgefield was home to 10 governors and five lieutenant governors).

Florence

Florence Air & Missile Museum, Rte. 301 north; take Exit 170 from I-95 or Rte. 76 east from I-20. (803) 665-5118. Adults: $5, seniors and military: $4, children: $3. Open daily, 9 a.m. to 5 p.m. Accessible to handicapped.

Aerial warfare, waged by aircraft or rockets, is a 20th-century contribution to a time-honored activity, and this museum runs the gamut, from a 98-foot Titan ICBM to a room devoted to World War I's Lafayette Escadrille. Founded in 1963, the museum is home base to more than three dozen airplanes, missiles, and related weapons and aircraft. You can climb aboard a C-124 Globemaster, check out astronaut Alan Shepherd's Apollo space suit, view instruments from a Saturn V rocket, marvel at a German V-2 rocket, and examine Apollo launch computers. Photos, art, and artifacts on various aspects of aviation complement the flying machines. All in all, a blast-off of a museum.

Georgetown

Rice Museum, intersection of Front and Screven Sts., between Rtes. 17 and 701 and the Sampit River. (803) 546-7423. Adults: $2, students: free. Open Mon. through Fri., 9:30 a.m. to 4:30 p.m.; Sun., 2 to 4:30 p.m.; Apr. through Sept., Sat., 10 a.m. to 4:30 p.m.; Oct. through Mar., Sat., 10 a.m. to 1 p.m.; closed major holidays. No facilities for handicapped.

For some 200 years, rice dominated the economy of this Low Country district which, in the 1840s, produced nearly half the nation's rice. Today, that culture and dependency on it have gone— rice is not commercially available in the area now—but the museum recaptures the flavor of a vanished era. Housed in a striking red brick clocktower building, the museum displays maps, photos, and other illustrations, plus dioramas of rice plantation structures, artifacts such as harvesters, and a scale model of a rice mill.

Rock Hill

Museum of York County, 4621 Mt. Gallant Rd.; take Exit 66-A from I-77 to Celeneese Bypass. (803) 329-2121. Adults: $2, seniors and students: $1. Open Tues. through Sat., 10 a.m. to 5 p.m.; Sun., 1 to 5 p.m.; closed major holidays. Accessible to handicapped.

A county museum, yes, but one with an emphasis on science and nature, and, more specifically, one of the largest collections of African mammals mounted by species in the United States. The Stans African Halls form a taxidermal habitat for hundreds of creatures, ranging from giraffes to ostriches to hippos. Even cobras and elephants find a still-life home here. There are also South American and North American halls. An interesting departure entails an ample collection of artwork by South Carolina resident Vernon Grant, creator of Snap, Crackle, and Pop of cereal fame. The exhibit includes the original puppets of the noisy trio.

Seneca

Duke Power's World of Energy, 7812 Rochester Hwy., adjacent to Oconee Nuclear Station, west of I-85 and Clemson. (803) 885-4600.

Free. Open Mon. through Sat., 9 a.m. to 5 p.m.; Sun., noon to 5 p.m.; June through Aug., open to 6 p.m.; closed Thanksgiving, Christmas Eve and Day, and New Year's Day. Accessible to handicapped.

Power to the people, after a fashion. This museum illustrates how water, coal, and uranium produce electricity and how energy can be conserved. A waterwheel, coal-fired steam operations, even a working model of a nuclear reactor, are on display. One room gives a nod to alternative energy sources such as solar and geothermal. Computer games test your knowledge of energy topics. Tours are also available of the nearby Oconee Nuclear Training Academy, which presents an exact replica of a control room at a nuclear power station. Large relief maps and a 400-gallon aquarium stocked with local fish give additional perspectives of the region.

Virginia

Alexandria

Stabler-Leadbeater Apothecary Museum, 105 Fairfax St., in the city's historic district. (703) 836-3713. Adults: $1, children: $.50. Open Tues. through Sat., 10 a.m. to 4 p.m.; Sun., noon to 4 p.m. No facilities for handicapped.

Edward Stabler founded this apothecary shop in 1792 and it remained in the same family until 1933. Over the years it was frequented by George Washington, Daniel Webster, Henry Clay, Robert E. Lee, and other notables. The building's exterior has been beautifully restored, and within you will find a complete and authentic line of pharmacy features—prescription orders, documents, instruments, eyeglasses, mortars and pestles, bottles, jars, medicines, mahogany cabinets, and glass cases—illustrating health and medical care during the 18th, 19th, and early 20th centuries. It is the only such museum with an original 19th-century pharmaceutical manufactory.

Berryville

Enders Funeral Home 1890s Mortuary Museum, 101 E. Main St., 2 blocks east of intersection with Rte. 340. (703) 955-1062. Free. Open Mon. through Fri., 9 a.m. to 5 p.m.; Sat., 9 a.m. to noon. Call in advance if possible, although no appointment is necessary. Accessible to handicapped.

Death is an inevitable part of living, and it seems only reasonable that among all the museums focusing on working, playing, and exploring, there should be a museum devoted to burial. Original equipment used by four generations of undertakers reflects changing means and methods dating back to the 1890s in this unusual, if not unique, museum. Among the exhibits are antique embalming equipment, a cast-iron sarcophagus, an 1889 horse-drawn hearse, make-up containers, caskets, old documents from funeral homes, and an antique printing press for producing forms and orders. There are also books with photos of funeral vehicles and explanations of mortuary methods.

Big Stone Gap

Harry W. Meador Jr. Coal Museum, E. 3rd St. & Shawnee Ave., off Rte. 23. (703) 523-4950. Free. Open Wed. through Sat., 10 a.m. to 5 p.m.; Sun., 1 to 5 p.m.; tours and groups other times by appointment; closed major holidays. Accessible to handicapped.

This was and is coal country. Harry Meador, a former employee of the Westmoreland Coal Co., conceived of this museum, dedicating it to the region's people, many of whom are associated with the industry. It reflects the life style of the old mining camps, with hundreds of historic photos depicting the town, its residents, and coal mining operations, from mule power to modern machinery. Artifacts range from shovels to drills. Also displayed are items donated by local folks, such as chandeliers, utensils, an old hand calculator, and other materials from home and work.

New Market

Bedrooms of America, 9386 Congress St.; take Exit 67 from I-81. (703) 740-3512. Adults: $2, seniors: $1.50, children 8 to 14: $1.25. Open daily Jan. 1 through Memorial Day, and Labor Day through Dec. 31, 9 a.m. to 5 p.m.; Memorial Day through Labor Day, 9 a.m. to 8 p.m. No facilities for handicapped.

To sleep, perchance to dream. Well, it helps if you've got a comfy bedroom, and given that we spend nearly one-third of our lives in slumberland, bedrooms acquire real importance. This museum takes that notion seriously, displaying 11 different American bedrooms outfitted with authentic period furniture, from William & Mary (circa 1650) to Art Deco (circa 1930). Furnishings, wall coverings, bedding and coverlets, window treatments, carpets, cabinets, and cradles add to the time-travel quality of these rooms. The museum is housed in a restored 18th-century building with ties to Abraham Lincoln and Gen. Jubal Early. It also holds an antique doll collection and a gift shop purveying various antiques and reproductions.

Paeonian Springs

American Work Horse Museum, Rte. 662, 4 miles west of Leesburg, between. Rtes. 9 and 7. (703) 338-6290. Donations suggested. Open Apr. through Oct., Wed., 9 a.m. to 5 p.m.; other times by appointment. Accessible to handicapped.

Some horses race, trot, and do historic things like help win the West. Others simply work. This museum, with illustrations, literature, and artifacts, pays tribute to the latter and to the types of labor work horses performed on farms, in cities, and at military posts before the arrival of the internal combustion engine and tractors, trucks, and trolleys. Seeders, threshers, harrows, plows, and reapers seem almost ready to return to work. Sleighs, hay wagons, surreys, a horse treadle, a carousel, and a U.S. Army gun cart also recall an earlier age. Blacksmith and harness shops and a veterinary building offer insights into other facets of this rather common laborer who, historically, has received comparatively little acclaim, but who helped move the nation forward for nearly 300 years.

Petersburg

U.S. Slo-Pitch Softball Association Hall of Fame Museum, 3935 S. Crater Rd.; take Rives Rd. Exit from I-95. (804) 732-4101. Adults: $1.50, seniors and students: $1. Open Mon. through Fri., 9 a.m. to 4 p.m.; Sat., 11 a.m. to 4 p.m.; Sun., 1 to 4 p.m. Accessible to handicapped.

Enjoyed by millions, softball is generally considered as much a fun game as competitive sport. And this museum demonstrates how popular and how competitive it is. Action photos, bats and balls, caps, biographies, and a 20-minute film bring the game back to anyone who has ever swung at, and possibly missed, one of those tempting spheres. Special exhibits focus on the 16-inch version of the game, umpires' programs, women's teams, and inductees to the hall of fame. It's nothing less than an invitation to "Play ball!"

Richmond

Museum of the Confederacy, 1201 E. Clay St.; take Exit 10 from I-95. (804) 649-1861. Adults: $3, children 7 to 12: $1.25. Open Mon. through Sat., 10 a.m. to 5 p.m.; Sun. 1 to 5 p.m. Accessible to handicapped.

No tour of the South can ignore the Civil War. This facility probably has the most comprehensive collection of documents and artifacts relating to that tragic episode. The main exhibit, Confederate Years, chronicles the war event by event, and a half dozen other exhibits provide details of the Confederate Cabinet, flags and firearms, and life on the home front. Items in the collection belong to the common soldier and to leaders such as Stonewall Jackson, Robert E. Lee, and J. E. B. Stuart—for example, a jacket of a Louisiana private wounded at Shiloh, telescope and pistol of an officer on the *Alabama*, tattered battle flags from Gettysburg, and the sword Lee wore at Appomattox.

Staunton

Museum of American Frontier Culture; take Exit 57 from I-81 to Rte. 250 west. (703) 332-7850. Adults: $4, children 6 to 12: $2. Open daily, 9 a.m. to 5 p.m.; closed Christmas and New Year's Day. Accessible to handicapped.

This region of the country, the rolling woods and meadows of the Shenandoah Valley, was settled by Germans, English, and Scots-Irish, and the museum recreates 18th- and 19th century farm life through faithful reconstruction of American and European farms of the settlement period. Tools, materials, crafts, methods, and architecture, all form a distant mirror. Demonstrations include plowing, cooking, spinning, and holiday celebrations particular to the various immigrant countries and to the synthesized American farm. Animals, sheds, barns, corn cribs, and costumes of guides are all authentic. A scholarly undertaking funded by the state, this rustic reconstruction may someday rival, and complement, elegant Williamsburg.

Virginia Beach

Life-Saving Museum, Atlantic Ave. & 24th St., in the old Coast Guard Station. (804) 422-1587. Adults: $2, seniors and military: $1.50. Open Memorial Day through Sept., Mon. through Sat., 10 a.m. to 9 p.m.; Sun., noon to 5 p.m.; Oct. to Memorial Day, Tues. through Sat., 10 a.m. to 5 p.m.; closed Christmas and New Year's Eve and Day.

Here on the edge of the sometimes unfriendly sea stands a museum dedicated to the Life-Saving Service and the Coast Guard that valiantly attempted so much, often with so few. Focusing on the Virginia coast from 1874 to the present, the exhibits recount shipwrecks and the feats of life-saving surfmen who plunged into the turbulent waves to rescue passengers and crews. Here are photos and paintings of men and boats, of rescue methods, of struggles with the sea. Artifacts range from ship models to breeches buoys. Also displayed are photos, posters, and other graphic reminders of German submarine threats, and Coast Guard horse and dog patrols of a wartime shore. The structure itself, built in 1903, is the second-oldest building on the Virginia Beach boardwalk.

Yorktown

Watermen's Museum, 309 Water St., on the York River, off Rte. 64. (804) 898-3180. Adults: $1, seniors and military: $.75, children: $.50. Open May through Dec., Tues. through Sat., 10 a.m. to 4 p.m.; Sun., 1 to 4 p.m. Accessible to handicapped.

In the United States, the term "watermen" refers primarily to the fishermen of Chesapeake Bay and this museum tells their story, one not typically recounted in history books. Photos, prints, models, exhibits, and demonstrations portray a vanishing way of life on this part of the coast, and retired watermen add texture to the tale by helping with tours. There are numerous models of different types of boats dating back to the late 1700s—from small fishing craft to large lumber schooners. Nets, traps, and oyster tongs are among the many artifacts, and an oyster-tonging platform gives visitors a chance to try their hand at this arduous labor. A children's hands-on exhibit area includes such items as ships' bells and portholes.

Washington, D.C.

National Geographic Society's Explorers Hall, 1145 17th St., NW, 4 blocks north of the White House. (202) 857-7000. Free. Open Mon. through Sat., 9 a.m. to 5 p.m.; Sun., 10 a.m. to 5 p.m.; closed Christmas. Accessible to handicapped.

If the Smithsonian is the universe, then Explorers Hall might fairly be called planet Earth, and that's appropriate, too, because the heart of its permanent exhibit is Earth Station One, an interactive, multimedia theater with an 11-foot free-standing globe. Visitors can touch and observe a model tornado, manipulate robotic microscopes, vicariously explore the continents and oceans, check satellite weather forecasts, and seek out clues to human evolution. Temporary exhibits have included the archaeological tales of a Swedish warship and a Mayan tomb. Dynamic, entertaining, and educational, Explorers Hall is nothing less than National Geographic magazine in 3-D with sound.

National Building Museum, Pension Bldg. on F St., NW, between 4th and 5th Sts. (202) 272-2448. Free. Open Mon. through Sat., 10 a.m. to 4 p.m.; Sun. and holidays, noon to 4 p.m.; closed Thanksgiving, Christmas, and New Year's Day. Elevators and entrance for the handicapped.

Established to commemorate American building arts, this museum is appropriately located in a magnificent century-old structure—its great hall has eight Corinthian columns, the largest in the world, supporting a clerestory to admit natural light, and there's a

1,200-foot-long terra cotta frieze depicting six Civil War units. The vast inner courtyard is the traditional site of presidential inaugural balls. The museum itself entails exhibits on architecture, design, urban planning, building trades, and historic preservation. Staff can even discuss the history of nails. In addition to the Pension Building itself, tours are available of nearby construction sites and unusual structures.

National Firearms Museum, 1600 Rhode Island Ave., NW, 5 blocks north of the White House. (202) 828-6253. Free. Open daily, 10 a.m. to 4 p.m.; closed Thanksgiving, Christmas, and New Year's Day. Limited facilities for handicapped.

In a country crazy about guns, it's sure-fire there'd be a museum devoted to firearms. Operated by the National Rifle Association, the two-story museum displays more than 1,000 weapons and exhibits illustrating firearms technology and development. In the celebrity category, you can find a pistol of Teddy Roosevelt, a rifle of Napoleon, and an air gun from England's Prince Charles. One exhibit depicts the operational mechanics of a rifle, another shows safari scenes. Temporary shows have covered sports pistols, hunting decoys, and shooting competition medals.

National Museum of Health and Medicine, Bldg. 54, Walter Reed Army Medical Center; take 16th St. from downtown to Georgia Ave. and Elder St. (202) 576-2348. Free. Open Mon. through Fri., 9:30 a.m. to 4:30 p.m.; weekends, 11:30 a.m. to 4:30 p.m.; closed Thanksgiving, Christmas Eve and Day, and New Year's Day. Accessible to handicapped.

Formerly the Armed Forces Medical Museum and born out of the Civil War when medical treatment was often chancy at best, this rejuvenated facility both tells and makes medical history. It houses numerous Civil War displays, including surgical instruments and a special exhibit on Lincoln's assassination and subsequent autopsy, even the bullet that killed him. But it also boasts the nation's first AIDS exhibit in a museum setting. Other items include the most comprehensive collection of microscopes in the U.S., Japanese medical manikins, various pathological specimens, and a circa 1900 horse-drawn ambulance. With some 325,000 artifacts, the museum has something for everyone interested in health, ranging from early electrotherapy machines to a shrunken head from the Amazon jungle.

Lincoln Museum, basement of Ford's Theater, 511 10th St., NW, near Metro Center, 1 block from FBI Bldg. and 2 blocks from Pennsylvania Ave. (202) 426-6927. Free. Open daily, 9 a.m. to 5 p.m.; closed Christmas. No wheelchair access to museum itself.

Now a National Park Service site, Ford's Theater is virtually synonymous with the murder of Abraham Lincoln by John Wilkes Booth in April 1865. The museum takes you a bit closer to that event than do pages in a history book. Here are the murder weapon, Booth's diary, the boot he was wearing when he broke his leg, the hoods of the executed conspirators; also the clothing the President wore that evening and the pillow on which his head lay, plus newspaper stories of the tragedy. But the collection is not all on the grisly or mournful side. It also includes memorabilia from Lincoln's youth, political cartoons, campaign materials, and other items related to his career.

Confederate Memorial Hall, 1322 Vermont Ave., NW, 8 blocks from the White House. (202) 483-5700. Free. Open weekdays, 9 a.m. to 5 p.m.; weekends, 10 a.m. to 4 p.m.; calling in advance for an appointment is advised. Limited access for handicapped.

Washington, D.C.'s single shrine to the losing side in the Civil War, this Richardson Romanesque structure is a former home for Confederate veterans that now serves as a gentle reminder of an era when the country was torn in two. The museum is more cultural than curatorial, heavier on anecdotes and perspective than artifacts. The latter include side chairs of Gen. Beauregard, a sideboard of Jefferson Davis, paintings of Southern leaders, photos of veterans, and an eclectic collection of their medals, Bibles, and other personal items. The highlight here is really curator John Edward Hurley who discusses not only the building and its objects, but provides historical context and recounts stories of cavalry raids, spies, intrigue, policy struggles, and the ebb and flow of the war, pegging it all to the background and interest of visitors.

West Virginia

Moundsville

Delf Norona Museum, 801 Jefferson Ave., 12 miles south of Wheeling and 2 blocks east of Rte. 2. (304) 843-1410. Adults: $1.50, students: $.75. Open Mon. through Sat., 10 a.m. to 4:30 p.m.; Sun., 1 to 5 p.m.; closed Thanksgiving, Christmas, and New Year's Day. Accessible to handicapped.

The Grave Creek Mound, constructed between 250 and 150 B.C., stands nearly 70 feet high and has a diameter of 295 feet at the base. Adjacent to this burial mound of the Adena tribe, the museum exhibits what is known of these prehistoric people. Most of the archaeological excavation occurred in the 1830s, and core drilling in 1974 revealed little to justify further digs. Exhibits include such artifacts as pottery and arrowheads. Maps, mounted text, and illustrations give further information about the site. If you're adventurous, you can hike to the top of the mound.

Wheeling

Oglebay Institute Mansion Museum, Oglebay Park; take Exit 2-A from I-70 to Rte. 40 east to Rte. 88 north. (304) 242-7272. Adults: $3.50, seniors: $3, ages 13 through college: $2.50, children under 12: free with paying adult. Open Mon. through Sat., 9:30 a.m. to 5 p.m.; Sun., 1 to 5 p.m.; special extended hours during holiday season. First floor accessible to handicapped.

Glass, china, and pottery are on display here, and in a big way—the Sweeney punch bowl stands nearly five feet tall, weighs 250 pounds, and holds 21 gallons of punch. It's believed to be the largest piece of cut glass in existence. Period rooms display antique furniture from the 1700s through the 1900s as well as portraits and furnishings. Formerly the summer home of the Oglebay family, the museum also houses some items of theirs, such as silverware, a tea set, a mirror, and a carpet. Rotating exhibits have included such things as Weimar German decorative pottery.

West Virginia Independence Hall, corner of 16th and Market; take Main St. Exit from I-70. (304) 233-1333. Free, except $2 guide fee for group tours. Open March through Dec., Mon. through Fri., 10 a.m. to 4 p.m.; Sun., 1 to 4 p.m.; closed Sat. and major holidays. Accessible to handicapped.

This fine sandstone structure, the former Wheeling Custom House (1859), was the birthplace of West Virginia, a state fashioned in the early 1860s from the North-South conflict. Restored rooms and exhibits focus on the formation of the state, for example, the furnished office of Governor Pierpont. Portraits, prints, documents, and an interpretive film add details to the story. Changing exhibits cover diverse aspects of West Virginia's heritage—a retrospective of the Blenko Glass Co., letters and memorabilia of abolitionist John Brown, historic photos of Wheeling, the first ladies of the state, and the warship U.S.S. *West Virginia.*

White Sulphur Springs

Presidents' Cottage Museum, at the Greenbrier resort, near junction of I-64 and Rte. 219. Free (and open to people not guests at the resort). Open Apr. 1 through Oct. 30, Mon. through Sat., 10 a.m. to noon and 1 to 4 p.m.; Sun., 10 a.m. to 3 p.m.; rest of year, Sat., 1 to 4:30 p.m. or by appointment. No facilities for handicapped.

Called the Presidents' Cottage because of its vacation use by Van Buren, Fillmore, Pierce, Buchanan, and Tyler, this structure was a premier cottage in the South's most fashionable resort prior to the Civil War, a meeting place for the political, military, and social elite. But other than the name, there's little within regarding the five chief executives. Rather, you will see items reflecting pre- and post-

Civil War life—marble-topped tables, musical instruments, different types of china, mementos of Robert E. Lee (a frequent postwar visitor to the resort, as was Ulysses S. Grant), photos of Confederate generals, and information about the Chesapeake & Ohio Railroad's purchase of Greenbrier in 1910.

III
NORTH
CENTRAL

Illinois

Arcola

Louis P. Klein Broom and Brush Museum, 115 N. Oak St., in
Arcola Depot; take Arcola Exit from I-57 and follow blue tourist
signs to depot. (217) 268-4530. Free. Open daily May through Oct.,
10 a.m. to 4 p.m. Ramp for handicapped, but no handicapped rest
room facilities.

Whoever thinks of brooms and brushes as ho-hum subjects for
viewing has never seen the Louis P. Klein collection. Housed in the
town's restored railroad depot, this sensational and unique collection of more than 1,000 pieces is a real eye-opener. Klein combed
the flea markets of London some years ago and came home with
the start of this extraordinary collection. Brushes come in an amazing variety of forms, as evidenced here, the most beautiful featuring finely-crafted bronze figures of animals—hedgehogs, mice,
boars, alligators, birds—with backs that bristle with brushes. Beau-
tifully-carved wooden animals also decorate curved clothes
brushes, and silver-backed hair brushes are artfully embossed with
filigree. There are American Indian paintbrushes, practical bath
and scrub brushes, and miniature brushes suitable for grooming
the tiniest doll. As for brooms, the hundreds on display here are
equally fascinating and as near to being classified artworks as the
brushes are.

Carthage

Show n' Tell Museum, 417 N. Madison, 2½ blocks north of 4-way stop at Rtes. 94 and 136. (217) 357-3456. Admission: $2 per person. Open daily by appointment only. No facilities for handicapped.

The 14 rooms of this Victorian house are the perfect setting for countless charming dolls, toys, teddy bears, and Christmas decorations, to say nothing of 35 dollhouses, including barns and churches, most furnished with authentic antiques. Notable among these are handcrafted log cabins, a house made of matchsticks, and a church of galvanized metal. The dolls and teddy bears run the gamut from mint condition models to well-hugged. Paper dolls, mechanical toys, antique clothing, books, games, and baskets round out this look at "200 years of childhood memories."

Chicago

American Police Center and Museum, 1705–25 S. State St. (312) 431-0005. Donation suggested. Open Mon. through Fri., 8:30 p.m. to 4:30 p.m. Accessible to handicapped.

"Do you have any exhibits on Al Capone?" is the most frequently asked question here. The answer is a decisive "Yes!" An entire room, dubbed Gangster Alley and featuring an electric chair, focuses on Chicago's most famous mobster and other Prohibition-era bad guys. They are only part of Chicago's police story, however. Other extensive exhibit areas focus on the development of police communications over the years, uniforms of all types, and a vast array of badges and insignia. Mug shots of past superintendents of police line one wall. Another wall serves as a memorial to officers killed in the line of duty.

Museum of Surgical Sciences and Hall of Fame, 1524 N. Lake Shore Dr.; from I-90/94, take North Ave. Exit east to Clark St., take right, go one block and left on Burton St. to Lake Shore Dr. and left to museum. (312) 642-3555. Adults: $1, seniors and children: $.50. Open Tues. through Sat., 10 a.m. to 4 p.m.; Sun., 11 a.m. to 5 p.m.; closed Mon. No facilities for handicapped.

Contributions to modern surgical science is the theme of this extensive collection, starting with evidence that brain surgery was performed by prehistoric man, through the development of the microscope and x-ray equipment, to heart surgery research, blood transfusions, and more. In fact, the three floors of this handsome building and annex contain more than 30 rooms of specialized exhibits—Greek Room, Turn-of-the-Century Apothecary Shop, Brazil Room, China Room (featuring acupuncture), Orthopedic Room, and so on. In the Hall of Murals original paintings depict surgical procedures, anatomy, and anesthesia. A Hall of Immortals contains life-sized sculptures of history's outstanding exponents of surgical science.

Des Plaines

McDonald's Museum, 400 N. Lee St., downtown, between Northwest Hwy. and Rand Rd. (708) 297-5022. Free. Open Mar., Apr., and Oct., Wed., Fri., and Sat., 10 a.m. to 4 p.m.; May and Sept., Tues., Wed., Fri., and Sat., 10 a.m. to 4 p.m.; June, July, and Aug., Tues. through Sat., 10 a.m. to 4 p.m. and Sun., 1 to 4 p.m. No facilities for handicapped.

The golden arches are the tip-off here. This is the birthplace of Ronald McDonald, or at least the original drive-in restaurant in Ray Kroc's omnipresent hamburger chain. Nineteen fifty-five is the featured year—with signs advertising hamburgers for 15 cents, gleaming vintage Chevies and Fords parked in front, and golden oldies on the jukebox. Downstairs, guided tours include a short video and a picture display of McDonald's lore.

Elmhurst

Lizzardo Museum of Lapidary Art, 220 Cottage Hill, 2 blocks west of York Rd., 2 blocks north of St. Charles Rd. (708) 833-1616. Adults: $1, seniors and children 13 to 19: $.50. Open Tues. through Sat., 10 a.m. to 5 p.m.; Sun., 1 to 5 p.m.; closed major holidays. Accessible to handicapped.

Lapidary art is the art of carving, polishing and engraving gemstones, and an enduring art it is, judging from exhibits that run the historical gamut from exquisite Chinese Ming Dynasty carved nephrite jade pieces to modern creations. Mosaics, intricately-carved stone art objects, and such decorative art pieces as snuff bottles, jewelry, bowls, and vases all testify to the skill and imagination that the craft requires and demonstrate how a rough lump of stone can be transformed into a work of beauty. Companion exhibits cover the geologic origins of rocks, with displays of rock specimens, meteorites, and fossils.

Galena

General Store Museum, 223 S. Main St., 4 blocks north of Rte. 20 in center of town. (815) 777-9129. Donation of $1 suggested. Open daily, June through Oct., 10 a.m. to 4 p.m.; weekends in May, Nov. and Dec. Accessible to handicapped.

Lucky for those interested in Americana that some things go out of style, for the bulk of the objects on view in this recreated 19th-century country store are outdated merchandise from the attic of Galena's downtown stores. The staff of this old-fashioned shop are papier-mâché manikins dressed in period clothing, and the goods filling shelves, hanging on walls, and overflowing floorspace include items that our grandparents would have expected to find stocking their favorite general store. An adjacent display recreates typical back-of-the-shop living quarters.

Vinegar Hill Lead Mine Museum, 8885 N. Three Pines Rd., 6 miles north of Galena on Rte. 84. (815) 777-0855. Adults: $3.50, students grades 1 through 12: $1.50. Open daily, June, July, and Aug., 9 a.m. to 5 p.m.; weekends in May, Sept. and Oct. No facilities for handicapped.

Claustrophobes may wish to confine their visit to this museum to the first half of the 40-minute guided tour—the half that takes place in the museum building above ground. Antique mining tools and lighting devices, artifacts, and mineral samples are offered here, as is a general history of the mine itself. The second half of the tour takes you 50 feet down and 200 feet laterally. Here, guides point out lead deposits and explain the different methods of mining used since the early 1800s. The area around Galena was once known as the lead-mining capital of the world. Vinegar Hill Lead Mine has been owned and operated since 1824 through five generations of one family and is the only lead mine in Illinois open to the public.

Glenview

Hartung's License Plate and Auto Museum, 3623 Westlake, ½ mile west of Glenview Naval Air Station main gate. (708) 724-4354.

Donation suggested. Open daily; call for hours. No facilities for handicapped.

License plate buffs can enjoy their favorite subject to their hearts' content here. On display are license plates of all 50 states, starting with first date of issue, plus examples from many other countries, including Canada. Also on hand are unrestored antique cars—a 1926 Hertz Touring car, a 1932 Essex Terraplane, Ford trucks, a 1950 Veritas convertible, and numerous others. You can see motorcycles, too, starting with a 1901 Wagner, through Sears, Indian, and Henderson models, plus sidecars. And 75 antique bicycles are part of the permanent collection. In addition, hundreds of spark plugs, radiator caps, emblems, badges, hub caps, hood ornaments, toys, and model cars create a little bit of heaven for earth-bound car enthusiasts.

Lockport

Illinois and Michigan Canal Museum, 803 S. State St., downtown, 1 block north of junction of Rtes. 7 and 171. (815) 838-5080. Free. Open daily, 1 to 4 p.m.; closed federal holidays, Thanksgiving week, and Dec. 15 through Jan. 2. Handicapped access to lower level.

Through pictures, records, documents and artifacts, this museum, located in an 1837 building that served as office and home to canal commissioners, tells the complete story of the planning, construction, operation, and demise of the Illinois and Michigan Canal. Costumed docents take you through the canal's history, starting in 1848 through 62 years of operation and more than 10 million tons of commerce. The tour then explores the nine remaining rooms, filled with authentic period furnishings, tools, and household items used by canal commissioners and their families.

Moline

John Deere Company Museum, Deere & Company Display Floor, John Deer Rd., in product display building just east of main office building. (309) 765-5838. Free. Display floor open daily, 9 a.m. to 5:30 p.m. No facilities for handicapped.

John Deere tractors—bright green with yellow wheels—are a familiar sight on American farmlands. Here they are shown in all their many models—from antique machinery dating back to the company's first product line to modern tractors and riding lawn mowers to monstrous machines possibly more at home on a road construction site than on the south forty. A unique addition to this display of hardware is a three-dimensional mural, designed by Alexander Girard, of more than 2,000 historical items—advertisements, souvenirs, photographs, and non-Deere farm items from the period 1837 to 1918.

Peoria

Wheels O' Time, 11923 N. Knoxville Ave., on Rte. 88, 8 miles north of downtown Peoria. (309) 243-9020 or 691-3470. Adults: $2.50, children through age 11: $1. Open May through Oct. and summer holidays, Wed. through Sun., noon to 5 p.m. Accessible to handicapped, except for balcony in one building.

Wheels? Yes, many of the objects on display in these three buildings depend on the wheel in one form or another—30 beautifully preserved vintage automobiles certainly do, as do a steam locomotive, a fire engine, Caterpillar tractors, and even a reproduction of the Red Baron's WWI fighter plane. But juke boxes? Toys? Miniature circuses, dolls, woodworking tools, clocks, and musical instruments? Wheels or no, it's a fascinating, mostly hands-on collection that is both entertaining and educational.

Quincy

Gardner Museum of Architecture and Design, 332 Maine St., at intersection of Fourth and Maine Sts. (Rtes. 57 and 24). (217) 224-6873. Adults: $2, seniors: $1, students: $.50. Regular gallery open weekend afternoons, 1 to 5 p.m.; gallery of stained glass open year round by appointment; two major exhibits: Apr. through June, and Oct. through Dec. Handicapped assistance available.

This museum, organized in 1974, is dedicated to the presentation and preservation of Quincy's architectural heritage, and an outstanding heritage it is, with numerous fine 19th-century buildings dotting the city, including the Richardsonian Romanesque former library in which the museum is housed. Changing exhibits focus on architectural ornamentation, photographs, and special design exhibits—for example, a Best Seats in the House exhibit of chairs and a Made in Quincy exhibit of products made locally. A permanent gallery of stained glass features windows from area churches and residences—including a glorious Tiffany window—all from the great age of American stained glass, 1860 to 1910.

Lincoln Douglas Valentine Museum, 101 N. 4th St., on Rte. 24, on northwest corner of Fourth and Maine. (217) 224-3355. Donation appreciated. Open daily, 9 a.m. to 9 p.m., by appointment only. Accessible to handicapped.

To set things straight, this is a museum of valentines, although not sentimental exchanges between Abraham Lincoln and Stephen Douglas; they are simply on display in the Lincoln Douglas apartment building. Valentines—romantic, funny, ornate, corny, elegant, gaudy, hand-colored in crayon—have found a home here, and comprise a very beautiful collection of sweet sentiment. Also on display are albums of century-old news items and collections of old postcards and calling cards. The museum is the project of building residents. The building has a security guard, which accounts for the visitor having to call first for an appointment.

Pharmacy Museum of Quincy and Adams County, Fifth and Chestnut Sts., 1 block east of Rte. 24. (217) 224-1000. Adults: $2, children: $.50. Open May 1 through Sept., Sat. and Sun., 1 to 4 p.m.; Oct. through Apr. by appointment. Accessible to handicapped.

Housed in another of Quincy's fine older buildings—the 1906 Heidbreder Hagemann Drug Store—is a remarkable collection of pharmaceutical artifacts: scales, old bottles, suppository machines, microscopes, mortars and pestles, and a variety of apothecary tools. When the drug store closed its doors after 80 years of business, its contents and its owner's collection of pharmaceutical memorabilia remained intact—all furnishings, counters, and display cases are original.

Rock Island

Rock Island Arsenal Museum, Building 60, Rock Island Arsenal; from I-74, take 7th Ave. West Exit, turn north on 19th St. and west on Second Ave. (309) 782-5021 or -5182. Free. Open daily, 10 a.m. to 4 p.m.; closed Thanksgiving, Christmas, and New Year's Day. Accessible to handicapped.

Rock Island Arsenal is an active U.S. Army factory that has manufactured military ordnance—weapons, ammunition, and equipment—since 1905. Themed displays here, labeled People, Processes, and Products, trace the history of Arsenal Island and its role in the manufacturing processes used at the arsenal and the equipment it has produced. Photographs eloquently tell the story of the people who have worked there—aproned men in 1898, for instance, and brightly-clad women in 1943—as well as what was made and how. There is an extensive collection of military firearms, foreign and domestic. A new exhibit entitled Indian Guns of the Little Big Horn features six rifles used by the Indians at that battle. Other buildings that may be visited at the arsenal include an 1816 fort and a Confederate prison camp.

Rockford

The Time Museum, 7801 E. State St., on premises of Clock Tower Resort, at junction of Business Rte. 20 and I-90. (815) 398-6000. Adults: $3, seniors and college students: $2, children 6 to 18: $1. Open Tues. through Sun., 10 a.m. to 5 p.m.; closed Mon. Accessible to handicapped.

Time-measuring devices come in a lot more forms than the ubiquitous clock on the wall. This diverse collection contains sundials, nocturnals, fire clocks, water clocks, sand glasses, chronometers and other navigational instruments, along with a huge and comprehensive selection of clocks and watches from all parts of the world. One of many highlights here is a 10-foot German astronomical clock designed in the late 1800s that features a mechanized procession of the Apostles at noon each day. Fourteen separate display areas divide the vast collection into time periods, starting with calendar stones and other early devices in Area 2, down to modern quartz and atomic clocks and novelty watches in Area 14. Instruments by famous makers are represented throughout.

Zitelman Scout Museum, 708 Seminary St.; take Business Rte. 20 to downtown, turn south at Second St. to end; make S-curve at Camelot Towers to Seminary St.; museum is 1 block past Morgan St. stoplight. (815) 962-3999. Free. Open Wed., 9 a.m. to 4 p.m., and Sat., 9 a.m. to 3 p.m. No facilities for handicapped.

Scouting uniforms are the uniform of the day here—Boy Scout uniforms dating back to 1910, as well as those of Girl Scouts, Air Scouts, Sea Scouts, Lone Scouts, Daisies, Brownies, and Scouts from many foreign countries. But patches, badges, scrapbooks, handbooks, stamps, flags, knives, and neckerchiefs are also part of this voluminous collection, as is an autographed picture of Lord Baden-Powell. Of particular interest is a series of photographs depicting one man's life in Scouting, from Cubs to adult Scouting. An entire room is devoted to Girl Scouts. Be prepared for an absorbing visit.

Teutopolis

Teutopolis Monastery Museum, 110 S. Garrott St., south from Rte. 40; museum is just west of St. Francis Catholic Church. (217) 857-3328. Adults: $1.50, grade school children: $.50. Open first Sun. of each month, Apr. through Nov., 1 to 4 p.m.; special tours for groups of 10 or more by appointment. No facilities for handicapped.

For the pious and the merely curious alike, this monastery-turned-museum is a fascinating peek at monastic life. The Franciscan monastery and the town of Teutopolis are historically entwined. The town was founded by German Catholics and the Franciscans were invited to help fulfill the villagers' spiritual needs. The 37 rooms on view feature a novice's cell, old books, Bibles, kneelers, lecterns, furnishings, and other articles from austere day-to-day monastic life. In one room is a collection of 65 dolls, dressed to depict scenes in the life of St. Francis. A tour includes a demonstration of the cord machine, a device utilizing 62 spools to weave the strong cords that Franciscans wear around the waist. The history of the town is not neglected—there is an exhibit of original tools used by pioneers to fashion the wooden shoes they habitually wore and which they manufactured for sale.

Indiana

Jeffersonville

Howard Steamboat Museum, 1101 E. Market St., on Ohio River across from Louisville; take Exit 10 off I-65. (812) 283-3328. Adults: $2.50, seniors and students over 12: $2. Open Tues. through Sat., 10 a.m. to 3 p.m.; Sun., 1 to 3 p.m.; closed Mon. and major holidays. No facilities for handicapped.

James Howard launched a shipyard in 1834 with his first steamer *Hyperion*. Sleek and durable, his vessels came to dominate the nation's interior river traffic. Purchased by the federal government in 1941, the family-run shipyard built some 3,000 river steamboats over its century of operation. The house, which holds the museum, was built in the Chateauesque style of the 1890s. Its grand stairway, carved arches, brass chandeliers, 15 types of wood, and exquisite furniture (including a 100-year-old rolltop desk) reflect the family's success and position. The tools, scale models of riverboats, pilot's wheels, paintings, photos, documents, gear, and furnishings—such as a medicine chest from the *Natchez*—place the museum in its own special transportation niche.

Kokomo

Elwood Haynes Museum, 1915 S. Webster, at intersection with Boulevard. (317) 452-3471. Donations welcome. Open Tues.

through Sat., 1 to 4 p.m.; Sun., 1 to 5 p.m.; closed Mon. and holidays. No facilities for handicapped.

Elwood Haynes—scientist, educator, and industrialist—built the country's first commercially successful gasoline-powered automobile in 1894 and later invented satellite alloy and stainless steel. Indeed, at age 15 he designed a blower-furnace for melting brass and cast iron. The inventor's home is now a museum, with the first floor devoted to documents, photos, family furnishings, and items related to Haynes' inventions and business ventures. The second floor contains Kokomo-area industrial displays and the basement shows a film on automotive history. Four antique cars grace the premises.

Muncie

Ball Corporation Museum, 345 High St., off I-69. (317) 747-6100. Free. Open Mon. through Fri., 8 a.m. to 5 p.m.; closed weekends and holidays. Accessible to handicapped.

This firm began more than a century ago making cans and has since leaped into the Space Age. It is perhaps most widely identified with its jars, but more than 20 percent of its activity today is in aerospace. Exhibits in this one-room facility chronicle the company's evolution, first displaying jacketed kerosene cans, then fruit jars and metal containers, plastic and aluminum packaging, and finally the more recent endeavors represented by models and photos of satellites and other aerospace and astronomical technology. Descriptive plaques and labels provide details of the company story, and groups can see a film that supplements the displays.

Nashville

John Dillinger Historical Wax Museum, 104 S. Van Buren, on Rte. 46, 16 miles west of I-65. (812) 988-7172. Adults: $3, seniors and children 6 to 12: $2. Open Mar. through Nov., 10 a.m. to 6 p.m.; Dec. through Feb., 1 to 5 p.m. (weather permitting). No facilities for handicapped.

And what could be more American than gangsters, especially the machine-gun marauders of the 1930s? John Dillinger robbed banks from Ohio to South Dakota, stole weapons from police departments, and reputedly broke out of an escape-proof jail with a wooden gun. Here in the peaceful landscape of southern Indiana a museum puts the violent Dillinger on display "without social or moral comment." Yes, some of the exhibits are wax figures—Dillinger, "Pretty Boy" Floyd, Ma Baker, and FBI agent Melvin Purvis, et. al.—but it also holds striking artifacts such as the fatally-shot outlaw's blood-stained trousers, the infamous wooden pistol, his first (and vandalized) tombstone, letters, family photos, period newspaper clippings, and a reporter's diary. The owners claim a certain expertise—one is a former FBI agent and the other is co-author of a book on Dillinger.

Peru

Circus Museum, 154 N. Broadway, downtown at intersection with 7th St. (317) 472-3918. Donations welcome. Open Apr. through Oct., Mon. through Fri., 9 a.m. to noon and 1 to 4 p.m.; special hours during second and third week in July. Accessible to handicapped.

Everyone loves a parade, and the circus. Peru bills itself as "the circus capital of the world" and this museum adds another dimension to circus entertainment. Lithographs, photos, and uniforms illustrate performers and performances. Rigging, harnesses, trapezes, furniture, and animal cages offer a quieter perspective of the circus' muscle and bones. In addition, there are miniature circus wagons and miniature circuses made to scale, and it's all against a background of authentic circus music.

Richmond

Indiana Football Hall of Fame, 815 N. "A" St., off I-70 and Rte. 27 south. (317) 966-2235. Adults: $1, children under 15: $.50. Open May through Oct., Mon. through Fri., 10 a.m. to 4 p.m.; Nov. through Apr., Mon. through Fri., 10 a.m. to 2 p.m.; weekend and evening hours by appointment. Accessible to handicapped.

In a state more oriented to hoops than pigskin, this museum pays unabashed homage to gridiron glory. It focuses on Indiana coaches (such as Knute Rockne, Ara Parseghian, Weeb Ewbank), college players (Indy racer Tony Hullman, an All-American at Yale), players who went to the pros from an Indiana team, high school players (a 1926 high school team had four sets of brothers), even Hoosier sportswriters and announcers. A coaches room, players room, and history room (dating to 1892) are filled with photos, footballs, and assorted memorabilia. Lamar Lundy of Richmond, Purdue, and the Los Angeles Rams often serves as a guide.

South Bend

Studebaker National Museum, 120 S. St. Joseph St. and 525 S. Main St., both off Rte. 31 south of I-80/90. (219) 284-9714. Adults: $3.50, seniors: $2.50, children 12 and under: $1.50 (fee good for both locations). Open Mon. through Fri., 10 a.m. to 4:30 p.m.; Sat., 10 a.m. to 4 p.m.; Sun., noon to 4 p.m. Accessible to handicapped.

For those who started driving in the past two decades, Studebaker may sound like something connected with ovens and bread. But older folks recognize the name as an innovative automaker with roots in mid-19th-century carriage and wagon manufacture. One location contains some 20 vehicles and recounts corporate history and South Bend industrial growth. The other houses an additional 60 Studebakers, including carriages of four U.S. presidents and military vehicles. The collection counts the first carriage built by Clem and Henry Studebaker in 1857 and the final car model in the mid-1960s.

Wakarusa

Bird's Eye View Museum, 325 S. Elkhart, 1 mile west of Rte. 19. (219) 862-2367. Ages 16 to 80: $2.50, 8 to 16: $1.25. Open year round, evenings and weekends by chance or appointment. No facilities for handicapped.

Toothpicks and popsicle sticks may be scrap lumber to some folks, but for DeVon Rose and his sons these and other common items have been building materials, which, when combined with large measures of precision and patience, have produced a "believe-it-or-not" scale replica of much of their community—churches, homes, schools, shops, and more. Begun as a hobby to accompany electric trains, the collection burgeoned. According to the owner and chief architect, Ripley's Believe It Or Not wanted to buy the display, which has won numerous awards. This is a true labor of love and about as personal as a museum can get.

Iowa

Amana

Museum of Amana History, ½ block east of junction of Rtes. 151 and 220. (319) 622-3567. Adults: $2, children: $1. Open Apr. 15 through Nov. 15, Mon. through Sat., 10 a.m. to 5 p.m.; Sun. noon to 5 p.m. Limited facilities for handicapped.

Religious persecution in Europe gave birth to many communities in 19th-century America. One such place was Amana, where True Inspirationists established a communal society on the Iowa River in 1855. All land was owned by the community. Families were assigned houses and individuals were designated to labor in factories, fields, kitchens, or shops. The museum comprises three 19th-century buildings. One, the Noe House, was originally a communal kitchen and later a doctor's residence. Exhibits here trace the development of Amana, depict a church interior, and show the sect's crafts and trades. The schoolhouse holds toys, carpet-weaving items, and the tools of education. A washhouse/woodshed has wine-making and gardening displays. Temporary exhibits focus on various aspects of Amana culture.

Colfax

Trainland USA, Rte. 117, Exit 155 off I-80. (515) 674-3813. Adults: $3, seniors: $2.50, children 4 to 12: $1.50. Open Memorial Day through Labor Day, 9 a.m. to 7 p.m.; weekends during Sept., and the three days after Thanksgiving; tours available by appointment, Apr. through Oct. Accessible to handicapped.

Railroads run a powerful track through our national nostalgia, and here you can see the whole development of American railways—from the frontier Iron Horse to the transcontinental flyers—all in model form. Starting as a hobby in 1964, the Lionel collection of Red Atwood has reached epic proportions. Two dozen trains may run at any one time, coursing through hand-painted scenes of America's past—Western gunfight, medicine shows, road crews, operating crane, lumberjacks, trolley cars, drive-in movie, operating oil wells, stockyards, antique cars, moonshine still, and more. Some 600 lights and 200 buildings are included in the overall operation, which comprises 4,000 feet of track and 25,000 feet of wire. Display cases contain original railroad memorabilia and toy trains dating to 1916.

Decorah

Versterheim Norwegian-American Museum, 502 Water St., on Rte. 52, 65 miles south of Rochester, Minn. (319) 382-9681. Summer season (includes outdoor division)—adults: $4, seniors and groups: $3, children 7 to 18: $2, youth groups: $1.50, family: $10. Winter season—adults: $3, seniors and groups: $2, children: $1.50, youth groups: $1, family: $7. Open daily, May 1 through Oct. 31, 9 a.m. to 5 p.m.; Nov. 1 through Apr. 30, 10 a.m. to 4 p.m.; closed Easter, Thanksgiving, Christmas, and New Year's Day. Accessible to handicapped.

The upper Midwest was settled by northern Europeans, and here the Norwegian-American experience finds expression. That expression, of course, connects to the old country, and one whole floor is devoted to Norwegian folk culture, with numerous examples from the 18th, 19th, and 20th centuries. Other areas display arts, crafts, and industries of the immigrants. There are examples of painting, clothing, embroidery, woodburning, and woodcarving—some 16,000 artifacts in all. The outdoor division consists of 12 authentic buildings, including a blacksmith shop, log houses, stone mill, and a 1795 Norwegian house. Architecture and implements complement one another in this portrait of immigrant life.

Keokuk

Keokuk River Museum, Victory Park and Johnson St., on the banks of the Mississippi River, off Rte. 136. (319) 524-4765. Ages 15 and up: $1.50, 6 to 14: $.75. Open daily, Apr. through Oct. (including holidays), 9 a.m. to 5 p.m.; last ticket sold at 4:30 p.m. No facilities for handicapped.

The *George M. Verity* is a 1920s paddlewheel steam towboat built to revive river transport on the upper Mississippi. It moved barges from St. Louis to St. Paul and later worked on the Ohio River. It now labors in quieter currents, as a museum to regional river history. Visitors get a first-hand look at the boat's boilers, smokestacks, crew quarters, pilot house, and machinery. Also displayed are pilot wheels, whistles, and other artifacts, plus photos of 19th- and 20th-century riverboats and literature on river history.

Mason City

Van Horn Truck Museum, Rte. 65 north, 8 miles east of I-35. (515) 423-0550. Adults: $3.50, children 6 to 12: $1.50. Open May 25 through Sept. 22, Mon. through Sat., 10:30 a.m. to 4 p.m.; Sun., 11 a.m. to 6 p.m. Accessible to handicapped.

The phrase "Keep on truckin'" acquires added meaning at this unusual "truck stop." Lloyd Van Horn has spent four decades collecting and restoring antique trucks, those successors to the wagons that once coursed across the heartland. The vehicles are all pre-1930 vintage and include models by Nash, Packard, Hawkeye, Republic, Diamond T, Kelly Springfield, and Defiance. Solid rubber tires, chain drive, and right-hand steering characterize many of these old-timers. A 1915 Buick truck, with its white tires and gleaming lamps, seems the forerunner of today's fancy pickups. But there are specific workhorse types, too, such as a Douglas truck outfitted with an early model Holmes wrecker and a 1919 Olds gasoline delivery truck. A 1930 storefront street and garage, tools, early gas pumps, and old automotive signs give period patina to the collection.

Mt. Pleasant

Museum of Repertoire Americana, Threshers Rd., south on Locust or Walnut from junction of Rtes. 218 and 34. (319) 385-8937. Admission: $2. Open by appointment only. Accessible to handicapped.

All the world's a stage, and here is located the country's largest collection of early-day tent, repertoire theater, opera house, and Chautauqua memorabilia, with emphasis on touring companies in the Midwest from the 1850s to the 1940s. Photos, posters, flyers, scrapbooks, scripts, costumes, and other colorful items beckon anyone who has ever enjoyed theatrical performances. The museum has a remarkable number of curtains and moveable drops. It also boasts the Toby Hall of Fame; the Toby character was a sort of country bumpkin hero of traveling moralistic plays where good usually triumphed.

Midwest Old Threshers Heritage Museum, Threshers Rd., south on Locust or Walnut from junction of Rtes. 218 and 34. (319) 385-8937. (Same location and telephone number as above.) Adults: $2.50, children under 10: free. Open daily, Memorial Day through Labor Day, and Mon. through Fri., mid-Apr. to mid-Oct., 9 a.m. to 4:30 p.m. Accessible to handicapped.

This museum reveals the rugged face of farming. The period focus is 1880 to 1925 when steam engines and tractors were replacing horse-drawn implements. There are harvesters, threshers, plows, and tractors from the early days of mechanized farming, a full-size farmhouse (circa 1915), the new Wilkie machine tool exhibit, and an annual threshers show. Other exhibits show the evolution of the family farm, the beginnings of electrification, and the value of water. One of them highlights the role of farm women past and present via historical and contemporary photos as well as handicrafts, looms, stoves, spinning wheels, and other domestic gear.

Winterset

John Wayne Birthplace, 224 S. 2nd St., southwest of Des Moines, off Rte. 169. Adults: $2, children 5 to 12: $1, under 5: $.50. Open daily, Mar. through Dec., 10 a.m. to 5 p.m.; Jan. and Feb., noon to 4 p.m.; closed major holidays. Accessible to handicapped.

Perhaps the ultimate movie image of American patriotism, justice, and toughness, John Wayne was born here in 1907. His real name: Marion Robert Morrison. Opened in 1982, the museum shows a non-Hollywood side of The Duke, with a kitchen, parlor, and back porch restored to their early 1900s appearance with furniture and furnishings. Lest the connection be lost, the homestead also displays photos, awards, and other memorabilia, including items from his films, such as firearms and the eyepatch he wore in *True Grit*.

Michigan

Acme

The Music House, 7377 Rte. 31 north, 8 miles north of Traverse City, just off Rte. 72. (616) 938-9300. Adults: $5, children 6 to 18: $2. Open May through Oct., and weekends in Dec., Mon. through Sat., 10 a.m. to 4 p.m.; Sun. 1 to 6 p.m. Accessible to handicapped.

Amply filling several galleries in this turn-of-the-century village setting are examples of some of the finest and most beautiful automated antique musical instruments in the world. Hour-long guided tours, that include discussions of various instruments' histories and working mechanisms as well as a sample tune or two, take visitors past such rarities as elegant six-foot-high music boxes that play steel discs nearly 30 inches in diameter. There are band organs that make music with a system similar to computer punch cards, an automated violin, and all manner of pipe organs, the most spectacular of which is the 30-foot-wide white Amaryllis that once graced a palace in Belgium. Modern music-makers are not neglected: Victrolas, radios, and a delightful collection of gaudy juke boxes round out 200 years of automated music.

Ann Arbor

Stearns Collection of Musical Instruments, School of Music, Baits Dr., in North Campus area of University of Michigan; take Plymouth Exit west from Rte. 23 to Broadway to Baits Dr. (313)

763-4389. Free. Open during school year, Tues. and Fri., 10 a.m. to 5 p.m.; Sat. and Sun., 1 to 8 p.m. Accessible to handicapped.

While the rare and revered—a Stradivarius violin, a crystal flute, a harpsichord owned by Johann Sebastian Bach—are found in this fine collection, the emphasis is not so much on the antique as the experimental, specifically European and American musical instruments from the 19th and 20th centuries. Among examples likely to show up in changing exhibits are a saxophone made by Adolph Saxe himself and a Loomis, of which Saxe made only eight in his lifetime and of which only three are now in existence. You may also see a 1924 Theramin, the first electronic musical instrument and producer of the weird sound that opened the *Green Hornet* radio show and provided background scariness for Alfred Hitchcock's movie *Spellbound*; and the first Moog synthesizer, which predates the Hammond organ and is considered as significant to the world of music as the Wright brothers' first airplane was to manned flight. Tibetan drums, a Japanese ensemble, and instruments to outfit a complete Indonesian orchestra are also counted among the strong holdings, but the motto here is "Preserve the 20th century before it slips away."

Caspian

Iron County Museum, Museum Rd., on grounds of Old Caspian Mine, about 2 miles from Rte. 2. (906) 265-2617. Adults: $2, children: $1. Open June 1 through Aug. 31, Mon. through Sat., 9 a.m. to 5 p.m.; Sun., 1 to 5 p.m.; month of May and month of Sept., Mon. through Sat., 10 a.m. to 4 p.m.; Sun., 1 to 4 p.m.; and by appointment. Accessible to handicapped.

Eighteen buildings and five outdoor complexes make up this extensive folk museum on Michigan's Upper Peninsula. Of special note among the full-size log homestead buildings, mining complex, and logging camp are some miniaturized representations. One, consisting of more than 2,000 hand-carved pieces, depicts a lumber camp typical of those that flourished locally in the late 19th century. Another, a series of six glass dioramas, features a working scale model mine. Some of the more intriguing life-sized exhibits include a collection of Indian highway signs, a colorful display on a local rum rebellion from the Prohibition era, and the home of

Carrie Jacobs-Bond who composed, among 400 parlor songs, "Perfect Day" and "I Love You Truly."

Detroit

Motown Museum, 2648 W. Grand Blvd.; exit west on W. Grand Blvd. from Rte. 10.; 1 mile west of General Motors World Headquarters. (313) 875-2264. Adults: $3, children 12 and under: $2. Open Tues. through Sat., 10 a.m. to 5 p.m.; Sun., 2 to 5 p.m.; and by appointment. Accessible to handicapped.

Hitsville, U.S.A. was the name Berry Gordy, Jr., gave this modest house when he recorded the songs of his many discoveries during the 1950s and 1960s—The Four Tops, The Miracles, Diana Ross and The Supremes, Marvin Gaye, and Stevie Wonder who recorded such million-dollar hits as "Shop Around," "Just My Imagination," and "Stop in the Name of Love" here. Today, it is the museum of soul music. The original Motown recording Studio A still looks as though a recording session is about to begin, and throughout the rest of the house rare photographs, memorabilia, vintage clothing, gold and platinum records, souvenir programs, handbills, posters, album covers, awards, and plaques commemorate the success of the many groups and vocalists who came under the Motown umbrella. One of the largest exhibits is the Michael Jackson Room where a hat and jeweled glove donated by that showbiz superstar help celebrate a musical heritage whose roots are right here in the Motor City.

Hanover

Conklin Antique Reed Organ Museum, Hanover Rd., just west of intersection with Moscow Rd. (517) 563-2311. Adults: $1.50, seniors and students: $1. Open Apr. through Sept., first and third Sun. of the month, 1 to 5 p.m.; also first Sun. in Oct. and second Sun. in Dec. Accessible to handicapped.

More music! Specifically, the melodious sounds that emanate from reed organs, keyboard instruments that depend on foot-operated bellows and utilize metal reeds instead of pipes. Lee Conklin, a retired farmer whose collection this was, completely restored these 80 instruments, some of which date back to the Civil

War. Walnut, cherry, and rosewood are among the fine woods used in the cabinetry of parlor, cottage, and church organs here. One rare reed organ features bells that sound with the notes; another, a unique suitcase organ, saw service on the battlefields of World War I; yet another was used by a circuit-riding minister. Housing this outstanding collection is a circa 1920 schoolhouse constructed with bricks from an earlier school that burned down, and a gymnasium built by Work Projects Administration workers in 1933 from beams, roof decks, woodwork, and tongue-and-groove wainscoting from an old church.

Marshall

American Museum of Magic, 107 E. Michigan, near intersection of I-94 and I-69. (616) 781-7666 or -7674. Admission: $3 per person. Open by appointment only. Accessible to handicapped.

Now you see it, now you don't! Actually, now you *do* see it in this elegant Victorian storefront, a former bakery. Inside, posters and handbills along the walls chronicle the enchantment of magic performances held worldwide over the years. Gleaming glass display cases throughout the ground floor and in a large upstairs auditorium unveil the mysteries of magic through props, illusions, toys, books, coins and tokens, figures, and magic kits, old and new. Magician's sets, costumes, and apparatus offer a glimpse into the powers of prestidigitation, and films, videos, letters, diaries, and scrapbooks illuminate the lives of famous conjurers. With more than 250,000 pieces in this collection assembled by museum founder Robert Lund, this is almost certainly the world's largest public display of ledgerdemain lore.

Minnesota

Duluth

Canal Park Marine Museum, next to the ship canal, Lake Ave. Exit from I-35. (218) 727-2497. Free. Open spring and fall daily, 10 a.m. to 6 p.m.; summer daily, 10 a.m. to 9 p.m.; winter, Fri. through Sun., 10 a.m. to 4:30 p.m.; closed Thanksgiving, Christmas, and New Year's Day. Accessible to handicapped.

The story of waterways complements that of the rails (see below). Operated by the U.S. Army Corps of Engineers, this museum focuses on Great Lakes shipping and the Duluth-Superior harbor. Two slide programs feature formation of the lakes and bulk loading of ships at Twin Ports, among the busiest in the nation. Exhibits include replicas of pilot houses and three different ship cabins, a working steam engine, photos, historic cargo samples, ship models, and ship and weather instruments. A public address system gives statistics of ships traversing the nearby Duluth Ship Canal, as the historical and contemporary merge at the edge of Lake Superior.

Lake Superior Museum of Transportation, 506 W. Michigan St.; exit that street from I-35. (218) 727-0687. Adults: $4, seniors: $3, children 6 to 17: $2. Open summer months, Mon. through Sat., 10 a.m. to 5 p.m.; Sun., 1 to 5 p.m. Accessible to handicapped.

Hauling ore from the Iron Range to Duluth's docks was labor not lightly undertaken. It took tough workers and heavy machinery.

This facility gives a glimpse of that effort, and houses 72 pieces of full-size railroad equipment—diesel, electric, and steam locomotives, gondolas, tank cars, flat cars, passenger cars, cabooses, and related gear. Contrasted to this is the nation's largest collection of rare railway china and silver, displayed in a 1908 wood-sided, 78-seat passenger car replete with arched entry and stained glass clerestory windows.

Le Sueur

Le Sueur Museum, 709 N. 2nd St., Rte. 93 Exit from Rte. 169. (612) 655-2087. Free. Open daily, Memorial Day through Labor Day, 1 to 4:30 p.m. Limited facilities for handicapped.

This community, situated in the Minnesota River Valley, is home to that jolly "Ho Ho Ho, Green Giant," and the museum, essentially a local history type, has a Green Giant Room devoted to vegetable canning and this particular corporate giant. The firm started as a small corn-packing plant in 1902 and the giant came aboard in 1926 with the introduction of canned peas. Photos, labels, artifacts, and film recount the evolving technologies of this facet of the food industry.

Minneapolis

The Bakken: A Museum and Library of Electricity in Life, 3537 Zenith Ave. S; take 36th St. Exit from Rte. 35 west. (612) 927-6508. Suggested donation: $3. Open by appointment, Mon. through Fri., 9 a.m. to 5 p.m.; closed major holidays. No facilities for handicapped.

Science fans may get a charge out of this museum which grew from the collection of Earl Bakken, inventor of the first cardiac pacemaker. It contains some 12,000 books and manuscripts and more than 2,000 instruments concerning the development and applications of electromagnetism. Holdings include Benjamin Franklin's writings on electricity, plus works by Galvani, Duchenne, Volta, and Nollet. Among the many electrifying artifacts are Franklin's glass harmonica, Duchenne's medical coil for faradic stimulation, and a graphic methods exhibit illustrating the rise of recording instruments in 19th-century physiology.

Nebraska

Brownville

Missouri River History Museum, off Rte. 136. (402) 825-3341. Ages 12 and over: $1. Open daily Memorial Day through Labor Day, 10 a.m. to 5:30 p.m.; weekends Labor Day to Oct. 15 and Apr. 15 to Memorial Day. No facilities for handicapped.

This is about crossing, and working on, the wide Missouri, and the highlight here is the *Meriwether Lewis,* a 300-foot dredge steamer. The vessel labored from the 1930s to the 1960s, helping to make the river navigable between Sioux City and Kansas City. Visitors get a close-up view of the paddlewheel from the wheelhouse and feel the muscle of the dredge as its triple expansion engine is demonstrated at 5 rpm. The upper deck exhibits historical materials related to the Missouri, such as Indian and fur trade artifacts and early steamboat photos and paintings. There's also a map showing meteorological and topographical features of the entire river basin. In the former officers' cabin are additional items, including before-and-after photos of Army Corps of Engineers' work on the Missouri River.

Chadron

Museum of the Fur Trade, on Rte. 20, 3 miles east of town. (308) 432-3843. Adults: $1, under 18 with parent: free. Open daily June 1 through Labor Day, 8 a.m. to 5 p.m.; rest of year by appointment. Accessible to handicapped.

Northwest Nebraska first drew Spanish fur traders from Santa Fe, followed in the 1830s by Americans who established a regular trail along the Missouri River. This museum documents the historic North American fur trade conducted by British, French, Swedish, Spanish, and American trading companies. Exhibits include buffalo robes, beaver pelts, and mink and badger furs; trade goods such as kettles, traps, beads, cloth, vermilion, and hatchets; and an incomparable array of period weapons, such as Hawken rifles and Bowie knives. Galleries also portray the lives of the voyageurs, trappers, Indians, and buffalo hunters. Here, too, is a faithfully recreated and outfitted 19th-century trading post.

Gothenburg

Sod House Museum, on Rte. 47, just north of I-80. (308) 537-2628. Free. Open May and Sept., 9 a.m. to 6 p.m.; June through Aug., 8 a.m. to 9 p.m. Accessible to handicapped.

A 19th-century farmstead reflects the West that is not generally part of "shoot 'em up" television shows. The museum, founded in 1988, consists of a replica sod house simply furnished with log table and cornhusk mattress, two century-old windmills, and a 28-foot by 12-foot sod-breaking plow, giving a hard-edged picture of settlers' lives circa 1875. The barn has three stalls displaying materials characteristic of the region before the settlers arrived, such as Indian artifacts and buffalo items, Solomon Butcher photos of local and area people, and sundry materials illustrating life and times, such as a washboard, guns, even letters from a Swedish immigrant.

Pony Express Station, in Ehman Park, on Rte. 47, 1 mile north of I-80. (308) 536-2680. Free. Open May and Sept., 9 a.m. to 6 p.m.; June through Aug., 8 a.m. to 9 p.m. Accessible to handicapped.

Built in 1854, this single-room cabin served as one of the 192 original Pony Express stations in 1860–61. It contains numerous artifacts from that era, including a mochila or mailbag, a 120-year-old saddle, Indian trappings, tack and equipment vital to the station's purpose, stamps, letters, and related materials. Visitors can mail a card or letter from here stamped with the Pony Express seal. Other items on display include flatirons, bottles, and similar period pieces donated by area residents.

Lincoln

National Museum of Roller Skating, 7700 A St.; take 84th St. Exit from I-80. (402) 489-8811. Free. Open Mon. through Fri., 9 a.m. to 5 p.m.; closed holidays and weekends, but special weekend tours can be arranged in advance. Accessible to handicapped.

Roller skating has rolled a long way since the mid-1800s. This unique museum not only houses the world's largest collection of roller skates and the amateur roller skating hall of fame, it presents the history and technology of skating as well. Here are the 1863 Plimpton skates that enabled skaters to steer by leaning left or right, six-wheel models, skates with stilts, even skates made for a horse. Photos, videotapes, costumes, trophies, and posters illustrate speed skating, artistic skating, and roller hockey. Film footage rolls visitors back to the 1940s and that era's championship skating events.

Omaha

Union Pacific Historical Museum, 1416 Dodge St.; take 14th St. Exit from east I-480. (402) 271-5457. Free. Open Mon. through Fri., 9 a.m. to 5 p.m.; Sat., 9 a.m. to 1 p.m.; closed Sun. and holidays. Accessible to handicapped.

Tracks of famous railroads run through American history, but no line perhaps is more renowned than the Union Pacific, which during the 1860s opened the central plains and in 1869 joined the Central Pacific in Utah to form the nation's first transcontinental rail line. Founded in 1921, following discovery of silver holloware from Abraham Lincoln's funeral car in a Union Pacific vault, this museum recreates that car furnished with original items. It also displays the surveying instruments of Gen. Grenville Dodge, chief engineer during the line's construction, as well as his original telegram announcing completion of the transcontinental route. Other exhibits include an authentically furnished railroad auditor's office, a hotel parlor, and several model trains.

Wilber

Wilber Czech Museum, at junction of Rtes. 41 and 103, about 20 miles north of I-80. (402) 821-2183 or -2585. Free. Open daily, 1 to 4 p.m.; closed holidays. Accessible to handicapped.

The community bills itself as "the Czech capital of the USA" and the museum houses a colorful collection of Czech dolls, costumes, and dishes as well as quilts, laces, and prints. Period rooms reflect immigrant life, at home and at work. An annual Czech festival in early August offers a chance to savor Czech music, dance, history, and traditions.

North Dakota

Fargo

Roger Maris Museum, West Acres Mall, 13th Ave. S., Exit 63 or 64 from I-29. Mall office telephone: (701) 282-2222. Free. Open during mall business hours: Mon. through Fri., 10 a.m. to 9 p.m.; Sat., 9:30 a.m. to 9 p.m.; closed Sun. Accessible to handicapped.

For those who don't follow America's pastime, Roger Maris is the New York Yankee slugger who broke Babe Ruth's season home run mark by hitting 61 roundtrippers in 1961. He grew up in Fargo and played American Legion and minor league baseball here. The museum contains more than 150 items including balls, bats, uniforms, his 1960 Golden Glove, Sultan of Swat awards, minor and major league records, minor league championship pennant, and individual and team photos. There's also a film narrated by famed announcer Mel Allen of Maris' last 12 home runs of his dramatic record-breaking season.

Fort Totten

Fort Totten State Historic Site & Pioneer Daughters Museum, between Rtes. 57 and 20, 12 miles south of Devils Lake. (701) 766-4382. Free. Historic site open Memorial Day through Labor Day, 8 a.m. to 5 p.m.; museum open 1 to 5 p.m. Limited access for handicapped.

Fort Totten, built between 1868 and 1871, was a U.S. Army

headquarters for patrolling the international border and protecting settlers. Units of Custer's fated 7th Cavalry came from Fort Totten. From 1891 to 1935, the site was a Bureau of Indian Affairs boarding school for Northern Plains tribes, and later became a tuberculosis sanitarium. Today, the restored fort is considered one of the best-preserved military posts west of the Mississippi River. Displays and an interpretive program recount this mixed heritage. The Pioneer Daughters Museum, housed in the fort's former hospital, exhibits period clothing, tools, and furniture of the surrounding region.

Hatton

Hatton-Eielson Museum, 405 8th St., off Rte. 18 from Rte. 15 or 200, west of I-29. (701) 543-3726. Adults: $1.50, children under 12: $.50. Open Memorial Day to Oct. 1, Sun., 1 to 4:30 p.m.; other days by appointment. No facilities for handicapped.

Carl Ben Eielson, pilot for the 1928 Wilkins Arctic Expedition and flyer of Alaska's first airmail, was raised in this Queen Anne-style house and flew into aviation history. The first to fly over the Arctic Ocean, he received the Harmon Trophy the year after Charles Lindbergh. The rooms hold family mementos and furnishings and the library displays the aviator's photos, honors, books, and memorabilia, as well as information associated with the early days of flying. Eielson died in 1929 on a mercy mission to an icebound ship in the Bering Strait, but memory and tribute survive here for one of North Dakota's heroic sons.

Makoti

Makoti Threshing Museum, 1 mile south of Rte. 23. (701) 726-5693 or -5622. Donation requested; $5 fee for Annual Threshing Show the first weekend in Oct. Open May into Oct., Mon. through Sat.; call ahead for tour guide. No facilities for handicapped.

The museum embodies the very grain-belt fiber of America, comprising six buildings in a pioneer village setting and one of the world's largest collections of antique motorized farm implements. There are gas and steam tractors, trucks, cars, threshers, stationary engines, and other vehicles related to the planting and harvesting of the amber waves of grain. During the Annual Threshing Show, some 350 units roar to life, and the event includes the world championship John Deere two-cylinder slow race.

Waterford City

Pioneer Museum, 109 Park Ave., off Rtes. 85 and 23. (701) 842-2990. Adults: $1, children: $.50. Open Memorial Day to Labor Day, Tues. through Sun., 1 to 5:30 p.m.; closed Mon. Accessible to handicapped.

This museum is dedicated to those homesteading settlers of the early 1900s who "stuck it out" on the Northern Plains, surviving loneliness, blizzards, back-breaking labor, and financial plight. Sod huts and tar paper shanties were typical abodes in this harsh, wind-swept land. The facility reflects the spare and sturdy life style of time and place—bottles and other glassware, tins, tools, utensils, garments, and gear. Justice matched the landscape here. One exhibit features Charles Bannon, who was lynched for murdering an entire family, and includes the hemp that hanged him.

Ohio

Akron

Goodyear World of Rubber, Goodyear Hall, E. Market St. Exit from I-76. (216) 796-2044. Free. Open Mon. through Fri., 8:30 a.m. to 4:30 p.m. No facilities for handicapped.

The hub of the American rubber industry for many years, Akron is home to Goodyear, of blimp and tire fame. The company was founded in 1898, nearly four decades after the death of Charles Goodyear, inventor of vulcanized rubber. One highlight here is the assemblage of paintings, mementos, and other items acquired from heirs of the inventor. Other exhibits encompass a replica of Goodyear's workshop, a simulated rubber plantation, an artificial heart, a moon tire display, various Goodyear products, and representations of rubber-making and tire-building processes. Films and dioramas add bounce to the presentation.

Cleveland

Howard Dittrick Museum of Medical History, 11000 Euclid Ave., third floor of Allen Medical Library, on campus of Case Western Reserve University. (216) 368-3648. Free. Open Mon. through Fri., 10 a.m. to 5 p.m.; Sat., noon to 5 p.m.; closed Sun. and major holidays. No facilities for handicapped.

The museum gives an examination of medical history, displaying instruments and procedures primarily from the 19th century.

These include the string galvanometer, an early electrocardiograph; early cylindrical stethoscopes; sphygmomanometers; x-rays; thermometers; and blood study procedures. You learn that before the 19th century, urinalysis involved color, odor, sediment, and—ahem—taste. And that otoscopes for the ear have changed little in design in 300 years, but their light sources once were candles and oil lamps. Early reflex hammers and ivory tongue depressors are among the more routine, yet still intriguing, items.

Ukranian Museum-Archives, 1202 Kenilworth Ave.; take W. 14th St. from I-71 or I-90. (216) 781-4329. Donation requested. Open Mon. through Fri., 9 a.m. to noon; Sat., 10 a.m. to noon; other times by appointment. No facilities for handicapped.

The Ukraine is one of those Eastern European lands that's been at the mercy of powerful neighbors for centuries and has known more than its share of brutality, especially in the 1930s and '40s. Founded in 1952 by a post-World War II refugee, this museum and archive preserve the cultural heritage and integrity of the Ukraine. Folk arts include embroidered clothing, textiles, religious vestments, and ceramics; fine arts comprise sculpture and paintings. Stamps, coins, treasury bonds, bank notes, maps, and political manifestos range from the Hapsburg Empire to the short-lived post-World War I Ukranian Republic. Also housed here are books, periodicals, clippings, and memorabilia concerning Ukranian poet laureate Taras Shevchenko. All in all, an insightful glimpse into (for most Americans) an obscure land and culturescape.

Dayton

Dayton Power & Light Company Museum, 1900 Dryden Rd.; take Nicholas Rd. Exit from I-75. (513) 227-2241. Free. Tours are by appointment and are normally conducted during business hours, Mon. through Fri., 9 a.m. to 4 p.m. Accessible to handicapped.

Begun by company employees more than 40 years ago, this museum offers an illuminating look at the formative days of electricity, with a jolting array of early light bulbs, irons, toasters, lamps, dryers, and other appliances. Of course, power and light predate commercial electricity, and the collection also includes an 1860s gas-powered fan, oil lamps, and hand-powered washers. The museum covers company history, profiles local inventors, and is attached to an archive filled with photos and literature. Visitors can turn hand-crank generators, grasp a static electricity generator, and check out equipment used by linemen in the early 1900s.

East Liverpool

East Liverpool Museum of Ceramics, 400 E. 5th St., at Broadway intersection. (216) 386-6001. Adults: $3, seniors: $2.40, children: $1.50. Open Mar. 1 through Nov. 30, Wed. through Sun., 9:30 a.m. to 5 p.m.; holidays, noon to 5 p.m.; open Dec., Jan. and Feb. by appointment; closed Thanksgiving. Accessible to handicapped.

By 1900, the East Liverpool ceramics industry was producing more than 47 percent of the dinnerware made in the United States. Abundant supplies of the proper clay, efforts of pioneer potters such as Benjamin Harker and William Bloor, and the immigration of skilled English pottery workers combined to make this community America's "crockery city." The museum, which occupies a former post office, tells the story of East Liverpool's ceramics industry and the lives of its people. Life-size dioramas illustrate manufacturing processes, and exhibits include numerous examples of products, such as Lotus Ware, a popular artificial bone china considered the finest made in North America.

Glenford

Flint Ridge State Memorial, 7091 Brownsville Rd. SE, 4 miles north of I-70 on Rte. 668. (614) 787-2476. Ages 13 and over: $2, 6 to 12: $1. Open Memorial Day through Labor Day, Wed. through Sat., 9:30 a.m. to 5 p.m.; Sun. and holidays, noon to 5 p.m.; weekends only through Sept. and Oct. Facilities for handicapped, including Braille signs and guide ropes.

Although not industrial by white colonists' standards, American Indians effectively plied the crafts and industries necessary to their culture. One such trade involved the points and blades used for scraping, cutting, and killing. Flint deposits here were among the finest known, and tools and weapons from Flint Ridge—believed to have been a neutral quarrying zone—have been found from the Atlantic coast to Kansas City. White settlers later used the flint for making millstones and small-scale grinders. The museum, built over an original flint pit, explains the geological and anthropological facets of the Flint Ridge stone, including flint formation, chipping techniques, and distribution of projectile points and other items throughout the eastern United States.

Marietta

Ohio River Museum, 601 Front St., just off Rte. 7 near I-77. (614) 373-3750. Ages 13 and over: $3, 6 to 12: $1. Open May through Sept., Mon. through Sat., 9:30 a.m. to 5 p.m.; Sun. and holidays, noon to 5 p.m.; Mar. and Apr., and Oct. and Nov., Wed. through Sat., 9:30 a.m. to 5 p.m.; and Sun., noon to 5 p.m. Accessible to handicapped.

America's big rivers played a major role in the development of the nation's interior. The geological and commercial histories of the Ohio River find expression here in three exhibit buildings. Models, maps, dioramas, and audiovisuals define and describe the river and its role. Steamboat displays, paintings, posters, and artifacts illustrate river transport. The third exhibit dwells on ecological aspects—what man has done to the river. Visitors can also explore a genuine steam-powered, stern-wheeled towboat, the *W. P. Snyder.* Also, there are replicas of the once ubiquitous river flatboats that carried people and cargo to points south and west during the nation's formative years.

Marion

Wyandot Popcorn Museum, Heritage Hall, 169 E. Church St., at junction of Rtes. 423 north and 95. (614) 387-4255. Free. Open Wed. through Sun., 1 to 4 p.m. No facilities for handicapped.

Is there a soul among us who occasionally doesn't yearn to munch a bunch of popcorn? Recently proclaimed nutritious, at least for a snack food, popcorn has been around for quite a while. In fact, Native Americans reportedly hooked the Pilgrims on it. Wyandot, named for an Ohio tribe, makes snack foods and began collecting antique popcorn machines and peanut roasters while researching the history of the industry. The collection includes antique Kingery poppers from Cincinnati and Cretors from Chicago (one circa 1899). There also are Holcomb and Hoke machines and Manley theater poppers that helped make the old movie matinees so tempting. If you time your visit right, you can sample products of the annual festival held in Marion the weekend following Labor Day.

Milan

Thomas A. Edison Birthplace Museum, 9 N. Edison Dr.; take Exit 7 south from Ohio Tnpk. to Rte. 113. (419) 499-2135. Adults: $2, children 6 to 12: $1. Open Feb. through May, Tues. through Sun., 1 to 5 p.m.; June to Labor Day, Tues. through Sat., 10 a.m. to 5 p.m. and Sun., 1 to 5 p.m.; Labor Day through Nov., Tues. through Sat., 1 to 5 p.m.; Jan. by appointment. No facilities for handicapped.

Renowned inventor Thomas Edison was born here in 1847 and the house, restored and furnished in the period style, is a National Historic Landmark. A 45-minute tour through the home deals with Edison's life and, of course, his myriad inventions. Two rooms display some of the latter, including a talking doll, mimeograph machine, rare chalk telephone receiver, folding pole ladder, root mixer, and rare electric pen. There's also an Edison movie billboard from 1913.

Norwich

National Road/Zane Grey Museum, 8850 East Pike; take Exit 164 from I-70. (614) 872-3143. Adults: $3, children 6 to 12: $1. Open daily, May through Sept., 9:30 a.m. to 5 p.m., and Sun., noon to 5 p.m.; Mar. and Apr., and Oct. and Nov., Wed. through Sat., 9:30 a.m. to 5 p.m. and Sun., noon to 5 p.m. Accessible to handicapped.

Ah, the old days of highway travel prior to the sterile inter-states—to a great degree it is a vanished America. What could be more fitting than a museum to the old National Road? The route even predates the automotive age, and diverse displays illustrate developments of the road from 1811 to the coming of the car. One exhibit consists of a 136-foot-long diorama of construction and use of the road. Neighboring Zanesville was home to Western author Zane Grey, and the museum incorporates this American tradition as well, with presentations of the writer's personal items as well as book and movie memorabilia.

Toledo

Blair Museum of Lithopanes and Wax Carvings, 2032 Robinwood, off I-75 and Ohio Tnpk. (419) 243-4115. Admission is $3 per person based on desired minimum of 10-person group; that is, four visitors would still pay $30. Open by appointment only. No facilities for handicapped.

Octogenarian Laurel Blair collected music boxes until about 30 years ago when he fell in love with lithopanes, 19th-century European porcelain transparencies. He now claims the world's largest collection (more than 2,000 pieces) of these rare decorative art objects which hung in windows and provided a three-dimensional image of scenes, portraits, religious events, and other subjects. In a way, they were precursors of today's more plebian stained-glass window objects. European artisans stopped making lithopanes in 1902, and according to Blair, 95 percent of people today have never heard of this delicate medium. He also collects paintings and mosaics in carved wax—flowers, portraits, battle scenes—an ancient art form; one of his pieces is a centuries-old depiction of the Egyptian god of the underworld. A private, personal, and possibly unique collection.

Vandalia

Trapshooting Hall of Fame and Museum, 601 W. National Rd., take I-75 from Dayton to Rte. 40 west. (513) 898-1945. Free. Open Mon. through Fri., 9 a.m. to 4 p.m.; closed weekends and holidays. No facilities for handicapped.

Trick shooting, demonstration shooting, sports shooting—they've all been as much a part of the firearms story as gunfights and warfare. This museum draws a bead on trapshooting champions and the tools of the trade, dating back more than 150 years. There are some hall-of-fame figures you would expect to find, such as sharpshooter Annie Oakley who won $9,000 in two years of trapshooting nearly a century ago, and some you might not, such as maestro John Philip Sousa who helped establish the American Amateur Trapshooting Association in 1916. The museum displays glass ball targets, old shells, personal guns of Olympic medal winners, early catapults, clothing, photos, posters, and more. It's a sure-shot for those with an eye for the sport.

Vermilion

Great Lakes Historical Society Museum, 480 Main St., on Lake Erie, 2 miles north of junction of Rtes. 2 and 60. (216) 967-3467.

Adults: $3, seniors: $2, children 6 to 15: $1. Open daily Apr. 1 through Dec. 31, 10 a.m. to 5 p.m.; Jan. through Mar., weekends only. Limited access for handicapped.

The Great Lakes are nothing less than an inland sea, navigated by explorers, naval crews, and merchantmen for 300 years and by Indians before that. Adventure, settlement, conflict, and trade converge here in a museum that relates the truly maritime cast of these lakes and their myriad vessels. In addition to the artifacts, models, and paintings you would expect, there are a huge light-house lens, a recreated freighter's pilothouse, marine engines, boat construction tools, engine room console, even yachting memo-rabilia. One of the more popular exhibits is the model, and atten-dant story, of the 729-foot *Edmund Fitzgerald*, sunk in a Lake Superior storm in 1975 and later memorialized in a popular song by Gordon Lightfoot.

Wapakoneta

Neil Armstrong Museum, Bellefontaines St.; take Exit 111 from I-75. (419) 738-8811. Adults: $3, children: $1. Open Mar. through Nov., Mon. through Sat., 9:30 a.m. to 5 p.m.; Sun., noon to 5 p.m. Accessible to handicapped.

On July 20, 1969, astronaut Neil Armstrong took "one small step for man, one giant step for mankind" on the surface of the moon. Manned flight had soared quite a way from Kitty Hawk. Opened in 1972, this museum pays tribute to a hometown boy, but it does much more than that. It covers Ohioans' flight achievements from balloons to dirigibles to the Wright brothers' model G Aero-boat. Dynamic audiovisuals chronicle progress in space travel. A Jupiter rocket engine, space suits, and aircraft flown by Armstrong also are on display.

South Dakota

Chamberlain

Old West Museum, Exit 260 from I-90, 3 miles west of town. (605) 734-6157. Adults: $4, children 6 to 14: $2, special rates for seniors and tour groups. Open daily, Apr. and May, 8 a.m. to 6 p.m.; June, July, and Aug., 7 a.m. to 9:30 p.m.; Sept. and Oct., 8 a.m. to 7 p.m. Accessible to handicapped.

This is one of those privately-owned eclectic places with a broad theme—the Old West—and considerable kitsch that nonetheless intrigues due to certain categories or mini-collections. Yes, there are Colt pistols and Indian baskets, old dolls and frontier dishes, but in a more uncommon vein are 200 fence tools, scores of branding irons, dozens of traps and varieties of barbed wire—all as much a part of winning the West as Winchester rifles. The museum also boasts the largest collection of horse-drawn vehicles in South Dakota, including a hearse, mail buggy, military ambulance, army caisson, covered wagon, and racing cart. And speaking of racing, there's also a rare western electric race horse piano that you can play.

Custer

National Museum of Woodcarving, Rte. 16 west, 2 miles west of town. (605) 673-4404. Adults: $4.75, children 6 to 14: $2.75. Open daily May through mid-Oct.; summer hours, 8 a.m. to 9 p.m.; other months, 9 a.m. to 5 p.m. Accessible to handicapped.

Shaping a piece of wood with a blade ranges from pastime to art, and this museum cuts to the heart of the skill. It comprises five distinct sections—36 scenes by a Disneyland animator, with a single scene having as many as 1,000 carvings; the Wooden Nickel theater, a special-exhibits gallery, an area dedicated to notable American woodcarvers, and a carving studio that offers instruction in the craft of carving. An unusual display, and that's not just whittlin' Dixie.

Lake Norden

South Dakota Amateur Baseball Hall of Fame, 515 Main Ave., on Rte. 28. (606) 785-3553. Free. Open daily May through Sept., 9 a.m. to 7 p.m. Accessible to handicapped.

In an era when players make millions, go on strike, and hype all manner of products, it's refreshing to reflect on what baseball once was—a game. And here it is, South-Dakota-style and for the fun of it, going back to the early 1900s, all expressed in photos, gear, memorabilia, and biographical sketches of 90 hall of famers. One highlight is the Ed Powers exhibit of homemade equipment used during the youthful decades of this century when playing was the important thing.

Mitchell

Enchanted World Doll Museum, 615 N. Main St.; take Exit 332 from I-90. (605) 996-9896. Adults: $2.50, seniors: $2, young people 13 to 20: $1, children 6 to 12: $.65. Open daily mid-May to late Sept., 8 a.m. to 8 p.m.; early Apr. through mid-May and late Sept. through late Nov., Mon. through Sat., 9 a.m. to 5 p.m.; and Sun., 1 to 5 p.m.; open rest of year by appointment. Accessible to handicapped.

In the beginning was the hobby of Sheldon F. Reese, collecting native or ethnic dolls on trips abroad. Today, it's the 9,000-square-foot museum housing more than 4,000 dolls from 120 countries in some 400 scenes from fairy tales and real life. Here stands King Henry VIII and all of his wives, and there Jack and the Beanstalk. A kewpie doll party, the Dionne quintuplets, Paul Bunyan, some

Cabbage Patch kids, early bent-limb dolls, an Oriental bazaar, even "naughty nudies" all make an appearance. Dollhouses, furniture, buggies, and other accessories supply suitable accompaniment.

Sioux Falls

Sioux Empire Medical Museum, Sioux Valley Hospital, 1100 S. Euclid Ave.; take 12th St. Exit from I-90. (605) 333-6397. Free. Open Mon. through Fri., 11 a.m. to 4 p.m.; closed weekends and major holidays. Accessible to handicapped.

Founded by alumni of the hospital's School of Nursing, the museum gives glimpses of health care in the early decades of the 20th century and medical history of the region. An iron lung reminds visitors of dreaded polio epidemics. An authentically replicated patient's room circa 1930 and a simulated surgery scene show the medical road we've traveled. Pediatrics and dentistry are also represented, and photos, uniforms, and lab equipment provide added touches to the story.

Spearfish

D. C. Booth Historic Fish Hatchery and Museum, 423 Hatchery Cir.; take Exit 14 from I-90. (605) 642-7730. Adults: $1.50, children: $1. Open daily May 20 through Sept. 20, 10 a.m. to 8 p.m. Accessible to handicapped.

This is no fish story. A working national trout hatchery from 1899 to 1983, the museum and hall of fame present perhaps the world's largest collection of fishery artifacts. The technology developed at hatcheries in the 19th and early 20th centuries contributed much to contemporary aquaculture, a growing part of the food industry. Housed in the original hatchery building, exhibits include antique hatchery jars, troughs, and trays as well as antique lab gear, early fish preparation equipment, and old incubation units. Donations have come from around the country, and the photo collection alone illustrates hatchery developments dating back to the mid-1800s. The hall of fame features prominent fish culture figures such as Seth Green and Livingston Stone, reportedly comparable in stature to baseball's Babe Ruth. There are ponds on the grounds where kids can feed the fish still residing here.

Vermillion

Shrine to Music Museum, 414 E. Clark St., on campus of University of South Dakota; take Rte. 50 west from I-29. (605) 677-5306. Free. Open Mon. through Fri., 9 a.m. to 4:30 p.m.; Sat., 10 a.m. to 4:30 p.m.; Sun., 2 to 4:30 p.m.; closed Thanksgiving, Christmas, and New Year's Day. Accessible to handicapped.

Music hath charms to soothe and, indeed, the instruments that make it have their own special charms. This trove of music makers has something of appeal to almost everyone, from concert cellist to those of us who could never learn to play the cornet. More than 5,000 instruments reside here, covering the globe and the centuries—bugles, music boxes, echo horns, flutes, lutes, banjos, drums, violins, melodeons, clavichords, conch-shell horns, ivory oboes, pianos, harmonicas, cigar-box fiddles, and stringed and wind instruments from Asia, Africa, and Latin America—a magnificent tuneful alphabet from arched harp to zither. Most are playable, but they are mainly here for viewing and preservation; however, the museum does host concerts on historical instruments.

Wisconsin

Ashippun

Honey of a Museum, Honey Acres, Rte. 67, off I-94 and 2 miles north of town. (414) 474-4411. Free. Open Mon. through Fri., 9 a.m. to 3:30 p.m.; also open weekends, noon to 4 p.m., May 15 through Oct. 30; closed holidays. Accessible to handicapped.

This sweet museum, opened in 1983, is part of a business that has been run by four generations of beekeepers. The entrance recreates a centuries-old method of protecting skeps, or domed beehives, namely by means of niches, or bee boles, in a masonry wall. Inside, you get a closeup view of a bee tree, and a 20-minute color film shows how bees live and work. There are displays of pollination and beeswax, and photos give a glimpse of honey production, processing, and packaging. In an exhibit of beekeeping yesterday, today, and around the world you see photos of previous generations of this company's owners and workers plus items such as old beehives and beekeeping gear and clothing; a cross section of a modern hive; and items related to beekeeping in Lebanon, Japan, Yugoslavia, and England. A stuffed black bear makes an eternal assault on a bee community to dramatize enemies of the hive. Honey tasting and nature walks are available, too.

Baraboo

Circus World Museum, 426 Water St.; take Rte. 33 from I-90/94. (608) 356-0880. Adults: $8.95, seniors: $7.65, children 3 to 12: $5.50.

Open daily, May through Sept. 16, 9 a.m. to 6 p.m. (July 21 through Aug. 22, open to 9:30 p.m.) Exhibit hall and visitor center open year round. Accessible to handicapped.

Five brothers from Baraboo, Ringling by name, hit it big with the big top in the last quarter of the 19th century, and from 1884 to 1919 their winter quarters were where this museum now stands. In summer months, animal acts, trapeze derring-do, and clowning around bring the circus world to life here. You can ride an elephant and learn how clowns put on make-up. The museum itself, in four major exhibit buildings, recounts the history of the American circus. In one football-field-size pavilion stand 170 circus wagons. There's a steam calliope, too, and other sounds of the circus provide a lilting backdrop. Featured as well are some 10,000 circus posters dating back to the 1830s.

Fort Atkinson

Dairy Shrine, 407 Merchants Ave., on Rte. 12 between Chicago and Madison. (414) 563-7769. Free. Open Sept. through May, Tues. through Sat., 9:30 a.m. to 3:30 p.m.; June through Aug., Tues. through Sat., 9:30 a.m. to 4:30 p.m., and Sun., 1 to 5 p.m. Accessible to handicapped.

The state's license plates remind us that Wisconsin is America's dairyland, so it's only fitting that there should be a dairy museum in this land of milk and honey; milk has been good food for thousands of years. Part of the Hoard Historical Museum, the shrine offers a 20-minute self-guided tour that includes a slide presentation, photos of "big cheeses" in the dairy industry, and various displays and artifacts depicting dairy farming yesterday, today, and tomorrow. Items on display comprise early testing and measuring equipment, prototypical milk cans, ladles, barrels, old butter churns, a dog-powered treadmill, even a photo gallery of champion dairy cows.

Hayward

National Freshwater Fishing Hall of Fame, 2 blocks south of junction of Rtes. 37 and 63. (715) 634-4440. Adults: $3.50, children under 18: $2.50, under 10: $1. Open Apr. 15 through Nov. 1, 10 a.m. to 5 p.m. Accessible to handicapped.

Nuts, nut art, and nut lore are the focus of the Nut Museum in Old Lyme, Connecticut.   Credit: John Harvey, Waterbury *Republican*

Nutcracker in hand, Elizabeth Tashjian shows the subject for her painting "Cracker Chase" at her Nut Museum in Old Lyme, Connecticut. Credit: Michael DeCicco, *Yankee*

The din of operating textile machinery lends atmosphere to The Museum of American Textile History in North Andover, Massachusetts.
Credit: Warren Jagger

A swan for soup --this 18th century porcelain soup tureen from Meissen, Germany, is only one of the many exquisite tureens at the Campbell Museum in Camden, New Jersey.

"Trash and You" is the name of this arresting exhibit at the Hackensack Meadowlands Development Commission Environment Center in Lyndhurst, New Jersey. Photo credit: HMDC

Franz Streitwieser honors old brass musical instruments in his Streitwieser Trumpet Museum in Pottstown, Pennsylvania. Credit: Foto Gabriele Christ

Among the 700 old brass instruments displayed in the Streitwieser Trumpet Museum in Pottstown, Pennsylvania are Viking trumpets, Civil War bugles, and steer horns.

A retired police car, suspended from the facade of the American Police Hall of Fame and Museum in Miami, Florida, symbolizes the precarious position of officers on patrol.

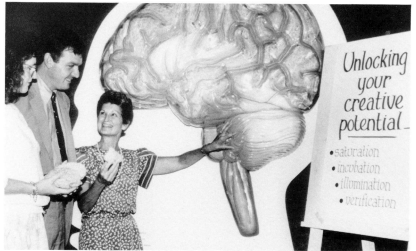

At the Health Adventure in Asheville, North Carolina, a giant brain lights up areas that control various body functions.

Bailey, North Carolina's Country Doctor Museum is housed in a building composed of two restored doctor's offices.

The Watermen's Museum in Yorktown Virginia, occupies 12 rooms of this large wood frame building on the banks of the York River.

The Howard Steamboat Museum is housed in an elegant 1890's Chateauesque-style home in Jeffersonville, Indiana.

As in olden times, bee skeps are sheltered in wall niches at Honey of a Museum in Ashippun, Wisconsin.
Credit: Conomawoc Enterprises

At the Trapshooting Hall of Fame and Museum in Vandalia, Ohio, an exhibit on the evolution of the clay target features early traps and barrels used to launch targets.

Thirty-five years in the making, the collection of the Miles Musical Museum in Eureka Springs, Arkansas, includes a Wurlitzer Golden Trumpet band organ (center).

The replica of America's first patented helicopter, on display at the High Plains Museum in Goodland, Kansas, was built by using only patent plans and this photo.

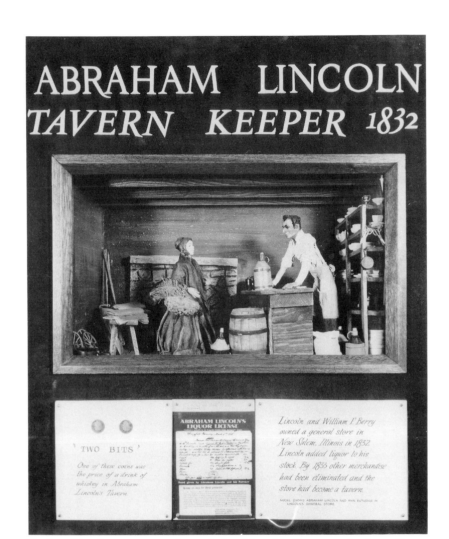

Abraham Lincoln was a tavern keeper? So claims this diorama at the Oscar Getz Museum of Whiskey History in Bardstown, Kentucky.

Banners hanging in the Great Hall of the Kentucky Derby Museum in Louisville, Kentucky, honor Derby winners through the years.

Nineteenth-century hand-made paper dolls are on display at the Toy and Miniature Museum in Kansas City, Missouri.

Scrimshaw walrus ivory pieces accompany 32 exhibits tracing Alaska history at Corrington's Eskimo Museum in Skagway, Alaska.

This fish "travel lock" from the Orient was made during the Middle Ages and is part of the Schlage Antique Lock Collection in San Francisco, California.

The Lingerie Museum at Frederick's of Hollywood, California, features undergarments of Cher, Zsa Zsa Gabor and other celebrities in its Hall of Fame.

The working scale model of sugar factory machinery is a popular exhibit at the Alexander & Baldwin Sugar Museum in Puunene, Hawaii.

Liberty Bell, grandaddy of nickel slot machines, is part of the Liberty Belle Antique Slot Machine Collection in Reno, Nevada.

Charles Fey goes down in history as the inventor of the nickel slot machine, an example of which is in the Liberty Belle Antique Slot Machine Collection in Reno, Nevada.

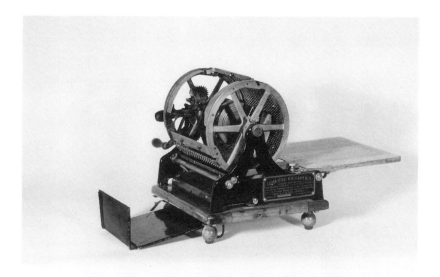

This portable mimeograph machine designed for the A.B. Dick Co. is only one of several Thomas A. Edison inventions featured at the Edison Plaza Museum in Beaumont, Texas.

This mounted longhorn steer is only one of the big attractions at the Cattleman's Museum in Fort Worth, Texas.

Maryhill Museum of Art in Golden, Washington, boasts a fine collection of chess sets. These Eskimo chess figures are carved from walrus ivory.
Photo credit: Maryhill Museum of Art

Rosaries from all parts of the New World surround a portrait of Christopher Columbus as part of Don Brown's Rosary Collection at the Skamania County Museum in Stevenson, Washington.
Photo credit: Richard Weaver.

Don't let this be the one that got away. One of the buildings alone is worth a cast—five-stories high, in the shape of a 143-foot-long muskie, complete with eyes, fins, and teeth, and a mouth that is an observation deck. A rotunda building holds photos and write-ups on anglers elected to the hall of fame. Other structures display fishing-related items such as rods, reels, lures, even some 350 fishing boat motors. More than 200 mounted salt water and fresh-water fish augment the piscatorial splendor. A library stores fish facts, and the museum is the official recorder of world-record freshwater catches.

Mineral Point

The Looms, far end of Shake Rag St., off Rte. 151. (608) 987-2277. Adults: $3, children: $2.50. Open daily, May into Oct., 10 a.m. to 4 p.m. Limited facilities for handicapped.

Located in an old stone brewery, this is part museum and part weaving school, and in both parts it preserves one of our civiliza-tion's oldest skills. The facility holds a major collection of old hand looms, and much of the antique textile equipment is operable. You can see demonstrations of the entire process, from fibers to finished fabric. It also contains a collection of 19th-century coverlets, or handwoven bed covers.

Neenah

Bergstrom-Mahler Museum, 165 N. Park Ave.; take Main St. Exit from Rte. 41. (414) 729-4658. Free. Open Tues. through Fri., 10 a.m. to 4:30 p.m.; Sat. and Sun., 1 to 4:30 p.m.; closed Mon. and major holidays. First floor accessible to handicapped.

A Tudor-style manse on the shores of Lake Winnebago houses this museum devoted to decorative glass paperweights, a trove started by Evangeline Hoysradt Bergstrom in 1935. Reputedly one of the world's best such collections, it comprises some 1,800 an-tique and contemporary pieces, containing brilliantly-colored fruit clusters, floral designs, cameos, animal designs, and other artistic renderings. In addition, the museum houses a remarkable collec-tion of Germanic glass and glassware dating to the 1500s. It also offers exhibits by regional artists, studio classes, and demonstra-tions. Eight temporary exhibits are staged each year.

Oneida

Oneida Nation Museum, 7 miles west of Green Bay, between Rtes. 41 and 55. (414) 869-2768. Adults: $1, children under 18: $.50, higher rates for guided tours. Accessible to handicapped.

The Oneida left the Iroquois Confederacy in New York in the 1820s, migrating to new lands in Wisconsin and taking with them their matrilineal tradition as well as their arts, crafts, and customs. Hands-on exhibits enable you to heft war clubs and stone drills, feel the texture of baskets and beadwork, listen to the drums and rattles of this Indian people, and view foodstuffs and cooking implements. Diagrams and displays discuss the migration, myths, and methods of the Oneida, and a longhouse fenced by a sturdy stockade helps illustrate styles of shelter, defense, and social organization.

Platteville

The Mining Museum, 405 E. Main St.; take Virginia Ave. from Rte. 151. (605) 348-3301. Adults: $3.50, seniors: $3, children 5 to 15: $1.50. Open daily, May through Oct., 9 a.m. to 5 p.m.; Nov. through Apr., Mon. through Fri., 9 a.m. to 4 p.m. No facilities for handicapped.

In the mid-1800s lead and zinc mining were major industries in this region. The Bevans Mine alone produced more than 2 million pounds of lead in a single year. Using photos, dioramas, models, and artifacts, this museum recaptures that era, and a visit includes a trek into the mine where manikins simulate mining techniques. The tour also entails a visit to a headframe, where zinc ore was hoisted and sorted, and a train ride around the site in ore cars.

Prairie du Chien

Fort Crawford Medical Museum, 717 S. Beaumont Rd., near Rtes. 35 and 27 and the confluence of the Mississippi and Wisconsin Rivers. (608) 326-6960. Adults: $2, children 6 to 12: $.50, families: $5, senior bus tours: $1.50. Open daily, May 1 through Oct. 31, 10 a.m. to 5 p.m. Accessible to handicapped.

Dr. William Beaumont, a military surgeon, practiced here during the 1830s, and his experiments formed the basis of developing knowledge of the human digestive system. But, in addition to Beaumont materials, the museum also includes an 1890s pharmacy, horse-and-buggy doctor days mementos, Indian herbal remedies, dioramas on surgical techniques (for example, a leg amputation), and a more contemporary display—Transparent Twins, two life-size plastic female models showing organs, skeleton, and nervous system.

Reedsburg

Museum of Norman Rockwell Art, 227 S. Park St., Rte. 23/33 from I-90/94. (608) 524-2123. Adults and children over 12: $3, seniors: $2. Open daily May 25 through Sept. 15, 9 a.m. to 7 p.m.; rest of year, 9 a.m. to 5 p.m. No facilities for handicapped.

For some folks, Norman Rockwell *is* Americana, or at least he cannot be excluded from any definition of it. This museum boasts the largest collection of Rockwell memorabilia anywhere, plus more than 500 Rockwell prints. Located in a former chapel, the museum displays original magazine covers, book illustrations, posters, and advertisements, some 4,000 pieces in all. It's somewhat of an extension of the Rockwell Museum in Rutland, Vt., getting its start via an exhibition from the latter museum in 1982.

Rhinelander

Rhinelander Logging Museum, Pioneer Park, Rtes. 8 and 47. (715) 369-5004. Donations accepted. Open Memorial Day through Labor Day, 10 a.m. to 6:30 p.m. Accessible to handicapped.

Billed as "America's oldest logging museum," this facility, established in 1932, recalls the 1870s when logging reigned in the upper Wisconsin River Valley. Every lumber company in the region was solicited for artifacts and old logging camps throughout northern Wisconsin were scoured for abandoned relics. Buildings consist of bunkhouse, cook shanty, and blacksmith shop. On display are all manner of tools—pike poles, peavies, cant hooks, crosscut saws, and more—as well as photos illustrating the face of the old-time logger, his life and work and times. Other equipment includes a narrow-gauge locomotive, a steam-powered snow snake to haul log-filled sleds, boats, and a road icer. In addition, you can watch an electrically-operated miniature sawmill.

Wisconsin Dells

H. H. Bennett Studio Museum, 215 Broadway; take Exit 87 from I-90/94 to Rte. 13. (608) 253-2261. Free. Open daily from last Sat. in May through Labor Day, noon to 6 p.m.; rest of year by appointment. No facilities for handicapped.

H. H. Bennett was a premier landscape photographer in the last three decades of the 19th century and he was among the first photojournalists. He made and modified camera equipment, designing, among other things, a rubberband-powered shutter that permitted him "instantaneous" exposures. The museum, housed in Bennett's original studio (circa 1865), stores more than 8,000 glass plates from which it makes Bennett prints for collectors. It displays Bennett's cameras and gear, numerous original images, and century-old furnishings. These items, plus America's oldest darkroom, give a sharp picture of 19th-century American photography, quite a distance in time and technique from Polaroids and "the mind of Minolta."

IV
SOUTH
CENTRAL

Alabama

Birmingham

Southern Museum of Flight, 4342 N. 73rd St., Airport Blvd. from Rte. 59. (205) 833-8226 or 836-2439. Adults: $2, students: $1. Open Tues. through Sat., 9 a.m. to 5 p.m.; Sun., 1 to 5 p.m.; closed Mon. and major holidays. Accessible to handicapped.

Flying has fascinated us since at least the days of Icarus, and the aeronautical accomplishments of our own century have stimulated that interest—global flights, moon voyages, space shuttles. Still, we love to look back. This museum is chock full of things aeronautical, such as engines, props, helmets, uniforms, awards, trophies, books, and publications. It also houses hundreds of model aircraft, including radio-controlled types, and is the home of the Alabama Aviation Hall of Fame. Best of all are the 14 planes, including an AT-6 trainer, a 1912 Douglas pusher, and various home-built and experimental aircraft.

Fort McClellan

U.S. Army Chemical Corps Museum, take Rte. 21 from I-20. (205) 848-3355. Free. Open Mon. through Fri., 7:45 a.m. to 4 p.m.; closed weekends and holidays. Accessible to handicapped.

The concept and its primitive practice stretch back over the centuries, but the message is as contemporary as datelines from the Middle East—chemical warfare is hazardous to your health.

This collection of the Army Chemical Corps, and not all materials are exhibited, contains more than 4,000 artifacts and covers chemical and biological warfare from biblical times to the present. The ancients, lacking our advanced technologies, resorted to such methods as throwing skunk cabbage or decomposing bodies into the enemy's water supply to contaminate it, illustrated here in dioramas. The modern era is represented mostly by artifacts from World War I and personal items donated by retired personnel of the First Gas Regiment, such as medals and paybooks. Also displayed are gas masks, flame-throwers, and mortars, and such specialty items as a World War I gas mask to cover the coops of carrier pigeons, a Mickey Mouse-faced World War II-era mask for children, and a Nazi nerve gas cylinder.

Women's Army Corps Museum, take Rte. 21 from I-20. (205) 848-3512. Free. Open weekdays, 8 a.m. to 4 p.m., and weekends by appointment. Accessible to handicapped.

Women in the military have marched a considerable distance, and while debate continues over possible combat roles, there's no question that female GIs have found their way into most other service roles—from computers, public relations, and medicine to law enforcement and management—considerable progress from World War II duty as cooks, clerks, drivers, and nurses. In fact, the Women's Army Corps (WAC) was disestablished in 1978; a female recruit is now just another GI. This museum honors the 36-year-history of the WAC and its transition to the contemporary niche. Uniforms, posters, photos, caps, plaques, films, archives, and displays trace the Corps from its establishment in 1942 as the Women's Auxiliary Army Corps through Korea and Vietnam. The contribution of the WAC is vividly portrayed in scenes of barracks life, recollections of overseas posts, awards and decorations, musical instruments, fatigues with bloomers, and oral history tapes.

McCalla

Iron & Steel Museum of Alabama, 12632 Confederate Pkwy., in Tannehill State Park; take Exit 100 from I-59/20. (205) 477-5711. Adults: $1, children: $.50. Open Mon. through Fri., 8 a.m. to 5 p.m.; weekends, 10 a.m. to 5 p.m.; closed Christmas and New Year's Day. Accessible to handicapped.

Not so much the metal of today as the mettle of yesterday, this museum represents the earlier days of the state's renowned iron industry, focusing on early 1800s technology—from the stone tools of the Indians through the weapons of the Civil War. A main attraction is the cold-blast iron furnace that daily produced 20 tons of pig iron and heavy ordnance during the height of the Civil War. The site began operations in the 1830s as a small forge, evolving into a charcoal blast furnace in the mid-1850s, and later giving birth to the Birmingham steel mills. Photos, exhibits, and artifacts from those formative days recount this iron-clad story.

Tuscaloosa

Paul W. Bryant Museum, on campus of University of Alabama, 300 Paul W. Bryant Dr.; take University Blvd. Exit from Rte. 82 off I-59. (205) 348-4668. Adults: $2, children 6 to 17: $1. Open Tues. through Sat., 10 a.m. to 4 p.m.; Sun., 2 to 5 p.m.; special hours for holidays and spring break. Accessible to handicapped.

Only someone ignorant of football or dwelling outside Alabama would not know that this is really the "Bear" Bryant Museum, named for and dedicated to a coach whose reputation is unsurpassed in college gridiron annals. In fairness, the museum chronicles the careers of other University of Alabama football coaches as well, and highlights great moments in Crimson Tide history from its 1926 Rose Bowl victory to the era of Joe Namath and beyond. Rosters, photos, film clips, trophies, balls, letter sweaters, old radio recordings, and a video on the Bear's life and career are here, and there's even one of his trademark houndstooth hats.

Tuscambia

Alabama Music Hall of Fame, on Rte. 72 west of junction with Rte. 43. (205) 381-4417. Adults: $6, seniors: $5, children: $3. Open daily, 10 a.m. to 6 p.m. Accessible to handicapped.

A musical back home Alabama, this museum highlights the state's singers, songwriters, musical pioneers, and industry go-getters. You can walk through a giant juke box and a guitar, and there's a recording facility where you can indulge your recording fantasies. Portraits, showcases, guitars, and other instruments, even one of Jim Nabor's suits, add distinctive notes to this score.

Exhibits include the tour bus of the group Alabama, and there are homages to Hank Williams, Jr., The Commodores, and Lionel Ritchie, among others.

Tuskegee

George Washington Carver Museum, Tuskegee Institute, Old Montgomery Rd.; take Rte. 81 from I-85. (205) 727-3201. Free. Open daily, 9 a.m. to 5 p.m.; closed Thanksgiving, Christmas, and New Year's Day. Accessible to handicapped.

Agronomist, educator, and artist, George Washington Carver was born a slave but died a renowned scientist and head of Tuskegee Institute's Agriculture Department. The school established the museum in 1938 to honor Carver and his work. Here you see historic photos, microscopes, and other lab equipment; jars of vegetable specimens; peanut grinders; and products he derived from peanuts, sweet potatoes, sand, and feathers, to name a few. His paintings and needlework are on display, as well, and you can hear recordings of his voice. This National Historic Site also has materials related to Booker T. Washington, famous educator and author, and Tuskegee Institute's first principal.

Arkansas

Eureka Springs

The Castle and Museum at Inspiration Point, Rte. 62, 5½ miles west of Eureka Springs. (501) 253-9462. Adults: $4, children 7 to 12: $.50. Open daily, mid-Apr. through Oct., with tours from 9 a.m. to 4:45 p.m. Ramps for handicapped in museum building.

If this castle, with its unique stonework and spectacular view, conjures up images of castles on the Rhine, there's a reason: It was designed and built in the early 1900s by a German immigrant, nostalgic for his homeland. The Castle's current owners, Annella and Vernon Baker, have turned it into a museum of family living and technology of the early 1900s. Although the castle itself, with its unique construction, period furnishings, and colorful history, is unusual, it is the museum—actually five separate buildings on the site—that is most interesting, for this is a collection of the mundane. A walk through the exhibits of early phonographs and radios, business machines, household appliances and machines, ladies' and men's fashions, and old cameras, all dating from earlier in this century, will be a stroll down memory lane for older visitors and a glimpse into the recent domestic past for younger visitors. There is a nice feeling here that everyday items are every bit as admirable as exotic objects.

Gay Nineties Button and Doll Museum, Onyx Cave Park, near entrance to cave, 3 miles east of Eureka Springs. (501) 253-9321.

Free. Open daily, 8:30 a.m. to 5:30 p.m.; closed Jan., Feb., and Christmas Day. Accessible to handicapped, but no handicapped rest room facilities.

There was a time when every woman had a button box—a tin filled with colorful little gems gleaned from discarded family clothing. Mrs. Victor Solberg had just such a collection, but over the years it grew to such proportions that it needed a building all to itself. Here, in a tidy red and white one-room structure, is Mrs. Solberg's button collection. Mounted on display cards filling nearly every available square inch of the building are more than 100 types of antique buttons made from ivory, lace, wood, brass, steel, glass. They are round, square, oblong; shanked and holed; plain and fancy. They include an outstanding collection of Japanese netsukes, a rare Liverpool transfer, and a unique habitat button from Belgium that contains, under glass, dried flowers, twigs, and even a tiny dried worm. Dolls, baskets, and other bits of old-time memorabilia also find a home here, but mostly there are examples of decorative yet practical devices for fastening one's clothing.

Hammond Museum of Bells, 2 Pine St., corner of Spring and Pine Sts. across from local post office. (501) 253-7411. Adults: $2.50, students: free with adult. Open Apr. 10 through Nov. 10, Mon. through Sat., 9:30 a.m. to 5 p.m.; Sun., 11 a.m. to 4 p.m. Limited access for handicapped.

Thirty years of bell collecting have resulted in 30 lighted exhibits of bells old and new from virtually every corner of the globe. Primitive sound makers, carillons, dinner bells, cow bells, art pieces, and all types of sweet-sounding bells of blown glass, brass, china, and many other materials are described in a taped narrated tour. Of special note is a display and demonstration of tuned wind chimes, precisely-tuned tubes that duplicate the sounds of familiar cathedral chimes and natural harmonies. The museum adjoins a "collectabells" shop featuring bells both functional and artistic, as well as books.

Miles Musical Museum, Rte. 62 west. (501) 253-8961. Adults: $5, children 6 to 15: $2.50. Open May 1 to Nov. 1, daily, 8:30 a.m. to 4:30 p.m. Limited access for handicapped.

A musical museum this certainly is, for it contains an enormous collection of musical instruments. Scores of organs are on display (including pump, automatic, and roller) as are examples of the familiar and the arcane, musically speaking—pianos galore, gramophones, nickel grabbers, a street barrel piano, unusual stringed instruments, music boxes, and singing bird boxes. But, beyond the musical are exhibits of items collected in the Far East, some very interesting clocks, an animated miniature circus, dioramas made from local onyx, and some fine locally-made art made from buttons sewn to canvas.

Fort Smith

Patent Model Museum, 400 N. Eighth, in Historic District, 4 blocks from downtown. (501) 782-9014. Free. Open Mon. through Fri., 9 a.m. to 4 p.m., unless owner is out of town. Limited access for handicapped.

What happens to models submitted with applications to the U.S. Patent Office? Eighty-five of the most intricate and ingenious ended up in the hands of Arkansas State Representative Carolyn Pollan and now occupy two rooms of the handsome 1840 historic Fort Smith house that she has restored. Dating from 1836 through the 1870s, these unique, mostly mechanical, models represent both American ingenuity and optimism. Not all the inventions depicted as models here won a patent—a transparent window shade was of dubious value, for instance. But many of them, such as the familiar spring roller shade, were patented and became part of everyday American life. Other curiosities filling the museum's lighted cabinets include models of a steam rotary engine, toys, refrigerators, printing presses, and devices such as a combination ironing table/clothes rack, designed to ease the drudgery of wash day. Along the walls are 17 drawings of models that were destroyed in the Patent Office fire of 1836.

Murfreesboro

Crater of Diamonds State Park Museum, Rte. 301, 2½ miles southeast of Murfreesboro. (501) 285-3113. Adults: $3.50, children 6 to 12: $1.25. Open Dec. 1 through Feb., 8 a.m. to 4:30 p.m.; Mar. to Memorial Day, and Labor Day to Dec. 1, 8 a.m. to 5 p.m.; Memorial Day through Labor Day, 8 a.m. to 7 p.m. Accessible to handicapped.

Diamond mining in the United States? Yes! More than 70,000 diamonds have been found in this crater (actually an eroded volcanic pipe) since John Huddleston dug up the first sparkler in 1906, and there are thousands just waiting to be discovered. The 40.32-carat Uncle Sam was found here, as were the 34.25-carat Star of Murfreesboro and other notable lumps of "ice." The museum, located in the park's visitor center, offers exhibits on the history of the mine and the people historically connected with it, information on the geologic formation, actual diamonds and other semiprecious gems and minerals found on the site, and displays on diamond cutting and lapidary. Most important, perhaps, are the displays on how to effectively search for and recognize diamonds—it is open season for diamond hunting at the park all year round, and finders, keepers.

Pine Ridge

Lum & Abner Museum & Jot 'Em Down Store, Rte. 88, between Mena and Pencil Bluff. (501) 326-4442. Adults: $.50, children: $.20. Open Mar. 1 to Nov. 15, Tues. through Sat., 9 a.m. to 5 p.m.; Sun., noon to 5 p.m. Ramp for handicapped at rear door.

Lum & Abner, whose real names were Chester Lauck and Norris Goff, were enormously popular radio personalities in the 1930s who literally put the name of their small Arkansas hometown on the map. Patterning their radio town of Pine Ridge on their real hometown of Waters and peopling it with characters inspired by people they knew, Lum & Abner created a community so well known that in 1936 the name of Waters was officially changed to Pine Ridge. The Jot 'Em Down Store was the radio setting for their humorous exchanges, and it, too, was based on a real grocery store that they knew from their youth. The tiny wood structure, now called the Lum & Abner Museum, originally a store, contains memorabilia from Lauck and Goff's radio careers, and from their subsequent careers in the movies.

Pottsville

Potts Tavern, 8 miles east of Russellville, just off Rte. 64 and I-40. (501) 968-1147. Adults: $2, children: $.50. Open daily, 10 a.m. to 5 p.m.; closed major holidays. Ramp to main building, but otherwise not geared to handicapped.

Like the Castle at Inspiration Point, Potts Tavern consists of one main building with period furnishings and several outbuildings, one of them a small museum with an unusual exhibit or two. At Potts Tavern, which 150 years ago served the stagecoach line, ladies' hats are the very special draw. This collection of feminine headgear spans 100 years, although most of them were designed by a local man, Michael McLain, who went on to fame and fortune by creating headwear for such fashion-conscious clients as the wife of President Warren G. Harding and the Queen of Romania. More than 100 hats hang here, mostly dressy and bedecked with feathers of all kinds, lace, and artificial flowers. Several charming period frocks are also displayed and posters offer biographical information on Mr. McLain, whose career was associated with Marshall Fields department stores.

Kansas

Abilene

Museum of Independent Telephony, 412 S. Campbell, downtown, across from Eisenhower Presidential Library. (913) 263-2681. Adults: $1, children under 12: free. Open Apr. 15 through Oct. 15, Mon. through Fri., 1 to 8 p.m.; Sat., 10 a.m. to 8 p.m.; Sun., 1 to 5 p.m.; closed Thanksgiving and Christmas. Accessible to handicapped.

Between 1893, when Alexander Graham Bell's telephone patents expired, and the 1984 divestiture of AT&T, independent telephone companies flourished in communities across the U.S. Their heyday and their contribution to communications in suburban America is commemorated here in an organized and entertaining manner. A well-labeled exhibit covering two walls traces the evolution of the telephone instrument with representative phones arranged by decades; another exhibit traces the evolution of the telephone dial. A typical telephone exchange office dating from the days of magneto switchboards is manned by a costumed guide, and at a kiosk decorated with sheet music visitors can call up some of the many songs that celebrate America's love affair with the telephone. Of special interest to hobbyists is an artistically presented collection of glass insulators.

Chanute

Martin and Osa Johnson Safari Museum, 16 S. Grant Ave.; follow signs from Cherry St. Exit off Rte. 169. (316) 431-2730. Adults: $2.50, students: $1, children under 12 with adult: free. Open Mon. through Sat., 10 a.m. to 5 p.m.; Sun., 1 to 5 p.m. No facilities for handicapped.

From 1917 to 1936, Martin and Osa Johnson traveled the world and recorded on film and in books the people and wildlife of the South Seas, East Africa, and Borneo, among other faraway places. Their treasure trove of photographs, films, musical instruments, and artifacts form the core of this museum, where visitors can browse through scrapbooks, view film footage, and enjoy looking at exotic artifacts and such personal memorabilia as Osa's fishing hat and Martin's cigar holder. A complementary adjunct to the Johnsons' collection is a collection of West African artifacts—masks (some of them 15 feet tall), headdresses, carved wooden figures, statues, and elaborate door locks—contributed by their friend Dr. Pascal Imperato. In addition, the museum holds fabrics, jewelry, weapons, and other artifacts from Africa, and, in a separate gallery, paintings and sketches of wildlife by well-known artists. The most important holding, however, is the Johnsons' film documentation of cultures, creatures, and wildernesses that have long since vanished.

Coffeyville

Dalton Museum, 113 W. Eighth St., 2 blocks north of junction of Rtes. 166 and 169. No telephone. Adults: $2, children under 16: free. Open daily year round. Accessible to handicapped.

On October 5, 1892, the infamous Dalton gang galloped into Coffeyville planning to rob the two local banks. Their nefarious plot went awry, however, when armed citizens blocked their escape. Four gang members and four citizens died in the shootout. The raid is commemorated by plaques all over town and in the Dalton Museum, which contains pictures, guns, saddles and other possessions that belonged to gang members. In a completely different vein, separate rooms in the museum are given over to mementos of baseball great Walter Johnson (a hometown boy) and to memorabilia of Wendell Willkie, GOP presidential candidate who lived and taught in Coffeyville.

Colby

Prairie Museum of Art and History, 1905 S. Franklin, on frontage road off Exit 53 or 54 from I-70. (913) 462-6972. Adults: $3, children: $.50. Open Tues. through Fri., 9 a.m. to 5 p.m.; Sat. and Sun., 1 to 5 p.m.; closed Mon. and holidays. Accessible to handicapped.

One family's generosity makes up the bulk of this museum's outstanding holdings. Nicely housed in a modern building is the collection of fine antiques of the Kuska family, whose interests included fine china and porcelain, dolls, and art glass. Among the 2,000 dolls in the collection, many of them quite rare, are French fashion dolls, an ermine-clad doll whose necklace is composed of miniatures of famous paintings from the Louvre, and a charming mechanical Jumeau called The Sorceress. The hundreds of china and porcelain pieces on display came from all over the world and include Quimper, Wedgewood, Sevres, Royal Worcester, Flow Blue, and Gaudy Welsh. One entire gallery displays 18th-century figurines from Meissen. Exhibits of cloisonne, Oriental porcelain, early American glass, and art glass round out the collections.

El Dorado

Butler County Historical Museum, 383 E. Central; take El Dorado Exit east from I-35; two blocks east of downtown; look for oil derrick landmark. (316) 321-9333. Free. Open Tues. through Sat., 1 to 5 p.m.; closed Sun., Mon., and holidays. Accessible to handicapped.

A 100-foot steel oil derrick announces the main emphasis of this county historical museum—oil. The El Dorado field, discovered in 1915, proved to be the greatest oil field in Kansas. Full-sized exhibits include a 24-foot band wheel used for pumping wells, a 1929 railroad tank car, and a modern pumping unit and tank battery. Drill bits, cable tools, a lazy bench, and other equipment necessary for drilling an oil well in 1916 are also featured.

Fort Riley

U.S. Cavalry Museum, 205 Sheridan Ave.; take Holbrook Ave. (Exit 301) from I-70 to left on Custer Ave.; museum is on next corner. (913) 239-2737, -2743. Open Mon. through Sat., 9 a.m. to 4:30 p.m.; closed Easter, Thanksgiving, Christmas, and New Year's Day. Accessible to handicapped.

Heroes of countless Western movies, the U.S. Cavalry figured in some of the more colorful chapters of America's history. Fort Riley, a strategic point along the Santa Fe Trail, later became cavalry headquarters for the U.S. Army and therefore has a museum dedicated to its own special breed of soldier. Uniforms, hats, saddlery, and insignia are shown in their evolution over the years, roughly 1775 to 1950 when the mounted soldier played an important role. Special exhibits, such as one of buffalo soldiers, as black troopers were called by the Indians, are featured, as are heroic murals and some rare artifacts, such as a shaggy buffalo coat. A picture and sculpture gallery displays works by such renowned Western artists as Frederic Remington, Jim Muir, and Don Stivers.

Goodland

High Plains Museum, 1717 Cherry; take Exit 17 or 19 from I-70 to Rte. 24 and follow signs to museum. (913) 899-3351. Donation suggested. Open June through Aug., Mon. through Sat., 9 a.m. to 5 p.m.; Sun., 1 to 5 p.m.; closed Mon., Sept. through May; closed major holidays. Accessible to handicapped, but no handicapped rest room facilities.

While the focus here is on the history of Goodland and of Sherman County, with HO-scale dioramas and exhibits on sod house building and pioneer life, the main attractions are two very different vehicles. One is a 1902 rope-driven Holsman car, manufactured in Chicago, gasoline-powered but propelled by ropes and pulleys up to 23 miles per hour. The other is a full-sized replica of America's first patented helicopter, the 1909 invention of two Rock Island Railroad engineers that used two counter-rotating rotors to offset engine torque, as opposed to the modern tail rotor. Unfortunately, it never flew. The replica, rather spindly and delicate-looking compared to its modern-day counterparts, was built in 1976 using patent plans and the only existing photo.

Kansas City

Clendening History of Medicine Museum, 39th and Rainbow Blvd., Univ. of Kansas Medical Center, south on 7th St. Exit from I-35. (913) 588-7040. Free. Open Mon. through Fri., 8 a.m. to 4 p.m. Accessible to handicapped.

The foyer of the building that holds Dr. Logan Clendening's world-famous collection of medical books and treatises is the setting for his outstanding collection of medically-related objects. Starting with a replica Babylonian stele on which the Code of Hammurabi is inscribed in cuneiform script, through disease-fighting amulets from many cultures, Egyptian charms, and rare Etruscan specimens of heart, uterus, breast, and eye votives designed to secure religious services for diseases of those particular organs, the collection documents man's attempts to cope with medical and surgical problems through the ages. From China there is an ancient model of a human body showing acupuncture points and a charming figure of a woman lying on a bed—for use by her maid in showing the doctor where the pain was without embarrassing exposure. From Bavaria, there is an 18th-century obstetric chair. A small collection of microscopes traces the development of that important instrument. South America is represented by pre-Columbian pottery portraying medical scenes and a skull that has been trephined to release evil spirits. America's chapter in the history of medicine is represented by a pair of Perkins Patent Tractors—two pieces of metal, brass, and iron, utilized by Connecticut doctor Elisha Perkins in the 1700s to draw away pain.

LaCrosse

Barbed Wire Museum, 614 Main St., 23 miles south of Hays, near junction of Rtes. 183 and 4. (913) 222-3116. Free. Open in winter, Wed. and Fri., 8 a.m. to noon; in summer, Mon. through Fri., 10 a.m. to noon and 1 to 3 p.m. No facilities for handicapped.

Some would say that it was barbed wire that tamed the West, effectively putting the land in the hands of farmers, bringing to an end the era of long cattle trains sweeping over the Great Plains. Barbed wire came in an amazing variety of forms, at least 400 of which are on display here, mounted on boards, in wall cases, and in free-standing exhibits. All are identified with popular name and probable origin. Nearly all date from the 19th century and are no longer made. Several types of specialized tools for stringing barbed wire are also showcased.

Post Rock Museum, 202 W. 1st St., 23 miles south of Hays, near junction of Rtes. 183 and 4. (913) 222-3560. Donation welcome. Open mid-Apr. through mid-Oct., Mon. through Sat., 10 a.m. to 4:30 p.m.; Sun., 1 to 4:30 p.m.

Native stone posts, strung with barbed wire, have marked boundaries in north central Kansas since the 1870s, creating a distinctive regional landscape. Exhibits in this restored stone house, circa 1883, tell the story of the native limestone and how it was quarried and split to form fence posts roughly 5 feet long and 9 inches on each side. Sledges, feathers, wedges, and other quarrying equipment are on display here, as are pictorial examples of other ways in which the stone was used—for construction of homes, schools, and churches, to build bridges, and as decorative touches. Limestone was so extensively used in the area that many homes even had stone clothesline poles.

Lawrence

University of Kansas Ryther Printing Museum, University of Kansas Printing Building, 2425 W. 15th St.; from I-70 take West Exit, then turn south on Iowa St.; turn right at 3rd traffic light; museum is large brick building 2 blocks down on left. (913) 864-4341. Free. Open Mon. through Fri., 8 a.m. to 5 p.m.; closed holidays. Accessible to handicapped.

Back before computerized typesetting, the business of printing was a cumbersome one indeed, as evidenced by the kinds of equipment on exhibit here. A cylinder press, various kinds of platens, racks of foundry and wood type in 4- to 60-point sizes, lithographic stones, and other instruments and machinery historically necessary for turning out the printed page are on view. There are also bulky linotype machines and a Simplex typesetting machine—motorized and still operable—that is the only one of its kind in existence: Linotype company machinists were instructed to take a sledge hammer to the Simplex machines they were replacing. Because the man who owned the Simplex on display here bought his linotype second hand, the Simplex was spared.

Liberal

Coronado Historical Museum and Dorothy's House, 567 E. Cedar,
1 block east of Rte. 54; follow the yellow brick road. (316) 624-7624.
Free. Open Sept. through May, Tues. through Sat., 9 a.m. to 5 p.m.;
Sun., 1 to 5 p.m.; June through Aug., Mon. through Sat., 9 a.m. to
7:30 p.m.; Sun., 1 to 5 p.m. Limited access for handicapped.

When Don Francisco Vasquez de Coronado and 36 soldiers
entered what is now Kansas over 400 years ago, they didn't find
the gold they were looking for, but they did leave behind what
were to become artifacts on display in this converted 1918 mansion:
spurs, a helmet, a horse bit, and a few other items. The rest of the
museum features items that helped tame the area—weapons,
household items, toys. Nearby is something celebrating a more
modern Kansas phenomenon—L. Frank Baum's story of the *Wizard
of Oz*—in the form of a 1907 farm house restored to duplicate the
era and the warmth of the house where Dorothy discovered that
"there's no place like home." Overstuffed chairs in the parlor, a
wood burning stove in the kitchen, and other period furnishings
tell of a simpler life style just after the turn of the century, and in
Dorothy's room is an exact reproduction of her room as depicted in
the 1939 movie, complete with ruby slippers and Toto's bed. Also
on display is the original model house used for filming the movie.
A yellow brick road marks the pathway to the front door of Dorothy's House.

Norton

Gallery of Also-Rans, First State Bank, 105 W. Main, just off Hwy.
283. (913) 877-3341. Free. Open during banking hours, 9 a.m. to 3
p.m. No particular facilities for handicapped.

Successful presidential candidates have their likenesses hung in
the halls of the White House, carved into mountainsides in South
Dakota, and reproduced on legal tender. Unsuccessful presidential
candidates are rarely recognized after election day. The Gallery of
Also-Rans, an assemblage of handsomely-framed portraits on the
mezzanine of a bank, gives them the attention that they perhaps
deserve. Framed biographical sketches of each candidate contain
some interesting tidbits: The first Also Ran, Thomas Jefferson, was
defeated by John Adams, whom he later defeated; Henry Clay was

the most consistent loser, having run and lost for three different parties between 1824 and 1848; Grover Cleveland was the only candidate to make a successful comeback after a loss; and Wendell Willkie, in 1940 the third of four losers to Franklin Delano Roosevelt, "captured the imagination of thousands who knew nothing, or cared little about the issues." The gallery was started by W. W. Rouse, former president of the First State Bank. Ann Hazlett, his daughter and current curator, claims that the portrait of reputedly accident-prone Gerald Ford keeps falling off the wall.

Ottawa

Old Depot Museum, Tecumseh St., 1 block west of Main St. (913) 242-8478. Free. Open May through Sept., Sun., 1 to 5 p.m., or by appointment. Difficult access for handicapped.

This 1888 Santa Fe Railroad depot contains the expected—a model train room, and photos of trains that have stopped in Ottawa over the past 100 years. But it also offers the unexpected. On permanent display in the military room here is a fine collection of framed World War II-era political and military cartoons. Another exhibit is devoted to the Chautauqua adult education movement that swept the country from about 1875 to 1924. Books, tickets, photos, old newspapers, diplomas, and awards testify that the Ottawa Chautauqua summertime seminars were second in size and success only to the original seminars in Chautauqua, New York. Also, of particular interest to collectors and nostalgia buffs is an exhibit of novelty post cards by Ottawan William "Dad" Martin, a pioneer in photographic techniques just after the turn of the century, who specialized in post cards depicting "jackalopes," people perched on giant watermelons, and other humorous claims that life is lived on a larger scale in the Midwest.

Sedan

Emmett Kelly Historical Museum, 202-204 E. Main St., 1 block east of town's main intersection. (316) 725-3470. Donation suggested. Open from Memorial Day weekend to Labor Day weekend, Sun. through Fri., 1 to 5 p.m.; Sat., 10 a.m. to 5 p.m. Ramp at entrance, but no rest room facilities for handicapped.

Sedan's favorite son is a tramp, or at least a make-believe tramp called Willy, as portrayed by the celebrated circus clown and Sedan native Emmett Kelly. Little wonder, then, that the focal point of this museum's several collections is memorabilia from Kelly's 50-year career playing the sad little hobo in derby hat and big shoes for the Ringling Brothers circus. Other exhibits of note in these three connecting buildings are a spectacular 1,500-piece decanter collection, a complete 1908 print shop, and a shell collection from faraway Guam.

Wichita

Fellow-Reeve Museum of History and Science, 2100 University St., Friends University, on 4th and 5th floors of Davis Administration Bldg. in center of campus; north of Rte. 54. (316) 292-5594. Adults: $1, children under 12: $.50. Open Sept. through May, Tues. through Fri., 1 to 4 p.m.; closed last 2 weeks of Dec. and first 2 weeks of Jan. Elevator from first floor.

The special aspect of this museum is that, in a way, it isn't unusual at all—it typifies the best in small museums that got their start with the natural human urge to acquire a bunch of interesting things and put them on public display. Occupying two floors of a Quaker university administration building, this museum contains thousands of artifacts and specimens that can roughly be lumped under the categories of history, natural history, and science. Many relics—such as a full-scale replica Indian teepee and campsite and hundreds of pioneer domestic items—relate to the early residents of Kansas. Among the hundreds of arrowheads on display is one approximately 11,500 years old. Other items relate to Quakers—African drums, weapons, and other artifacts from the Dark Continent that were brought back by missionaries. Under the heading "natural history" are many fossils and stuffed animals, both foreign and domestic. Among other items too numerous to mention are a collection of shoes (exotic and otherwise), carved chess sets, a collection of 4,000 buttons, and a cane collection.

Kentucky

Bardstown

Oscar Getz Museum of Whiskey History, 114 N. Fifth St., in Spalding Hall. (502) 348-2999. Free. Open May 1 through Oct. 31, Mon. through Sat., 9 a.m. to 5 p.m.; and Sun., 1 to 5 p.m.; Nov. 1 through Apr. 30, Tues. through Sat., 10 a.m. to 4 p.m., and Sun., 1 to 4 p.m. No facilities for handicapped.

Whiskey, a Kentucky nectar, is well decanted in this small, compact museum in the heart of bourbon country. It covers whiskey manufacture from colonial days through Prohibition. The process is concisely outlined in poster format, and artifacts such as vats, cookers, and yeast samplers bring it three-dimensional form. There's a whiskey thief (circa 1900), a device to sample a barrel's contents for gauging proof, and an illicit still that once operated in the Kentucky hills. Patents, licenses, ads, books, and labels help document the beverage's lineage, including an 19th-century sales permit. An amazing array of jugs, decanters, and bottles calls the roll—from Old Overholt and J. W. Dant to Mattingly & Moore and Mud Lick. Best of all is an antebellum bottle from Philadelphia dealer E. C. Booz who gave his name to the world of drink.

Berea

Berea College Appalachian Museum, on campus of Berea College, take Exit 76 or 77 from I-75. (606) 986-9341. Adults: $1.50, seniors and students: $1, children 6 to 12: $.50. Open year round, except Jan., Mon. through Sat., 9 a.m. to 6 p.m.; Sun., 1 to 6 p.m.; closed Christmas and Thanksgiving. Entrance ramp but no rest room facilities for handicapped.

The past is special here, in the sense of traditional folkways infusing a culture, be they weaving, music, or methods of farming. In Appalachia, it's said, people don't live in the past; the past lives in them. This museum reflects regional life in the 19th and early 20th centuries, and exhibits feature spinning wheels, blacksmith tools, handmade baskets, muzzle-loading rifles, and other traditional objects. Temporary exhibits examine contemporary and historical issues facing Appalachia. A major attraction is the demonstration of crafts and skills, such as splitting rails, dyeing yarn, playing dulcimers, and weaving cloth. Eighteen slide/tape programs, produced by the museum, reinforce the living, working nature of these arts and crafts.

Elizabethtown

Schmidt's Coca-Cola Museum, in bottling plant, 1201 N. Dixie Ave., off I-65 and Western Kentucky Pkwy. (502) 737-4000. Adults: $2, seniors: $1.50, students: $.50. Open Mon. through Fri., 9 a.m. to 4 p.m.; closed weekends and major holidays. No facilities for handicapped.

Billed as the world's largest privately-owned collection of Coca-Cola memorabilia, this is the real thing, at least in advertising terms. Ads for the ubiquitous soft drink have appeared on trays, calendars, glasses, cards, knives, and sheet music, and also on thermometers, cigar bands, bubblegum wrappers, and clocks. The museum displays signs, posters, magazine ads, stained glass, even an 1890s soda fountain that served Coke at the Columbian Exhibition. The Schmidt family has been bottling Coca-Cola in Kentucky since 1901, and a visit here includes a glimpse of plant operations and free Coke to boot.

Henderson

John James Audubon Memorial Museum, on Rte. 41 between Western Kentucky Pkwy. and I-64. (502) 826-2247. Adults: $2.50, children: $.75. Open daily, Apr. 1 through Oct. 31, 9 a.m. to 5 p.m.;

weekends only in Feb., Mar., Nov., and Dec.; closed in Jan. Limited facilities for handicapped.

The famed wildlife artist lived in this area for more than nine years and his children were born here; he was merchant and property owner as well as an incomparable illustrator. The museum is situated in Audubon State Park, a sylvan locale that Audubon often visited to study birds and other animals. He discovered the spot was a migratory stopover and he studied and painted eight local birds here. French Norman architecture envelops a collection of the artist's works, books, and journals, as well as family silver, jewelry, and portraits. Highlights are an elephant folio collection of Audubon's bird engravings and an array of watercolor hummingbirds. Original prints are also on view.

Lexington

American Saddle Horse Museum, 4093 Iron Works Pike; take Exit 120 from I-75. (606) 259-2746. Adults: $2, seniors: $1.50, children 6 to 12: $1. Open daily, Apr. through Oct., 9 a.m. to 5 p.m.; Memorial Day through Labor Day, 9 a.m. to 6 p.m.; Nov. through Mar., Wed. through Sun., 9 a.m. to 5 p.m. Accessible to handicapped.

Kentucky, the "bluegrass state," is horse country and what more appropriate place for a museum dedicated to equine endeavors. This is a specialized horse museum, describing the history and uses of the American Saddlebred Horse, Kentucky's only native breed and the oldest registered American breed of horse. Artifacts, posters, paintings, dioramas, and sculpture provide a dynamic view of this renowned breed, a famous representative of which was Gen. Robert E. Lee's Traveler; others were film star Fury and TV's Mr. Ed. A touch-screen video setup features "Scrapbook of World Champions" and "The Right Horse for You," the latter enabling a visitor to "see" himself riding a horse. A wraparound theater offers a 10-minute multi-image presentation of the breed's history and the pageantry of a contemporary horse show.

International Museum of the Horse, 4089 Iron Works Pike; take Exit 120 from I-75. (606) 233-4303, ext. 231. Adults: $7.95, children: $3.95, special rates for groups and seniors. Open daily, Apr. 1 through Oct. 31, 9 a.m. to 5 p.m.; Nov. 1 through Mar. 31, Wed. through Sun., 9 a.m. to 5 p.m. Accessible to handicapped.

In the neighboring stable, so to speak, is a horse museum that runs the gamut at a winner's pace. It's devoted to all breeds of horses and spans some 50 million years from the fox-sized proto horse Eohippus to stately stagecoach steeds. Some 30 horse-drawn vehicles represent diverse modes of transportation associated with horses. Other galleries and exhibits focus on horses in sport and art. The historical canter is truly intriguing, offering fascinating facts from around the world and across the centuries—for example, in ancient Rome bookmakers flew chariot-race results to off-track bettors by carrier pigeon.

Louisville

Kentucky Derby Museum, 704 Central Ave., next to Churchill Downs; take Taylor Blvd. from I-264. (502) 637-1111. Adults: $3, seniors: $2.50, children 5 to 12: $1.50. Open daily, 9 a.m. to 5 p.m.; closed Thanksgiving, Christmas and Kentucky Oaks and Derby Days. Accessible to handicapped.

Opened in 1985, this colorful, three-floor museum places you inside the famous Kentucky Derby, from mint julep cups to racing silks to trophies, and to the jockeys, trainers, and horses themselves. A 360-degree multimedia presentation takes you through Derby Day, from sunup in the stables to the thundering run for the roses. One exhibit features betting windows and instruction on the art, or science, of wagering on the ponies. You can learn how to read a tote board and weigh in on authentic jockey scales. One floor is devoted to the horse racing industry and the breeding, training, and even running mechanics of these magnificent animals. A visit to the museum also includes a tour of Churchill Downs, the nation's oldest continuously-operating track.

Murray

National Scouting Museum of the Boy Scouts of America, campus of Murray State University, off I-24. (502) 762-3383. Adults: $4.50, seniors: $4, children 6 to 12: $3.50, Scouts: $3. Open daily, 9 a.m. to 5 p.m., June 1 through Labor Day. Accessible to handicapped.

Scouting ranks up there in the American pantheon with motherhood and apple pie, and this museum recounts the Scouting story from its beginning eight decades ago. Interactive exhibits, such as Murray the Robot, and touch-screen videos place the goals and values of Scouting in a contemporary technological context. Other displays offer uniforms, photos, and gear that reflect a more traditional cast. A special Norman Rockwell exhibit features more than two dozen of the artist's paintings, each depicting a Scout.

Louisiana

Marthaville

Louisiana Country Music Museum, Rte. 1221, in Rebel State Commemorative Area, about 22 miles from I-49. (318) 472-6255. Ages 13 to 62: $2; over and under: free. Open Wed. through Sun., 9 a.m. to 5 p.m. Accessible to handicapped.

A state-owned facility opened in 1988, this museum tells the tuneful story of Louisiana people and their music—bluegrass, Cajun, gospel, and more. A 13-minute film introduces you to the music makers and transmitters, and listening posts enable you to tune in to music from different eras, dating all the way back to the late 1800s. Items on display encompass guitars, fiddles, banjos, zithers, and other instruments as well as clothing and mementos from artists and entertainers. The museum is home to the Louisiana state fiddling championship and its amphitheater hosts gospel concerts and other live samples of regional sounds of music.

New Orleans

New Orleans Historic Voodoo Museum, 724 Dumaine St., edge of the French Quarter. (504) 523-7685. Adults: $4, students: $3, children: $2; additional charges for rituals, lectures, readings, and tours. Open daily, 10 a.m. to dusk. No facilities for handicapped.

The only privately-owned museum dedicated to voodoo culture and tradition, this stop is a decided departure from the usual bend

and browse. Exhibit rooms transport you into a world of synthesized African and European cultures and faiths with Caribbean
and Latin-American transmutations dating back several hundred
years. Here you see voodoo artifacts from Africa, Haiti, Louisiana,
and elsewhere—masks, carvings, drums, staffs, garb, amulets,
potions, and charms. Photos and paintings add colorful details to
the display. There's also a live 11-foot-long python and an altar for
offerings and rituals. In addition, the museum gives voodoo-
related tours of the area, including the swamp, if you're daring
enough.

New Orleans Pharmacy Museum, 514 Chartres St., the French
Quarter. (504) 524-9077. Donation: $1. Open Tues. through Sun., 10
a.m. to 5 p.m.; closed Mon. and holidays. Accessible to handicapped.

This museum opened in 1950, but the building's genesis dates
back to 1823 when it was constructed for Louis Defilho, America's
first licensed pharmacist. A tour of this establishment gives you a
good dose of 19th-century pharmacy, medicine and health care,
and what people endured when they had to take their medicine.
German hand-carved rosewood cabinets (circa 1850) hold hand-
blown glass apothecary jars filled with medicinal herbs, voodoo
gris-gris potions, and patent medicines. Here, too, are leech jars,
trade literature, journals, and Civil War surgical instruments. A
period seaman's medicine chest is juxtaposed with a curved glass
cosmetic counter where perfumes and rouges were sold. The Cre-
ole-American townhouse also boasts a black and rose marble soda
fountain and an interior courtyard with herb garden.

Confederate Museum, 929 Camp St., below I-10 between Super-
dome and the river, not far from French Quarter. (504) 523-4522.
Adults: $3, seniors and students: $2, children under 12: $1. Open
Mon. through Sat., 10 a.m. to 4 p.m.; closed Sun. and major
holidays. No facilities for handicapped.

Dedicated in 1891, this is the oldest museum in Louisiana. The
Romanesque structure designed by Thomas Sully houses manuscripts and memorabilia from the Civil War, with emphasis on
Louisiana's role. The exterior is brown pressed brick, and interior
woodwork consists of hearty cypress. Exhibits include paintings
and uniforms of Confederate leaders, regimental banners, litho-

graphs and tintypes of the era, medical gear, and a variety of weapons and ammunition. Prints and manuscripts describe secession and the subsequent capture of the city by Union troops.

Old U.S. Mint, 400 Esplanade, near French Market and the river. (504) 568-6968. Adults: $3, seniors and students: $1.50. Open Wed. through Sun., 10 a.m. to 5 p.m. Accessible to handicapped.

Sure, they used to make money here, but the glitter of interest today is the music they make, New Orleans jazz style, and the parties they throw. The Old Mint Building, part of the Louisiana State Museum, houses a couple of singular collections—development of jazz in the Crescent City and memorabilia related to the festival to top all festivals, Mardi Gras. The latter displays several types of colorful costumes, ornaments, and accessories, a portion of a float, invitations, and photos illustrating the revel of Carnival through the years. The former houses photos of jazz greats, the first jazz record—a 78-rpm recording by the Dixieland Jazz Band in 1917—a Dizzy Gillespie horn, a Pete Fountain clarinet, a Louis Armstrong cornet, and other instruments and items of jazz artists. There are also videos of jazz performances, and the sounds of jazz provide suitable backdrop for viewing the entire display.

St. Martinville

Acadian House, 1200 N. Main St., off Rte. 31. (318) 394-3754. Admission: $2, seniors and children under 13: free, all school children free during regular school sessions. Open Wed. through Sun., 9 a.m. to 5 p.m.; tours on the hour, 10 a.m. to 4 p.m. No facilities for handicapped.

No trip to Louisiana would be complete without an exploration of the Acadian and Creole cultures. The Acadians, refugees from Nova Scotia in the mid-1700s, settled in Louisiana which at the time belonged to France. In this locale where the swamp meets the prairie, they mingled with Creoles, or native-born Louisianans of French descent. The site itself is a former indigo and sugar plantation, a principal feature of which is a Creole raised cottage (circa 1836) constructed of brick, cypress, and bousillage (a mud and moss mixture). Legend links the house to Longfellow's "Evangeline." A visitors center exhibits Acadian and Creole tools, looms, utensils, and other items. Artisans demonstrate traditional crafts, such as building a pirogue.

Sulphur

Brimstone Museum, 800 Picard Rd.; take Sulphur Exit from I-10, then north on Rte. 27. (318) 525-7142. Free. Open Mon. through Fri., 9:30 a.m. to 5:30 p.m.; closed weekends and major holidays. No facilities for handicapped.

This has nothing to do, as the name might suggest, with sinners or Satan's aftershave. The locale gave birth to American sulphur mining a century ago, and this museum commemorates that industry and the pioneering efforts of Herman Frasch who developed the process of melting sulphur below the ground with forced hot water and pumping it to the surface. During the first quarter of the 20th century, area mines produced millions of tons of the mineral. On exhibit are a one-ton block of sulphur, a display of the Frasch process, artifacts and memorabilia, and photos of the community from the sulphur mining days.

Mississippi

Biloxi

Seafood Industry Museum, near Point Cadet Marina off Rte. 90. (601) 435-6320. Adults: $2.50, seniors and children 6 to 15: $1.50. Open Mon. through Sat., 9 a.m. to 5 p.m.; closed Sun. Accessible to handicapped.

Opened in 1986 in a renovated Coast Guard barracks, the museum focuses on the people, tools, technology, and products of the Gulf Coast seafood industry. Maps, photos, models, diagrams, nets, labels, cooking gear, and other items span more than 300 years of regional fishing and shellfishing and processing of seafood. Shrimping, crabbing, and oystering have been particularly important here, and the museum presents live demonstrations of oyster shucking as well as net knitting and model-boat building. The museum also owns a replica of a topsail oyster schooner, the *Glen L. Swetman,* and offers exhibits on sailmaking and fishing boat construction.

Clarksdale

Delta Blues Museum, 114 Delta Ave., downtown in Public Library, off Rte. 61/49 and Desoto Ave. (601) 624-4461. Free. Open Mon. through Fri., 9 a.m. to 5 p.m. (closed noon to 1 p.m.) Accessible to handicapped.

The blues, a truly American contribution to music, arose in the

Mississippi Delta and influenced jazz, country, and rock 'n' roll. Bluesmen such as W. C. Handy, Muddy Waters, and John Lee Hooker called the Delta home. Established in 1979, the museum has permanent and changing exhibits in the form of photos, books, recordings, videos, instruments, archives, and memorabilia devoted to the origins, development, and impact of the blues and the very roots of American music. It is a tuneful heritage fittingly preserved and fostered in Delta country.

Jackson

Dizzy Dean Museum, 1204 Lakeland Dr., off I-55 north. (601) 960-2404. Admission: $1. Open Apr. 1 through Sept. 30, Tues. through Sat., 11 a.m. to 6 p.m.; Sun., 1 to 6 p.m. Accessible to handicapped.

His real name was Jay Hanna Dean, but he's better known to baseball fans as Dizzy, a 30-game winner for the St. Louis Cardinals' famed Gas House Gang. He was a star pitcher with a blazing fastball and a talent for mangling the mother tongue, something he cultivated further in a post-playing days broadcast career. Although a native of Arkansas, Dizzy considered Mississippi his home state in his later years, and the museum is fittingly located near a minor league baseball park. Exhibits include photos, videos, uniforms, bats and other equipment, rings and watches and assorted mementos, and some of his golf gear.

Smith Robertson Museum, 528 Bloom St.; take High St. Exit from I-55. (601) 960-1457. Adults: $1, children: $.50. Open Tues. through Fri., 9 a.m. to 5 p.m.; Sat., 9 a.m. to noon, and Sun., 2 to 5 p.m. Accessible to handicapped.

Housed in this city's first public school for black children (circa 1894), the museum relates the life, history, and culture of black Mississippians from early settlement and slavery to the present, a story of pain as well as progress. Exhibits are divided into periods and topics—prints of slaves aboard ship, cotton sacks and bales from plantation days, Civil War artifacts and information about blacks in that conflict, photos and materials from Reconstruction and from civil rights successes in the 1960s. There are clothing, books, and photos regarding education of blacks in Mississippi, and biographical information and photos of the first black women in the state legislature. Other materials include artifacts from the local historical district as well as quilts and ceramics, letters and books of author Richard Wright, and a tuxedo made by a self-taught tailor.

Meridian

Jimmie Rodgers Museum, in Highland Park, off 39th Ave., south of I-20. (601) 485-1808. Admission: $2, children under 10: free with parent. Open Mon. through Sat., 10 a.m. to 4 p.m.; Sun., 1 to 5 p.m.; closed Thanksgiving, Christmas, and New Year's Day. Accessible to handicapped.

Known as "The Singing Brakeman," Jimmie Rodgers was a railroad man forced to turn to a less strenuous life by tuberculosis. He parlayed his musical talent and railroad songs into unshakeable fame, eventually becoming memorialized in Nashville as the man who started country music. He died in 1933 at age 35. Established in 1975 in his hometown, this museum displays photos, clothing, sheet music, instruments, records, correspondence, railroad paraphernalia, and other items from the singer's short life. On hand, for example, are his straw hat and Martin guitar. There's also a biographical video. In late May the town hosts a country music fest to commemorate the singer's music.

Pascagoula

Scranton Floating Museum, Pascagoula River Park, off Rte. 90, just west of town across the river. (601) 762-6017. Suggested donation: $1 for adults and $.50 for children. Open Tues. through Sat., 10 a.m. to 5 p.m.; Sun., 1 to 5 p.m.; closed Mon. and major holidays. Limited access for handicapped.

A converted 26-year-old, 70-foot-long shrimp boat, this museum reflects regional shrimping activity and provides insights into the local coastal environment. The vessel is typical of large Southern shrimpers and you get a close-up look at the rigging, trawls, galley, wheelhouse, crew quarters, navigational and electronic gear, even a turtle excluder device mandated for shrimp boats by the federal government. Below decks are exhibits concerning beachcombing and area natural history and aquariums filled with local fish. All in all, this is a loud and clear echo of shrimping and boatbuilding still active in this locale.

Petal

International Checker Hall of Fame, 220 Lynnray Rd., 2 miles from downtown. (601) 582-7090. Adults: $2, seniors and children: $1. Open by appointment, Mon. through Fri., 10 a.m. to 3 p.m. Accessible to handicapped.

This 40,000-square-foot tribute to the game, or sport, of checkers is an elegant venue for world tournaments every other year (one in 1991) and an interesting glimpse into the popularity and challenge of checkers. The two King Halls have checkerboard floors and ceilings, and a Hall of Flags testifies to the scores of nations that play some version of checkers. There's also a checkers library, and the artifacts room contains sets and boards from around the world as well as other games and dolls. The Hall of Fame honors writers, masters, and other people associated with checkers. Part of the Walker estate, the hall is cast in medieval decor and is compelling in architectural, as well as sporting, terms.

Missouri

Florissant

St. Stanislaus Jesuit Historical Museum, 700 Howdershell Rd.; take McDonnell Blvd. from I-270. (314) 837-3525. Donation of $1 suggested. Open Mar. 15 to Dec. 15, Sun., 1 to 4 p.m., and Wed., 10 a.m. to 3 p.m.; other days by appointment for groups. No facilities for handicapped.

Leading the westward tide of trappers, traders, soldiers, and settlers were friars seeking to Christianize and educate the Indians, claiming hearts and minds and souls, if not territory. Prominent among them were the Black Robes. This museum focuses on the Jesuit missionary effort in the Great Plains and Northern Rockies and displays tools, church vessels, and religious books spanning five centuries. Woodcarvings, silverwork, period maps, and the oldest organ made in St. Louis highlight the collections of this truly pioneering museum on the threshold of the Old and Wild West.

Hamilton

J. C. Penney Museum, N. Davis St., on Rte. 13, in middle of town. (816) 583-9997. Donations welcome. Open Tues. through Sat., 10 a.m. to noon, and 1 to 5 p.m. No facilities for handicapped.

Housed in the J. C. Penney Bldg., which is also home to the public library, this museum honors the department store founder who was born near Hamilton. He began his entrepreneurial efforts with the Golden Rule stores in Wyoming in 1902, and the rest is retail history. The museum displays family photos, photos of the early stores, and examples of early advertising; plus personal mementos, books he wrote, and items related to his Masonic activities. He also was an accomplished farmer, and other parts of the collection consist of farm implements and other items related to these endeavors.

Kansas City

Hallmark Visitors Center, Crown Center Complex, Hallmark Square (parking available off Gillham Rd. at 25th St.) (816) 274-5672. Free. Open Mon. through Fri., 9 a.m. to 5 p.m.; Sat., 9:30 a.m. to 4:30 p.m., and most holidays. Accessible to handicapped.

When you care enough about cards—their history and how they're made—this is the place to see. The 10,000-square-foot Hallmark Center includes 12 major exhibits recounting the story of Hallmark cards, from memorabilia dating back 75 years to contemporary craftsmen at work. Sculpture, paintings, audiovisuals, and interactive displays give the collection a multimedia cast. Artisans demonstrate die-cutting and printing techniques, and machines make ribbon bows. In addition to greeting cards, you will find posters, puzzles, Crayola crayons, and other products made by Hallmark.

The Toy and Miniature Museum of Kansas City, 5235 Oak St., near I-435 and campus of University of Missouri at Kansas City. (816) 333-2055. Adults: $2.50, seniors: $2, students: $1.75, children 5 to 12: $1.50. Open Wed. through Sat., 10 a.m. to 4 p.m., and Sun., 1 to 5 p.m.; closed Mon., Tues., major holidays, and the first two weeks after Labor Day. Accessible to handicapped.

In this museum, toys transcend mere playthings. Made-to-scale working miniatures, such as clocks and scissors, are precisely fashioned for the adult collector. Indeed, the craftsmanship is such that a tiny violin strung with human hair is playable. Exhibits include lead soldiers, cast-iron farm implements, cars and trains, peep shows, and more than 85 antique dollhouses. The houses date from the mid-19th century to the mid-20th and the architecture of some, to say nothing of the furnishings, is amazing—mansard roofs, turrets, and spires, fan and bay windows, intricate molding.

This is truly a place for all those who don't wish to put away the things of childhood.

St. Joseph

Pony Express Museum, 914 Penn St.; take 10th St. Exit from Rte. 36. (816) 232-8471. Adults: $1, children 7 to 15: $.50. Open Oct. 1 to Mar. 31, Tues. through Sat., 1 to 5 p.m., and Sun. and holidays, 2 to 5 p.m.; Apr. 1 through Sept. 30, Mon. through Sat., 9 a.m. to 5 p.m., and Sun. and holidays, 2 to 5 p.m.; closed Thanksgiving, Christmas Eve and Day, and New Year's Eve and Day. Ramp for wheelchair access provided on request.

Today, you can send a document from the East to California almost instantly by fax; 130 years ago the facts were quite different. It took almost four weeks for mail to travel from "rail's end" to San Francisco. The Pony Express, launched here in 1860, sought to cut that time in half with relay riders and fast horses. Dedicated to that brief but heroic episode, this museum occupies the Pike's Peak Stables, original eastern terminus of the Pony Express. A satellite of the St. Joseph Museum, the facility displays diverse mementos of the Pony Express operation—photos, fliers, weapons, saddles, blacksmith and wheelwright tools, and the most comprehensive photographic exhibit of the known trail and station sites. It is a gallop back in time.

Jesse James Home, 12th and Penn Sts.; take 10th St. Exit from Rte. 36. (816) 232-8206. Adults: $2, students: $.50. Open Apr., May, Sept., and Oct., Mon. through Fri., 10 a.m. to 4 p.m., and weekends, 1 to 5 p.m.; June through Aug., Mon. through Fri., 10 a.m. to 5 p.m., and weekends, 1 to 5 p.m.; weekends only during Jan., Feb., Mar., and Nov. Limited facilities for handicapped.

The old axiom about living and dying by the gun was never more true than for Jesse James, arguably America's most famous, or infamous, outlaw. Jesse died in this house at age 34, shot by former gang member Bob Ford. The bullet hole from the fatal shot still marks the wall where Jesse fell. The house, now a complete museum devoted to the bandit, contains original furnishings—stove, chairs, spinning wheel—as well as weapons, newspapers, photos, clothing, and other artifacts. Publications and an audiotape give added information on Jesse's life and times.

St. Joseph State Hospital Psychiatric Museum, 3400 Frederick Ave., less than 1 mile west of I-29. (816) 387-2300. Donations welcome. Open Mon. through Fri., 8:30 a.m. to 4 p.m.; also open weekends, 1 to 5 p.m., Apr. through Sept.; closed holidays. Accessible to handicapped.

Would someone be crazy to run a psychiatric museum? Not if it illustrates how far we've come in treating the mentally ill. An early tranquilizer was a club. Another was an upright wood coffin-like device called the clock case or mad box in which a patient might be confined for days. There are reproductions of the 17th-century "bath of surprise," where a patient was dropped through a platform into a tub of cold water, and a 19th-century O'Halloran's swing, where a strapped-in patient was spun around. Dioramas show use of crude straight jackets and blood-letting, and there's a ceramic skull which illustrates how the ancients dealt with mental illness— by opening a hole in the skull to permit evil spirits to exit. The museum has an intact seclusion room and a 1920s surgical display presenting hundreds of objects removed from one patient who swallowed bolts, pins, thimbles, and more. One section focuses on history of the hospital, with century-old photos, fine wood furnishings, hydrotherapy tubs, ECT devices, and patients' artwork.

St. Louis

Decorating Products Industry Museum, 1050 N. Lindbergh Blvd., near corner of Olive Blvd., off Rte. 270. (314) 991-3470. Free. Open Mon. through Fri., 8:30 a.m. to 4:30 p.m.; closed holidays. Accessible to handicapped.

Located on the second floor of the National Decorating Products Association building, this collection consists of items donated by manufacturers and retailers in the paint and wallpaper industry. Among materials exhibited are Dutch Boy paint dolls, old clip art, retailers' scrapbooks, signs, paints, swatchbooks, wallpaper stands, the first paint trays and rollers, and other tools and tidbits of the trade.

National Association of Civilian Conservation Corps Alumni Museum, 16 Hancock Ave., Jefferson Barracks Historic Park. (314) 487-8666. Free. Open Mon. through Fri., 8 a.m. to 4 p.m. Accessible to handicapped.

Established in 1987 and located in a World War II Army officers' quarters, this museum pays homage to Franklin D. Roosevelt's tree army, the Civilian Conservation Corps, established in 1933 to pit unemployed young men in the fight against erosion of natural resources. Over the decade of its tree planting (and some 3 billion were planted), road building, and land reclamation, nearly 3 million people served in the CCC. There were CCC camps in every state, and the museum draws on alumni across the country to collect maps, posters, jackets, banners, surveying gear, and other artifacts from the various camps. It's still gathering materials and is working on a history of the CCC.

The Dog Museum, 1721 S. Mason Rd., off I-64 and I-270. (314) 821-3647. Adults: $2, children 5 to 14: $.50. Open Mon. through Sat., 9 a.m. to 5 p.m., and Sun., 1 to 4 p.m. No facilities for handicapped.

Despite the popularity of cats, pigs, and other animals for pets, the dog remains man's best friend. It's only fitting there should be a museum devoted to this age-old companion. Galleries and exhibits primarily feature prints, paintings, and sculpture of various breeds of canines. A video theater makes available a choice of 80 tapes on pure-bred, guide, and hunting dogs, with tips on selection, care, training and showing. Every Sun. afternoon a dog-of-the-week program features an actual dog and dog owner.

Oklahoma

Beaver

Beaver City Museum, Main St., near junction of Rtes. 83 and 270. No telephone. Donation requested. Open Mon. through Sat., 11 a.m. to 5 p.m.; Sun., 1 to 5 p.m. Accessible to handicapped.

With one exception, the displays here are nicely representative of the kinds of things that small local Oklahoma museums offer. Occupying two rooms of what began as a sod house are cases of Indian articles, including examples of rock wampum; the skull of a buffalo that was part of the huge herds that once dominated the area; and dolls, eyeglasses, and other relics of early life here along the Jones and Plummer Trail, a major artery for hide traders, freighters, and cattle drovers. The exceptional part of this museum's offerings is its collection of beads—6,300 strands in all—that fill two large showcases in one room. There are beads of every imaginable type made from virtually every material, and, seen in such quantity, they create an unusually colorful display. Two strands of beads each hail from all the states in the Union, hundreds represent the state of Oklahoma, and hundreds more come from all corners of the world.

Catoosa

Arkansas River Historical Society's Museum at Tulsa Port of Catoosa, 5350 Cimmarron Rd., 4 miles north of I-44 on 193rd and E

Aves. (918) 266-2291. Free. Open Mon. through Fri., 8 a.m. to 4:30 p.m.; closed Sat., Sun., and all major holidays. Accessible to handicapped.

Oklahoma only looks like a landlocked state. Actually, along with sister state Arkansas, it is connected through a remarkable system of 25,000 miles of inland waterways to the Mississippi River, the Gulf of Mexico, the Great Lakes, and the St. Lawrence Seaway. The Tulsa Port of Catoosa has handled millions of tons of shipping since the area was developed in the early 1970s. Central to exhibits devoted to the history of the Arkansas River, and the most popular exhibit in this small museum, is a working scale model of a river lock and dam. Other interesting exhibits include items recovered from a steamboat that sank in the river in 1900 and a pictorial documentation of the shipment of 134 wheeled military vehicles from the Port of Catoosa to Camp McCoy in Wisconsin. Collections of local historical interest include Indian tools and weapons found along the Arkansas River.

Claremore

J. M. Davis Gun Museum, 333 N. Lynn Riggs Blvd.; take Claremore Exit off I-44. (918) 341-5707. Free. Open Mon. through Sat., 8:30 a.m. to 5 p.m.; Sun. and holidays, 1 to 5 p.m.; closed Thanksgiving and Christmas. Accessible to handicapped.

Twenty thousand firearms are showcased in this 40,000-square-foot facility. They span the historic spectrum from the 1300s to the present and cover such themes as the evolution of ignition systems to guns of outlaws. Outstanding individual specimens abound: the world's tiniest manufactured gun, the Kolibri, weighing 2½ ounces; cased sets of rat-tail dueling pistols; a Chinese hand cannon; whaling guns; Kentucky rifles; and many more. Despite the museum's name, guns are not all there is. Collector J. M. Davis also specialized in fine beer steins (Bavarian salt glaze, Villeroy and Boch, Mettlach), music boxes (cylinder, disc and hand-pump), swords, knives, animal horns, musical instruments, Rogers sculpture, and World War I posters. The high quality of presentation and the diversity of subjects at this museum combine to make this a rewarding stop for people of all ages and interests.

Dewey

Tom Mix Museum, 721 N. Delaware, off Rte. 75, 5 miles north of Bartlesville. (918) 534-1555. Free. Open Tues. through Fri., 9 a.m. to 5 p.m.; Sat. and Sun., 2 to 5 p.m.; closed Mon., all major holidays, and on Tues. when holiday falls on a Mon. Accessible to handicapped.

"King of the Cowboys" was the title bestowed on Tom Mix, the immensely popular star of Western movies whose 30-year Hollywood career actually started in Guthrie, Oklahoma. His careers as soldier (he was wounded on San Juan Hill during the Spanish-American War), prize fighter, bartender, band major, and trick roper that preceded a stint as movie stunt rider, are all glimpsed in exhibits here, but his years as movie idol are the main focus. Saddles used by this superb horseman, movie stills, posters, clothes from his extravagant Western-style wardrobe, and other personal items all pay tribute to the original "good guy in the white hat," a handsome, fascinating figure who led a most colorful life.

Guthrie

State Capital Publishing Museum, 301 W. Harrison; from I-35, take Rte. 33 west to 2nd St., go south 4 blocks. (405) 282-4123. Free. Open Tues. through Fri., 9 a.m. to 5 p.m.; Sat., 10 a.m. to 4 p.m.; Sun., 1 to 4 p.m. Facilities for handicapped soon to be completed.

"State Capital" here refers to the town of Guthrie's role as original capital of Oklahoma, since relocated to Oklahoma City. The 1902 building housing this museum, site of the largest printing plant in the Southwest from 1900 to 1910, was the fourth home of the first newspaper published in Oklahoma Territory, and has been mostly restored. Nineteenth-century prints, bookbinding technology, Victorian commercial architecture, publisher Frank Hilton Greer, and capital relocation are all topics interpreted in this printing house museum. This was also the largest stationery supply house west of the Mississippi, and the original sales gallery has been returned to the way it was in 1904.

Oklahoma City

International Photography Hall of Fame and Museum, 2100 NE 52nd St., in Kirkpatrick Center, ¾ mile from I-35 or I-44. (405) 424-4055. Adults: $5, seniors and children over 5: $3.50. Open June through Aug., Mon. through Sat., 9 a.m. to 6 p.m., and Sun., noon to 6 p.m.; Sept. through May, Mon. through Fri., 9:30 a.m. to 5 p.m., and Sat., 9 a.m. to 6 p.m., and Sun., noon to 6 p.m.; closed Thanksgiving and Christmas. Accessible to handicapped.

Only one of several museums, galleries, and exhibits in the Kirkpatrick Center, this museum features traveling photo exhibits from around the world, montages from its own permanent collection of more than 3,000 works of major photographers, NASA prints, antique cameras by the hundreds, antique photography equipment, and memorabilia. Most fascinating, perhaps, is the museum's 50-foot-wide landscape laserscape of the Grand Canyon, billed as the world's largest photo-mural.

Sanamu African Gallery, 2100 NE 52nd St., in Kirkpatrick Center. (405) 424-7760. Adults: $5, children: $3. Open Mon. through Sat., 10 a.m. to 5 p.m.; Sun., 1 to 5 p.m. Accessible to handicapped.

African traditional arts, crafts and artifacts in the middle of Mid-America? Yes, indeed, for here is a unique collection of antique musical instruments, sculpture, paintings, masks, crosses, basketry, textiles, and carved doors from West Africa, Ethiopia, Sierra Leone, and other nations on the Dark Continent. Other attractions in the Kirkpatrick Center include the International Photography Hall of Fame and Museum (above), the Center of the American Indian, a Japanese garden and greenhouse, the U.S. Navy Galleries, and the Oklahoma Artists' Gallery.

Pawnee

Pawnee Bill Museum, Rte. 64, ½ mile west of Pawnee. (918) 762-2513. Free. Open during summer, Tues. through Sat., 9 a.m. to 5 p.m., and Sun., 1 to 5 p.m.; winter, Wed. through Sun., same hours. Accessible to handicapped.

Major Gordon W. Lille, better known as Pawnee Bill, was a Wild West show entrepreneur extraordinaire, and started his traveling spectacle in the 1880s with six Indians and his wife May who charmed audiences with her marksmanship and graceful bronc riding. Some years later he merged his show with that of his friend Buffalo Bill, and together they toured the world for several years. Housed here in Pawnee Bill's ranch home are personal effects and, more interesting, mementos from his famous Wild West show, including a huge billboard reputedly painted by Frederic Remington. Early on in his career Pawnee Bill became concerned about the plight of the American bison and started his own large herd of buffalo. Descendents of that herd still roam the ranch today.

Wagoner

Fashion House Museum, 804 Cherokee, in center of town. (918) 485-3642. Donation requested. Open by appointment only. Accessible to handicapped.

Two hundred years of fashion are unveiled in a 1902 Victorian house in this historic lakeside village. The collection of designer gowns, dresses, and other modish articles of clothing stems from the years that museum owner Lucille Carpenter spent at MGM Studios in Hollywood. High style is the common denominator here among clothing that ranges from women's antique frocks to the fashions of such *haute couture* designers as Adrian—there are 16 of his dresses in the collection. The fun side of fashion hasn't been neglected; there is the raincoat that Gene Kelly wore in the movie *Singing in the Rain,* for instance. A group of rare fashion dolls rounds out the collection. A fashion show gleaned from the collection highlights an annual town-wide festival in July.

Tennessee

Bristol

Grand Guitar Music Museum, 875 New Kingsport Hwy., immediately off Exit 74-A from I-81. (615) 968-2277. Adults: $1. Open daily, 10 a.m. to 5 p.m. No facilities for handicapped.

Some 25 years ago, Joe Morrell, a retail music man, began collecting old and unusual stringed instruments. In 1983 he built a museum for his collection, erecting a structure that could not fail to get attention—a three-story, 70-foot-long guitar. A monument to stringed instruments is not out of place here; he figures more than 50 nationally-known country and bluegrass artists live within a 100-mile radius of Bristol. The museum contains instruments shaped like a shovel, a pig, and an elephant, a fiddle made of matchsticks, and another instrument made from an armadillo. There are auto-harps, violins, dulcimers, mandolins, and ukuleles; in all, 250 to 300 stringed instruments from across the country and around the world. In addition, there are old wire recorders, cylinder machines, and transcription devices predating the era of platters and tapes, and old microphones from a recently acquired radio station that first aired in 1929. Other exhibits include clothing and memorabilia from country and bluegrass entertainers.

Chattanooga

National Knife Museum, 7201 Shallowford Rd.; take Exit 5 from

I-75. (615) 892-5007. Free. Open Mon. through Fri., 9 a.m. to 4 p.m.; Sat., 10 a.m. to 4 p.m. First floor accessible to handicapped.

Situated in the headquarters of the National Knife Collectors Association, and started in 1981, this museum occupies two floors and consists primarily of cold steel—at least 20,000 blades dating from the 17th century, representing cultures and countries around the world and worth $6 million to $10 million. There are swords and bayonets from various wars and armies as well as all manner of knives. The collection does not attempt to show the evolution of the knife or tell a story as such. Rather, the blades are grouped by donor and displayed in cases or on walls. A few accoutrements are included—some sheaths and scabbards and some old honing implements from the days of itinerant sharpeners.

Crossville

Cumberland Homestead Tower Museum, Rte. 96C; take Rte. 127 from I-40; about halfway between Knoxville and Nashville. (615) 456-9663. Free. Open Mon., Tues., Thurs., and Sat., 10 a.m. to 5 p.m., and Sun., 1 to 5 p.m.; closed Wed., Easter, Thanksgiving, and Labor Day. No facilities for handicapped.

Franklin D. Roosevelt's New Deal, among other things, generated a huge homesteading effort on rural lands throughout the country for the years 1934–1946. Crossville was one of more than 100 such homesteading units, but is believed to be the only one remaining intact. People from Tennessee, Georgia, Alabama, and North Carolina settled on homesteads of five to 50 acres and worked cooperatively. Located in the administration building, the museum displays letters of application and complaint, receipts, photos of houses, floor plans, old wood stoves, homemade toys, curtain stretchers, washboards and soap, utensils, appliances, locally-made furniture, and other items reflecting the rugged life and modest life style of these 20th-century settlers. The octagonal sandstone tower, which once contained water for the homestead, can be climbed for a $.50 fee.

Goodletsville

Museum of Beverage Containers and Advertising, Ridgecrest Dr.; take Exit 98 from I-65. (615) 859-5237. Admission: $2. Open Mon.

through Sat., 9 a.m. to 5 p.m., and Sun., 1 to 5 p.m.; closed major holidays. Accessible to handicapped.

This is another one of those museums that burgeoned from a personal collection—what was once a modest stash of beer and soda cans has become a 28,000-item assemblage, including rare and limited containers, both full and empty. Acquisition has been varied and often fruitful. Reportedly, a former inspector at the Panama Canal donated his collection of 30- to 50-year-old beer bottles. The advertising art comprises clocks with logos, neon signs, pool table lamps, and old beer ads, among other pieces. The collection is forever changing and growing and the owner offers duplicates and leftovers for sale in an adjacent shop.

Johnson City

General Shale Museum of Ancient Brick, 3211 N. Roan St., off I-181. (615) 282-4661. Free. Open Mon. through Fri., 8 a.m. to 5 p.m.; closed holidays. No facilities for handicapped.

Tobacco gets a lot of bad press these days, but despite the furor over health and manners, tobacco itself is an authentic American product and the craftsmanship and artwork associated with it remain remarkable. Carved meerschaum pipes, elegant snuff boxes and mulls, silver tampers, colorful cigar labels, and handsome tobacco jars are among the antiques and collectibles gathered from around the world. It also exhibits cigar store figurines, glass pipes, a cigar ribbon quilt, and a coiled Staffordshire puzzle pipe. Photos, posters, and other displays convey the economic and social role of tobacco in the region, the country, and the world.

Pigeon Forge

Carbo's Smoky Mountain Police Museum, Rte. 441; take Exit 407 from I-40. (615) 453-1358. Adults: $4.50, children 10 and under: $2.50. Open 9:30 a.m. to 5 p.m., weekends in Apr., every day but Tues. in May, daily June through Aug., and every day but Thurs., Sept. through Oct.; closed Nov. through Feb. Limited facilities for handicapped.

This museum, originally in New Orleans, relocated to the Smoky Mountains in the mid-1970s—"Too much crime in New Orleans," according to owner Bert Carbo, a retired dentist who started his collection with a single badge in the 1950s. He now has four spacious aisles of display cases plus wall mounts showing scores of badges, billy clubs, firearms, handcuffs, uniforms, and other law enforcement items—mostly domestic but some foreign forces are represented, too. There's a drug display and some historic pieces, such as mementos from the Texas Rangers. One highlight involves material related to Sheriff Buford Pusser of *Walking Tall* fame, including the car in which he was killed.

Vonore

Sequoyah Birthplace Museum, on Rte. 360, 1 mile off Rte. 411. (615) 884-6246. Adults: $2.50, children 6 to 12: $1.25. Open Mar. 1 through Dec. 31, Mon. through Sat., 10 a.m. to 6 p.m., and Sun., noon to 6 p.m. Accessible to handicapped.

In 1821 a Cherokee named Sequoyah, who could not read or write in any language, introduced to the Cherokee nation an 85-character syllabary that enabled his people to become literate. His single-handed achievement is nothing short of extraordinary. This museum opened in 1987, honoring the man and his accomplishment and retracing the entire span of Cherokee culture. Here you will find centuries-old arrowheads and pottery; textiles, implements and clothing from pre-European and post-European contact; and a section on Sequoyah where you can read the syllabary and hear it pronounced on "hearphones" and encounter literature and artifacts relating to his life. A final exhibit deals with the Trail of Tears, the Cherokees' bitter and brutal exile to Oklahoma.

Waverly

World O' Tools Museum, on Rte. 13, 2 miles south of Waverly Courthouse. (615) 296-3218. Free. Open by appointment, advance notice is requested. Accessible to handicapped.

A private, one-man museum, this collection covers what its name suggests, but it's far from a few clamps and mallets and chisels. The 2,400-square-foot building contains more than 20,000 tools, ranging from the trades of cooper and tinsmith to those of welder and machinist. The antique, the odd, and the common all find a home here and span decades of development and use. In addition, the collection includes tool-related art, figurines, miniatures, books, and catalogs, some a century old.

General Shale is one of the country's largest brick manufacturers and it wouldn't be surprising if the corporate lobby displayed a few samples of the product line. However, the size of this collection is what an entire building might be to a single brick. Certainly unusual and possibly unique, at least for an industry display, this collection embraces bricks from notable structures around the world—the Great Wall of China, Egyptian tombs, the Roman Forum, even two 10,000-year-old blocks from beneath the ancient walls of Jericho. Included, too, are samples from Colonial Williamsburg, from ballast on the *Mayflower*, and from Jefferson Davis's home. For several years, the firm's marketing director and self-taught archaeologist had carte blanche to retrieve ancient bricks from Europe to Asia to the Americas. Good conversation pieces, sure, but they also convey a message about the durability of brick, and that's some solid advertising.

Memphis

National Ornamental Metal Museum, 374 W. California Ave.; take Delaware St. Exit from I-55 north. (901) 774-6380. Adults: $1.50, seniors: $1, children 5 to 18: $.75. Open Tues. through Sat., 10 a.m. to 5 p.m., and Sun., noon to 5 p.m.; closed Mon. and major holidays. First-floor galleries accessible to handicapped.

The importance of metals and metalworking trades spans the centuries, from tools and weapons to ornaments to building and transportation. This museum is devoted to the preservation of fine metalwork from the past, be it jewelry or architectural design, and to the encouragement of contemporary artisans. Exhibitions change, and recent showings have included silver holloware and flatware, 19th-century French ironwork, and a collection of handmade knives. You can watch blacksmiths work at a fully-operational forge, and each fall the museum holds two repair days when it will fix metal items brought in by the public.

Morristown

Crockett Tavern Museum, 2002 Morningside Dr.; take Rte. 25 from I-81, then 11-E Bypass to town. (615) 581-8585. Adults: $2, children

5 to 16: $1. Open May 1 through Oct. 30, Mon. through Sat., 10 a.m. to 5 p.m., and Sun., 1 to 5 p.m. No facilities for handicapped.

Davy Crockett was the quintessential American hero—frontiersman, politician, adventurer, legend in his own time. This tavern, a replica of that established by Davy's parents, was a stage and wagon stop for people pushing west, and this area was his boyhood home. Authentic construction and furnishings and utensils give the structure a true early 19th-century flavor. The loom room beneath the kitchen holds the most complete example of pioneer flax-making equipment in the country, and includes loom, spinning wheels, winding blades, warping bars, and scutching knives.

Nashville

Museum of Tobacco Art and History, 800 Harrison St., downtown, 4 blocks north of the state capitol. (615) 271-2349. Free. Open Tues. through Sat., 10 a.m. to 4 p.m.; closed Mon., Sun., and major holidays. Accessible to handicapped.

V
WEST

Alaska

Fort Richardson

Fort Richardson Wildlife Center, Room 114, Bldg. 600, 2½ miles north of Anchorage on Glenn Hwy. (907) 863-8288 or -8113. Free. Open Mon., Tues., Thurs. and Fri., 8:30 a.m. to 5 p.m.; Wed., 8:30 to 11:30 a.m.; closed weekends and national holidays. Accessible to handicapped.

Alaska boasts countless museums and exhibits, both large and small, devoted to displaying the state's abundant variety of wildlife. Sometimes specimens are part of habitat displays, sometimes they merely line the walls of a room. The modestly presented, but comprehensive collection here (like the collection at nearby Elmendorf Air Force Base) is typical in the variety of its offerings. What is atypical among these mounted native birds, mammals, and sportfish is that so many are recordbook trophies. The world record Dall's sheep is here, as are world-record-class brown bears, a rare glacier bear, and several other "biggest" specimens.

Haines

Sheldon Museum and Cultural Center, corner of Front and Main Sts., next to the small boat harbor. (907) 766-2366. Adults: $2, children under 18: free. Open daily during summer, 1 to 5 p.m., and to 10 p.m. on Mon.; open during winter on Sun., Mon. and Wed., 1 to 4 p.m., and by appointment. Accessible to handicapped.

Outstanding among this museum's nicely-rounded exhibits that trace area history is its Chilkat Dance Blanket collection, fine blankets woven in traditional ways only by Tlingit women and frequently used for traditional ceremonies. Since weaving a blanket was each woman's personal statement, all in the collection are different, and all are exemplary. An exceptionally rare example is one that was never finished—according to tradition, if a woman died before completing a blanket it was buried with her. Other historical aspects of the Chilkat Valley finding focus in this rustic wooden building are the history and culture of the Tlingit Indian people, the unique transportation history of the area, and pioneer history, including gold rush days and the fishing and logging industries. Wall exhibits, recreated rooms, and short movies adequately cover the latter two aspects of the valley's history, but it's in the telling of the intricate culture of the Tlingits that the museum really shines.

Homer

Miller Museum, East Rd., off Williams St. (907) 235-8819. Admission: $3. Open May through Oct., Mon. through Sat., 10 a.m. to 5 p.m. No facilities for handicapped.

Who would expect to find the world's largest collection of fancy ornamental hair combs and hair art in Homer, Alaska? Then again, where would you expect to find such a collection? Artistically mounted in wall cases here are some 3,800 delicately-wrought combs from the Orient, Africa, and Europe, dating from 800 B.C. and including many tall Spanish combs worn with mantillas. They are fashioned from ivory, tortoise shell, lacquered wood, and celluloid, just to name a few materials. They are embellished with precious metals, precious and semi-precious stones, cutwork, inlay, carving, and extinct Blue Kingfisher feathers. Hair art? That's art made from human hair, most of it dating from before 1850. A particularly fine example here is a picture composed of locks of hair donated by women in memory of a friend who died. In addition, the museum contains materials of historic and prehistoric Alaskan cultures.

Kodiak

Baranov Museum, 101 Marine Way, downtown near the Alaska ferry dock. (907) 486-5920. Admission: $1, children under 12: free.

Open mid-May through mid-Sept., Mon. through Fri., 10 a.m. to 3
p.m.; Sat. and Sun., noon to 4 p.m.; mid-Sept. through mid-May,
Mon. through Fri., 11 a.m. to 3 p.m., and Sat., noon to 3 p.m.
Accessible to handicapped.

Among the Koniag, Aleut, Russian, and American objects
showcased in this 1808 woodframe residence/store/warehouse the
Russian items stand out. Lustrous brass samovars, silverware,
icons, money (including a sealskin note), trading beads, figurines,
and a fine collection of elaborately hand-painted eggs testify to the
wealth and the richly-textured life led by members of early Russian
commercial companies in the area. The building also contains
pioneer furnishings, including a piano that traveled by sailing ship
around Cape Horn, and objects from pre-history of bone, slate,
graywacke, gut, and grass.

Palmer

Museum of Alaska Transportation and Industry, Mile 40 Glenn
Highway. (907) 745-4493. Adults: $3. Open Tues. through Sat., 8
a.m. to 4 p.m. Limited facilities for handicapped.

Be warned: This museum is mostly outdoors, so dress for the
weather. Parked along pathways throughout these extensive
grounds are all manner of wheeled and winged vehicles. Railroad
engines and cars, farm equipment, horse-drawn wagons, automobiles of many makes and models, fire trucks, helicopters, am-
bulances, and airplanes ranging from a 1928 Curtiss Wright Travel
Air 6000 to a modern jet—these make up the bulk of this spectacular display and are augmented by the occasional boat, buzz
bomb, missile, and road grader. A detailed brochure lets you be
your own guide through the collection, and for indoor types the
Don Sheldon Building houses historical photographs, portraits of
bush pilots, and more vehicles and engines.

Skagway

Corrington's Eskimo Museum, 5th and Broadway, downtown.
(907) 983-2580, or -2579. Admission: $.50 per person or $1 per
family. Open May 25 through Sept. 25, 9 a.m. to 7 p.m. Accessible
to handicapped.

For people wishing to get a broad overview of Alaska history,
this museum is a good place to start. More than 1,000 artifacts

make up 32 exhibits tracing Alaska history from the crossing of early travelers over the Asian land bridge 10,000 years ago to the construction of the trans-Alaska oil pipeline. Tour guides lead visitors past displays portraying the state's story through early explorers, whaling days, 100 years of Russian rule, the Civil War, gold rush days, and more. Accompanying each exhibit are scrimshaw walrus ivory pieces that depict stories, songs, and legends relevant to the event. The 800 ivory sculptures represent the work of more than 90 Eskimo artists living and dead, and are a unique adjunct to the story of a unique part of the world.

Valdez

The Valdez Museum, 101 Chenega, 307 miles from Anchorage on the Glenn and Richard Hwy. (907) 835-2764. Suggested donation: $1. Open May through Sept., daily, 10 a.m. to 7 p.m.; Oct. through Apr., Tues. through Sat., 1 to 6 p.m. Accessible to handicapped.

The Valdez area gained world renown for the oil spill that took place off its shores in 1989, and the event has not been forgotten here. This local museum, which naturally focuses on such local historical highlights as the gold rush, mining, maritime activities, and the growth of the community, has installed a display telling the grim story of the spill and the cleanup operations that followed. The Alaska pipeline, for which Valdez is a port, is also the subject of an exhibit, as is the tremendous earthquake that rocked the area in 1964.

Arizona

Green Valley

Titan Missile Museum, Duval Mine Rd.; take Exit 69 from I-19 south of Tucson, which is well marked. (602) 791-2929. Adults: $4, seniors and military: $3, juniors 10 to 17: $2. Open daily, Nov. 1 through Apr. 30, 9 a.m. to 5 p.m.; May 1 through Oct. 31, Wed. through Sun.; closed Christmas Day; last tour 4 p.m. Limited access for handicapped.

Operated under the auspices of the Pima Air Museum at nearby Davis Monthan Air Force Base, this is the world's only intercontinental ballistic missile museum. Part of the exhibit at this missile complex is above ground; the rest is a tour—definitely a guided tour—of the below-ground missile silo and support systems. For the tourist, it is certainly awesome, and possibly disturbing, considering the capabilities and possible uses of such firepower. Tempering such mixed feelings is the knowledge that the military opened the site to the public so that it might stand as "a memorial to all loyal Americans who served their country so valiantly in peace and war."

Kingman

Mohave Museum of History and Arts, 400 W. Beale, ¼ mile from Exit 48 off I-40. (602) 753-3195. Adults and children over 12: $1. Open Mon. through Fri., 10 a.m. to 5 p.m., and Sat. and Sun., 1 to

5 p.m.; closed major holidays. Ramps for wheelchairs; wheelchair available.

Specializing in the history of northwestern Arizona might seem to preclude exhibits on out-of-the-ordinary subjects, but such is not the case here. Local History, Prehistory to Present includes exhibits of locally-mined carved turquoise, a fine collection of historic Kachina dolls, and, in the Indian Room, a life-size wikiup, a type of Indian dwelling. Local history also includes Andy Devine, who was born and raised in the area and who went on to become the consummate cinematic cowboy sidekick. The Good Guys Wore White Hats is the name of the special exhibit that features movie posters and photos, family photos, personal memorabilia, and tributes to other famous cowboy actors with whom Devine starred. Out of the local domain is a collection of paintings of the U.S. presidents and their wives.

Mesa

Champlin Fighter Museum, 4636 Fighter Aces Dr., at Falcon Field (Mesa Airport), 5 miles east of Scottsdale, 10 miles east of Phoenix. (602) 830-4540. Adults: $5, young people: $2.50. Open daily, 10 a.m. to 5 p.m.; closed Easter, Thanksgiving, Christmas, and New Year's Day. Accessible to handicapped.

Airplane museums and collections abound in the U.S., but this is the world's only museum dedicated to showing the evolution of the fighter plane through World War I, World War II, Korea, and Vietnam. More than 30 fighter planes trace that evolution here, and fighter pilot memorabilia are also featured. A separate gun room is given over to more than 200 machine guns of various origins. For airplane art lovers, there is a large oil painting collection.

Patagonia

Stradling Museum of the Horse, Inc., 350 McKeown Ave., 1 block off Rte. 82. (602) 394-2264. Adults: $2, children 6 to 12: $.50. Open 9 a.m. to 5 p.m. daily, most of the year; closed Wed. from June 1 to Oct. 1; closed Thanksgiving and Christmas. Accessible to handicapped.

As a young girl, Anne Stradling, fascinated by her grandfather's beautiful carriages and silver-mounted harnesses, vowed that the automobile would never replace the horse in her heart. This museum is her tribute to the animal that carried our past on his back. Some 45 horse-drawn vehicles, ranging from stagecoaches to sleighs to fine carriages, fill one large barnlike room; saddles, harnesses, bits, and spurs from all over the world, including ancient Greece and Rome, fill another. Equine art includes works by well-known Western painters Frederic Remington, C.M. Russell, and Frank Tenney Johnson. An extensive Indian Room documents the close association between the American Indian and the horse.

Phoenix

Medical Museum, Phoenix Baptist Hospital Lobby, 6025 N. 20 Ave., entrance on Bethany, 1 block from ChrisTown Shopping Center. (602) 249-0212. Free. Open daily, 8 a.m. to 9 p.m. Accessible to handicapped.

Twelve glass-fronted cases make up this interesting exhibit of medical artifacts collected by Robert Kravetz, a physician with an interest in the medical practices of previous generations. Relatively tame medical antiquities, such as a physician's drug case and medicine chest from the 1700s, an 1870 English ophthalmoscope, and a 1929 blood pressure machine are on display here, as are some more provocative items, such as an English leech jar and a bleeding bowl. Shelves in other cases hold herbal, patent, and quack medicines—samples of licorice root, stomach bitters, Pluto water, and Hamlin's Wizard Oil Liniment among them—and exhibits of specific medicines include laxatives as well as medications for arthritis sufferers.

Telephone Pioneer Museum, 20 E. Thomas Rd., downtown, in U.S. West Plaza. (602) 630-2062. Free; garage parking next door at $1 per hour. Open Mon. through Fri., 8:30 a.m. to 4:30 p.m.; evenings and weekends by appointment. Accessible to handicapped.

One way to trace the changes in American culture from the turn of the century to the present is by looking at the different ways Americans have communicated over those years, especially by telephone. Among other pieces of primitive and sophisticated telephone and telegraph equipment here is one of the largest collections of old coin phones. There are prototype telephones—

experiments that for one reason or another never went into production—a large display of military communications equipment, and working telegraphs and teletype machines. Many of the displays, all of which track the story of telecommunications in the Southwest since the 1870s, are hands-on.

Scottsdale

Mouse House Museum, 3634 Civic Center Blvd., across from Senior Center and public parking structure; entrance in rear. (602) 990-2481. Free. Open Mon. through Thurs., 10 a.m. to 4 p.m.; closed month of August. Accessible to handicapped.

If you grew up with the nickname "Mouse," as did Olive Atwater Getz, you might have a special affection for those small rodents, at least in their more winsome forms. The focal point of Getz's collection of more than 3,000 mouse figures is a nine-room Victorian dollhouse that swarms with toy mice—dancing on the picnic table, soaking in the hot tub, sitting down to a hearty breakfast, and, in general, occupying the house from ground floor to attic. There are mice from all walks of life: factory mice, churchmice, housewife mice. And they are made of all sorts of materials; ivory, ceramic, wood, fabric. One wall is dedicated to the most famous mouse of all, with stuffed Mickeys, Mickey Mouse pillows, Mickey mugs, and Mickey buttons surrounding framed original celluloids from Walt Disney cartoons.

California

Boron

Twenty Mule Team Museum, 26962 Twenty Mule Team Rd.; take Boron Ave. Exit south from Rte. 58, 6 blocks to museum. (619) 762-5810. Donation suggested. Open daily, 10 a.m. to 4 p.m.; closed Easter, Thanksgiving, Christmas, and New Year's Day. Accessible to handicapped.

This is a small local museum with a very specific focus: the borax-laden wagons pulled by teams of 20 mules that once plied the trails of the California high desert and that were featured on an early television show hosted by, among others, Ronald Reagan. A highlight here is a large illuminated mural of a 20-mule team hauling a set of wagons in Death Valley; for years, the picture graced the bar of Boron's Silver Dollar Saloon. In addition to displays on the local borax mining industry (still in operation), the Santa Fe Railroad, local Indian tribes, and homesteading, there are exhibits on nearby Edwards Air Force Base and NASA and information on an innovative solar energy plant that operates in the locale.

Buena Park

Museum of Torture, 7662 Beach Blvd., on premises of Medieval Times Restaurant/Tournament, north of Lincoln Ave., south of Rte. 91, west of I-5, 1 block north of Knott's Berry Farm. (714) 521-4740.

Admission: $1. Open Mon. through Sat., 9 a.m. to 3 p.m. Accessible to handicapped.

This is not a museum for small children or for the faint of heart. Iron maidens, stretching racks, and 28 other authentic reproductions of inhumane devices commonly found in medieval dungeons and jails are featured here, most of them dating from the Spanish Inquisition. You can see, among other instruments of torture and ridicule, a hanging cage, complete with female manikin in a blood-soaked frock, where the victim was shackled, raised above the ground and left to starve to death. Another manikin is chained to a Judas Cradle, a gruesome device involving ropes, pulleys, and a sharp wooden pyramid. The museum is intended to add to the Spanish medieval history recreated in the restaurant-tournament performance.

Cherry Valley

Edward Dean Museum of Decorative Arts, 9401 Oak Glen Rd.; take Cherry Valley Exit from I-10 left to Beaumont Ave., which becomes Oak Glen Rd. (714) 845-2626. Admission: $1. Open Tues. through Fri., 1 to 4 p.m.; Sat. and Sun., 10 a.m. to 4:30 p.m.; closed Aug. and major holidays. Accessible to handicapped.

Nestled in the foothills, definitely off the beaten California track, is this gem of a museum that specializes in 17th- to 19-century European and Asian furniture, ceramics, glass, paintings, sculpture, accessories, and unusual objects. There is a unique collection of 18th-century sewing cabinets, for example, as well as snuff boxes, paperweights, wax portraits, and what has been called one of the best collections of Far Eastern bronzes in the United States. The setting is homelike—but a very fine home—with ornately carved English paneling, elaborate chandeliers, Persian carpets, and beautifully landscaped gardens.

Hollywood

Hollywood Studio Museum, 2100 N. Highland Ave.; from Rte. 101 south take Highland Ave. Exit to Odin St., left; from Rte. 101 north take Hollywood Bowl Exit right onto Odin. (213) 874-2276. Adults: $3.50, seniors and students: $2.50, children: $1. Open Sat. and Sun., 10 a.m. to 4 p.m. Accessible to handicapped.

Hooray for Hollywood! In 1913 director Cecil B. DeMille rented the barn that constitutes this museum, started a movie studio, and an industry was born. The building was moved in 1982 from its location between Hollywood and Sunset Boulevards to its present site across from the Hollywood Bowl, becoming a repository of costumes, props, and equipment from the pioneering days of film making. A pictorial gallery documents the history of the barn; there is a screening room and a reproduction of DeMille's office; and videos, posters, photogaphs, and personal memorabilia salute such early movie makers and stars as Charlie Chaplin, Mary Pickford, Douglas Fairbanks, and Rudolph Valentino.

Lingerie Museum, 6608 Hollywood Blvd., in Frederick's of Hollywood store; from Rte. 101, take Hollywood Blvd. west. (213) 466-5151. Free. Open daily, 10 a.m. to 6 p.m. No facilities for handicapped.

Naughty but nice. How else to describe Zsa Zsa Gabor's bra and lace panties from the movie *Lilly,* Cyd Charisse's leotard from *Silk Stockings,* Ethel Merman's foundation garments, Loretta Young's movie nightgowns, and a 1950s lacy corselette worn by Mamie Van Doren? All these and much more, including a black lace bra worn by Tony Curtis in *Some Like It Hot* and lingerie donated by such current celebrities as Madonna and Cher, are on show in the Celebrity Lingerie Hall of Fame behind the bold Art Deco facade of Frederick's of Hollywood's famous lingerie store. As if that weren't enough, the museum offers a retrospective exhibit of vintage Frederick's under fashions dating back to 1946. It could only happen in Hollywood.

Max Factor Museum of Beauty, 1666 N. Highland Ave.; from Rte. 101, take Hollywood Blvd. west, north ½ block on Highland Ave. (213) 463-6668. Free. Open daily, 10 a.m. to 4 p.m. No facilities for handicapped.

Max Factor began as wig maker and make-up artist to the Royal Ballet in czarist Russia, but left his mark on Hollywood, first creating the heavy make-up needed to render strong images in early black-and-white and color films, and later producing cosmetics for streetwear. He is said to have invented the false eyelash and the eyebrow pencil, original examples of which, along with other Factor cosmetics, are on display here. An entire wall showcases glamorous ads featuring famous movie stars, and hundreds of rare autographed photos of Hollywood's best-known faces line other walls. Among other artifacts and memorabilia that trace Hollywood cosmetic history are two devices that, fortunately, never reached the general public: a beauty calibrator, with screws and metal rods protruding from all points of the head, resembling an instrument of torture, but designed to pinpoint flaws on faces of screen beauties; and a kissing machine that tests the indelibility of lipstick by smacking two pairs of rubberized lips together to simulate a kiss.

Mr. Science Fiction's Fantastic Universe, 2495 Glendower Ave.; enter Griffith Park at Vermont and Los Feliz Aves., go 2 blocks to Cromwell, left, 2 short blocks to stop sign at Glendower Ave.; up Glendower, staying on avenue. (213) 666-6326. Donation suggested. Open most Sats., 1:30 to 3 p.m., and by appointment. No facilities for handicapped.

Bela Lugosi'a Dracula cape; life masks of Boris Karloff, Peter Lorre, and Vincent Price; a reconstruction of the robotrix from the 1927 movie classic *Metropolis;* Lon Chaney's make-up kit; Stephen King's first story manuscript—these rare items are only a few of the thousands of pieces of science fiction and horror film memorabilia displayed throughout this 18-room home of former horror movie magazine editor Forrest Ackerman. Ackerman considers the *Creature from the Black Lagoon* model from the 1952 film and the Martian war machine from *War of the Worlds* among his most valuable pieces, but he is also proud of his collections of horror and sci-fi related stamps, books, magazines, autographs (Mary Shelley, Jules Verne, and H.G. Wells), theater lobby cards, movie stills, games, toys, props, costumes, and paintings.

Julian

Julian Pioneer Museum, 2811 Washington St., on Rte. 78 near junction with Rte. 79. (619) 765-0227. Suggested adult contribution: $1. Open Apr. through Nov., Tues. through Sun., 10 a.m. to 4 p.m.; Dec. through Mar., Sat., Sun., and holidays, 10 a.m. to 4 p.m.; closed Mon. No facilities for handicapped.

Mounted animals and birds indigenous to the chaparral, a mountainous area not far from the coast with its own special climate, find abode here. All the more interesting, perhaps, to find in this small community museum a collection of lace that is considered the best in California, possibly in the West. Mounted on black felt in six-foot-long cases are samples of Battenburg lace, tatting, hand-made lace, and machine-made pieces, more than 200 different types. All are identified with labels, and such a comprehensive display shows the amazing variety of trims that can be created from thin air, some thread, and a needle or two. The museum also contains collections of local Indian artifacts, period clothing, and mining memorabilia.

Los Angeles

Museum of Neon Art, 704 Traction Ave., near Union Station, between 2nd and 3rd Sts. (213) 617-1580. Adults: $2.50, children under 15: free. Open Tues. through Sat., 11 a.m. to 5 p.m. No handicapped facilities in rest rooms.

This museum is just where it should be—right in the middle of downtown Los Angeles, a city whose history might be said to be written in neon. On permanent display are vintage pieces, many of them from old theater marquees, and many of them animated. The Melrose Theater lady, an example of Hollywood Byzantine architectural art dating from the 1920s, is sketched in bright neon; the crest-shaped Fox Venice theater marquee dates from the 1950s; a dairy sign features a calf that wags its tail; a woman dives into a pool on a motel sign; and Nipper the dog poses on a 1920s RCA Victor sign. All are large, and certainly colorful. The museum also offers changing exhibits of contemporary neon electric and kinetic art.

Wells Fargo History Museum, 333 S. Grand Ave.; from Rte. 110 take 4th St. Exit east to Hope St.; turn left. (213) 253-7166. Free. Open Mon. through Fri., 9 a.m. to 5 p.m.; closed bank holidays. Accessible to handicapped.

Any fan of Western movies recognizes a Wells Fargo wagon, and in this bank museum, and in its sister museum in San Francisco, you get the opportunity to journey back to the Gold Rush days in an authentic 1890 stagecoach—by taped tour, anyway. Also helping to capture a bygone era are a collection of gold ore, a working Wells Fargo agent's office, gold scales, a hands-on telegraph key, mining tools and other artifacts, and photos that trace Wells Fargo history from its founding in 1852 (making it the oldest bank in the West) through the 1906 San Francisco earthquake and fire to today's electronic age.

National City

Museum of American Treasures, 1315 E. 4th St.; take 8th St. Exit east from I-5 to M Ave. for 4 blocks. (619) 477-7489. Adults: $3, children: $1. Open Sun., 11 a.m. to 4 p.m., and by appointment. No facilities for handicapped.

Most impressive here, among an interesting mix of old-time paraphernalia, are thousands of pieces of desert glass. Also called amethyst glass, desert glass is created by the effect of the sun's rays on clear glass containing traces of manganese. Many of the pieces—ink wells, candle holders, bottles, a complete 100-year-old table setting, paperweights, massive jars, delicate vases, figurines—were purposely left out in the sun for a couple of years to take on their characteristic color, but many were dug from desert trash dumps. Since manganese hasn't been used in glass manufacture since World War I, all of the pieces are old. Augmenting this glance at America of two generations ago are gadgets from Grandmother's kitchen (including an iron heated by charcoal), old-time educational materials, toys, voting artifacts, souvenirs from hotels and restaurants, and men's and women's personal items. There is even a smokers' corner filled with old-fashioned smoking memorabilia.

Oakland

Museum of Robotics, 4026 Martin Luther King, Jr. Way, 1 block from McArthur BART station. (415) 547-3579. Adults: $2.50, seniors and children to 18: $1.50. By appointment only. Accessible to handicapped.

While displays of computers, electrostatics, and holography will intrigue any electronic enthusiast, the robot is king at this unusual museum. Robots of all persuasions strut their stuff here—there is a robot carousel, a robot ferris wheel, robot toys, and even robot rides for children, including a trip on a robot train. Robotropolis, a city of robots, features mechanical creatures in a variety of settings—working out in a gym, walking along the street, toiling in a robot factory. Part of the museum's 10-year plan is to build the world's tallest robot that will be 10 stories high.

Orange

Museum of Dentistry, 295 S. Flower, in Orange County Dental Society building; take Chapman Ave. Exit east from I-5, then right on Flower. (714) 634-8944. Free. Open Mon. through Fri., 9 a.m. to 5 p.m. Accessible to handicapped.

While people afflicted with dentistphobia might equate this exhibit to a museum of torture, the exhibits here at least don't employ bloodied manikins. Yes, there are numerous picks, probes, forceps, and other dental tools that were the precursors of implements used nowadays to inspect and repair teeth, and there is even a foot-operated drill. But there are also dentures made from a variety of materials, bridges (including one made for George Washington), and a relatively cozy fringed dental chair, circa 1876. Photos of evidence of bygone practices—such as a leather saddlebag fitted out for the tools of a traveling dentist—round out this glimpse of historical American dentistry.

Palm Springs

Ruddy's General Store Museum, 221 S. Palm Canyon Dr., in center of town. (619) 327-2156. Admission: $.50. Open Oct. through June, Thurs. through Sun., 10 a.m. to 4 p.m.; July through Sept., Sat. and Sun., noon to 6 p.m. Ramp for wheelchairs.

Sarsaparilla, fly ribbons, Mazda lamps, Rinso, Lux, silk stockings—authentic groceries and household products from the 1930s and '40s, mostly in their unopened original containers—are among the 6,000 pieces of merchandise not really for sale here. Authentic period shelves and cases in this recreated general store of 50 years ago are literally filled with goods. Fixtures are right out of the Depression era and nostalgic advertising touts products that Mother and Grandmother couldn't do without. There are no reproductions—bins are actually filled with dried peas and beans; a cracker barrel contains Uneeda biscuits; and hardware, beauty aids, soaps, and notions appear ready to be tucked into your shopping basket.

Portola Valley

Foothill Electronic Museum, Perham Foundation, 101 First St., Suite 394, on campus of Foothill College; take El Monte Exit east from Rte. 280 to campus entrance, turn right or left and continue around campus to museum. (415) 949-7383. Nominal admission fee. Open Thurs. and Fri., 9:30 a.m. to 4:30 p.m.; Sun., 1 to 4:30 p.m. Accessible to handicapped.

Here is an opportunity to learn a lot about electronics in a short time—from the phenomenon of static electricity to the techniques used in the manufacture of large-scale integrated circuits. This is a hands-on museum that traces electronic equipment from early spark-gap transmitters, coherers, "cat's whisker" crystal detectors, and pre-World War II television receivers to modern video recorders, calculators, and computers. The first radio station the world ever listened to is here, as are materials documenting the contribution of West Coast electronics inventors and entrepreneurs—rightly so, as the museum is located in California's famed Silicon Valley.

Redlands

San Bernardino County Museum, 2024 Orange Tree Lane, east on California St. Exit from I-10, north to Orange Tree Lane, then right. (714) 798-8570. Donation requested; varying admission fees for special exhibits. Open Tues. through Sat., 9 a.m. to 5 p.m.; Sun., 1 to 5 p.m.; closed Mon. Accessible to handicapped.

History, natural history, and anthropology are the main subject areas of this large county museum, and among the many fine exhibits covering those subjects are some containing artifacts from prehistoric times. What is really outstanding here, however, is an egg collection—40,000 sets of eggs (all labeled, of course)—from those of the tiniest hummingbird to those of the giant ostrich. The collection dates back to the mid-19th century, and is one of the largest in the nation.

Riverside

California Museum of Photography, 3824 Main St., Downtown Pedestrian Mall, near historic Mission Inn. (714) 784-4787. Adults: $2, seniors, students, and youth 13 to 18: $1. Open Tues. through

Sat., 10 a.m. to 5 p.m.; Sun., noon to 5 p.m.; closed Mon. Accessible to handicapped.

To walk onto the indoor balcony of this converted five-and-dime store is to walk into a huge camera. You enter a giant camera obscura in the form of a big black box that projects images on the far wall. Other permanent hands-on exhibits include the Light Island containing prisms and lenses that bend light and mix colors, a Colored Shadows exhibit that has you mixing colors with your own shadow, and a Praxinoscope where mirrors turn still images into moving pictures. Changing exhibits throughout four floors of display area tap the museum's enormous resources—18,000 photographs by such masters as Ansel Adams, Walker Evans, and Barbara Morgan; more than 100,000 stereoscopic prints; and a collection of 6,000 cameras.

San Diego

Model Railroad Museum, 1649 El Prado, Casa de Balboa Bldg., Balboa Park. (619) 696-0199. Adults: $1, children under 15: free. Open June through Sept., and last week of Nov. through Mar. 31, Wed. through Fri., 11 a.m. to 4 p.m.; Sat. and Sun., 11 a.m. to 5 p.m.; first Tues. of month, 11 a.m. to 4 p.m.; Apr., May, Oct., and most of Nov., Fri. 11 a.m. to 4 p.m., and Sat. and Sun 11 a.m. to 5 p.m.; closed Martin Luther King Day, Thanksgiving and Christmas. Handicapped access through back door from parking lot.

Four giant permanent exhibits here present an entertaining look at the heritage of American railroads in miniature, with model trains of various scales running through hand-crafted landscapes. One exhibit features the Cabrillo and Southwestern Railroad in O scale; another, in HO scale, runs the Southern Pacific-Sante Fe line through California's scenic Tehachapi Pass; yet another HO scale train crosses a model of the Goat Canyon trestle, at one time the largest wooden railroad trestle in the world. Layouts are the work of local model railroad clubs, and temporary displays occupy the rest of the exhibit space.

San Francisco

American Carousel Museum, 633 Beach St., on Fisherman's Wharf across from the Cannery. (415) 928-0550. Adults: $2, seniors and children 12 to 17: $1. Open daily, Apr. through Oct., 10 a.m. to 6

p.m.; Nov. through Mar., 10 a.m. to 5 p.m.; closed Christmas and
New Year's Day. Accessible to handicapped.

Hand-carved carousel horses and menagerie figures are a vanishing breed, and the beautifully crafted carousel horses, tigers,
giraffes, and other appealing animals on display here are virtually
national treasures. Gleaned from the so-called Golden Age of carousels—between 1876 and 1930—these examples of American
dramatic free-flowing carved figures (as opposed to the stiff stereo-
types that populated European carousels) represent the American
spirit translated by immigrant craftsmen into works of entertainment art. Exhibits demonstrate differences in carving styles and
painting techniques. You can see skilled restorers at work and
listen to lively band organs supplying authentic carousel music.

Esprit Quilt Collection, 900 Minnesota St., in Potrero Hill District;
from I-280 north, go right on Mariposa St., then right on Minnesota
St.; from I-280 south, take 18th St. Exit, go left on 18th St., then
right onto Minnesota St. (415) 648-6900. Admission: $4, includes
color catalog for self-guided tour. Open Mon. through Fri., 9 a.m.
to 4:30 p.m. Accessible to handicapped.

Three floors of the handsome corporate offices of the Esprit de
Corps line of sports clothing are the repository of some 200 fine
antique (1870–1950) Amish quilts, most of them from Pennsylvania's Lancaster County. Amish women have traditionally
shunned gaudy colors and pictoral designs in their quiltmaking,
skillfully combining tiny cloth squares of blue, purple, black, and
other muted colors into such designs as Sunshine and Shadow, and
Diamond in the Square. To see their creations hanging on the walls
of a starkly modern building is to appreciate their profound under-
standing of graphic art.

Museum of Ophthalmology, 655 Beach St., third floor of American
Academy of Ophthalmology headquarters, across from the Cannery. (415) 561-8500. Free. Open Mon. through Fri., 8:30 a.m. to 5
p.m.; closed holidays. Accessible to handicapped.

A fitted case containing 50 hand-blown glass eyes (circa 1850) is
a bit startling on first view, but eye cups and pharmaceutical bottles
on display here are almost works of art. Trade signs, advertising
literature, photographs, and documents trace individuals, historical moments, and developments in professional medical eye care
and mix nicely with display cases of finely-crafted spectacles,

monocles, lorgnettes, and other visual aids. There are stamps, coins, and medallions honoring pioneers and milestones in ophthalmic research and exhibits of diagnostic and surgical instruments that date back to the 1800s before sterilization or electricity.

Old Mint Museum, Fifth and Mission Sts., 1 block south of Market St. (415) 744-6830. Free. Open Mon. through Fri., 10 a.m. to 4 p.m.; closed major holidays. Accessible to handicapped, elevator entrance on Jessie St.

Here in an outstanding example of Federal Classical Revival architecture are restored Victorian rooms as well as exhibits on things monetary. Numismatic samples of the mint's special coins and medals division are the main draw, as are a Million Dollar Gold display, a real stagecoach, an authentic 1869 coin press, a pyramid of gold bars, and other monetary treasures and artifacts of California and the Old West. You can also view a ½-hour movie that traces the mint's history.

Schlage Antique Lock Collection, 2401 Bayshore Blvd., at Leland. (415) 467-1100. Free. Open by appointment only. Limited access for handicapped.

Filling nine display cases in this corporate cafeteria are 4,000 years of history in the form of locks and other security devices. The oldest is a wooden specimen reputedly used in ancient Egypt, its mechanism remarkably similar to that of a modern pin lock. The most fascinating is a necklace of 89 tiny padlocks, given to Catherine the Great by a locksmith she had imprisoned—she subsequently freed him. You'll also see American locks from colonial times, medieval travel locks that were the precursors of padlocks, and numerous examples of modern locks designed to resist picking. The collection was started by the great-great-nephew of Jules Verne and includes the push-button cylinder lock invented by company owner Walter Schlage.

Tattoo Art Museum, 839 Columbus Ave., on Mission St. cable car line near Lombard St. (415) 775-4991. Free. Open daily, noon to 6 p.m. No facilities for handicapped.

"Next to religion and politics, tattoos are the most controversial subject," claims museum owner/tattoo artist Lyle Tuttle, who goes on to say that tattooing dates back thousands of years and was often the privilege of nobility. After the Battle of Hastings, for instance, the body of England's King Harold was identified by a tattoo. On display in flip racks here are hundreds of "flash sales aids," hand-drawn designs from which customers could select a tattoo. The oldest dated sheet is 1898, and some are signed by the artist. You'll also see old equipment—a pre-Columbian transfer cylinder that imprints three monkeys; hand-, spring-, and electric-powered needles; and what Tuttle claims is the world's largest tattoo machine.

Wells Fargo History Museum, 420 Montgomery St., between California and Sacramento Sts., on mezzanine of bank building. (415) 396-2619. Free. Open Mon through Fri., 9 a.m. to 5 p.m.; closed banking holidays. Accessible to handicapped.

The story of Wells Fargo, from its 1852 founding in San Francisco to the present day, concerns both banking and transportation, so there is a 122-year-old Concord stagecoach in this two-story showroom, as well as such Gold Rush-related items as mining tools, gold specimens, and gold coins. You will find a recreated early Wells Fargo office and a collection of Western stamps and postal franks. This is the sister museum to the Los Angeles Wells Fargo Museum.

San Jose

Military Medals Museum and Research Center, 448 N. San Pedro St., on southeast corner of N. San Pedro St. and Fox Ave. (408) 298-1100. Free. Open Mon. through Sat.; closed major holidays. Accessible to handicapped.

This is the only museum in the world devoted exclusively to military medals. It is not a military museum in the strictest sense, in that it does not contain general military memorabilia, but concentrates on medals, awards, commendations, documents, and books. The medals represent 50 countries, and free pamphlets on the subject are available. The owner, who has been collecting for more than 25 years, will answer questions that you may have about the many ways in which nations honor their military heroes.

San Luis Obispo

Shakespeare Press Museum, Room 116, Graphic Arts Building, on campus of California Polytechnic State University; take Grand Ave.

Exit (Rte. 1) from Rte. 101. (805) 756-1108. Free. Open by appointment only. Accessible to handicapped.

Among the turn-of-the-century presses and printing equipment exhibited here are hundreds of styles of foundry type, wood engravings, lead and rule cutters, and composing sticks. There are three hand presses (one of them dated 1850), six platen presses (one a floor model), and assorted table model presses. An especially rare artifact, called the Printer's Favorite, is an 1858 paper and card cutter, one of only three known to exist. Paper cutters, perforators, staplers, and linotype and linograph machines round out the museum, and for book lovers, the university library features a special collections section with examples of fine book printing, one-of-a-kind books, and classics.

Santa Cruz

The Santa Cruz Surfing Museum, West Cliff Dr., Lighthouse Point, south of Municipal Pier. (408) 429-3429. Donation suggested. Open Thurs. through Mon., noon to 4 p.m. Two low steps, then accessible to handicapped.

"Surf's up!" is the cry heard along the Santa Cruz coastline when the swells are swell. Santa Cruz is considered the birthplace of the modern surfboard. Housed in a working lighthouse, this small museum traces the history of the sport through the decades since the 1920s. One exhibit offers visitors an appreciation of the evolution of the surfboard, starting with a huge 95-pound redwood behemoth, and ending with a modern 7-pound version. A rather grisly specimen is the so-called Shark Board, a polyfoam board bitten by a shark who left behind a complete bite imprint. Other photo and artifact displays are devoted to Hawaiian surfers, especially the famed Duke Kahanamoku and his brothers; celebrated local surfers; and the wet suit, invented by a man from Santa Cruz.

Victorville

Roy Rogers and Dale Evans Museum, 15650 Seneca Rd.; take Palmdale Rd. Exit from I-15 to Kentwood, turn right to Civic Dr., then left to Seneca Rd. (619) 243-4547. Adults: $3, seniors and children 13 to 16: $2, children 6 to 12: $1. Open daily, 9 a.m. to 5

p.m.; closed Thanksgiving and Christmas. Accessible to handicapped.

"This is our life," reads the rustic sign over the entrance to this
museum, and, indeed, the professional and personal lives of Roy
Rogers and Dale Evans, popular Western stars of movies and
television, are very much on display here. Souvenirs, including
family furniture, handcrafts, and awards; mounted hunting trophies; an extensive hand gun and rifle collection; and a collection of
scale-model western vehicles, all add to the Roy/Dale lore. But, by
far the most popular display is the one featuring the mounted
figures of Trigger ("The Smartest Horse in the Movies," ridden by
Rogers in every picture he made), Buttermilk (Evans's famous
buckskin horse), Trigger, Jr., and Bullet, the dog.

Colorado

Colorado Springs

Money Museum of the American Numismatic Association, 818 N. Cascade Ave.; take Exit 143 east from I-25, turn right onto Cascade Ave. (719) 632-2646. Adults: $1, children 10 to 17: $.50, ANA members, accompanying family members, and children under 10: free. Open Mon. through Sat., 8:30 a.m. to 4 p.m.; closed Sun. and national holidays. Accessible to handicapped.

Who says a nickel isn't worth anything these days? Among the rarities in this foremost collection of U.S. currency is a 1913 Liberty head nickel valued at $1 million. Numismatics—coins, tokens, medals, paper money, and related items—is the focus here, and with more than 400,000 items in its collection, the museum can display less than 1 percent of its holdings at any time. Eight changing exhibits offer themed displays covering such topics as paper money relating to Abraham Lincoln, symbolic monies of non-western bartering cultures, coins of a particular nation, or medals, badges, orders, and decorations of modern society. There are also a hands-on Hall of Nations with large three-dimensional models of the world's coins, a Colorado Gallery dedicated to the Centennial State's abundance of precious metals, a Modern Medallic Art Hall, and a Hall of Presidents that presents numismatic memorabilia of the birth, death, and inaugural years of every American president.

National Carvers Museum, 14960 Woodcarver Rd., on Rte. 25 north. (719) 481-2656. Adults: $3, seniors and children under 12: $2. Open daily, 9 a.m. to 5 p.m.; closed Christmas and New Year's Day. Completely accessible to handicapped.

Whittlers from all over America have contributed to the permanent exhibit of more than 3,000 woodcarvings in this striking modern building. Half-round, full-round, plaques, and bas-reliefs, the works cover a wide range of subjects and styles. Carvings are mostly representational—animal, human, or inanimate object—and have been finished in natural wood tones. Some, however, are free-form, and the grain or texture of the wood itself is the design. Some, such as a fine series on Western wild animals, have been painted. Changing exhibits on varying themes have a separate room.

Pro Rodeo Hall of Champions and Museum of the American Cowboy, 101 Pro Rodeo Dr., at north end of town, south of Air Force Academy; take Exit 147 from I-25. (719) 593-8847 or -8840. Adults: $4, seniors: $3.75, children 5 to 12: $1.25. Open Memorial Day to Labor Day, daily, 9 a.m. to 5 p.m.; in winter, Tues. through Sat., 9 a.m. to 4:30 p.m., and Sun., noon to 4:30 p.m.; closed Easter, Thanksgiving, Christmas, and New Year's Day. Accessible to handicapped.

The life of the rodeo rider is documented here along with that of the humble cowboy, and artworks and exhibits of memorabilia from typical trail rides and roundups tell the latter's story effectively and sympathetically. On the rodeo side, cases are packed with goodies—posters, trophies, personality exhibits, clothing, and different types of equipment favored through the years in rodeo and show riding. Other exhibits tend to be action packed: You can touch a 100-year-old saddle and you can stare a Brahma bull in the eye. A guided tour takes you on a historic trek through the Old West and plaques name hall of fame members and National Rodeo Champions.

Denver

Black American West Museum, 3091 California St., on southwest corner of California and 31st Sts. (303) 292-2566. Adults: $2, seniors: $1.50, children 13 to 16: $.75, children 12 and under: $.50. Open Wed. through Fri., 10 a.m. to 2 p.m., and Sat., noon to 5 p.m., and Sun., 2 to 5 p.m.; closed Mon and Tues. No facilities for handicapped.

Nearly one-third of the cowboys in the Wild West were black. Black families came West in covered wagons, established all-black towns, filled jobs in communities including doctors and state legislators, and owned much of the West's most valuable real estate. Until Denver native Paul Stewart opened this museum dedicated to the role of Black Americans in the Old West, their story had never been fully told. Personal artifacts, newspapers, legal documents, letters, photographs, and oral histories make up the collection of 35,000 items here documenting Western blacks from early fur trade until today. You'll learn that Louis Price, a black Denver millionaire, had five white servants; black cowboys bulldogged, roped, and branded on the trail and in rodeos; and black pioneers defended their homesteads against marauding Indians and white men. Exhibits are nicely laid out in this restored home of Dr. Justina L. Ford, a black female physician who delivered some 7,000 babies during her 60-year practice in Denver.

Evergreen

International Bell Museum, 30213 Upper Bear Creek Canyon Rd., 1 mile west of town. (303) 674-3422. Adults: $4, children under 12: $2. Open Tues. through Sun., 10 a.m. to 5 p.m. Indoor display not accessible to handicapped.

Bells for calling people to work, to dinner, to worship; bells for locating livestock; alarm bells; bells just for show—they adorn walls, line every flat surface, spill out of glass cases, and festoon the ceilings of two rooms in this private home. Many, such as bells owned by the Medici family, Francis I of France, and the Hohenzollerns, have a royal ring to them. Some were owned by famous people of other than royal blood: Amelia Earhart, Houdini, Lillian Russell. There are pieces of Sarah Bernhardt's bell jewelry, temple bells from the Orient, and decorative examples from Austria. The outdoor display includes a fine campanile of three historic bells from Nebraska.

Golden

Buffalo Bill Memorial Museum and Grave, Lookout Mountain between Rte. 40 and Golden. (303) 526-0747. Adults: $2, children 6 to 15: $1. Open Tues. through Sun., 9 a.m. to 4 p.m. Accessible to handicapped.

Established four years after Buffalo Bill Cody's death in 1917, this museum covers his times a well as his life. Cody's boyhood, Pony Express, military, and showman days are commemorated. Especially colorful are posters advertising Cody's Wild West show, along with his show saddle, guns, and costumes. Exhibits not based directly on his life include a display of antique barbed wire and a collection of the kinds of guns that won the West. While a number of artworks throughout the building depict the familiar goateed figure, many other pieces come from Cody's own extensive collection of American Western artists and include works by Frederic Remington and Charles Schreyvogel.

Colorado Railroad Museum, 17155 W. 44th Ave., (known as 10th St. within Golden), on Rte. 58. (303) 279-4591. Adults: $3, children 6 through 16: $1.50. Open daily 9 a.m. to 5 p.m.; closed Thanksgiving and Christmas.

Sixty pieces of antique railroad equipment are not the only items on display at this large railroad yard: Various kinds of yard switches, two roundhouses, and different types of yard trackage and layouts are also part of the exhibit. Some of the cars, locomotives, and trackage are standard gauge, but most (as well as most of the artifacts, photos, and mementos on display in the replica 1880s depot) relate to Colorado's flamboyant narrow gauge railroading days. Before being overtaken by standard gauge lines at the turn of the century, 2,000 miles of narrow gauge tracks probed canyons and crossed mountains to serve Colorado's booming mining industry.

La Junta

Koshare Indian Kiva Museum, 115 W. 18th St., on campus of Otero Junior College. (719) 384-4411. Adults: $2, seniors and students: $1. Open daily, Sept. through May, 12:30 to 4:30 p.m.; June through Aug., 9 a.m. to 5 p.m.; and show evenings. Accessible to handicapped.

The Indian as artist and as subject of art are twin themes of Koshare's extensive collection of Western and Indian paintings; nicely mounted displays of historic and present-day Native American arts, crafts, and costumes represent tribes from Alaska, the Northwest coast, and South America, as well as from the Southwest. The kiva (a domed ceremonial room for Indian dancing) and museum exhibit rooms, plus most of the artifacts and works on display, have been financed by the Koshare Indian Dancers, a group of Explorer Scouts nationally acclaimed for their authentic Indian dancing.

Vail

Colorado Ski Museum and Ski Hall of Fame, 15 Vail Rd., in center of town. (303) 476-1876. Adults: $1, children 12 to 18: $.50. Open Thanksgiving through Easter, Tues. through Sun., 10 a.m. to 6 p.m.; Memorial Day through Sept., Mon. through Fri., by appointment only. Accessible to handicapped.

Photographs and artifacts in this attractive mountainside museum illustrate more than 100 years of Colorado skiing. Filling six galleries are exhibits on presidential skiing (featuring replicas of Teddy Roosevelt's skis and authentic skis used by Gerald Ford), the U.S. Army 10th Mountain Division (ski troopers trained in Colorado for World War II action), cross-country skiing, and numerous displays tracing the development of skis, poles, boots, and bindings—from pine boards and bailing wire to today's high-tech gear. Slide shows and racing movies are shown in the museum theater, and one large room serves as the Colorado Ski Hall of Fame. Outdoor exhibits include a World War II Army snow tank and primitive snow-grooming equipment.

Hawaii

Captain Cook

Mauna Kea Royal Kona Coffee Mill and Museum, on island of Hawaii, Napoopoo Rd., just above Kealakekua Bay, south of Captain Cook. (808) 367-8047, ext. 150. Free. Open daily, 8 a.m. to 4:30 p.m.; closed Christmas Day. Accessible to handicapped.

Along with pineapples, sugar, and macadamia nuts, coffee is one of the traditional agricultural products of Hawaii. Coffee has been grown in the Kona district of the big island of Hawaii for more than 150 years; in fact, this is the only area in the U. S. where coffee is grown. Old-time roasters and grinders, posters, and instructive photo exhibits make up the museum part of this rustic building. In the business half of the building, depending on the time of day, the coffee roaster may actually be in operation, filling the air with a rich aroma. There is a three-minute film on the processing of coffee, and visitors are offered a sample cup of pure Royal Kona brew.

Kilauea

Guava Visitors Center and Display Pavilion, Guava Kai Plantation, on island of Kauai, end of Kuawa Rd., about 5 miles inland from Kilauea Lighthouse. (808) 828-1862. Free. Open daily, 9 a.m. to 5 p.m. Accessible to handicapped.

Visitors to this, the world's largest commercial guava farm, are greeted at the lovely visitors pavilion with a free sample of guava juice and fresh fruit slices. From there, it's on to a replica 1930s plantation kitchen and a look at some of the kinds of equipment used for harvesting the fruit in years gone by. Along the way, a series of panels documents guava production and uses and the people involved in the industry. A visit includes a walk through a guava orchard and a view of the processing plant.

Lahaina

Whaler's Village Museum, on island of Maui, 2435 Kaanapali Pkwy., G-8, in Whaler Village Shopping Complex. (808) 661-5992. Free. Open daily, 9:30 a.m. to 10 p.m. Accessible to handicapped.

This nicely-designed tribute to the golden age of whaling (circa 1825 to 1860) includes an interpretation of how Hawaii was forever changed by the ships that called at her ports. The skeleton of a 40-foot-long sperm whale forms an impressive centerpiece here, and nearby displays relate to the biology of more than 70 species of this marine mammal. The men who hunted the whales are not forgotten: A fully fitted-out whale boat, fine examples of scrimshaw, wood carvings, and other pieces of sailors' art are also featured. In addition, other artifacts, photo murals, graphics, and films guide the visitor through the days when whaling was one of the most important industries in the world.

Lihue

Kaua'i Museum, on island of Kauai, 4428 Rice St., adjacent to state and county buildings. (808) 245-6931. Adults: $3, children under 18: free. Open Mon. through Fri., 9 a.m. to 4:30 p.m.; Sat., 9 a.m. to 1 p.m.; closed Sun., July 4, Labor Day, Thanksgiving, Christmas, and New Year's Day. Accessible to handicapped.

Occupying a 1924 building that was originally the Kauai public library, this museum concentrates on the history of what Hawaiians call the Garden Island. At the same time, it offers a good overall picture of the geological, ethnological, and historical heritages of all the islands, starting with Hawaii's volcanic genesis some 5 million years ago. Artifacts of ancient Hawaiian culture are on display here, along with exhibits on Captain Cook's 1778 discovery trip, attempted Russian expansion, missionaries, Oriental influences, and plantation life. There are examples of folk art, such as shell leis and beautiful Hawaiian quilts, and photographs of the recent past. An aerial film offers visitors a look at parts of the island that are seldom seen.

Puunene

Alexander & Baldwin Sugar Museum, on island of Maui, 3957 Hansen Rd., ½ mile east of junction of Rtes. 380 and 350. (808) 871-8058. Adults: $2, children 6 to 17: $1. Open 9:30 a.m. to 4:30 p.m., daily in summer, Mon. through Sat., during rest of year. Accessible to handicapped.

Until the 1960s, when it was edged out by tourism, sugar production was the dominant industry in Hawaii. The Sugar Museum, housed in the former home of a sugar plantation superintendent, presents a comprehensive view of the island's sugar industry. You learn about geologic origins of the island, pioneer life, sugar plantations, and the production of sugar. In one room, a 12-foot-high photo mural illustrates how water was brought from the mountains to Maui's dry central plain. Another room is devoted to family photographs, furniture, and personal memorabilia of sugar pioneers. Other rooms pay tribute to the people who worked the plantations—laborers from Japan, Portugal, and other faraway lands. Plantation life is chronicled with a scale model of a workers' camp, a Japanese household Buddhist altar, field and factory tools, and photographs. Most arresting is a manikin of a Japanese woman field worker, dressed in heavy sun-proof, dust-proof clothing that also acted as armor against sharp sugar cane leaves and eight-inch-long centipedes. An unusual and entertaining working scale model of a nine-roller mill, with sound effects and recorded narration, completes the experience.

Wailuku

Maui Historical Society Museum, on island of Maui, 2314-A Main St., near junction of Rtes. 32 and 30. (808) 244-3326. Suggested donation for adults: $2, children: $.50. Open Mon. through Sat., 10 a.m. to 4:30 p.m.; closed Sun. and most major holidays. No facilities for handicapped.

This is a museum of contrasts. The building is a mission home, part of what was originally a female seminary. Articles from the missionary era—furniture, clothing, toys, china, and other items—document the pioneering way of life of late 19th-century missionary Edward Bailey and his family. But also housed here is Maui's largest collection of pre-Western-contact artifacts, including stone and shell implements, examples of tapa (barkcloth), cordage, woodwork, and feather and bone articles, testaments to the Hawaiians' ingenuity in using limited indigenous materials. Bailey's oil paintings and copper engravings document 19th-century island life. Outdoors are other, very diversified, displays: rare plants, varieties of sugar cane brought to the islands by Polynesians, stone implements used by ancient Hawaiians, huge gourds from plants that are now extinct, a hand-hewn outrigger canoe fashioned from a single log, and a redwood surfboad used by legendary surfer Duke Kahanamoku.

Idaho

Boise

History of Electricity in Idaho Museum, Old Idaho Penitentiary, 2445 Old Penitentiary Rd.; take Broadway Exit north from I-84 to Warm Springs Ave., then east to Old Penitentiary Rd. (208) 334-2844. Adults: $3, seniors and children: $2. Open daily, noon to 4 p.m.; closed state holidays. Accessible to handicapped.

In 1955, Arco, Idaho, was the world's first city to be entirely lit by nuclear energy. This fact, and many others relating the history of electricity in Idaho, is the subject of one of many interpretive exhibits here. Others include such topics as how a hydroelectric dam works, the lineman's tools, lightning, radios, and reading electric meters. Visitors can generate some electricity of their own—six light bulbs' worth, to be exact—by pedaling a bicycle; other interactive displays include Numbers Please and Dial-a-Friend. The penitentiary itself, built of hand-cut stone in 1870 and used for over 100 years, is open for self-guided tours.

Hailey

Blaine County Historical Museum, N. Main St., between Bellevue and Hailey. No telephone. Adults: $1, children 6 to 15: $.50. Open Memorial Day weekend and June 15 through Sept. 15, Wed. through Mon., 10 a.m. to 5 p.m. Accessible to handicapped.

Once in a while something really special hides among the regional memorabilia of a local historical museum. Here, among relics and artifacts from Blaine County's mining glory days, is an impressive collection of American political items. Numerous display cases hold hundreds of badges, pennants, buttons, and other souvenirs of American political (mostly presidential) campaigns. The collection starts with campaigns as far back as the early 1800s and traces the hoopla through "Win with Willkie" and "I Like Ike" right up to today.

Moscow

Appaloosa Horse Museum, Moscow-Pullman Hwy. (208) 882-5578. Free. Open Mon. through Fri., 8 a.m. to 5 p.m.; closed holidays. Accessible to handicapped.

The Appaloosa horse, admired for its intelligence, speed, and stamina, has a large and loyal following. Proof of its popularity is here in the Appaloosa's very own museum, where artifacts and paintings link Appaloosas historically to both Indians and cowboys. Nez Perce Indians, who developed the breed, are represented by exhibits of clothing and tools. Early cowboy equipment and an excellent saddle collection round out the story. The Appaloosa Horse Club, Inc. has its headquarters here.

Rexburg

Teton Flood Museum, 51 N. Center, 25 miles north of Idaho Falls, off I-20. (208) 356-9109. Free. Open June through Sept. 1, Mon. through Sat., 10 a.m. to 5 p.m.; Sept. 2 through Memorial Day, Mon. through Fri., 11 a.m. to 4 p.m. No facilities for handicaped.

At 11:57 a.m., Sat., June 5, 1976, the newly-constructed Teton Dam with full reservoir burst with little warning. Thousands of people fled their homes in the small communities below the dam, and 11 people died from the flood. Damage to homes, businesses, farms, and livestock was estimated at $1 billion. Pictures, artifacts, and videos tell the story of the day when 80 billion gallons of water left Rexburg eight feet deep in water. The museum, housed in the Rexburg Tabernacle basement, which the flood completely filled with mud and debris, was opened in 1982. Other displays here depict the history of the Upper Snake River Valley prior to the flood.

Sandpoint

Vintage Wheel Museum, 218 Cedar St., at corner of Cedar and Third, downtown. (208) 263-7173. Adults: $2.50, seniors: $2, high school students: $1, grade school students: $.50. Open daily, 9:30 a.m. to 5:30 p.m. Ramps for handicapped.

Museums devoted to old vehicles are not uncommon, but this museum's approach is novel: chronologically—from horse-drawn to steam to internal combustion—the history of powered vehicles is dramatically presented in a series of period settings. Artwork, antique clothing, signs, and period accessories all contribute to placing groups of vehicles in authentic historic context. Logging equipment is featured, along with classic cars, buggies, and steam engines. An adjacent gallery features art and furniture from the 1920s, '30s, and '40s.

Weiser

National Fiddler's Hall of Fame, 8 E. Idaho, 1 block east of State St. (208) 549-0452. Free. Open Mon. through Fri., 9 a.m. to 5 p.m. Accessible to handicapped.

Each June, the town of Weiser hosts the National Oldtime Fiddlers' Contest, and this museum has grown out of that annual event. As expected, there are photos of past champion fiddlers and a scrapbook of the town's involvement over the years. Of note, however, are the broken bows, the sheet music, and the costumes from past fiddlers' contests; displays of folk music items and instruments; and, especially, a large collection of old-time fiddles, some of them homemade.

Montana

Browning

Museum of the Plains Indians, Rte. 89, at junction with Rte. 2, west of Browning. (406) 338-2230. Free. Open Mon. through Fri., June through Sept., 9 a.m. to 5 p.m.; Oct. through May, 10 a.m. to 4:30 p.m.; closed Thanksgiving, Christmas, and New Year's Day. Accessible to handicapped.

The artistic and creative achievements of the Blackfeet, Crow, Northern Cheyenne, Sioux, Assiniboine, Arapaho, Shoshone, Nez Perce, Flathead, Chippewa, and Cree Indian tribes are documented here in a permanent historic exhibition and in changing exhibits of present-day crafts. Highlights in the permanent gallery are examples of different types of tribal dress on life-size figures of men, women, and children; arts and crafts connected with ceremonial events; and leather items meant for everyday use but beautifully decorated with bead- and quillwork. Design motifs repeated on the handicrafts, as well as painted on tepees displayed outdoors during the summer, illustrate the rich artistic diversity among the different tribes collectively called the Northern Plains Indians.

Great Falls

Charles M. Russell Museum, 1201 4th Ave. North. (406) 727-8787. Adults: $3, seniors and students: $1.50. Summer hours Mon. through Sat., 9 a.m. to 6 p.m., and Sun., 1 to 5 p.m.; winter hours

Tues. through Sat., 10 a.m. to 5 p.m., and Sun., 1 to 5 p.m.; closed Easter, Thanksgiving, Christmas, and New Year's Day. Accessible to handicapped.

Western artist Charles M. Russell claimed friendship with preachers, priests, cowpunchers, trappers, Indians, and other residents of the Far West, many of whom he put on canvas. The nucleus of this museum's holdings is the Josephine Trigg collection of Russell paintings, bronzes, and wax models, and these alone make a visit worthwhile. Extra attractions are Russell's private collection of Indian costumes, his illustrated letters, and a display of outstanding works by several of Russell's contemporaries. The artist's home and original studio are nearby.

Helena

Gold Collection, 350 N. Last Chance Gulch, in lobby of Norwest Bank Helena, downtown. (406) 442-5050. Free. Open during regular banking hours, Mon. through Thurs., 9:30 a.m. to 4 p.m., and Fri., 9:30 a.m. to 5 p.m.; closed holidays. Easily accessible to handicapped.

One of finest collections of gold specimens in the country graces the lobby of this Helena bank. From gold dust to graded nuggets, acquired from as far away as California and Alaska or as near as next door, most of the specimens were assembled by the bank's first president in 1900. Detailed labeling clears up some quaint and puzzling assay nomenclature: pumpkin seed gold, gold in quartz, sheet gold, crystallized gold, flake gold, scads, flour gold, and black gold. Included in the collection is the 46-troy-ounce Dragon Nugget found only 20 years ago in placer operations on Alaska's Long Creek.

Miles City

Range Riders Museum and Huffman Pictures, W. Main St., Rtes. 10 and 12, west of city. (406) 232-6146. Adults: $3, high school students: $1, grade school students: $.50. Open daily, Apr. to Nov. 1, 7 a.m. to 7 p.m. No facilities for handicapped.

Two separate but related exhibits offer a good historical perspective of Montana's wide open spaces. Displays of branding irons, different types of fencing wire, riding equipment, and related memorabilia recreate the area's cattle boom era—the mid-19th century when land was fenced into grazing ranges for cattle and range riders kept lonely vigil over them. The Huffman period photos eloquently recount the next era, the years following the decline in beef ranching when the land was thrown open to homesteaders eager to try to farm this semi-arid land.

West Yellowstone

Museum of Fly Fishing, Main St. Town located at west entrance to Yellowstone National Park. (406) 646-9541. Free. Open summer only, 9 a.m. to 8 p.m., daily. Accessible to handicapped.

The history of fly fishing and the value of a conservation-oriented approach to the sport are the subjects of this small museum. Antique fly rods and reels, rare and delicate flies, technical materials, and other fishing gear are on exhibit, not only for whatever historic value they may have, but also as examples of tools used in the science of angling. Fly rods of celebrity fishermen—Dwight D. Eisenhower, Ernest Hemingway, even Daniel Webster from far away New England—are displayed in one gallery; another gallery holds a collection of angling art. An especially interesting exhibit shows what several different kinds of flies are composed of (fur, feathers, thread) and how they are tied so as to resemble a tasty insect.

Nevada

Las Vegas

Liberace Museum, 1775 E. Tropicana, at corner of Tropicana and Spencer in Liberace Plaza, 2½ miles east of Tropicana Hotel. (702) 798-5595. Adults: $6.50, seniors: $4.50, students: $4.50, children 6 to 12: $2. Open Mon. through Sat., 10 a.m. to 5 p.m., and Sun., 1 to 5 p.m.; closed Thanksgiving, Christmas and New Year's Day. Accessible to handicapped.

Liberace, this country's most flamboyant entertainer, was as extravagant in his personal collecting as he was on stage. Presented here in a relatively low-profile white brick building are Mr. Showmanship's dazzling collections: rare and antique pianos, including a concert piano once owned by George Gershwin and one played by Chopin; custom-ornamented cars, such as a Rolls-Royce covered in rhinestones and another finished in thousands of mirror tiles; his own costumes—befeathered, befurred, and encrusted with rhinestones and sequins; and his stage jewelry, featuring such custom-designed pieces as a candelabra ring with platinum candlesticks and diamond flames, and a piano ring with keys of black jade and ivory. Liberace also collected rare Moser crystal from Czechoslovakia, miniature pianos, and musical instruments; these are also showcased here, along with recreations of the pianist's office and bedroom from his Palm Springs, California, home.

Reno

Harolds Club Gun Collection and Museum, 250 N. Virginia St., located on second floor and mezzanine of Harolds Club, under Reno arch. (702) 729-0881. Free. Museum is in a casino; open 24 hours a day. Accessible to handicapped.

Before newspaper photographer Ray Stagg's beloved gun collection found a permanent home in 1978 at Reno's Harolds Club, it was a popular success on national road tour, traveling in a colorfully decorated 1949 Buick "woodie" station wagon. Nowadays, Stagg's 500 firearms, representing 500 years of gun technology, look very much at home in their permanent setting, where they share space with shiny nickelodeons, phonographs, automatic musical instruments, and other antiques, some of which were also collected by Stagg. The guns are the main draw, however, and they run the gamut from Gatling gun to dueling pistols to such curiosities as a cannon sundial and an all-purpose dagger/brass knuckles/revolver.

Liberty Belle Antique Slot Machine Collection, 4250 S. Virginia St., in front of the Convention Hall. (702) 825-1776. Free. Open Mon. through Sat., 11 a.m. to 11 p.m., and Sun., 4 to 11 p.m.; closed Thanksgiving and Christmas.

Charles Fey was the first person to hit the jackpot with the nickel slot machine. He invented the Liberty Bell nickel slot in 1887, and made his fortune by manufacturing and operating it and numerous other gaming machines he invented. Seventy years later two of his grandsons opened a saloon/restaurant in Reno, reserving part of it as a museum of gambling devices, many of them designed by their grandfather and their father. The first silver-dollar slot machine, dating from the 1920s, is here, as are the first draw poker machine, a dice machine dated 1895, roulette wheels, a gambling clock, and even a nickel slot craftily disguised as a chewing gum dispenser. As one-armed bandits go, these are all handsomely ornate and all are rare examples of their breed.

Wilbur D. May Museum, 1502 Washington St.; from downtown, take Fifth St. west to Washington St., then north to Rancho San Rafael Park where museum is located, just inside main entrance. (702) 785-5961. Adults: $2, seniors and children 12 and under: $1.

Open year round, Wed. through Sun., 10 a.m. to 5 p.m.; in summer, Tues. through Sun., 10 a.m. to 5 p.m. Handicapped parking, entrance, drinking fountain, and rest rooms.

Son of the May Company department store founder, Wilbur D. May was the ultimate souvenir hunter, circling the globe more than 40 times on trips and safaris seeking items to augment his eclectic collection. Wild animal trophies (some in habitat dioramas), African folk art, shrunken heads from South America, exquisite Chinese pottery, samurai swords, and Russian and English sterling silver are just some of the artifacts that fill this replica Western-style ranch house. Gallery displays are arranged geographically and an atrium acts as a setting for a number of big-game specimens. On display in the Tack Room is another type of trophy—ribbons won by May's purebred cattle and prize-winning horses—as well as some of his own saddles.

New Mexico

Albuquerque

Meteorite Museum, main floor of Northrop Hall, on campus of University of New Mexico, on Central between Girard and University Blvd. (505) 277-2747. Free. Open during school year, Mon. through Fri., 9 a.m. to 4 p.m. (usualy closed noon to 1 p.m.) Accessible to handicapped.

The first institute to study meteorites (circa 1940), the university's geology department has accumulated more than 100 specimens from around the world. Perhaps the star attraction is the Northrop County, a one-ton meteorite believed to be the world's third largest and displaying all the features of its passage and impact. One case holds New Mexico specimens, many cut and polished, including one from Glorieta shaped like a long staff. The museum also holds a collection of tectites, material of terrestrial origin shot into the air by a meteorite's impact and melting on reentry. One from Czechoslovakia is green and glassy, and another from Texas is black.

Capitan

Smokey Bear Museum, on Rte. 380. (505) 354-2612. Free. Open daily, 8 a.m. to 6 p.m. in summer; 9 a.m. to 5 p.m. in spring; 9 a.m.

to 4 p.m. in winter; closed Christmas and New Year's Day, and sometimes by snow. Accessible to handicapped.

Operated by the city, this museum is dedicated to that famous firefighting bear who was born in the area and is buried nearby. The Smokey concept began in 1944 in poster form as part of the war effort. The actual bear was found in a nearby forest fire in 1950 and sent to Washington, D.C., where the fire prevention program began and has been going like blazes ever since. The museum's materials comprise photos and stories of the real Smokey, excerpts from the Congressional Record, posters, firefighting materials, even the commemorative Smokey the Bear stamp—more than the bare facts about a singular bear.

Deming

Deming Luna Mimbres Museum, 301 S. Silver St., the old brick armory, off I-10. (505) 546-2382. Donation requested. Open Mon. through Sat., 9 a.m. to 4 p.m., and Sun., 1:30 to 4:30 p.m.; closed Thanksgiving, Christmas, and New Year's Day. Accessible to handicapped.

Housed in a former National Guard Armory established when Pancho Villa terrorized the border, the museum was founded in 1977 and since has put together some distinctive exhibits reflecting the grand tableau of the Southwest. Chief among these are Mimbres Indian pottery dating back 900 years; a superb array of saddles, bridles, blankets, quirts, and stirrups; an authentic chuck wagon; and quilts made in the 1840s.

Hobbs

Lea County Cowboy Hall of Fame & Western Heritage Center, 5317 Lovington Hwy., on campus of New Mexico Junior College. (505) 392-4510. Free. Open Mon. through Fri., 8 a.m. to 5 p.m.; Sat., 9 a.m. to 5 p.m., and Sun., 1 to 5 p.m.; closed major holidays, spring break, and Christmas break. Accessible to handicapped.

A home on the range for ranching and rodeo buffs, this museum focuses on the region's cowboys and homesteaders and honors rodeo champs of Lea County which reportedly has more than any other county in the United States, dating back to 1901. The rodeo section displays trophies, saddles, buckles, and photos. There are also quilts, furniture, branding irons, and other artifacts from the region's pioneer days. There's even a simulated barn dance tunefully done to the tapes of old-time fiddle music. Other exhibits offer Indian relics and regalia and discuss buffalo hunters and buffalo soldiers.

Lincoln

Lincoln County Heritage Trust Historical Center Museum, Main St., Rte. 380 east from I-25. (505) 653-4529.An admission of $4.50 covers this and other community museums; under age 16 are free. Open daily, 9 a.m. to 5 p.m., mid-Mar. to mid-Dec. Accessible to handicapped.

This is Billy the Kid turf and the highlights of the museum focus on that infamous fellow who developed his reputation during the Lincoln County War. There are two letters written by Billy, plus his knife and set of spurs, and the original tintype of the outlaw. Also displayed are photos that may be of William Bonney, and the museum is participating in a computer study to determine authentic photos of the Kid. In addition, the museum has exhibits on Apaches and buffalo soldiers, showing uniforms, weapons, hats, and paintings. Staff wear period garb, and from May through Sept. conduct tours of the town, pointing out such landmarks as the store that kicked off the county conflict and the courthouse from which Billy the Kid escaped.

Los Alamos

Bradbury Science Museum, Diamond Dr.; take the Bandelier Exit off Rte. 502. (505) 667-4444. Free. Open Tues. through Fri., 9 a.m. to 5 p.m., and Sat. through Mon., 1 p.m. to 5 p.m.; closed national holidays. Accessible to handicapped.

There are science museums and there are science museums; most of them in some fashion focus on the creative side of science and technology. This one tells a grimmer story, namely that of the Manhattan Project or construction of the atomic bomb. Prominently displayed are production models of Fat Man and Little Boy, the two bombs dropped on Japan in World War II. To be fair, other defense-related research has occurred at the Los Alamos National Laboratory, and the museum also offers interactive exhibits on computing, lasers, and other projects.

Santa Fe

Museum of International Folk Art, 706 Camino Lejo; take Old Pecos Trail Exit from I-25. (505) 827-8350. Adults: $3, children 6 to 16: $1.25. Open daily, 10 a.m. to 5 p.m., except Jan. and Feb. when it is closed Mon. Accessible to handicapped.

Part of the Museum of New Mexico, this facility fills a niche here because of its extensive collection of Hispanic folk art from the entire Spanish colonial world, quite fitting for Sante Fe. Opened in 1989, the Hispanic Heritage wing reaches back to the 1500s for five centuries of clothing, carved wood, metalwork, weavings, utensils, construction, religious sculpture, music, and more.

Taos

Kit Carson Home & Historical Museum, Kit Carson Rd., just off Taos Plaza. (505) 758-4741. Adults: $2.50, children: $1.50. Open daily in summer, 8 a.m. to 6 p.m., and winter, 9 a.m. to 5 p.m. Limited facilities for handicapped.

Famed mountain man and scout Kit Carson bought this 12-room adobe home for his wife in 1843, and his family lived here for 25 years. The area was a spicy mix of Spanish, Indian, and Anglo cultures. Period living room, bedroom, and kitchen convey the flavor of that era and recount important chapters in Carson's life. Weapons, textiles, traps, furniture, paintings, documents, and other artifacts illustrate how Carson lived. A biographical sketch in the reception room introduces visitors to Carson and his exploits. Other rooms in the museum focus on regional Indian culture and life and life styles of Taos 150 years ago, ranging from beautifully fashioned saddles to women's clothing.

Martines Hacienda, Rte. 240 (Ranchitos Rd.), 2 miles west of Taos Plaza. (505) 758-1000. Adults: $2.50, seniors: $2, children: $1.50. Open 9 a.m. to 5 p.m. No facilities for handicapped.

The Spaniards were here long before the mountain men arrived, and this 21-room fortress-like edifice captures the Spanish colonial flavor. Windowless adobe walls surround two inner courtyards, and the home's exhibits include tools, gear, and funishings of the era. In late Sept., the hacienda hosts the Old Taos Trade Fair, a two-day festival reliving the 1820s when trappers, merchants, padres, and Indians convened to talk, trade, dance, drink, and sing. Authentic food, crafts, music, and costumes help recreate a bygone time.

Oregon

Baker City

Gold Collection, U. S. National Bank of Oregon, 2000 Main St.; take Exit 304 from I-84, follow Campbell St. to first stop light, turn left to Main St.; museum is on northeast corner. (503) 523-7791. Free. Open Mon. through Thurs., 10 a.m. to 5 p.m., and Fri., 10 a.m. to 6 p.m.; closed holidays and weekends. Accessible to handicapped.

Baker County experienced a gold rush at the turn of the century, and the modest showcase at this bank displays some typical finds. On view are various ore and gold nuggets found locally during the gold rush, plus a few mining-related artifacts, such as old newspapers with headlines announcing yet another rich strike. Notable among the gold specimens is the Armstrong Nugget, weighing in at a whopping 6¾ pounds. Found in 1913 by George Armstrong and his son, it was worth $1,408.75 at the time. Its approximate value today is $32,160.

Central Point

Crater Rock Museum, 2021 Scenic Ave.; from I-5, head into town on Pine St., turn right on 10th and proceed ½ mile to stop sign; enter Scenic Ave. straight ahead; museum is on S-curve in ¼ mile. No telephone. Donation suggested. Open Tues., Thurs., and Sat., 10 a.m. to 4 p.m. Accessible to handicapped.

Thousands of examples of Oregon's rich mineral lode are on view here. Agate, crystals, minerals, petrified wood, fossils, and Indian artifacts, including exquisitely crafted Rogue River Indian arrowheads, crowd lighted showcases. In one case fluorescent light reveals the hidden beauty of otherwise common-looking rocks, and another features huge Oregon Thundereggs—volcanically-formed egg-shaped agates—that, split open, reveal all the colors of the rainbow. Most of the specimens here are in the rough, but one display is of cut gemstones of such semiprecious rocks as tourmaline, amethyst, quartz, and sunstone, the state's official gemstone.

Chiloquin

Logging Museum, Collier Memorial State Park, Rte. 97 north, 5 miles north of Chiloquin and 30 miles north of Klamath Falls. (503) 783-2471. Free. Open daylight to dark, year round. Limited access for handicapped.

This is one museum that lives up to Oregon's outdoor image. A huge steam-powered engine that hauled logs out of the woods in the late 1800s can be inspected at close range, as can pieces of railroad equipment. Inside the cabins are other types of logging equipment. Skidding and transporting equipment; peaveys, levers, felling axes, and other hand tools; barbed wire; blacksmithing equipment; and some curiosities, such as a slab of tree trunk that had grown around a metal fence post—all these and more trace the area's timbering industry from pioneer days to modern times.

Florence

Dolly Wares Doll Museum, 3620 Rte. 101, at northwest corner of 36th St. (503) 997-3391. Adults: $3.50, children 5 to 12: $2. Open Mar. through Oct., Tues. through Sun., 10 a.m. to 5 p.m.; Nov. through Feb., Wed. through Sun., 10 a.m. to 5 p.m. Accessible to handicapped.

Few doll museums have quite the scope of this collection, with dolls ranging from a crude pre-Columbian clay figure to a 17th-century Spanish royal fashion doll to a very modern doll made of vinyl. In size, they go from six-footers to "dressed fleas." Bisque, wood, china, papier mâché, wax, and even tin dolls are all represented here, and groupings include ethnic, personalities, advertising, rag dolls, and Kewpies. Rare items filling a large well-lighted hall include a French stump doll, comic strip dolls, and an elaborately carved wooden soldier of Rome that served as a plaything, circa 1604.

Klamath Falls

Favell Museum of Western Art and Indian Artifacts, 125 W. Main, west of Rte. 97 at Link River Bridge. (503) 882-9996. Adults: $4, seniors: $3, children 6 to 16: $1. Open Mon. through Sat., 9:30 to 5:30; closed Sun., 4th of July, Thanksgiving, Christmas, and New Year's Day. No facilities for handicapped.

Artifacts of Indians who roamed the land before the coming of the white man and works by contemporary Western artists work well side by side in this modern fieldstone building. In sheer numbers, the Indian artifacts are outstanding, especially for a private collection: Scores of stone ceremonial knives are nicely mounted and labeled in cases and frames, as are 60,000 arrowheads, including a rare arrowhead of fire opal. Stonework, beadwork, quillwork, basketry, bone and shellwork, pottery, and North Coast Indian carvings round out this superb collection. Some 300 works emphasize Oregon painters and sculptors.

Portland

The American Advertising Museum, 9 NW 2nd Ave., on western bank of river, between Burnside and Couch Sts., on second floor of Erickson Building. (503) 226-0000. Adults: $1.50, children under 12: free. Open Wed. through Fri., 11 a.m. to 5 p.m.; Sat. and Sun., noon to 5 p.m. Accessible to handicapped.

Not surprisingly, this is the only museum in the world devoted exclusively to advertising; what is surprising is to find it here instead of New York City. The museum's goal—to preserve artifacts of the industry and to educate the public about its role in America's cultural and business history—is well met in sleekly-mounted exhibits. More than that, it is entertaining. A highlight is an exhibit of All-Time Best advertising campaigns, with print advertisements and television storyboards of such familiar ads as Volkswagen's wry pitches and Hathaway Shirts' campaign starring the man in the eyepatch. Another exhibit traces famous company logos through the years, such as the Quaker Oats man, and visitors are invited to identify other popular logos. The development of broadcast, outdoor, and specialty advertising is also presented, and a timeline illustrates the evolution of the business from the 1400s to the present.

International Museum of Carousel Art, NE 7th Ave. and Holladay St., just north of junction of I-5 and I-84. (503) 235-2252. Admission: $1, includes ride on carousel. Open daily mid-Apr. through mid-Oct., 11 a.m. to 4 p.m.; call for information on winter schedule. Accessible to handicapped.

Portland is a city of carousels, boasting five restored antique wooden merry-go-rounds, four of which are listed as National Historic Places. Entrance to this engaging museum is through a courtyard where the pipings of a calliope set the pace for a ride on a carousel created in 1895 by Charles Looff. Inside the museum are over 60 wonderful carousel figures, including works of the 10 best-known carvers of turn-of-the century America. Placards identify the carver and offer tips for identifying the works of various craftsmen. Nine splendidly carved horses prance along one wall. Another wall is devoted to works by Looff, with explanations of his finishing techniques. A menagerie corner holds elaborately-carved zebras, elephants, giraffes, lions, and a magnificent tiger; a separate room holds European figures. (The locations of Portland's other restored working carousels are: World Forestry Center [see below]; Burger King, 7601 SW Barbur Blvd.; Oaks Park at east end of Sellwood Bridge; and Jantzen Beach shopping center.)

World Forestry Center, 4033 SW Canyon Rd.; take Zoo/OMSI/Forestry Center Exit from Rte. 26 west. (503) 228-1367. Adults: $3, seniors: $2, students 6 to 18: $2. Open daily, 9 a.m. to 5 p.m. in summer, and 10 a.m. to 5 p.m. after Labor Day; closed Christmas Day. Accessible to handicapped.

A 70-foot-tall talking tree is merely the largest wooden object among this fascinating group of exhibits promoting awareness of forest management and the use of forest products. Showcased in this beautiful wooden building are the Jessup Wood Collection—actual samples of each type of tree found in North America, informatively labeled. Equally striking is the Langdon Plate Collection—600 plates made from woods from all around the world. Logging equipment is also featured and a multi-image presentation introduces visitors to many different kinds of world forests, their beauty and their usefulness. One of Portland's restored working antique carousels is also located here (see above).

Texas

Bandera

Frontier Times Museum, 506 13th St., 4 blocks from Rte. 16. (512) 796-3864. Adults: $1.50, children 6 to 18: $.25. Open Mon. through Sat., 10 a.m. to 4:30 p.m., and Sun., 1 to 4:30 p.m. Accessible to handicapped.

Not only are there some diverting relics here from early local settlers—canes, buggy whips, powder horns, bullet molds, moustache cups, celluloid cuffs and collars—there are some most unusual collections not related to frontier times. The Charles Fagan South American collection, for instance, includes a shrunken human head, the shrunken head of a wild Ecuadorean jungle dog, a pair of copper conquistador stirrups, lace from a lacewood tree, rubber novelties from Jamaica, pre-Inca items from Peru, vegetable ivory, butterflies, and a necklace of alligator teeth. The Gordon collection contains a totem pole, Oriental art objects, and 500 bells from all parts of the world, some dating to the 6th century B.C. An assemblage of old and rare bottles that will delight collectors contains some quart-size bottles allegedly from Judge Roy Bean's saloon.

Beaumont

Edison Plaza Museum, 350 Pine St., next to Gulf States Utilities corporate headquarters; take Downtown Exit from I-10. (409) 839-3089. Free. Open Mon. through Fri.; in summer, 7:30 a.m. to

4:30 p.m.; rest of year, 8 a.m. to 5 p.m.; closed holidays. Accessible to handicapped.

Housed in a working power substation is one of the country's largest collections of Thomas A. Edison inventions, occupying the bulk of the Yesterday section of the museum's displays on the electric industry. The early cylinder Edison standard phonograph showcased here is one of the inventor's more recognizable creations, but who would recognize the Cure All—the Master Violet Ray Machine invented by Edison circa 1925 to treat every ailment? Or the Carry and Sell miniature mimeograph machine that he designed for A.B. Dick Co.? Or how about a phonographic doll? The Today section of the museum treats factors that influence electrical rates and costs; the Tomorrow section looks at possible supplemental sources of energy, such as superconductors.

Corpus Christi

International Kite Museum, on grounds of Best Western Sandy Shores Resort, 3200 Surfside, on Rte. 181 north. (512) 883-7456 ext. 7162. Free. Open Mon. through Sat., 10 a.m. to 5 p.m., and Sun., 10 a.m. to 3 p.m. Accessible to handicapped.

Chinese legend has it that in an attempt to overthrow his emperor, Han Hsin dispatched a kite over enemy lines to measure the distance to defensive walls. The strategy not only worked, but it also marked the first recorded kite flight. In a colorful and absorbing fashion, this museum looks at kites as military weapons, scientific tools, ceremonial objects, recreational equipment, and kinetic works of art tracing their history from the Orient to Europe and the United States. One display deals with the Wright brothers' tests of theories on controlled flight. Another is devoted to Paul Garber, credited with inventing the maneuverable stunt target kite for the U.S. Navy in World War II. Naturally, there are also many toy kites, as well as such specialty models as an antique straw Chinese devil kite meant to carry away evil spirits.

Museum of Oriental Cultures, 418 Peoples St., second floor of Furman Plaza, at intersection of Peoples and Mesquite Sts., 3 blocks west of Shoreline Dr. (512) 883-1303. Adults: $1, seniors: $.75, students and children: $.50. Open Tues. through Sat., 10 a.m. to 4 p.m.; closed most holidays. Accessible to handicapped.

A five-foot-tall bronze Buddha, entitled Moon over Mountain, is a highlight at this museum devoted to the magic of the Orient. Other exhibits from Japan, China, Korea, the Philippines, and India include exquisite kimonos and hapi coats, masks, shrines, utensils, games, toys, and art objects. Oriental cultures and crafts are illuminated with fine Japanese Hakata figures, architectural scale-model dioramas of festivals, bronzeware, lacquerware, and porcelains. Changing exhibits focus on particular Oriental countries.

Denton

DAR Gowns of the First Ladies of Texas Museum, ground floor of Human Development Bldg., on campus of Texas Woman's University, off I-35. (817) 898-2683. Free. Open 8 a.m. to 4:30 p.m., Mon. through Fri., during fall and spring semesters; Mon. through Thurs., during summer semester; closed holidays and during university recesses. Accessible to handicapped.

The pioneer spirit of frontier Texas, the graceful lifestyle of the antebellum South, the robust growth of the Lone Star State from wagon trains to railroads to space ships, the election of the first woman governor of Texas—evidence of all these facets of Texas history are on view here, in the form of gowns worn by wives of the governors of Texas and presidents of the Republic of Texas, dating from 1836. In addition, the collection contains dresses worn at formal White House events by wives of two presidents and the wife of a vice president of the United States. On view, too, are assorted historic pieces of silver, books, jewelry, personal mementos, and pictures. Some of the garments are originals, others are faithful copies, and manikins have been carefully outfitted with period hairstyles.

Forth Worth

Cattleman's Museum, 1301 W. Seventh St.; take Summit St. North Exit from I-30, turn right on Seventh St. (817) 332-7064. Free. Open Mon. through Fri., 8:30 a.m. to 4:30 p.m. Accessible to handicapped.

This is the museum for people whose imagination is captured by cowboys and cattle. The story of longhorns, cattle drives, and ranching is told with artifacts, interactive displays, photographs, and dioramas complete with longhorn cattle and life-size human figures in period clothing. The ranch woman, the cowboy, the rustler, and the cattle baron are all commemorated here, with exhibits of branding irons, chaps, barbed wire, chuckwagon utensils, domestic items, and a wall of brands. A talking bull tells his side of the story and a memorial hall honors cattlemen and women who contributed to the growth of the cattle industry. A special section and film illuminate the role of brand inspectors, the corps of men who have diligently pursued cattle thieves for more than 100 years; an official brand inspector's book and badge are on display, and a life-size bronze entitled "The Brand Inspector" stands before the museum's entrance. At a colorful push-button wall display you can learn the history of today's cattle and horse breeds.

Greenville

Audie Murphy Room, W. Walworth Harrison Public Library, 3716 Lee St.; take Greenville/Terrell Exit from I-30, follow Wesley St. and turn left on Lee St. (214) 457-2992. Free. Open Mon., 10 a.m. to 8:30 p.m.; Tues. through Thurs., 9 a.m. to 8:30 p.m.; Fri., 9 a.m. to 5:30 p.m.; Sat., 9 a.m. to 4 p.m.; closed Sun. and major holidays. Accessible to handicapped.

In a state whose history is replete with heroes, Audie Murphy stands at the top of the list. Murphy, a native of the Greenville area, was World War II's most-decorated GI, receiving 24 decorations, including the Congressional Medal of Honor. Murphy died in a plane crash in 1971, and one room in this library is dedicated to his memory. Replicas of his medals are on display here, along with his Army footlocker. His youth in Hunt County is traced with black-and-white photographs and a few personal mementos. After the war, Murphy went on to Hollywood, where he played himself in the movie *To Hell and Back* and starred in many Westerns. Posters and stills from many of his movies are exhibited here.

Hereford

National Cowgirl Hall of Fame, 515 Avenue B, east of Rte. 385. (806) 364-5252. Admission: $3 for ages 12 and over. Open Mon. through Fri., 8 a.m. to 5 p.m. No facilities for handicapped.

"In praise of the strength, spirit, stamina, and courage of the Western Woman" is the theme of this unique museum, where memorabilia of Western women and cowgirls—costumes, chaps, boots, spurs, belts, buckles, trophies, and photographs—celebrate the exciting and important events that make up the distaff side of the story of the West. In addition, an extensive collection of photographs and a Western art collection fill a hall of fame honoring women who exemplify the pioneer spirit and cowgirls who have promoted the sport of rodeo.

Irving

National Museum of Communications, Four Dallas Communications Complex, 6305 N. O'Connor, Suite 123; west on Royal Ln. from I-35. (214) 556-1234. Adults: $2, seniors and children 10 to 18: $1. Open Tues. through Sun., 10 a.m. to 4 p.m. Accessible to handicapped.

The history of mass communications is the history of the printing press, broadcasting, telecommunications, photography, and the computer. How we arrived at today's Information Age is traced here in exhibits covering language and printing (from cave paintings to modern newspapers), telegraphy and telephone, the phonograph and broadcasting (including a rare 1939 RCA television set), and photography and film. There are also transitions (from amateur radio to computers, laser technology, and CDs), nostalgia and celebrity items, and recreated vintage television and radio studios where you can play deejay for a day, sit behind a camera, or listen to recreations of old radio shows. Many of the exhibits are hands-on, and among the rarities showcased in various sections are a first edition King James Bible, a hand-cranked movie camera that belonged to Charles Chaplin's film company, and a giant Voice of America central control console.

Midland

The Petroleum Museum, 1500 I-20 west, on north access road of I-20 at Exit 136. (915) 683-4403. Adults: $3, seniors: $2.50, students: $1.50. Open Mon. through Sat., 9 a.m. to 5 p.m., and Sun., 2 to 5 p.m.; closed Thanksgiving, Christmas Eve, and Christmas Day. Accessible to handicapped.

A full-size indoor oil-well fire illuminates the story of oil and gas exploration and drilling, from exploration through production here. As if that weren't enlightening enough, the world's largest marine diorama recreates a 230 million-year-old sea. Another unique exhibit allows visitors to "fly" over a petroleum pipeline in search of leaks, and a simulated nitro blast recreates early oil exploration techniques. Other exhibits in this very contemporary museum trace 20,000 years of regional history. Historical paintings act as backdrop.

New Braunfels

Museum of Texas Handmade Furniture, Breustedt Haus, 1370 Church Hill Dr.; take Rte. 337 north, then right on Rte. 81 and right on Church Hill Dr. (512) 629-6504. Adults: $2, children 6 to 12: $1. Open Memorial Day through Labor Day, Tues. through Sat., 10 a.m. to 4 p.m., and Sun., 1 to 4 p.m.; closed Mon., except holiday Mon.; Labor Day through Memorial Day, open Sat. and Sun. only, 1 to 4 p.m. Accessible to handicapped.

Beginning in 1845, many German immigrant cabinetmakers settled in the Hill Country of Texas and left their mark on the area, if not always on their furniture. More than 75 original pieces of furniture handmade in Texas, dating from 1850 to the late 1860s, form the core of the exhibits in this 1858 *fachwerk* (frame) house. Most of the furniture was fashioned from local woods—elm, pine, walnut, even mesquite—and most imitated styles of famous European furniture makers. A rounded corner cupboard for instance, copies a Biedemeier design; a pine cupboard has a painted-grain finish simulating fine woods available to Old World cabinetmakers. The furniture is shown in appropriate settings throughout the house, and is augmented by period accessories, such as beer steins, a Munich clock, pewter, and a large collection of English ironstone.

Odessa

The Presidential Museum, 622 N. Lee, at intersection of 7th and Lee Sts., 1 block west of Grant St. (Rte. 385). (915) 332-7123. Free. Open Tues. through Sat., 10 a.m. to 5 p.m. Accessible to handicapped.

Created in 1963, shortly after the assassination of President

John F. Kennedy, this one-of-a-kind museum relates the story of the American presidency through exhibits of first-lady dolls, recreations of first-lady inaugural gowns, and memorabilia of this country's 41 presidents—household items, articles of clothing, personal copies of books. Every four years a special exhibit documents presidental campaigns, from George Washington to George Bush. The museum library contains general works on the presidency and books on each president and his administration.

San Antonio

Buckhorn Hall of Horns and Hall of Texas History, Lone Star Brewing Company, 600 Lone Star Blvd., 1½ miles from downtown, off S. St. Mary's St. (512) 270-9400 or -9467. Adults: $3, children 6 to 11: $1. Open daily, 9:30 a.m. to 5 p.m.; closed Thanksgiving and Christmas. Accessible to handicapped.

It all began in 1881 when saloonkeeper Albert Friedrich started collecting rattlesnake rattles. Thirty years, 20,000 rattles, and 32,000 antlers later, Friedrich's collection filled his Buckhorn Saloon and San Antonio had acquired another landmark. Today, Friedrich's collection has been augmented by hundreds of additional specimens and exhibits. Cattlehorn furniture, scrimshaw horns, and stuffed animal, bird, and fish specimens are displayed alongside such oddities as a portrait of an Indian "drawn" on tin by a local sharpshooter with his .22 rifle and a photograph of Albert Friedrich framed in a star created by Mrs. Friedrich from rattlesnake skins and rattles. "Old Tex," the steer with the world's record-length longhorns is here, stuffed, as is a yawning gorilla. There is also the relocated Buckhorn Bar, along with a cash register so old that the largest total it can ring up is $6.99. This being a brewery, there's also a collection of over 200 different beer bottles.

Hertzberg Circus Collection and Museum, San Antonio Public Library Annex, 210 Market St., 3 blocks from Alamo; from I-10 take Downtown Exit east on Dolorosa, which becomes Market St.; from I-35 take Commerce St. Exit west; validated parking at River Bend Garage across street. (512) 299-7810. Free. Open Mon. through Sat., 9 a.m. to 5:30 p.m.; additional summer hours, Sun. and holidays, 1 to 5 p.m. No facilities for handicapped.

This extraordinary collection traces more than two centuries of circus history, starting with a rare 1793 handbill from America's first circus advertising that President George Washington and his wife would attend the show. Donated by collector Harry Herzberg to the San Antonio Public Library, it contains hundreds of whimsical circus-related treasures—a ring large enough to slip over a baby's wrist that belonged to Ringling Brothers' Texas giant Jack Earle, Clyde Beatty's white uniform and jungle hat, Tom Thumb's miniature carriage that was built for him in 1843 at age five. Side show personalities are showcased, as are such circus celebrities as Jenny Lind, P.T. Barnum, and aerialist Lillian Leitzel. Collections of miniatures, including a complete vintage 1920 scale-model five-ring circus complex, fill whole rooms. Posters, photographs, playbills, ticket wagons, and countless other items add up to one of the largest—and undoubtedly best—circus collections in the world.

Edward H. White II Memorial Museum, Hangar 9, Brooks Air Force Base, 1 block west of I-37 on SW Military Dr. (512) 536-2203. Free. Open Mon. through Fri., 8 a.m. to 4 p.m.; closed holidays. Accessible to handicapped.

Housed inside the last remaining military World War I hangar in the United States is the U.S. Air Force's museum of flight medicine, dedicated to astronaut Edward H. White II, who lost his life at Cape Kennedy in 1967. Exhibit space is primarily devoted to the development of manned flight and the evolution of aerospace medicine. The original Barany Chair, first utilized in 1918 to test the equilibrium of student pilots, is here, as are the oldest (1918) low-pressure chamber and the first space cabin simulator. Other exhibits include a rotational flight simulator used in early training of astronauts; a Jenny aircraft used by flight students; a World War I wicker balloon basket; early flight nurse combat and training uniforms and equipment; examples of space equipment, suits, and foods; and White memorabilia and decorations.

Pioneer Hall, Pioneer, Trail Driver, and Texas Ranger Museum, 3805 Broadway; from Rte. 77/281 north, take Hildebrand Exit to Broadway. (512) 822-9011 or 824-2537. Adults: $1, children 6 to 12: $.25. Open Sept. 1 through Apr. 30, Wed. through Sun., 11 a.m. to 4 p.m.; May 1 through Aug. 31, 10 a.m. to 5 p.m. Accessible to handicapped.

"Three rooms of Texas history" is the modest claim of this museum, but it is a particular history—that of the men who tamed Texas—frontiersmen, trail drivers, and Texas Rangers. The buildings' central rotunda is a miniature of the one in the state capitol, with branching exhibit rooms. One of these, the Pioneer Parlor, focuses on the life of early settlers. Another, the Trail Driver Room, houses memorabilia from the raw era of ranching and cattle drives—saddles, early pistols and rifles, barbed wire, branding irons. Dominating the room are more than 250 photographs, portraits of the kinds of men who established the ranches and rode the dusty trails. Exhibits in the Texas Ranger Room trace Rangers' history and heroism, from 1823 to today. Handcuffs from the 1800s, shackles, weapons, and photos commemorate the legendary men in the white hats.

Temple

SPJST Museum of Czech Heritage, 520 N. Main, in basement of Slavonic Benevolent Order of State of Texas building, at intersection with French St. (817) 773-1575. Free. Open Mon. through Fri., 8 a.m. to noon and 1 to 5 p.m.; closed holidays. Accessible to handicapped.

Outstanding here are two collections of Czech handiwork—a priceless collection of handmade puppets, made by an immigrant in 1875 and dressed as characters from popular puppet plays; and a glass showcase of exquisitely hand-carved miniature wooden horse-drawn vehicles—stagecoaches, farm wagons, sleighs, Conestoga wagons. The purpose of this museum is to preserve the heritage of the Czech pioneers who settled this part of Texas, a purpose that it serves nicely with recreated pioneer doctor's office, kitchen, blacksmith shop, and log cabin, along with colorful native Czech costumes and vintage pioneer clothing. But it's the puppets and wooden vehicles that represent the quality of craftsmanship that those settlers brought with them from their home country.

Utah

Ogden

Union Station, 25th St. & Wall Ave., east of I-15. (801) 629-8535. Adults: $2, seniors: $1.50, children under 12: $1. Open year round, Mon. through Sat., 10 a.m. to 6 p.m.; Memorial Day through Labor Day, also open Sun., 1 to 5 p.m.; closed Thanksgiving, Christmas, and New Year's Day. Accessible to handicapped.

This handsome 1924 depot is exhibit hall, working railroad station, and three museums in one:

Browning Kimball Car Museum displays only a dozen classic American cars at any given time, but they are all 1920s and '30s gems exhibited in suitable settings. There are also numerous antique gas pumps and a license plate collection spanning 60 years that features a 1944 Utah plate made from compressed soybeans.

Browning Firearms Museum contains a re-creation of inventor John M. Browning's firearms workshop, as well as a display of Browning production firearms mounted in glass cases for 360-degree viewing.

Wattis-Dumke Railroad Museum has a unique approach to railroad history: A dozen HO scale model trains running on eight track layouts recreate Ogden's railroading heyday. Depicted are the construction and geography of the 1,776-mile transcontinental route that made Ogden a railroad hub. Within the railroad museum is a display of topaz, coral, fossils, and other gems and minerals from Utah's rich geological lode.

Price

College of Eastern Utah Prehistoric Museum, Price Municipal Bldg., 2nd East & Main Sts., in north end of City Hall. (801) 637-5060. Donation requested. Open Memorial Day through Labor Day, Mon. through Sat., 10 a.m. to 5 p.m., and Sun., 11 a.m. to 4 p.m.; closed major holidays. Accessible to handicapped.

Some of the finest fossils and dinosaur bones in the world—dug from nearby Cleveland-Lloyd Quarry (originally a coal mine)—are assembled here, literally. Four complete dinosaur skeletons (Allosauraus, Camarasaurus, Camptosaurus, Stegosaurus), composed of up to 70 percent real bone, are displayed in all their awesome glory. Fossilized footprints of various reptiles and dinosaurs, petrified wood, and bone samples are also part of this well-mounted geological exhibit. Other artifacts of prehistoric times on display include the mysterious Pilling figurines (a collection of unbaked clay Indian ornaments estimated to be 900 years old), a reproduction of an ancient Indian rock mural dubbed "Holy Ghost and Attendants," and a life-sized display of Ute, Navajo, and Pueblo Indian dwellings.

Provo

McCurdy Historical Doll Museum, 246 North 100 East, east of I-15. (801) 377-9935. Adults: $2, children under 12: $1. Open Apr. through Dec., Tues. through Sat., noon to 6 p.m.; Jan. through Mar., Tues. through Sat., 1 to 5 p.m.; closed Christmas, Thanksgiving, and New Year's Day. Assistance available for handicapped.

From Barbie dolls to 300-year-old antiques, more than 3,000 dolls fill two floors of this restored 1894 carriage house. They are grouped into 13 collections by maker or subject—Folk Dress of the World, Laura Alleman kid leather dolls, Lewis Sorensen wax dolls, Women of the Bible, Madame Alexander dolls, Nancy Ann Storybook dolls, Boy Dolls, First Ladies of America, etc. Also on display are 47 miniature rooms of dollhouse furniture, as well as doll accessories, buggies, and other toys.

Wendover

Bonneville Speedway Museum, 950 State Hwy., on old Rte. 40 in east end of town. (801) 665-7721. Adults: $1.50, children: $.50. Open Memorial Day through Oct. 31, daily 10 a.m. to 6 p.m. No facilities for handicapped.

Bonneville Speedway, close by the Bonneville Salt Flats, is the site of auto speed trials and racing competitions. Among the antique and collectible automobiles assembled here are a 1963 Rolls-Royce Silver Cloud III, a 1948 MG-TC, a 1957 T-Bird, a 1928 Essex Boattail, and a 1955 Mercedes 300SL Gullwing. More interesting, perhaps, are the Bonneville race cars, including the famous *Goldenrod*, holder of the land speed record—409 mph—for wheel-driven cars.

Washington

Bremerton

Bremerton Naval Museum, 130 Washington Ave., at entrance to Puget Sound Naval Shipyard, off Rte. 3, 1 block north of Seattle ferry terminal. (206) 479-7447. Donations accepted. Open Tues. through Sat., 10 a.m. to 5 p.m., and Sun., 1 to 5 p.m.; closed Thanksgiving, Christmas, and New Year's Day. Accessible to handicapped.

The Puget Sound Naval Shipyard, the subject of this museum, has a proud history, serving as Navy base and repair yard until the needs of the two world wars turned it to shipbuilding. Ship models are among the featured exhibits here, as are Pearl Harbor photos, a collection of ship bells, and extensive ordnance exhibits. Of special note is the exhibit on "Big E," the aircraft carrier *Enterprise* of World War II fame, and even non-sailors will enjoy the museum's large collection of hats from navies around the world.

Goldendale

Maryhill Museum of Art, 35 Maryhill Museum Dr., on Rte. 14; take Exit 104 west from I-84. (509) 773-3733. Adults: $3, seniors: $2.50, students 6 to 16: $1.50. Open Mar. 15 through Nov. 15, daily 9 a.m. to 5 p.m. Accessible to handicapped.

On a remote bluff overlooking the Columbia River sits a 1914 mansion conceived as a home for wealthy entrepreneur Sam Hill, now a museum housing a most unusual accumulation of attractions, among them an extensive collection of works and drawings by French sculptor August Rodin. Fine art aside, the museum also boasts one of the finest collections of chess pieces anywhere, over 100 sets, ranging from elephant-mounted ivory chessmen from India, to plastic figures of presidential campaigners Richard Nixon and George McGovern. Queen Marie of Romania's throne, coronation gown, crown, and dozens of personal items and furnishings also have found a niche here, as have a number of 30-inch-high French manikins attired in post-World War I fashion and a choice collection of Columbia River Indian artifacts. This is truly a rewarding detour off the beaten path.

Port Gamble

Of Sea and Shore Museum, General Store Building, Rainier Ave., east of Rte. 104, on right at end of street. (206) 297-2426. Free. Open May 15 through Sept. 15, Tues. through Fri., 11 a.m. to 4 p.m., and Sat. and Sun., 11 a.m. to 5 p.m.; Sept. 16 through May 14, weekends only, 11 a.m. to 4 p.m.; closed Christmas and New Year's Day if they fall on a weekend. No facilities for handicapped.

Port Gamble, one of the few company towns left in the U.S. and classified in its entirety as a National Historic Site, is home to one of the nation's largest shell collections. The thousands of mollusks displayed here were all collected by Port Gamble native Tom Rice through beachcombing and exchanges with collectors from more than 100 countries. In addition to the many beautiful and captivating shells—presented unpolished, just as they were found—are numerous displays of other marine life, such as crabs, sea urchins, and sharks.

Port Townsend

The Coast Artillery Museum at Fort Worden, 30 miles northwest of Seattle on northeast corner of Olympic Peninsula. (206) 385-2021. Adults: $1. Open Memorial Day through third weekend in Oct., daily, 11 a.m. to 5 p.m.; third weekend in Feb. to Memorial Day, noon to 4 p.m. Accessible to handicapped.

Coastal defense, dating from the turn of the century, is the order of the day here, and the emphasis is on anti-battleship artillery:

massive rifled cannons, shore mines, huge rifled mortars. Greeting the visitor at the front steps of the museum are two 16-inch target shells weighing 2,340 pounds each that, using 750 pounds of powder, could be fired 30 miles. Inside are other projectiles and cannons, such as a fully-operational 12-inch disappearing gun and a 12-inch mortar. Several rooms throughout the museum feature color reproductions of U.S. Army regimental insignia, photographs of big guns, maps, rifles, regimental flags, and manikins dressed in uniforms typical of coastal defense fortifications, 1884–1948, along with other peacetime and wartime artifacts.

Seattle

Memory Lane Museum, 1400 S. Lane St., in Goodwill Store, on corner of Rainier Ave. S and S. Dearborn, at south side of Capital Hill. (206) 329-1000. Free. Open during regular store hours, Mon. through Fri., 10 a.m. to 8 p.m.; Sat. and Sun., 10 a.m. to 6 p.m.; closed July 4, Christmas, and New Year's Day. Accessible to handicapped.

What more appropriate setting for a trip down memory lane than a Goodwill Store, repository of household goods that we've abandoned along the way? Some of the exhibits here—such as the *Miss Bardahl* hydroplane, a repeat world champion racing boat, and Bruce the Bear, a 10-foot stuffed Alaskan brown bear estimated to have weighed 1,500 pounds—may not be the stuff of most people's personal memories, but the bulk of the items on display are. Tools and equipment that fill an old-time service station, musical instruments, quaint toys, period photos, outmoded furniture, china, glassware, needlework, vintage clothes, and old-fashioned household items trace the American domestic scene from the turn of the century to 1930. A retrospective fashion show is occasionally presented.

Seattle-King County Camp Fire Museum, 8511 15th Ave. NE, east of I-5; heading north on 15th Ave. NE, turn left on 85th St. NE, turn left; Camp Fire Office is only building on right. (206) 461-8550. Free. Office open weekdays 9 a.m. to 5 p.m., and one Sat. a month; call in advance to be sure museum is open. Accessible to handicapped.

Camp Fire girls—and, recently, Camp Fire boys—are accorded

their very own museum here in the hallways of the Seattle-King County Camp Council headquarters. Displays cover the 8 decades of Camp Fire history, with gowns from the early years, uniforms throughout the years, dolls dressed in different types of uniforms, and awards, Camp Fire beads, and books. Among the memorabilia that will no doubt trigger happy summer camp memories of former Camp Fire boys and girls are examples of leatherwork, beadwork, and other handicrafts.

Thorniley Collection of Type, West Coast Paper Company, 2203 First Ave. S, below Kingdome between I-5 and Rte. 99. (206) 623-1850. Free. Open Mon. through Fri., 8 a.m. to 5 p.m. Limited facilities for handicapped.

Type used to print Gold Rush newspapers, a ton of type from the Deep South, wood type carved in end-grain maple—these make up just a fraction of the collection of pre-1900 printing paraphernalia showcased in this recreated print shop. Printing presses, book presses, and job case layouts help unfold the story of American typography from Revolutionary days to the turn of this century, along with such rare items as a case of 20-point Union Pearl type introduced in 1690; 21-point Antique Pointed type, once hidden from Sherman's troops; a newspaper-addressing device from Alaska; and beautiful borders and ornaments. Cedar-paneled walls hold photos of old-time printers at work. Best of all, visitors can set type by hand, start up the old treadle press, and print something of their very own.

Stevenson

Skamania County Historical Society Museum, Vancouver Ave., Courthouse Annex, one block north of Rte. 14. (509) 427-5141, ext. 235. Free. Open Mon. through Sat., noon to 5 p.m., and Sun., 1 to 6 p.m.; closed national holidays. Accessible to handicapped, including Braille history of rosary collection.

This being a county museum, most exhibits reflect local history, particularly pioneer and Native American life in the Columbia River gorge. Absolutely unique, however, is a large permanent display of rosaries, 4,000 to be exact. Like many unusual collections, it was the work of one man, Don Brown. Religious connotations aren't necessarily a factor here; rather the general effect of such a dense display of so many beautiful pieces is like looking into a room-size jewel box. The rosaries, sent to Mr. Brown by people worldwide, range in size from one with beads as small as pin heads to one nearly 16 feet long. They are composed of all manner of materials—glass, precious metals, and woods of all types, but also seeds, stone, shells, and water chestnuts. Ironically, there's one made from bullets and shell casings. Surrounding a picture of Christopher Columbus in one large lighted case are rosaries from the New World; another contains rosaries donated by famous people. Prayer beads of other religious groups are also included in this singular exhibit.

Wyoming

Cheyenne

National First Day Cover Museum, 702 Randall Blvd., east of I-25, south of Pershing Blvd. (307) 771-3202. Free. Open Mon. through Fri., 9 a.m. to noon and 12:30 to 5 p.m.; closed weekends and holidays. Accessible to handicapped.

Self-guided tours explore the extensive exhibits of first day covers (first edition postage stamps) in this only museum of its kind. Featured in glass cases and framed displays are rare and old specimens, including the Penny Black, the world's first first day cover; the 1893 *Columbians,* America's first commemorative issue; and the 1930 *Graf Zeppelin Air Mail* first day cover issued for mail carried on the *Graf's* first Europe-Pan American round-trip flight. Theme exhibits include space exploration, birds and flowers of the 50 states, the wedding of Prince Charles and Lady Diana, China, and pioneers of flight. The museum also is an official post office.

Cody

Buffalo Bill Historical Center, 720 Sheridan Ave., on corner of 8th St. (307) 587-4771. Adults: $5, seniors: $4.75, students: $3.25, children 6 to 12: $1.50. Open daily in May, Sept. and Oct., 8 a.m. to 8 p.m.; and June through Aug., 7 a.m. to 10 p.m.; open Tues. through Sun., Mar. and Nov., 10 a.m. to 3 p.m.; and Apr., 10 a.m. to 5 p.m.; closed Dec. through Feb. Accessible to handicapped.

Four separate facilities make up this historical center, including: **Buffalo Bill Museum**, which contains, among other personal and professional effects of the showman, Buffalo Bill Cody's own valuable trophy collection, guns, saddles, and letters.

Plains Indian Museum, where preservation of culture of the six Plains tribes is documented with exhibits of clothing, weapons, tools, and ceremonial items.

Whitney Gallery of Western Art, containing what may be the best collection of the original works of such notable Western artists as Frederic Remington, Charles M. Russell, Edgar S. Paxton, Albert Bierstadt, and many others.

Winchester Arms Museum with more than 1,500 historic firearms, guns, cannons, and projectile weapons. The collection was begun in 1860 by Oliver Winchester.

Jackson

Jackson Hole Museum, 105 N. Glenwood, in center of town. (307) 733-2414. Adults: $2, seniors and children 6 to 12: $1. Open last weekend in May through Sept. 30, Mon. through Sat., 9 a.m. to 5:30 p.m., and Sun., 10 a.m. to 4 p.m. Accessible to handicaped.

In the midst of some of the most spectacular scenery on earth sits the town of Jackson, and in the middle of town sits an out-of-the-ordinary regional museum. Early Western life—pre-pioneer Indian days, and the era of trappers and mountain men—are commemorated here with the usual artifacts and other general memorabilia. Unique, however, is a large collection of hand-forged knives dating from pioneer and trapper days. An exhibit of guns of the era also has a separate display area, as does what is reputed to be the largest collection of mounted deer antlers in the West.

A Last Word

There's a measure of unpredictability with small museums. That, coupled with their diversity, lends to their appeal, but it does mean that it's difficult to provide a hard and fast list of the more intriguing ones.

Some good ones have apparently closed their doors—a museum on medical quackery in St. Louis, the Museum of Modern Mythology in San Francisco, the Slave Mart Museum in Charleston, South Carolina. Some, like the Lacrosse Foundation in Baltimore, which is moving to a new facility, and the Lace Museum of Mountain View, California, which is looking for a permanent home, are in transition, so can't yet be included here. Some were rumored, but proved impossible to track down. Others were in preparation, but not quite ready to open.

Here are some other American originals that you might look for when you're in the vicinity:

- A gourd museum in Angier, North Carolina.
- An international and antique shoe collection at the Pennsylvania College of Podiatric Medicine in Philadelphia.
- The Levi Strauss Museum in San Francisco.
- A new steel museum in Youngstown, Ohio.
- A Kentucky Fried Chicken Museum in Corbin, Kentucky, on the site of Col. Harland Sanders' first restaurant.
- The Medal of Honor Museum in Chattanooga, Tennessee.
- The Hawaii Bottle Museum in Honolulu.

- A new civil rights museum in Birmingham, complete with a jail cell that once held Rev. Martin Luther King, Jr.
- A bordello museum at The Chicken Ranch in LaGrange, Texas.
- The Potato Museum and International Food Museum in the Washington, D.C., area.
- A New Jersey corrections museum in Trenton, containing, among other things, the electric chair used to execute Bruno Hauptmann, who was convicted of kidnapping and killing Charles Lindbergh's baby.
- A museum in Omaha concerning the historic role of blacks on the Great Plains.
- The Dard Hunter Paper Museum in a new facility at the Institute of Paper Science and Technology in Atlanta.
- A rice museum in Crowley, Louisiana.
- Mom and Pop's Cap Museum in Marietta, Oklahoma.

Watch for them when you travel, and keep an eye out for others.

Index of Museums
by Name

Index of Museums
by Category

Agriculture

Animals

Architecture, Decoration, and Design

Art/Decorative Arts

Bottles and Other Containers

Carving and Sculpture

Clocks and Watches

Clothing and Textiles

History

Industry

Money and Stamps

Music

Natural History